Life with the
Little People

Life with the Little People

Robert Perry

Illustrations by
Chester Scott

THE GREENFIELD REVIEW PRESS

FRANK WATERS MEMORIAL SERIES, Volume #3

Publication of this volume has been made possible, in part,
through grants from the Literature Program of the
New York State Council on the Arts and from
The Bay Foundation to support this first in a series of volumes
of prose writing by Native American Authors. This series,
named in honor of the memory of Frank Waters,
consists of the annual winners of
The North American Native Authors First Book Award for Prose.

ISBN 0-912678-98-4

Library of Congress #98-72934

Cover Art Chester Scott

Cover and Interior Design and Composition by
Sans Serif, Inc., Saline, Michigan

Contents

Contents / vii

Introduction

The stories about the 'little people' were quite sacred. Not even in the same family was this a common subject. If a stranger came to an Indian home and asked in English, "What you know", there would be silence, shrug of the shoulder, or an 'Ugh'. Even in the old days, when a child was chosen by 'them', nothing would make him tell his parents what he knew. The reason these stories are offered now is because the contributor, Chester Scott, has found a better way. As a Christian, he has learned not to keep secrets with a select few but to openly share the good news. Chester grew up with the "little people". They are friends to children and teach medicine used in healing. Their price was perfection. Chester has learned he doesn't have to be perfect to be healed from sickness. This releases him to tell of fun with the "little people" to the Indian children, and through stories bond child, elder and God.

It's generally known that Indian docktors made natural medicines from herbs and plants. Healing of sick people had to occur to care for a large tribe. When modern man tries to duplicate the Indian medicines, results are poor at best. There must be some secret ingredient. For years researchers have sought to learn the secrets of plants in far away places such as the rain forests. They count leaves in the top of trees and run statistics to find the secret of natural medicines.[1] Others note North American bears that chew on a root, then rub it in their fur to repel fleas and other pests. [2] Some researchers look for the answer to healing from the old Indian shamans. They seem to concede the shaman linked the community to the almighty god, but look at his paraphernalia as the answer. One researcher couldn't find such spiritual power in churches of the United States and opted for a grant to study shamans in Siberia.[3] By contrast, the Muscogea Indian *docktors* (we will adopt this spelling) using the natural medicines are very plain and humble men. They go about their business without fanfare. For the most part, the phenomenon of native healing has been met with skeptics and the Indians keep on being silent.

In bringing information about the possibility of native cures touches on the differences of how cultures accept new knowledge. White Man depends on facts and proof, so the limit of believing is as far as his "headlights" reach. The Indian knows that he is one piece of a multi-dimensional world. Indians are observant of the constant change in Nature. Everything in his environment is important. You might say that an Indian lives in a world neither black nor white, mostly grey to be responsive to change. He remembers a lot of information because there was no written language. His memory was uncluttered with unnecessary words and questions. After gathering all the information with his "headlights", he chooses the "right path" by asking an elder. The elder is the "library". This is the link to the storehouse of knowledge from past generations. "Grandfather" would examine the evidence, "This is the way it's always been". This adds stability, a black or white line to the "grey". The elder added more than history. He teaches the child to reach beyond his "headlights". He teaches what's right, instilling integrity and morals. An Indian accepts far more on faith alone, which is beyond the known and in the future. This brings peace. Each time the peace comes, it builds more strength on faith. The Muscogea People were renown in olden days as the peace-makers.

For an Indian moving to a new place was a great crisis. To learn the new birds, animals and plants as well as the old home-place may take generations. In 1836, the Muscogea people were forcibly removed to Oklahoma. Intermarriage by White Men was often a means to get control of Indian land. The tribes treated the new spouse with full tribal rights. The new land-holder could have a voice in Oklahoma becoming a state. That happened in 1907. The Indian tribe gave up their land, soon after destruction of the buffalo. There was much pressure on the Indian people to be quiet about their culture and be assimilated. After Statehood, two generations didn't tell the old stories and use the ancient tongues. At the same time, the children were being taught to read and write in English and substitute books for the ancient knowledge of the elders.

Chester's stories go back four generations to when his tribe came to Oklahoma, then forward two generations, all from the same Indian family. None of the old Indians had any knowledge of their history, the kind with dates. Their stories were tied to the different generations. Our task was to weave Muscogea history with these people's stories. History was used to strengthen the oldest family stories, the ones with few facts. When the more recent family stories got shackled by too many facts, it was time to call this work "fiction, based on facts". A fictitious Indian boy was created: "ChaBon" means "boy", a curious boy. "B" is added here to show proper inflection. ChaBon can think and act for the story.

To the non-Indian reader, "medicine" is more than a spoonful of elixir. An Indian adds a prayer as part of the package. The one who receives has the faith that healing will occur. The spiritual component is more important than the plants. Then you will read of medicines, both 'good' and 'bad'. This is not a taste component. It goes back to their ancient history. A tribal history spanning 200 years before the migration was written as a *short* story with few dates (last story). The Peace clans gave 'good' medicine to care for their people, which is the realm of the 'little ones'. It's the War clans that made medicine used to defend the people from enemies. When the 'bad' medicine is used to do evil or counteract 'good' medicine, a battle ensues.

Through Chester's illustrations, we can see what the "little people" look like and how peaceful they seem. They come in two sizes. The bigger ones are serious and may have white beards. It's the littler ones that play pranks. To those who doubt their existence, they are invisible and quiet. Mischief can still occur. We

should say that not every Indian mother could submit to their child being taken by 'them'. In modern times one Chickasaw woman kept her boy at home after 'they' took him off the first time. This tribe no longer has any native docktors. As an adult, the son developed a dependency problem. The mother blamed herself for not letting 'them' train her boy.

The Indian learned much by observation in nature. When it comes to words, his stories are very short. There would be no introduction or summary. He would tell the middle of the story, lay it down for months, then continue another episode as if there was no break. A story taken out of the cultural text wouldn't be understood by a stranger. Seeking to introduce these stories to a general audience requires explanation. In effect, we started with bits of stories, connected 'dot-to-dot', then colored with word 'paints' to produce a broader picture.

We learned the pranks of "little people" went beyond North America. The British reported an encounter in the mid 16th century: [4] The Saxons had underground mines of silver, copper and lead. They believed their vast underground treasure was guarded by gnomes called "Kobalds". When the supply of ores suddenly failed, blame fell on the Kobalds. They were accused of transmuting the ore into rubbish called "cobalt". Disaster was averted when the British learned to make an expensive blue glassware, using the Saxon cobalt. The glassware is still called, "Cobalt Blue". For some reason, these "little people" no longer exist in Europe. Or do they?

One Northwest tribe knew that "little people" disciplined children, but had lost the part about healing.[5] The Chickasaw, Muscogea, and Cherokee tribes came to Oklahoma from the Southeast USA. Since the Muscogea people migrated from Georgia and Alabama, we were captivated to find a lost band of Tugaloo Cherokee living in Georgia. After the removal, it was illegal to be a Cherokee. We are indebted to Jerry King, the Tugaloo historian. He shared early-day history. When the Creeks were calling the Jamestown Colony traders 'Wacena', the Cherokee said, 'Watseni'. These two tribes probably traded stories over the same campfire. About one hundred years ago, the lost Cherokee band was hiding. To admit knowing the old stories would bring misery to an "illegal Indian". To stop questions, a story was leaked to a local newspaper: A tribe of 'little people' existed. However, they had emigrated 'out West' when the Cherokee people were forced from Georgia in 1837.[6]

Joe Bruchac told us about the 'little people' stories of the Abenaki tribe.[7] There are three bands of "little people". Some were "Stone Throwers" with heads shaped like an ax, "Underwater People" and another band called "Spreaders". Anyone defiling their sacred hunting grounds would be found with ash splints holding eyes and mouth open and fingers and toes spread apart. Ross John, Seneca, gave us Iroquois stories. [8] There were three bands, too. Some dwell underground and guard against spirits escaping to suffer mankind. Another band applies paint to the strawberries and Indian corn. The "Stone-Throwers" toss huge boulders but are very friendly to Earth-children. Kakujirakeron, historian of the Akwesasne Mohawk, told how his tribe migrated long ago through the Southeastern America. Mohawk and Seneca are part of the Iroquois Confederacy. Their 'little people' stories differ from the Southeastern versions. Crow Tribe of Montana has its own sacred stories about the 'little ones'. Just as there are 500 US tribes, there seems to be no Pan-Indian description. In the first place, man can't describe a spiritual being. The old Indians never attempted to do this in fear of placing rigid boundaries that destroyed rather than created. As small as this book is, it provides an introduction to a subject without precedent. Rather than to attempt to add stories from other tribes, we have provided a full treatment within the Muscogea people, specifically the "pure-bloods". All versions attribute a guardian spirit; only the Muscogea talk about healing the sick.

In the overview, these simple stories document a truth that may become more valuable in later years. There were no college-trained medical doctors and large hospitals. They lived far out in the woods. By their observation, there was a way to find the medicinal plants and work out dosage that would heal sick people. What follows are stories about Indian people living with the "little people". No attempt is made to define the particular plants used for healing. This book is not a pharmacopeia—on purpose. Frankly, we believe healing comes from God and not Man. Even physicians of today recognize the importance of prayer and faith.

Our advice is to read as a child. Remember your early days and any playmate or dog who was your best buddy. If you can do this, the stories that follow are possible. Read with skepticism and the same story is impossible. This simple faith can change your life. This brings peace. It's not so much that "little people" exist or even that herbs were used, it's that simple faith is enough for healing to occur.

Simple pleasures are the last refuge of the complex.
Oscar Wilde

Life with the Little People

They Named Him Little Jack

Little Jack

Introduction: *The Muscogea Nation had been named "Creeks" by the early English settlers as either "Upper" or "Lower" for where they lived on Okmulgee Creek (Georgia). Long respected as peace-makers, their war clans and peace clans were housed in separate towns to promote harmony. The "Lower Creek" Towns included the Coweta (peace clan) and Ka-sih-ta (war clan). As early as 1802, President Jefferson promised the white settlers of Georgia more land by peaceably removing Indians to territory out west. He had the western land but no treaty with the Indians. The Indians liked their ancient homelands. These peaceful Indians became model citizens and learned White Man's ways. This caused great anxiety to the white settlers, who wanted the Indians off "their" land. This situation became like dry wood awaiting a spark to start a fire. Thirty years later the US government announced a deal to soon move the Indians. Indian lands would be bought and they would receive land in kind in Oklahoma Territory. Details to be resolved. This news opened the door for land speculators. The Creeks who owned five million acres were besieged with evil schemers after title to the best land. Indians were treated badly, accused of wrong doings and evicted from their land. The US Army already battling Indians in Florida was ordered into Alabama to "control" Indians. In 1836, 15,000 Creeks were forcibly removed from their ancient homelands to Oklahoma Territory.*

Many soldiers had surged into the Lower Creek Town yelling warhoops of *Hos-tiles!* Justification to handcuff 500 people to a long chain and march over ninety miles in double file to a river-boat landing. Joined with other dissidents, 2500 people were crammed into the pitch-black holds of two river-boats built for 600 each—headed for Arkansas. Contagious incurable yellow fever was rampant. Those the fever spared then walked on to Oklahoma. As this epic unfolded, the rest of the tribe was electrified by fear. They had done their best to learn White Man's ways. How could this happen? Next, the soldiers divided the *non-hostiles* like sheep into five parties. Each party was counted, then an agent and military officer assigned to lead them to the Mississippi River. To avoid yellow fever that spread inside the boats, they would be walking. The rest of this story tells what happened when a little boy had to cross the big river. He was little Jack Lewis, seven years old.

One day the US Marine Corps Lieutenant J. T. Sprague showed up at Coweta Town, the home of the Peace Clan. It didn't take long for the people of both 'Lower Creek' towns to gather. With everyone assembled, he stated, "I am to lead you and Kasihta Town across the big river to Oklahoma Territory." No one was smiling. There were others with him, but not many. So no one was afraid. Chief Tuk-a-bat-chee Hadjo spoke softly, "You come too early". Soldiers don't understand Indian humor. This one didn't shout back at the Chief, so the people began to smile. He wouldn't be so bad. This thought helped their fear to leave. So, they talked. The few Indians with crops left to gather and cattle to sell begged him, "Just a little more time, please". The marine thought it senseless for these people to stay longer. There were marauding white men, who were stealing anything the Indians had left. Shrugging his shoulders, he granted the wish and left to find many horses and wagons for the long trip to the big river.

In one moon the lieutenant returned to Coweta Town with 500 ponies and 45 wagons. The noise of the approaching animals and wagons had brought all of the people to the village. When the convoy arrived, the Indians were surprised. They brought many cattle. There would be fresh meat for the trip, at least to the big river. The lieutenant said, "We are the last party to leave. Let's go". The chiefs gestured, "go". Everyone rushed for their bundles and returned ready. The soldiers had them stand in long lines to be counted. Counting finished, the sergeant called out, "Sir, 1,984 people ready to go". The long walk started.

The oldest people rode in wagons with the bundles and babies. As the wagons passed the walking people, the elders waved to the children and encouraged everyone. The weather was nice but the roads were terrible and there was little water to drink. When Jack, the little boy, tired of walking, someone offered a pony to ride. In a matter of days, he learned to ride the pony well.

It took a moon to walk to the great muddy river they knew as "We-o-gof-ke". Reaching Memphis, two parties had arrived earlier. Everyone camped south of the city on the high bluffs. Down below, We-o-gof-ke was violent and raging. The agent soothed them, "Big boats will come". The Creeks had all seen steam-boats on the Alabama River. The big boats would carry the people across the river and then around a big swamp on the other side. No wagon could cross the swamp, but boats could.

It was early one morning a week later, when the children were awakened by a loud call, "Whoo! Whoo-o-o!" The sound came from the river. Steamboat coming through the fog! Excited boys and girls raced to the high bluff to see. Elders followed to get a closer look. Even in the dense fog the sight made them sad. These boats were old and battered and weak! Not like the ones seen on the Alabama River. How could horses ride these old tubs?

The two earlier parties would get the first boats. Everyday the people spied from the high bluffs. They saw people counted and loaded, paddle wheels churning to float down steam. After a long wait, the boats returned for more people. People counted first, the boats turned and left. Critics on the bluff grumbled the boat was overloaded.

The lieutenant's party waited almost a moon for their turn on a boat. There was time to face the raging river and the setting sun. The chiefs told the story of the ancient Yamasee people.[1] When harassed by their enemy, these gentle people of old faced the river, too. All joined hands and humbly sang pretty songs. They peacefully walked into the river never to be seen again. As the Creeks waited, it helped to hear these stories to dispel fear of the river. Each day two or three of the cattle were killed for food. The women are good cooks and did everything to make the meal time pleasant. The roasted meat tasted so good and it prepared everyone for the strenuous tasks ahead. When the time was near to ride the boats, most of the cattle had been eaten.

This time when the boat returned, its captain talked to the agent, who talked to the lieutenant, who gathered the chiefs. Slowly the lieutenant explained, "The two earlier parties have blocked the White River". His plan was to bypass the White River and ride the boat further west to the Arkansas River, then up to Little Rock. His party would save 150 miles of walking. He expected agreement. After talking in their language, the chiefs replied, "We will not get on the boats". Upset now, Lt. Sprague stormed back, "And what would you do? Swim the river?" The chiefs consulted, then spoke, "Yes. Men take horses through the swamp. Leave wagons. You take women and children. Boat go around swamp. We meet at Little Rock". There was no mention of the river to cross. Nothing like this had been done before. The agent nodded in agreement, one boat rather than two would save him money. The lieutenant agreed, also.

At dawn the lieutenant gave the orders: load the riverboat *John Nelson* with the women and children, baggage and old sick men including Chief Hadjo. It was done. The soldier counted heads, then shouted out, "Sir, 1500 people loaded". After the wooden barrels of salt pork rations were rolled on deck, the boat's whistle blew. The paddle wheel churned the heavily laden boat away from the pier. Later, on reaching the shallow Arkansas River, the boat's bottom was dragging in the sand. The captain pulled to the side and put ashore 900 people and rations. This lightened the boat, which rode higher in the water. He steamed away with the rest of the Indians to Little Rock, then returned days later for Chief Hadjo and his people. It was easy to see there would have been no room for the horses or men.

After the boat left Memphis, the men were ready to begin this river crossing. Mr. Freeman the Assistant Agent was the leader. Although Mr. Freeman knew little about how to cross rivers, he wisely let the Indians take charge. These men had crossed rivers and knew well its power and strength. No one spoke the river's name. To speak of something very strong would only bring fear. Someone shouted, "What about this boy?" It was little Jack. The boy couldn't bear to leave his pony and besides, he wanted to go with the men. He was hiding to stay with his horse when the boat had left. Too late! There was no turning back now. The river must be crossed. Jack watched the elders at the water's edge praying for the safety of their people. The leader's horses plunged into the water. Other riders followed. Though concerned for the boy, the water raged so violently that no one could help.

Before his eyes, men and horses were being disastrously carried downstream, pulled under and dragged to the bottom. Jack nudged his pony into the water, "Let's go". Huge logs were careening down the river. Riders reaching the far bank turned to watch the little boy and his pony. Soon everyone was watching the drama. Midway, something large knocked him from the horse. Jack was swallowing water and gulping for air. No one could help the boy now. Somehow he was able to grab the pony's tail. The horse struggled through the heavy current until he was able to stand and walk to shore. Jack! Men lifted the boy in their arms. He had made it! Others who watched the boy's crossing, re-marked about seeing a tiny man sitting on the head of that pony. That was strange but the little man was also directing the pony across the raging river with little Jack in tow.

It took awhile for the ones swept the farthest to return up-stream. In gratitude, everyone gathered that evening on the west bank. Their tradition was to change the name of a child or man when something important happened in his life. Names were never given for a lifetime, but earned by deeds. Jack's new name was "Jock-O-Gee". Their mind says "Jack" but their tongue says "Jock". "Gee" means "little". This modest name would mark a small boy who overcame a mighty river. The name had a second unspoken but more powerful meaning. All knew of the 'little peo-ple'. No one had seen the 'little people' for at least four genera-tions. Yet, it was clear that the mark of the Great Spirit and the 'little people' were on Jock-O-*Gee*. No one had dared to speak the river's name. "Gee" was as close as they dared to speak the full name of the 'little people'. The knowledge and protection by the 'little people' reside with peace-makers. From the day the river was crossed, "they" were with Jock-O-Gee, teaching him how to docktor sick people in the new land with new herbs and plants.

Back in the old country, the War Clan people had warned, "All the White Man wants is the Indian's land". It was sad. Rather than hate the White Man for taking their land, they had come to the river and prayed. The Creator had brought them safely across the river. At this moment, they became Indians again. This was a good lesson and it made the rest of the trip go easier.

In one week, the men and horses crossed the river and swamp to meet the women and children at Little Rock. In 96 days, they were the second party to arrive in Indian Territory after being the last to leave. The agent would be happy! He gets paid $20 a head for every *live* Indian. One last time the line was formed to count. At the place where the sergeant shouts the final count, he stopped. Something was wrong. He asked for a recount and the line reformed. Recount. The soldier called out, "Sir, the count is

2,237". The party had started with less than 2,000. How is this possible!

The lieutenant gathered the chiefs. Their secret was now told: the 'hostiles' had been with them all the way. These were 'hostiles', never captured. Ones very frightened with whom the Indian people shared their food. Lt. Sprague replayed the journey in his mind. The boat count had been 1,500. That boat wouldn't have left if the count was 200 long. Still angry when the men refused the boat, he had skipped the count. By the boat count, there *had to be* 500 men swimming the horses. It was clear now there were 700 men and the boy. Fooled! Who would sneak a chance to swim a raging river and walk 1,200 miles! The lieutenant was duty-bound to act against the hostiles. He changed the count to 1,984 and paid the agent. This single act of kindness erased grudges against all White Men. The hostiles smiled, then went away to choose their land.

And so it was with the rest of the Tribe. The war clan, the Kasihta, are supposed to prepare for the next battle. The war clan's parting public message for the lieutenant was, "We will live in peace and friendship in the new country—if the White Man will let us." Everyone smiled, then went away to choose their land.

Shoo. Get outta here!

Big Chicken

It was 25 years after the Muscogea people crossed the big river to the western lands, when the white men started *their* war. It was strange how they called it *civil* and killed each other. The Indians had sold their land to move to Oklahoma Territory, but the federal government was still paying annuities. So the threat of non payment forced the tribe to carefully consider taking sides. No one could agree. Over 5,000 of the Upper Creeks left for Kansas, a Union state. The Lower Creeks, who stayed in Oklahoma, served with the Confederate Indian Troops under Colonel Daniel McIntosh and Lt. Colonel Chilly McIntosh.[1] As a respected docktor, they made Jock-o-gee a lieutenant. He was a good docktor. When an Indian would get shot in the arm by noon-time, the doctor had him ready for battle the next day. Jockogee was at the Battle of Honey Springs in 1863. The Creeks lost this battle, the last major skirmish in Oklahoma. Even though the Indians enjoyed battles, the White Man far away decided when the War ended. Their side, the Confederates lost.

After the War, it was rough on the Confederate veterans. They were treated as traitors, regardless of their role in the war. Not only did the white settlers treat them badly, but so did the tribesmen who returned from Kansas as part of the "winning side". This led to internal strife. As part of the war settlement, the tribes had to give right-of-way for railroads to cross the land. The old Butterfield coaches used to leave Ft. Smith going west to intersect with the Texas Road, which ran north to south, connecting Ft. Gibson to Eufaula and Texas. After 1872, the north-to-south railroad called "the Katy" was built on the same Texas Road. [2] This opened the gates for the white settlers coming to Indian Territory. From people traveling the Texas Road, Jockogee heard how easy it was for the old Confederates living in Choctaw Country. The Choctaws needed good doctors in southeast Oklahoma.

Jackson "Jockogee" Lewis had married Nancy Phillips about the time the Creeks joined the Confederacy. His daughter, Cindy, was born while he was off to battle. Now, he couldn't stand the thought of his baby being harmed. Yes, it would be best to leave his family with relatives, go doctor for the Choctaws. He was called to visit the Choctaws for several months. Even though his skills were greatly needed there, the docktor would get so lonely. He would ride his horse up the old Texas Road to Fallah to visit his loved ones.

When his wife Nancy died, there was a long time that Jockogee couldn't stand to return. He gave up his land and was once gone from Fallah for 12 years. Cindy, his daughter, had grown to be a beautiful woman. She had married George, who was a good farmer. With the railroad bringing white settlers, they moved to a farm four miles west of town. George couldn't stand to be around the white settlers, who wanted nothing but his farm. Sam & Nancy, George's parents, continued to live just west of Fallah close to other Indian families. Their place was between town and the old Indian Baptist Church. They used to call it Tulla-much-kea, but it's been gone for many years.

The years seemed to melt away. As grandfather Jockogee Lewis became older, his visits grew longer. And everyone was so glad to see him. He was sure glad to see them! The one who treasured his visits the most was his favorite grand-daughter, Susie. She was George and Cindy's second child, about six years old at the turn of the century. Grandfather would always ask her to scratch his back. He was 70 years old. At first, she didn't want to do this. Out of respect for the elders, she must do this task. After all, he had chosen her from all the children. Susie would get a stick to rub his back until he fell asleep. Susie loved that grandpa and he loved her.

Today was hot. Docktor Jockogee was on his way home. A letter had reached him in Choctaw Country. Cindy sure needed him to come. It was something wrong with George's father, Sam. He didn't like to travel in the hottest part of the Summer, but he felt a pressing need this time. The sweat poured from under his hat band and ran down his back. His horse was hot and white patches of sweat lathered his skin. They were both parched when he arrived in front of Sam's place. The dogs announced a stranger. This brought Susie out of the house to see who was coming. It was her grandpa! She ran to greet him with the barking dogs chasing behind. When the dogs recognized the rider, their tails started wagging. They were quiet again. Grandfather smiled at her and dismounted with his bag in hand. As he went into the house, Susie led the horse away to give it water. Then she removed the saddle and wiped off the lather. This chore was a delight because grandfather had come! Surely he would tell stories tonight after supper. They needed someone to bring joy. Everyone was sad because her other grandpa Sam was sick. Bad sick!

Cindy had brought Susie with her to care for the sick one. George and the other children had stayed on the farm. Corn crop ready to pick now. Cindy was so relieved that the ol' docktor had come. It didn't take long to tell him the bad news. As she spoke, he was shaking his head. Yes, he could see 'bad medicine' at work. Many thoughts rushed through his head. The ol' Indians know there is a battle of the 'good' and the 'bad' medicines. So they never made a show of emotions in public. They never

bragged much. Others were always listening. It's easy for someone to be jealous. The slightest affront may be warped out of
shape and they seek the witch docktor. Just a small gift or favor
would start work on an evil spell. What's bad is that few know
who the witch docktor is, or his victim. Those under attack are
not prepared to fight 'bad' medicine. They often aren't aware of
the problem before becoming very ill. If the docktor with 'good'
medicine can identify the cause, sometimes he can find a way to
block the spell or cure the sickness.

Old Sam was very ill. There was no cool place inside the
house, so they kept him on a bed under the trees. He was pro-
tected from the sun and the gentle breeze could blow across his
hot skin. With each passing day he became weaker. No medicine
gave comfort. The ol' docktor was angry with himself that he
couldn't figure out what to do. Sam was a good man and everyone *seemed* to like him a lot. He was fair and generous with
everyone. The docktor knew that the 'little people' had given him
good medicine to use. Their herbs and plants work well, but
these spells were hard to untangle.

As old Sam laid quietly, he called out, "We-o-jumba. We-o-
jumba." When the old ones realize death is near, there is only one
thing they want. That is the cold, sweet water from the little
spring on the tall hill. The old docktor would look at Sam, shake
his head. Nothing helping him. They would do their best to bring
spring water to him. The spring was maybe a half-a-mile away.
Jockogee and Susie walked to the hill and climbed the west side.
Its not a big spring, but there is a huge stone over it. The water
that flows from under the rock and down the hill is the coldest
and sweetest water around. Susie gently scooped up a bowl of
this water. It was nearly dark. Jockogee lit the lantern to see the
way as they walked reverently down the hill.

Soon Sam had his drink. He smiled weakly to thank them.
Then Jockogee hung the lantern on the porch. Every Indian
knows that the night belongs to the animal kingdom. You could
hear the calls of the night creatures, such as "chuck-bah-la-bah-

la", the whip-poor-will. The night locusts or "gah-zuh-zah" are singing loudly in the woods. They reach a crescendo, then fade away as another tribe of locusts answers their calls. After awhile both tribes tire of making such beautiful music. Then the crickets and tree frogs chime in with their peaceful languages so serene. Most nights you could hear the owl. To the Indians, the owl's screech was especially terrifying. One of its jobs is to warn of impending death. There are many noises of the night woods. Especially with someone deathly ill, the noise grows louder.

Indians know that some witch docktors change their physical form. When death is near for their victim, he tries to sneak inside the house when no one is watching. He could come disguised as a chicken, a dog, an owl or something else. They say [3] the creature comes to steal the last bit of life, while a person is too weak to fight back. This little bit of stolen life lets the witch docktor himself live longer.

To protect from these excursions of the evil ones from the edge of the night, the old Indian would rake the ground clean. Nothing was allowed to grow between the house and the woods. Anything in that clearing in the daylight could be identified as friend or foe. At night a lantern was lit and hung on the porch. It kept back the darkness and what it was hiding. The docktor would walk around the house with his pipe, laying down a smoke ring of protection. Tobacco smoke was one of the strongest medicines. The next morning Momma Cindy carefully swept around the house. Her sturdy broom was made from the buck brush. Back and forth. Back and forth. As the broom swished, she looked for tracks of strange creatures that had passed in the night. Finding strange tracks would lead to a search around the house with her broom in hand. Woe to whatever she found.

That night the lantern either wasn't bright or there was something mighty powerful in the darkness! A big fire was lit on the clean ground. It blazed all night. It's dancing flames cast shadows across the trees at the edge of the woods. The smoke kept away the "oke-we-yah", the big mosquitoes. More important, the fire kept away whatever evil was out there. These were called "watch fires" and for good reason. The docktor was doing everything that had worked before.

Sam laid still with only the light from the watch fires. It was near dusk and the locusts and tree frogs were singing. The owl was hooting. Suddenly all the noises stopped! Momma Cindy was in the house. In the middle of the silence, noise came though the screen door. The sound was that of "Dah-lo-se", a chicken. She knew that no animal was allowed near the house at night, much less a chicken. Besides, it was already past the time when chickens are asleep on their roosts. Cindy glanced out the door. There was a chicken standing just off the porch nearly three feet tall! No ordinary chicken. She rushed from the house with the broom. With the screen door slamming behind her, she was shouting, "Dah-lo-se, shoo! Get outta here! I no like you!" Swap! She swung her broom like a war club. Big chicken ran across the clearing and disappeared into the darkness. It was afraid of the light and the broom!

In spite of Cindy's courage and the docktor's best efforts, Sam died. They placed the casket in the little Fallah Indian church. Many people came for this last time to see him. Susie and her mother came. Along the way they must walk by the old graveyard, by the old church called "Tulla-much-kea". Just being near the graveyard was scary to Cindy. She held her mother's hand very tightly. It used to be ol' Sam's church long time ago, but there was nothing left of the old log cabin. When the women reached the Church house, they took turns to watch the casket the last few days to protect it from evil spirits. Over the casket, they carefully placed a blanket to keep the spirit warm. To prepare Sam for the long trip to the spirit land, they added little bits of his favorite food on the foot of the casket. Just a pinch of "tok-lake-dok-cea", the Indian sour bread and a little bit of "auh-pusk-kea", the parched corn. It doesn't take much for the journey in the sky.

A few days later, the night noises were calm again. There had been no time to tell stories. Jockogee took Susie out on the front porch. The lantern had been removed. It was near dusk and the "oke-we-yah" were buzzing around. Grandfather pays no attention to the mosquito and they leave. Susie asked, "What does Tulla-much-kea mean?" He answered, "Back in the times when our people came to this county, they didn't trust missionaries anymore. These people came and talked about God, but forced the Indian to give up his old ways, dancing, and playing flutes and drums. Losing their homelands, Indians felt they had been betrayed in Alabama and Georgia. At the River Crossing, the Creeks forgave the White Man. Yet here there were still grudges. Any Indian claiming to be a Christian was punished hard. The Christian always took punishment without flinching. After watching them thrive on hardship, our leaders could see they had been wrong. This new religion was a good one. They had been blaming God for all their troubles, when it was just man. It was another ten years or so before they let Indian churches meet. Tulla-much-kea was one of the first Indian churches built in Oklahoma Territory. I guess every evil witch docktor tried spells on those church members. Sam was one of the last ones, very brave and strong. He never flinched. You will be proud of him in the days to come". Susie smiled at grandfather. She would have to choose, whether to be tossed about by the battle of good and bad medicine or learn the new religion. These words were wise and they stuck.

Years later, Susie remembered the exact moment of Jocko-gee's death. From another room, she heard a spoon rattle in the kitchen. When she looked, no one was there. Then she recalled how he would "fix" a cup of coffee. He would add extra sugar, then stir and stir, while lost in his thoughts. Then he would lay the spoon on the table. It would rattle just like it did that day. With that noise, you knew it was his last visit.

Author's note: *Lieutenant Jackson Lewis of the First Creek Regiment, Confederate States of America, was buried in the old Church Cemetery on Southport Road. Later that year, young Susan, age 12 years old became a member of the new religion.*

Grandfathers Stories

A Squirrel Tree

Long ago but years after crossing the big river, the Muscogea Indian family moved to Fallah. They lived in a log house in the woods. There was no money but that didn't make them poor. That was because Earth Mother would give them plenty of good things to eat. Corn, squash and other vegetables were grown in the garden. Out in the woods beyond were other good things to eat such as wild berries, roots and nuts. The woods were filled with many wild game animals for meat. It took many tasks to gather, then prepare food for the family to eat. Everyone did their share gladly to help each other. The land was good to them.

After eating supper, the family talked. There was no television in those days. Even if there was, there was no electricity. For that matter, there were no pipes to supply such common things as running water. In those days, the water in the streams was clean and pure. They dipped water from the stream to drink. It was good. When the evening chores were done, everyone gathered around the fireplace to talk about the day's events.

Each child had two parents, but he also has four grand parents and many uncles and aunts. All or some may have come for supper that night. The young ones tell their tale of the day. Then one of the elders is reminded of an incident that happened long ago. Sharing what was learned in the past helps the child see the similarity to what happened this day. They learn something from beyond what their eyes can see or the fingers can touch. This is good! The children have much respect for the elders because they are the final source of knowledge on anything worth asking. Yes, all the children looked forward to the evening. It was the best time of the day!

ChaBon was a small boy in a large Indian family. "ChaBon" means "boy", when applied to a very curious boy. This boy was so smart and wondered about everything. Since an Indian's nature is not to ask many questions, the name fit the boy. ChaBon could hardly wait to tell what happened today, "I was walking in the woods and heard a squirrel in the tree. As I passed, he made talk in his language, 'ur-ur'. He was looking right at me and barked. Each 'word' he spoke, his tail would flip behind him. The squirrel wanted me to see something or to do something for him. Once he had my attention, the squirrel stared there in the bushes." ChaBon motioned in *that* direction and continued, "My eyes followed to where the squirrel was looking. Over there, I could see a wildcat sneaking in the bushes. I threw a rock and the cat ran away. The cat was sneaky and was going to eat the squirrel. That squirrel needed my help!"

Ah! Grandfather heard ChaBon's words. The boy told of helping others and was not thinking about himself. It is good. Now he is ready to hear something new.

Tonight, Grandfather was sitting in front of the fireplace. The light came over his shoulders. He was outlined by the dancing flames, but no one could see the features of his face. The words came out of the dark spot where his mouth should be. He said, "Stee-lo-booch-go-gee". ChaBon knew that these words in his language meant "little people". He had heard the elders use these words before. If he was nearby, they would stop talking or switch to some other subject. This had happened several times. ChaBon only knew little bits. Each instance they mentioned 'little people', he managed to collect a word or two. This was enough to cause a great thirst inside him to learn more. Yes, ChaBon was different from most other Indian children.

Grandfather puffed on his clay pipe. The smoke of the Indian tobacco mixed with other herbs smelled so good. Then he spoke to the children, "There are many strange things we do not know. 'Stee-lo-booch-go-gee', the 'little people' are always near us. We can't see them. Sometimes they sound like the little birds twittering or squirrels chattering. They look carefully for children who are curious and can learn fast. It takes a long time to be sure, so they don't decide quickly. Then, one day, the child is able to see one of the 'little people', maybe two or more. They always talk in our language just like you and me are talking."

ChaBon could feel Grandfather's words. They seemed to be directed at him. When he realized the message was meant for him, a winter chill passed across his back and down his legs. Oh! Grandfather could read the faces of people. He didn't need words to know which child was receiving the message. His voice was calm, "Now don't be frightened about the 'little fellows'. It's good that they come. It's their job to pick young ones who will grow up and be docktors that care for sick people. The 'little fellows' might ask *you* to go away with them for a few days."

The boy blinked his eyes. As Grandfather emphasized "you", he was looking right at ChaBon. Grandfather resumed, "If you do, the little ones will take care of you. They are going to teach you many things about what grows in the woods and meadows. After all that, they will bring you back to the family. There will be other visits. Too much to learn at once. It takes years to teach all the ways to docktor sick people. Even after teaching, they are never far away. 'Little people' are always around the good docktors to help them choose plants to make the good medicine." He says, "Next time you get sick and have to be taken to the docktor's place, look all around. His house could be next to a big tree."

Again Grandfather paused to puff on the pipe and talked to the boy, "ChaBon, it was good when you heard the squirrel talk, then threw the rock. That squirrel can run the trees faster than any other animal. Nothing can catch him. When he gets scared, his feet don't move. Then the cat can eat him. Sometimes we are supposed to be a 'rock' to chase away fear from someone else." ChaBon smiled. Grandfather's story was kind of a rock because it had removed his fear about 'little people'. Grandfather could have spoken earlier of ChaBon's squirrel story. Instead he waited to tell all the children about the little ones. ChaBon was captivated by every word that he heard.

The old man continued his story, "When you find the big tree at the docktor's house, look for squirrel holes. If the holes are in the tree, be sure to look for squirrels. If there are no squirrels, then you know that *something else* lives there." He puffed on his pipe. The children first looked at each other, then all whispered what must be there, "Stee-lo-booch-go-gee". Their little eyes got so big.

Finishing his story, Grandfather said, "The little people teach the docktor well. It takes a long time to learn to use the many plants. This is because people have so many different kinds of ills. Some times, a docktor thinks he knows more than his helpers. When this happens, the branches begin to die and fall off the Big tree. The little people leave. A docktor without his helpers can't do much for sick folks, and nothing for ones that are bad sick."

ChaBon would remember this story. He hoped soon to be sick enough to visit the docktor. But first he thanked Grandfather for this story, "Ma-to!", then added, "Tomorrow, I will remember to look closer at squirrels in the trees." It was time for bed. ChaBon was sure to dream about "Stee-lo-booch-go-gee" tonight.

They did an Honor Dance for me

Little People's Stomp Ground

After Grandfather's story, one of the children blurted out, "Steel-lo-booch————". The word was barely started from his mouth, when Grandfather cupped his hand over his own mouth. Then, he said, "Shoosh, they will hear you!" There was a pause, "Ahh, does anyone want to hear more?" Every child in the room was nodding his head, especially ChaBon.

Grandfather puffed his pipe a few times. The smoke curled up and into the room, making all sorts of shapes. All the children were captivated watching the smoke images. They watched until the smoke had disappeared to the farthest and darkest corners of the room. No child made a noise to hear what he was going to say next.

Grandfather pointed at the smoke and said, "Little people are like the smoke you see that disappears before your eyes. Most times only certain children can see them. They don't want to be seen by all the people. This story is about a man, who found the little people".

Strange things began to happen in the middle of the week

during the summer. The family noticed that after supper, Father would change his clothes to go somewhere. Just going anywhere except on Saturday was unusual but he was dressing special, too. He was wearing his boots and jeans and a shirt with ribbons with his wide-brimmed black hat. On his hat was the white feather, the special one, that was only worn in the Green Corn Dance. They call it the "water-bird" feather. Father even slicked down his black hair nice and smooth. It was obvious to everyone watching that he was going someplace special. Where? He didn't say where. He put on the black hat, turned, and walked out the door. No words. Later that night after everyone had gone to sleep, he came home. The next day, there was no mention of that escapade.

These strange visits kept on. One evening after supper, Father got dressed to leave. This time, he was carrying a little brown paper bag brought from the General store in town. It had to be something special. Before he reached the door, his wife's voice caught him, "Where are you going? It's the middle of the week and you are dressed up." He nodded as if to admit that he was cleaned up, then replied, "Goin' to the stomp dance". Father left them puzzling the mystery. Everyone knew that in Muscogea Country the stomp dances were held only on a weekend. Again, Father returned home late at night after every one was in bed.

His behavior lasted this way for several weeks. No one questions the man of the house in the old Indian families. The man of the house, the warrior, withholds information until he is sure of a blessing for his family and loved ones. So the family members have learned over time to resist questions. With each strange visit, the tension in the family increased.

One evening as he was getting ready to leave the house, the children were watching again. This time, mother couldn't stand it any longer. He knew it was time to tell his secret to the family. In that split second, everyone seemed to be alerted to what he would say. "This spring when I was hunting," he started, "I found a place deep in the woods. Strange place, it was. There, in the grass, was a big circle". As he spoke, his arms swung out to their full length, then swung in a huge imaginary circle. All the children's eyes seemed to follow the circle of his hands. He continued, "The grass that made the circle was darker in color than the rest of the grass in that place in the woods. There was a big 'x' that ran through the middle of the circle." His hands cut the air to show that the big 'x' went from one edge of the big imaginary circle to the other edge. He said, "After finding this place, I had an urge every day to go back to the same spot in the woods. I don't know why."

Father continued this strange story, "One day, I got to the place in the woods. Just beyond the circle, I could see many 'little men' dressed to dance. They were not in the circle, but milling around the outside. One little man noticed me standing there. He said, 'Hi, Man' like we had known each other for life. Many of the little fellers began to talk all at once in our language. It didn't take long for us to become friends. After a while, I didn't notice they were any different in size than me. I liked talking with them! One of the 'little ones' asked me to come back in a couple of days. He said, 'You will like to see what we do'. Oh, yes, I wanted to come back."

The children were as excited as Father and anxiously waited to hear more. He continued, "I left, then came back in two nights, after supper. There they were, waiting for me just outside the big circle. The leader waved his hand, motioning for me to rest and watch. I lay down on my side to watch what they would do. The little leader starting singing his songs, 'A-E-A, A-E-A, He-Hoe, He-Hoe, A-E-A, A-E-A!' as they all danced around the circle. It's kind of prayer for people they care about. On many other nights, I came back with my dance clothes on. I would watch the little people's stomp dance far into the night. One night, they did an honor dance for me. An honor dance is done for a chief, not an ordinary person such as me. It was great!"

Grandfather ended his story, "The Indian woman and her family were greatly relieved to learn that he wasn't crazy. He wasn't gambling and wasn't in any great trouble. It was *just* the 'little people'. From that day, no one in the family was ever sick. The man lived to be very old.

The biggest mystery that remained for the children sitting before Grandfather was what was inside the small brown paper bag. His story made it clear that no one should question the man of the house as to where he was going or especially about the little bag. As they wondered how to find the answer, Grandfather pulled out a small brown paper bag from his pocket. It was just like the one in the story. Every child scrambled to get closer to the bag but politely waited for Grandfather to speak. He smiled and held out the bag, "Here, try one." Each child dipped his hand deep into the sack. It rattled as the child chose one lump, placed it into his or her mouth. Peppermint! Grandfather knew that the children loved to hear stories and peppermint candy. As if to answer the question each child wanted to ask him, Grandfather smiled and said, "The 'little fellers' sure like candy, too."

Hi-Ho Silver, Away!

Tricksters

Tonight after supper, the children were hurrying to finish their chores and prepare for the next day's work. It was winter and cold outside tonight. More logs had been added to the fireplace. Tonight Grandfather was cold and sitting in front of the fire. As the logs burned down, he poked with a long stick to get the fire just right. He was waiting politely for the children to finish work. Their backs were toward him. Grandfather didn't have to be with them and see what they were doing to know when the work was done. He could hear them. They were all quiet at the same time. That signaled the work was about done. He whispered softly, "Stee-lo-bootch-go-gee". Oh, they were listening! Like a covey of quail, the children flocked into the darkened room to hear more.

The young ones gathered close together to keep warm. Grandfather started his story, "Some of the 'little ones' like to play tricks on people. Little ones come in two sizes. It's only the smaller little fellows that play tricks. Most any time that something strange happens and you can't figure out why, then one of the little fellows is close by, even if you can't see him."

One time there was an old man who lived in a small log cabin away from town. He was not a happy man and had no family. One day when he needed some groceries, he rode his horse to the General store in town. He left the horse tied out front, so as not to stray looking for grass to eat. Didn't stay long in the store. Didn't need much. When he came back to get the horse, someone had braided the mane and tail. The old man looked all around to see who was playing a trick on him. No one around. He glanced down at the braids. The knots were tied so small and tightly that his big fingers couldn't loosen them. Behind many of the knots were old yellow glass beads, so old that they were scratched and opaque. They were old Indian beads like the earliest traders had brought hundreds of years ago. The braids on his horse's mane were tied together with strings in a strange way—like reins. Those reins were too small to fit any child, much less a full-size man. Could be, some small person was riding the horse while he was inside the store. If so, the 'little man' would be urging the old horse to go faster, "Hi-ho Silver, away!"

All "this" had happened in a very short time. Unable to loosen the knots, he had to mount the horse and head toward his small log cabin. Riding through the town brought him a great deal of unwanted attention. The townspeople would stop walking where ever they might be going and stare at him. Here was a rather plainly dressed man riding that fancy tied horse. Where had this man got that fine horse? Was it stolen? This extra attention embarrassed the man. He yanked a long knife from his pocket, then cut off those braided knots and hurried away from their rude stares. The townspeople remembered the event for years and years. It's strange how these little fellers pick on people who don't smile much. Trying to bring a little joy into their lives, I suppose.

This story delighted the children. They were looking at each other. Their black eyes were flashing in the firelight. One of the children remembered the time when they were all playing in the pasture. One of the horses had tiny braids in its mane. At the time, he had blamed the other children. No one knew how this had happened. Now they knew that it was only the little people borrowing a horse for awhile. They never stole anything, only used what they could find. Telling the story had solved a great childhood mystery.

Grandfather nodded his head. He could see that the children understood what they had seen. Then he told this story, "Another time an old man was sitting in a chair on the front porch. It was a warm day. Soon he had closed his eyes. His head dropped to his chest as sleep came over him. His eyes were closed only a moment! When he awoke, his shoe laces were tied together. They were tied so tightly that he couldn't walk, nor could he untie the knots on his shoes. Out came his long knife. Snip. Snip. The laces were cut and he took off the shoes, tucked them under his arm. He wasn't taking any chances on those little pranksters getting hold of his shoes again".

Grandfather had a comment, "It's a surprise to wake up and be hobbled like a horse. Now, that old man didn't have any grandchildren to play tricks on him. So he knew those 'little people' were around his porch." He had brought the children into the story. When they realized this, they all laughed.

Grandfather went on with other stories, "There was a man who traveled a dirt road to meet a friend. Some 'little people' were tagging along even though no one could see them. He knew they were there. When the two men met, they got to talking about the *old days*. As they talked, the 'little ones' got to scuffling nearby. The dust was flying high in the air. The men stopped talking to see what was the cause. To the man who knew about the little ones, it was no surprise. The other man was startled. Not only were there two tiny men down on the ground before him, but they had suddenly appeared from nowhere. Most times the 'little ones' are very careful not to be seen by anyone. When it comes to scuffling, they must get careless—just like you and me."

The old man added, "There is something I need to tell you for use later in your life. When you happen to have a few crumbs or morsels left over from the evening meal, save them. Take them along with you on the next walk in the woods. Just drop a crumb or two as you leave. It doesn't have to be much. If you go hunting rabbits or fishing, drop a few crumbs. Keep walking. Don't look back. Watch out! The fish you catch gonna be bigger that day. The rabbits you catch gonna be bigger too." With that story, the children were yawning and Grandfather sent them to bed.

This was a big family. After the children heard that story, it seemed there were never any leftovers on the supper dishes and the fish that the children brought home—were bigger.

I'm Cutting This Horse Free From a Spell

McIntosh Cemetery

It was a cold and blustery day. All the livestock had stayed inside the barn. Someone was coming down the road. Good! It was Uncle Nathan, Dad's brother. Dad had always called him "Brother". He had come to spend a couple of days. It seemed to ChaBon that his coat pockets were bulging. All the children remembered that he sometimes brought them candy.

After the chores were done that night, the family sat around the fire to hear what Uncle Nathan had to say. Before speaking, he reached for his coat hanging in the kitchen. ChaBon remembered the big bulge in his coat pockets. He slowly brought out a bag of candy. The children's eyes grew bigger and bigger. He set the bag on the floor before the children. Everyone sat near the bag eating sweets and waiting for the stories to follow. This was a spooky story, but true.

One night, a few months ago, Brother had been to town visiting friends. He stayed much too late talking. Sometimes they get to drinking the beer made from peaches. This was called "choc" beer. The moon was shining brightly as he left the house. "Ah, yes, it would be easier to ride with a full-moon lighting my way," he thought. He mounted his white horse and starting riding south on the old Southport road. The road made a turn to the east. At the corner and on the other side of the fence was the McIntosh Cemetery. There is no older graveyard in the State of Oklahoma than that one. No one called it a "cemetery" and certainly not "graveyard". It was referred to as "Grandma's Corner". It's been there since 1827. Approaching the turn ahead, he was startled. In the bright moonlight, he could see the figure of a man suddenly stand up. He was dressed in black from head to toe. Because of the nearby graveyard, the man knew this could mean trouble. He stopped the horse, then kicked her in the flanks. "Ye-hah! Get out of here!" he shouted. Now in a rush to go west as fast as the horse could run.

That horse was making tracks as they went through a cross roads. Just ahead, Brother could again see the figure of a man standing. In the moonlight, he could see the man was dressed in black. Why it was the same man from Grandma's Corner! He realized that as fast as the horse ran, that spirit was faster! Chills ran all over his body! Again he turned the horse around to escape back to the cross roads just passed. "Ye-hah! he slapped the horse on the rump. She reared, then started running.

As the horse raced down the road, Brother remembered a second Indian cemetery further down Southport road. He was tired of messing with graveyards. He was more tired of messing with spirits at graveyards! He knew there was a pond about half way to that other cemetery. Tonight there was a mist or fog coming from the pond, which covered the road. He was a little afraid of going through the fog in front of him.

Brother stopped the horse to listen and smell for strange things to know what to do next. He knew that the pond is ringed with willow trees. The willows have long branches that hang to the water's edge. He imagined things that could be concealed beneath the willow limbs. Yes, he had heard other's call this pond "the Bear".

Suddenly his nose caught the pungent smell of a bear. In his mind, it was a big bear. He stood in the stirrups and whacked the horse's rump. Let's get out of here. The horse stood frozen stiff and wouldn't or couldn't move. Yes, he knew she had smelled the bear!

Brother carried a pistol for emergencies such as this. Under his breath, he muttered, "I'm not afraid! I'm not afraid!" He pulled his pistol and got off the horse. Walking in front of the horse, he cut the air swinging the big pistol. He shouted loud so that all could hear, "I'm cutting the horse free from the spell. Now she can run!" Shouting like that made him feel brave and strong again. Back on the horse, he kicked her in the flanks. Away she flew again. He had his pistol in his hand, so nothing better mess with him. Now that the horse was running fast, he hit her again, "Faster! Faster!"

Just ahead, he saw something white stand up! The horse kept running. As horse and rider rushed by the white object, he was afraid to look. Something swished by his hand and the cold chills returned. He feared to be chased by a spirit that could move so fast. There was just one chance. He shouted out, "I'm going to kill this thing!" He swung the pistol over his left shoulder. He could see the white spirit following him, floating in the air, getting nearer! Blam! Blam! Blam! Not looking backward again, he fired all the shots left in the pistol. The horse ran so fast! Fortunately, he was able to get home that night without more problems. As the horse trotted into the yard, he was so relieved to be home. Both he and the horse were drenched with sweat. Hot, but with cold chills shaking his body, he just rolled off the horse and hurried to bed.

The next morning, his wife woke Brother for breakfast. Just waking startled him. When she pulled off the blanket, he was still in his clothes. The pistol was gripped tightly in his hand. She could see the terror in his eyes. Gently, she pried his fingers loose and took the gun from him. He watched her check the pistol for bullets. It was empty. That frightened him more! To name his fear, she asked, "Did you see a ghost or something worse?" No answer. She looked out the window to see the horse. It was in the yard still saddled. When the wife and children went outside to care for the horse, they were surprised. This horse had no tail. What happened last night?

Brother slowly ate breakfast, dreading the questions sure to come about the horse's tail. Finally, he told the family what happened, "When that tail flipped up, I thought it was that old spirit chasing me." His voice got very low, "I guess I musta shot her tail off." Then he vowed to the family to never again touch that "chock" beer. And he would stay away from Grandma's Corner! To this day, on the last turn in the Southport road, you can sometimes see a little man. He will be dressed in black, standing there off the road—behind the fence of the old McIntosh Cemetery. If you look carefully, you will see a slight smile. Probably remembers the night of the full moon when the man shot off his horse's tail.

LITTLE PEOPLE HUNTER WITH TURKEY (GRASSHOPPER)

I Have Killed a Big Turkey for You to Eat

Strongest Man in the World

Dad's brother Nathan had the best stories about "little people". Uncle Nathan told this story about a good friend.

It had rained most of the night. The big thunder would shake the house, then lightening flashed. Sleep came in fits to the Indian man and his wife. Finally, the storm ended and both slept again. As the sun raised its face the next morning, the skies were clear. The man was awakened by the birds' wake-up songs. He put on his clothes and went outdoors. Ah, there was an early morning rainbow in the sky. Yes, today would be a good day!

His wife was still asleep. Maybe there was time to take a little walk. As he walked along, it was easy to imagine some of the good things that she would cook for his breakfast. Ham and biscuits and coffee. While distracted, he heard a small voice, "Ho, man, you want to come see our place?" He was startled by three tiny men standing in his path. "They are too small to hurt me," he thought. His curiosity overcame the thoughts of food. He followed the little men walking through the underbrush in a south and westerly direction.

Soon, the little men reached a small stream. The leader gathered them near the water. Their little voices sounded like many bumble bees. He gestured and talked, then turned and looked directly at the man. The leader spoke to him, "The rains last night have made the river too wide and deep for us to cross. We need your help to go home." The water may have been chest deep to the man. He didn't want to wade cold water, much less carry three little men. Instead, the man began the search for a felled tree. He returned with a sapling chewed to the ground by a beaver. It was just the right size, about six inches across. He dragged it to the edge of the stream, walked his hands up the trunk to make it stand erect. It toppled over, crashing down across the stream. The little men jumped up and down and shouted and cheered, "You are the strongest man in the World!" The man smiled. Their encouragement made him feel good. Next, the little men took up the line formation and led him safely across the "bridge". They looked like ants crossing the log. Reaching the other side of the stream, they again cried, "You are the strongest man in the World!"

This procession reached a big hill covered with trees. The leader stopped. He pointed to a hole in the side of the hill, "Ho, man, you want to go inside our house?" Even before an answer came, the men popped through the hole. Dropping to his knees, the man squeezed his head and shoulders through then struggled in. Once inside, he sat up. A good hunter learns to use his nose, especially when it's dark. What he smelled was danger! There was a heavy pungent, musky odor in the room.

In the rear of the dark hole, he could see light shining through another opening. Slowly his eyes began to adjust to the darkness. Snake! Big snake! His eyes locked on the snake, coiled, with its head in the air. It's tongue was flicking in and out as it peered into the man's eyes! Then he was aware of hissing. He didn't dare to move his head, but looked sideways. The room was filled with hundred's of snakes of all sizes. There were red and yellow and green and black snakes. Most of the big snakes were coiled and hissing at the man. Smaller snakes were entwined about others like little children playing.

The man was so frightened at the terrible sight of the snakes. He regretted following these little people. Maybe he could escape. Then his eye was attracted by the leader of the little men, waving his hand, "Stop, don't be afraid. We keep *them* here so that people won't bother us. You can see the guard snakes with rattle tails are quiet." Then, he gestured across the room to the second hole. He turned and walked with the others following. "Come with us," they cried out. The little men walked through the hissing snakes as if they were nothing but a field of daisies waving in the breeze.

The man backed against the wall of the cave to keep his eye on the snakes in front of him. With his fingers touching the cold damp wall, he inched his way. Reaching the opening, he turned and leaped headfirst through the hole. He fell to the floor of the second cave. The little men were standing near, looking him in the eye. One at a time, they would stick out their tongue at the big man and hiss—like one of the snakes. All laughed. They were making fun of him. After watching them walk through the snakes, he admired their courage. Lying on the floor, he no longer felt like the "Strongest man in the World". His heart was still pounding. He had much to learn about courage.

As he was prostrate on the floor, they turned to talk to themselves in their little voices. The leader walked up close to his face, "Ho, man, you hungry? Have you eaten today?" He answered, "Well, yes, I would eat. What do you eat, acorns and berries?" They were talking again to themselves. The leader turned to a little warrior. The underling drew himself to full attention as if to salute, then picked up his bow and arrows and left the room. The other two sat cross-legged on the floor and started a small fire. The flames danced and the smoke wisped from the room. "They" seemed to be waiting for the hunter to return.

It wasn't long until the hunter came back with the "kill" slung over his tiny shoulder. He entered the cave and threw it to the floor before the cooks. It was a big yellow grasshopper with a small arrow sticking from it's side. He said, "Man, I have killed a big turkey for you to eat. It will taste so good." The cooks began to roast the grasshopper. When it was done "just right", the head cook tore off a leg and passed it to the man. "Have you ever eaten grasshopper, even *roasted* grasshopper?" It took great courage for the man to take a small bite from the roasted leg. He was quite surprised to learn its taste *was* like wild turkey. He was hungry. It surprised him that his stomach was so full even though this grasshopper was so small—to him. The little men patiently waited and watched the man eat his fill. Then, each one ate small portions. When finished, they wiped the last trace of turkey grease from their little hands on their little bare legs. They smacked their little lips and clapped their little hands, and smiled. Once the meal was done the chattering began again. The leader stepped forward, "Man, you stay with us for a few days. We want to show you more of our ways." The man was captivated with their courage and skills and rather disappointed with his own. Leaving meant to cross that snake pit. He was pleased to stay with them.

Three days later, he returned home. His wife remembered the rainbow she saw the morning that he had left home. He left before breakfast and returned days later, happy and so peaceful. Not hungry and not talking about where he had been.

She would not have questioned the children and she wouldn't question him either. Breakfast was served and good luck seemed to follow them. The man was right. This had turned into a good day.

Treading on Sacred Ground

Intruder

A unt Loney was married to Robert Grayson, a Muscogea medicine man and interpreter. Robert knew both the Indian and English languages. The Graysons lived in a log house near the old McIntosh cemetery. After living a long time on the old home place Robert and Loney are buried in the old family cemetery. Long ago William McIntosh was one of the first White Men to come live with the Muscogea people in Georgia. His descendants were the first of the Muscogea Nation to travel to Indian Territory; that happened in 1828.[1]

Some of the relatives who came for supper at ChaBon's house were Uncle Robert and Aunt Loney. They would eat then spend the night. This custom is what people did back in those days because the distance was too far to travel that night. Roads were poor. The horses and wagons moved as slow as walking yourself, but not nearly as tiring.

After supper with the evening chores done, everyone gathered around the fire for their daily family talk. One of the children had found a large bunch of onions growing by the spring at the creek.

What a find! Everyone enjoyed eating eggs with wild onions. This food is very special food to Indians. Wild onions are like small roots or bulbs covered with a thin skin, growing in the dirt. All have an onion flavor but you look for the ones with longer green tops. That means that the onion in the ground below is a bit larger. Those big ones are the ones to dig. Let the smaller ones keep growing for another time. Yum. Tomorrow everyone would go to dig more onions.

Talk about the fun of onion hunting was enough to remind Uncle Robert about another time, when Aunt Loney went to dig onions. He told this story to the children. One spring day, it was time to dig wild onions. The 'place where the onions grow' was down in the meadow in the shade of the big mountain. To dig onions, she carried the kitchen butcher knife.

Loney walked briskly to the 'place where the onions grow'. She was looking forward to this. Seeing the place before her, she sat down on the ground ready to dig. There were so many onions in that place, she didn't have to move far. As she dug, the onions were dropped into the folds of her long dress. She would collect a pile of onions, then stop digging long enough to clean them with her big knife. The small root would be cut from the tiny white bulb. Then, peeling off the outer skin and leaving the long green tops.

After working awhile, Loney was aware of a buzzing noise in her ears. The noise kept getting louder as she gathered the onions. It was now a roaring noise. Finally to a crescendo, Loney could stand this no longer. She stopped digging and sat erect. As her eyes refocused far away, there in the distance was Robert. He was coming toward her, waving his arms. Even this far away, he seemed to have a scowl on his face. She wondered, "What is wrong?" He walked briskly and shouted at her. His lips were moving but she couldn't understand his words. As he came nearer, Loney called to him, "I have a roaring in my ears. Can't hear what you are saying!"

There was a long silence. Made no sense to keep shouting. Robert kept walking until he towered over Loney. He said, "Woman, you are sitting on the sacred ground of the little people.

They dance here." He spoke very calmly so as not to frighten her. Loney jumped like lightning had struck her. The onions that used to be on her lap flew in every direction. Her black eyes were flashing as she searched all around her for something strange. The roaring sound was now like a strong wind blowing from the northeast. The noise got louder in her ears.

Robert put his big arm around Loney to settle her. With his other hand, he pointed to a big circle on the ground. It was about fifteen feet in diameter. The earth in the circle was a different color than the rest of the onion patch. Spread across the big circle was a giant "X". Where she had been sitting to dig onions was right in the middle of the "X"! Loney was the intruder here!

Neither man nor woman saw anything, but they could feel *something* very close by. Gathering up her onions from the ground, Robert and Loney walked off the big circle. Loney was startled when the buzzing noise stopped as suddenly as it all started. When she looked back, they were beyond the edge of the big circle. Loney looked at Robert and they both looked in every direction for anyone who may be playing tricks with them. The sun was shining brightly and the gentle breeze lilted across the meadow.

No problem here. Robert left to go catch a big fish for supper that night. Loney positioned herself in a new spot to pick more onions. All day long as she worked to dig the bulbs, her mind replayed the old stories about "little people". Until *that* day those stories weren't so important. The roaring in her ears was now gone but not forgotten.

As Robert's story ended, Aunt Loney spoke softly, "even the smallest task you do is important". She offered to go along tomorrow and show the children how to dig onions. 'Digging onions' was spoken but each child's mind was focused on staying away from the little people's dancing place. Each pledged to be careful about where they would dig for onions the next day. This wild onion is small in size but big in taste. Tomorrow, everyone would eat eggs with lots of wild onion.

Why Can't I Move This Wagon?

Woman
with Wagon

Uncle Nathan had come to supper tonight. Aunt Alice had come, too. After a good meal, Nathan shared some stories about Aunt Alice: After Aunt Alice was married, she lived in a little house about a quarter mile east from the Fallah Indian Church. The road passed in front of her house on the way to the Church. At the road was a picket fence and a big tree in the front yard. The back yard behind the house melted into the forest to the south. Everyone respected Alice because she knew the "old ways" of the Muscogea People.

Aunt Alice enjoyed the many wild birds that lived near her home. In the olden days, the birds were not afraid and didn't fly away when someone walked near. The birds were too busy singing their hearts out. Every bird had a different job and a different song. Alice had studied them to see their many differences. They watched her, too. The little birds waited for her to come outdoors. In the olden days, the Indian families had no grass near the house. They took great pains to have a neat bare yard. Early each morning, Alice would sweep the earth clean with her big buck-brush broom. Swish. Swish. Swish.

As she swept the front yard, Alice talked to *her* birds. She called their names in the old language, "Fus-wah ja-dea". The red birds with black caps and their lighter colored mates would call back, "Sweet. Sweet. Sweet!" Oh, those pretty voices tickled her! The yellow birds with black wings were next. She called to them, "Fus-wah loni". A flock of the tiny yellow birds would fly just ahead of her feet and the swishing broom. They would be pecking at the last seed before the broom flipped it aside. There were the two little brown wrens perched on the porch. They watched, then the male sang out his song. So loud for such a small bird. Both the female bird and Alice admired this wonderful song. It gave them pleasure to watch the male wren look for a nice, nest site for his life-long mate. Alice kept on sweeping as the birds of all different color and song kept twittering. Few others in the area called out the bird's names in the old language. It was special to be called a familiar name. A variety of birds stayed around Aunt Alice's house. When she called out to them in her native tongue, they called back to her. The birds seemed to call her by a special name—"Sa-a-a-rah", "Sa-a-a-rah". Each time she came out to do chores or sweep the yard, they would call "Sa-a-a-rah", "Sa-a-a-rah". They loved her company as much as she loved having them around.

Back in Alabama,[1] the people would keep count of the new moons to keep track of the length of the Winter or Summer seasons. A notched counting stick was kept out in the barn. Six "notches" on the stick during Winter was about the time for Spring to start and crops to be planted. Aunt Alice didn't need a counting stick. She had the blue birds. Her Spring planting time was marked when the little blue-bird would show up to sing his song. "Fus-wah ho-lot-toe-gee" was the first bird of the Spring. He came before the grasses turned green or the buds started sprouting on the oak trees. With its red chest glimmering against the austere dull brown country side, the blue-bird was like the Sun shining. Its presence seemed to foretell the trees would be green soon and the Summer days would be hot again.

Alice's favorite birds were the pair of gray mockingbirds. During mating season, they serenaded everyone with the songs of all the birds and sometimes a squeaky gate. Alice would call to them, "fus-wah sa-ha-ya!", then she would laugh as they turned toward her and sang. When the baby birds were born, the parents would take turns watching to keep them safe. The mate would proudly sing from his perch in the front-yard tree. These babies heard melodies all day long and sometimes into the night. Papa bird would repeat each tune three or four times. The baby birds would soon be answering the calls. That made the parents happy. You could tell because they would jump high in the air, flashing the black and white tail feathers, then land again on their perch on the big tree. Just so happy! Then, the male would sing his song, mocking all the birds that he had heard that day. It was a joy to watch these birds. Oh, Summer was such a wonderful time for Alice.

During Sunday church services, the younger children would play outside. No one would scold them and they were not made to stay inside and keep quiet. Indian parents have an unusual way to discipline their children, only with words or stories. Never with force. In the summer, it was so hot inside the building even with the windows open. They were allowed to go outdoors to play, but never beyond the "branch" west of the church. To keep the children within a safe distance, stories were told to teach lessons: "At night, the branch is where you can hear a baby's cry". A little bit of fear keeps them within a quarter mile of the church. It was no surprise that the children didn't want to go to "that place". Instead, they chose to go in the opposite direction to Aunt Alice's house. Especially in the summer time and during Sunday and Wednesday Church meetings. Only the children could see the "little people" who came to watch the birds and play with them. It made no difference whether Alice was home or not.

Thanks to the "little people", the parents didn't have to discipline the children. With the younger children, the "little people" would pester and antagonize them until the child learned to submit to the parents warnings. When the child began to listen to his elders, then "they" encouraged his every action. You could see the sudden change as the child matured. The older children were no discipline problem. When they reached the age of 10 or 12 years, the child would decide to be grown-up. No more rolling or tussling for him! This is a sign that the "little people" were teaching him to obey. As the child reaches this point in his maturity, the parents tell him different types of stories. They tell about the owls and big chickens. These are grown-up stories and are not told to frighten the child. It is to prepare him for action so he will not run away, but face the situation bravely.

Today was Sunday. When Alice returned from church services, she saw the wagon on the path to her house. The children had come to play. Now they had left. The abandoned wagon was just an old hand-me-down contraption, too old to have any value except to a child. It had been given some rough treatment over the years. When the wagon tongue broke and there was no handle, the children tied a rope to pull the wagon. When the wheel broke, Alice asked her husband to make a new one. He had sawed a slab off a log to fix it one more time. The wagon somehow had held up to all the abuse. She could remember the face of each child who had claimed the wagon as his own. They used to play with the wagon for hours and laugh for no reason at all. There was so much pleasure for them with the old wagon. Then, Alice realized that someone would trip over the wagon if it was left on the path to her house.

Alice changed from her Church meeting clothes and returned to move the wagon from the path. As she tried to move the wagon, it seemed to be stuck to the ground. Alice tugged harder and harder. Then, she walked all around the wagon to see where the trouble was. Again she tried to pull it away, "Why can't I move this little wagon?" Then she could sense laughing from somewhere but couldn't see who or where it came from. Just faint, laughing voices. Oh my, that wagon was filled with "little people". Other "little people" were pulling on the wagon to tease

Aunt Alice. Had she been able to see "them", it would be clear why the children had been so fond of the wagon. The kids had as much fun pulling that wagon filled with "little people" as Alice had talking to her birds.

Now was Alice's turn. She laughed at remembering the first time she saw the "little people". Walking up the dusty road from Fallah church, she could see 'them' in front of the house sitting on the picket fence. So small, many would have fit in that little wagon. They called out as loud as the little wren did, "here comes Sa-a-a-rah!" Then, they would laugh and giggle. Now she knew they were the ones who had named her Sarah. She had thought it was the birds calling back. This was the first time they had shown themselves to her. Alice was the one who knew the names of all the birds in the old language and they wanted to give her a special name too. Sarah, it is a pretty name, isn't it!

The Toy Gun

The children looked forward to the special time in the evening when Grandfather told stories, especially about the 'little people". They were finishing their chores in the kitchen. It was an old time kitchen without running water. Drinking water was kept in a bucket beside an enamel pan on a wash stand. One dipper full of water in the pan was enough to wash your face and hands. After dirty water was thrown out the back door, the pan was ready for the next dirty face. The wood burning cook-stove had an oven that set next to the burners. Nearby was a cupboard with a porcelain counter-top, with drawers and a cabinet below. Up above, another cabinet for dishes and tea cups and to the side is a flour bin. At the bottom of the flour bin is a handle for the flour sifter. Mother sifted the flour to make many a good biscuit baked in that oven. As a little tyke, ChaBon couldn't reach the dish shelf. He had pulled out a drawer to use as a step ladder to climb up on the metal counter. By standing on the counter, he could reach high enough to place the clean cups on the shelf. At this height, he first spied the cut glass sugar bowl high on the top shelf. No sugar. Inside were coins that almost filled the bowl.

The cook stove had heated the house. Chores finished, the family gathered outside on the back porch. This Summer night was so pleasant. Grandfather began to tell 'little people' stories', "The little folks can make you forget things that you see them do. They also like gifts of food. Save your morsels from the table. Drop the bits of food on the trail in the forest. Don't look back! If they are around, it will be found. If not by them, then by other creatures that will enjoy your gift." The eyes of one child formed a question, which Grandfather caught. First, he repeated "If they are around". Then he explained, "Sometimes when children begin to grow up, they forget to leave morsels. The 'little ones' will forgive this for awhile. Sooner or later, they get an itching to find some child who leaves morsels. Usually they leave in the Spring or the Fall".

From the kitchen, the back entrance faced east. This part of the house was four feet off the ground. It took several steps to reach the ground. There was a water well located nearby. It was a rock-lined well and not very far to the water level. This was the drinking water supply. The well had a wood box cover with a lid. When water was drawn from the well, that pulley squeaked and the noise could be heard a great distance. In fact, that squeaky noise was one signal to the children that supper was being cooked. In the back yard, near the house, there was not a blade of grass. Mother is the one who kept this ground swept clean. It's tradition among the Muscogea to keep this kind of yard clean, as if it was part of the house.

Further behind the 'clean ground', the parents had planted some fruit trees and grass. After the fruit trees grew tall, it was a neat place back there. During the hot summer nights, father would sleep under the apple tree on an old Army cot, the kind with flat steel springs and mattress. It was dry under the fruit tree. The grass would get dewy during the early morning hours, so he would lay out a piece of cardboard near the cot to have a dry place for his shoes and socks. To the west of the fruit trees, was a garden devoted to corn. In the fall of the year, this was a good place to play "Cowboys and Indians". The corn stalks would make the finest tepees or the best spears.

There were other good places for the children to play. The front yard had huge oak trees, at least three feet in diameter. There were a few black oaks, some called "black jack's". There were also three big cedar trees near the front porch. One of the cedars was ChaBon's favorite tree to climb. He could be up in the tree in the thick green foliage and people walking below couldn't see him. On the east side of the house, only 12 feet from the home was a giant maple tree. It's thick roots had no place left to go except above the ground. Among these roots were one of the best places to play.

On past the fruit trees was Mother's chicken pen. She raised the chickens but it was ChaBon's duty to gather eggs. To keep the chickens laying eggs, you had to feed them chopped corn and mash with oyster shells. One thing for sure, they ate fried chicken some times. Mother would order the baby chicks by catalog for General Delivery to the local post office. She and the children would walk two miles to town to pick up the baby chicks.

On the way to town, the children were very aware of anything left or found on the trail. It was considered very good luck to find a penny or even two pennies. The path to the post office passed the General store. Mrs. Orr was a friendly, kind lady. Her home was right there at the west side of the store. It was just a small place where she sold bread, cookies, candies, crackers, can goods, things of that nature and a few key chain trinkets. To a child with a penny in his pocket, Mrs. Orr's store was a treasure trove. It was such a big decision to choose the best candy to buy with just one penny. Worse yet, where would the next penny come from!

On these walks, the children would see these strange new contraptions known as "automobiles". The old Indians called them "mo-bil-ga" and the children keyed on the last syllable "ga" or "car". ChaBon would return from these walks torn between dallying to find a penny or rushing home to play with his 'little friends' and toy cars among the roots of the old maple tree. Rushing home usually won. There on the gnarled roots of the giant tree, his cars—just blocks of wood—would rush around curved bridges and swoosh through "underpasses". He screeched the car to a halt. Dust flew. Parking it under another root, an imaginary garage, ChaBon's mind returned to the glass candy case at Mrs. Orr's store. He began to think of the many kinds of candy and his mouth began to water. It was then that he remembered the cut glass sugar bowl high on the kitchen cabinet filled with coins.

It was only a penny or two at the beginning because in those days a single penny would buy a lot of candy. For a nickel, he could get a small popcorn bag full of candy. Soon a single coin turned into more, though he would rarely take more than three or four cents. Seldom a nickel, never took a dime! That was too much for anybody. This went on all summer long whenever he got a chance to go to town. ChaBon began to think about the missing money and how the level in the sugar bowl was going down. He told himself, "Better quit. You will be caught and there will be great trouble!"

One day at Mrs. Orr's store his eye caught sight of something new. It was a little toy gun and a belt. The gun was only three or four inches long. The more he thought about this treasure, the more he had to have it. He left the store with a bag of candy. For the rest of the week in every quiet moment, the thought of the little gun nipped at his heart. ChaBon could stand it no longer. He vowed to go to the sugar bowl—one last time. Came the last day, he took a dime for the toy; then a nickel for a bag of candy. That was a bunch of money. Anyway, he bought the little toy gun and belt. Candy, too. He was happy. All the rest of the summer, he carried the gun strapped to the side of his overalls. Bang! Bang!

That was the *last* time he took money from the sugar bowl. The bowl must have been at least four and half inches tall. When the last coins were taken, it was down at least an inch and a half. The little pistol became his most prized possession. Somehow, by the end of the summer, he had lost the gun! School ended the days of playing outdoors from sun-up to sundown. ChaBon dared not ask the other children or his parents about the lost gun because of the guilt in his heart from taking coins from the sugar bowl.

His inseparable "little friends" were gone now and ChaBon wondered why. After a few years, he remembered the story about the little people taking the horse while the old man was inside the store. He found his horse mane braided in tiny knots. The 'little people' *never stole anything*. They returned the horse leaving their mark. That's why 'they' left him! Oh, his conscience couldn't stand the pain. He was ready to confess the theft. He would pay his parents what was taken and apologize. One evening he asked them about "the sugar bowl" and where the coins had come from. Both parents were mystified. What coins? Even the crystal sugar bowl was never a family possession!

After repenting, ChaBon could remember that summer again. How he and the 'little ones' played the whole summer. He had brothers and sisters. Playing with the 'little people" was different. They were inseparable buddies. Playing with the cars among the tree roots and hiding in the tree and shooting toy guns. Oh, what fun they had! As the day was approaching to go to Eufaula Boarding School, he had dreaded giving up endless play with his friends. When that day came, he could remember his playmates, the "little ones". Tears ran down their cheeks. They were saying good-by and waving to him. A certain 'little man' was standing tall because ChaBon had given him the little gun, his most prized possession. The 'little man' seemed so-o-o happy.

Then, ChaBon knew what had happened to the toy gun. It *was* the "little ones" who placed the sugar bowl high on the shelf for him to find. It was a test in honesty and trust. A "bear-trap"! To ever be trusted as an adult treating sick people, he must not give in to temptation even when no one was looking. Even though he failed the test, the 'little ones' cared so much for him, they had played the Summer. They accepted his special gift of candy bought with stolen coins because it made him happy. When it was time for ChaBon to go off to school, they were so sad. Then his 'little friends' were gone and his memory of them vanished. Yes, grandfather warned about this. Now that his memory had returned, ChaBon could only hope to see his 'little friends' again. He sure wished for the little toy gun. It was such a treasure!

MEDICINE MAKER

CHESTER
SCOTT

Nov. '79

Medicine Maker

Great Hunter

After an elder tells about the "little people", many Indian children never see or hear one. But they all look for signs of the little people! This is what ChaBon saw after sneaking up the bank over looking a little stream not far from the log house. What a tale to tell his family!

From over the hill, he could hear the little stream as the water gurgled over the rocks. The stream wasn't too far away. ChaBon thought he heard some noise other than the gurgling brook. Maybe it was a wild animal. Grandfather would be so proud that he was using his best training! He dropped to his knees, then down on all fours to not be seen. He crawled through the tall grass being careful not to make the tops wave and give him away. Reaching a tall tree, he carefully pushed aside dead branches lying on the ground, so that his knee wouldn't cause a snapping noise. And when the prickly wild rose bushes blocked his path, he parted the thorny branches and crawled through. This crawling and thinking so slowly is hard to do. After almost an hour, he crossed the open field and over the hill until the stream below was reached. Ahead was a raccoon walking along the stream. Since the coon was upwind and wouldn't smell him, he was safe. The ol' coon wouldn't give him away! Slowly, slowly, he inched closer to the stream. He felt strongly that something was there. Move a little bit closer. Stop. Listen. ChaBon forced his ears to reach far ahead and search for noises to guide which way to turn. Move a little bit closer. Stop. Listen.

Was that someone singing? The coon couldn't make that sound! It was such a low sound. Once his ears detected something unusual, he could focus. The noise seemed to get louder. It was—singing! Somehow his body moved quietly through the tall grass, closer to the stream. He crawled under the long branches of a willow tree. The branches hung to the ground below and concealed his path to reach the edge of the stream. The little boy looked from beneath the tree. "Who was singing?" he thought.

There! It *was* a little man, sitting cross-legged before an acorn. No, it was just the cap of an acorn, turned up like a tiny cup. This discovery made the sweat pour off his body. Then he realized that his lungs were like fire inside his chest. He had been holding his breath, trying so hard to be silent. ChaBon let out his breath so slowly. Uh-h-h-h! The little man was intently looking at the acorn pot. He held a thin tube of river cane. Tied around the cane was a ribbon. The ribbon was long, thin and red in color, but a very faded red color. The little man pointed the tube toward the pot. He raised his face to the morning sun. With his eyes closed, his song could be heard. Now that ChaBon could hear the singing, he knew the words were in his Muscogea language. The song was short. When it was ended, the tiny man bent closer to the acorn pot with both little hands on the thin reed. The gentle breeze would make the end of the faded red ribbon blow and flip on the ground.

The breeze seemed to give life to the ribbon. It was like a little snake reaching out. Tap, tap. Then he placed the tube into the pot and blew. Gurgle, gurgle, gurgle. There was liquid in the pot. He blew through the tube into the pot. Gurgle, gurgle, gurgle.

Then the tiny man stopped and rested the cane tube on the ground. He raised his face to the morning sun. With eyes closed, he began again to sing the little short song. When the song ended, he bent toward the acorn pot. Blow into the pot. Gurgle, gurgle, gurgle. He was making a good medicine!

ChaBon knew that what he saw was something new. In a flash, he knew that this song was *his* song. He knew that this song couldn't be shared with anyone. He turned and left his hiding place beneath the willow branches. He didn't look back. A while later walking toward home, he sang the song under his breath over and over. Never would he tell anyone his song!

ChaBon was so excited that he could hardly wait to tell Grandfather what he had seen. The old man heard the boy's story. Grandfather knew that it was no accident that ChaBon was able to sneak up on the little man. No one can see them unless they want to be seen. It was more likely the little man had enticed the child just to show him something that would not be used until years later. Grandfather asked ChaBon to tell the other children what had happened.

That night, ChaBon hurried through his chores so quickly. When all the children finished with their tasks, and gathered around the fire place, Grandfather said, "ChaBon has something to tell". ChaBon spoke in almost a whisper, "Stee-lo-booch-go-gee". The children's eyes got big and round. "What did you see?" they asked in awe. ChaBon chose his words carefully to tell what happened without the song.

It was years later and ChaBon had grown to manhood. That year the sun was angry and had baked the Earth. Everything that was normally green and could be eaten had been seared by the hot summer sun. All the people were hungry. Hunters in the tribe were asked to travel farther from the home place to kill game animals for the rest of the hungry people. ChaBon was not what others called a "good hunter". He would do his best. ChaBon still remembered the little song from his child-hood. He sang this song today walking through the woods. The words always seemed to make him feel stronger. He was able to walk a long time even though there was nothing to eat or shoot at. It was getting late in the day. ChaBon was very tired. He stopped to lay beside a hollow log for some protection and was soon asleep.

ChaBon slept a long, long time. Some sense awakened him. He raised up on his elbow to look beyond the hollow log. A hunter's eye always focuses far away for the unusual, then scans the horizon for some movement to refocus on. A hunter repeats his search many times and quickly. As his eyes searched all around, he saw in front of him an acorn. No, it was just the cap of the acorn, turned up like a cup. He was certain this acorn was not there before his sleep.

ChaBon picked up the little cup and looked inside. There was something inside! Then he put his finger inside the little cup. It was warm! Out came the finger, colored a faint red. He rubbed the finger across his chest, which left a long streak of paint. Then, a second streak was added. When the acorn cup was empty, he picked up his bow and arrows.

He left his place by the hollow log and began singing *his* song. After walking through the woods a little way, he would stop and listen, then move on. There were many animals now, when before, there were none. Hah! The hunter quickly used his arrows. Zing. Zing. Zing. The game animals were soon dressed. By that evening he returned to the home place with a heavy load of meat. All the people were so happy! From that day, ChaBon was known as a great hunter. He always kept that little acorn pot with him. When he needed to find game, the acorn was magically filled with the dull red paint. If the paint was put on the same way and he intended to find food for others, ChaBon could always find game animals. On these hunts, ChaBon always sang his special song and wore a long faded, red ribbon in his hair. The end of the ribbon flipped in the breeze as he walked.

Author's Note: *The Cherokee tell[1] of "the little men" who lived where the sun goes down. When they talk, we hear low rolling thunder in the west. "Thunder Boys" taught the people seven songs to call up the deer. At the first song, there was a roaring sound like a strong wind in the northwest. It grew louder and nearer. (the sound could have been in the ears of Aunt Loney.) As the seventh song was sung, a herd of deer came from the woods. The hunters shot all they needed. The "little people" in the olden days had to be much stronger than today.*

Indian Medicine

This is a story about "good" and "bad medicine" and winning. It happened fifty years ago. At the time, the teaching seemed vague. Sometimes it takes years of learning to understand something that happened long ago. ChaBon had grown to be a very large boy. His mother thought that ChaBon was lax about following her instructions. It would be harder for him when he grew up, if he wasn't responding now to words of the elders. She had cautioned him, "Pay attention to the words of the ol' medicine man". Momma didn't have a medicine man in mind when she said this. All she really wanted her boy to do was to listen to his elders to make good decisions and to follow the rules all the rest of his days.

Soon after hearing mother's words, ChaBon happened to meet an ol' Cherokee medicine man. The old Indians accept that the people we meet aren't by accident. When people are spiritually matched, even with strangers, something special will happen. If the boy didn't know this, the man did. In this manner, the Cherokee knew that the boy would someday have a spiritual need for medicine. Otherwise he and the boy wouldn't have met.

They talked about spirits and medicine, because the boy was so curious. When ChaBon had exhausted all his questions, the man handed him a stick. The ol' man told him, "You must take special care of this stick. If you don't, it will get away from you. Then it's magic will not be yours." This was not an ordinary stick, but one with some potency—for 'medicine'. No instructions were given on how to use the stick. ChaBon knew it was special, but nothing that he tried would release the power from the stick. As hard as he tried, it was still nothing more than a stick in his hands. Finally, the stick was put away in a safe place, waiting for the day when he would figure out how to properly use it. Several months later when he returned to the hiding place, the stick was gone. It was never found. No matter, he didn't understand how to use the power of the stick. ChaBon gave up the search.

The stick was a test! If the boy had discovered it's secret potency without instructions; then the ol' medicine man would have known the boy had natural ability and needed to be taught more. ChaBon would have come rushing back to tell him. Later, when he was sure that nothing special had happened in the boy's life, the ol' man suspected the gift was gone.

Next time their paths crossed the boy told the stick was lost. The Cherokee decided to try again. This time he gave ChaBon a bag of dry paint. "Indian paint has more power than a stick", he said. With this gift, he gave more directions: "Use the paint only for something important. I don't know what that will be, but you will." He added, "Put a little on your forehead or make an 'X' on your leg. Don't have to be dark enough to be seen. If it's there at all, that's enough. It will bring good luck" ChaBon's eyes got so big. A bag of magic dust! To keep from losing *this* important gift, he carried the bag in his pocket. This bag went everywhere with him, waiting for the right moment. Many days passed. No day ended without searching his pocket to be sure the bag was still there.

Team play with ball and stick has always been a popular sport with Indian boys. Softball was no different. It's packed with action and everyone likes to win. ChaBon played on an Indian Church Softball League. He was the pitcher for the Possums. They had lost every game this season. His team became so discouraged and dreaded the next game. Then, zap! The moment had arrived! He felt in his pocket to be sure the bag of paint was still there. At the end of the inning the teams switched positions on the playing field. He dabbed the ball with a little bit of magic paint. With a smile, he handed the ball to the pitcher of the other team. Walking toward the bench, ChaBon was *sure* that things would change in the next inning.

Their pitcher threw the first ball. Sock! At the sound of the bat, the ball was sent whizzing low into shallow right field. The right fielder started to run toward a spot where he judged the ball would hit the ground. As he reached down to scoop up the ball on the first bounce, it slowed down. It spun like a top, veering to the right circling around the dazed fielder. While he was trying to chase down the ball, the batter ran to first base and then around second. He stopped to see if the fielder was throwing the ball. He was standing up with a dazed look. At third base, the runner paused, then loped for home. He stood on home plate and raised his hands above his head. Yea! We all cheered. This was great!

The Cherokee medicine was working that ball real good for us. It was an easy victory. All the players were congratulating each other in ending the drouth of losses. There was excitement and talk of the Possums winning the rest of the games. Champions! ChaBon was the only one who knew for certain. The magic dust had made the difference. In a group of Indians who have seen spells of the medicine men, something odd was going on at these softball games. And so talk was started among the losing teams.

You would think that all it takes to win a ball game is the right kind of 'medicine', with little skill. ChaBon was obliged to keep his team winning. And so they did. Every game when the pitcher would hand the ball to the other side, ChaBon was smearing more paint on the ball. The ball would do skips and hops against the other side and act nicely for ChaBon's team. They kept on winning but at a great cost. The dust in the little bag was soon gone. There was one more game left to play, an important game. The winner would be Champion of the Church League.

The other contending team was from a little town on the outskirts of Seminole (OK). They were a young bunch of kids, but their pitcher was a veteran. He wasn't good enough to carry them to a championship on skill alone. The rumor was they couldn't win—without some outside help.

Even without the advantage of the Cherokee paint, ChaBon's team was playing the best team of the League and beating them badly. The balls he pitched were zipping over home base. Their batters could barely hit the ball that day. When it was our turn to bat, the ball was easy to hit. Their fielders were missing easy outs. It was near the end of the game. Score: Us 5, Them 0. The game was soon down to the last inning. ChaBon's team was excited, smelling victory. The boys on the other team were so sad as they warmed up ready to bat in the last inning. Soon the umpire would declare ChaBon's team the winner. Possums, champions of the Indian Church League!

Then out of the corner of his eye, ChaBon saw an ol' Indian man walk slowly to the edge of the playing field between first base and home-plate. He wasn't a coach, but his mouth was moving and arms were waving. ChaBon thought, "Probably cheering." The man held a leather-covered ball in his hand. It was much smaller than a soft-ball, an inch or so across. He threw it up in the air and caught it—several tosses. The ball had a little red tail. He couldn't hear his words, but all the players on the other team had their eyes on him. When his words were done, the other players seemed to be changed. They were standing more erect, with smiles of confidence. The first batter stood at home-plate, almost daring the pitcher to throw.

The red tail on the ball! This is the kind of ball used long ago in the Indian Stick-Ball games. Then, ChaBon realized that he knew this man and why he was there. He is the medicine man at

Fish Pond stomp ground. Oh-oh, this means trouble from 'bad' medicine. He pitched the ball. Blam! The ball was hit safely and they had a runner on base. They were all cheering. Next batter hit the first pitch long and to left field. Our fielder was under the ball. He fumbled the ball, then couldn't pick it up before the first runner crossed home-plate. Score: Us 5, Them 1. Before anyone could catch their breath, the score was tied. This was the *last* inning. One more run scored to beat the Possums. Oh, they were so happy! ChaBon could not complain about another team using 'medicine' to win. The losing team slowly left the playing field. Beaten at the last!

ChaBon had forgotten his mother's words, "Pay attention to the words of the ol' medicine man". She was trying to impress on him the importance of listening to the elders. The Cherokee had told ChaBon, "Use the paint only for something important." Winning can go to your head. The bag of paint had disappeared as surely as the stick by not responding to the words of the elders.

Fifty years later ChaBon was still playing the championship game in his mind. Had he learned to use the power in the stick or the bag of paint, the boy would have sought the Cherokee medicine man. Today, the rules of using 'medicine' in the ancient ball games aren't known; "when to" or "when not" and "how". Even then, those rules were lying in the graves of the old ball-players. Messing with 'good' and 'bad' medicines without rules leads to a battle that can't be won. They lost the game and quit using Indian medicine. Momma got her wish for him. He had lived the rest of his days by the rules and on his own skill, learned while playing softball in Indian Church League.

Robin is Coming Today

Docktoring Tree

Ol' Sam was a good Indian docktor until the day he died. I remember the time because it snowed. It was such a heavy snow on the day we buried him. His given name was "Sum-o-gee". All Indians like to give short 'nick-names'. His name was "Sam" for short, but they were long on respect for this docktor. When Sumogee was alive, people came from miles away for his advice about their pet ills and hurts. The old docktor lived in a small house that was comfortable enough for him and his wife. When Indians made houses, the ceiling was no higher than the tallest person of the family. The front door pointed toward the rising sun. It stayed warmer this way and the sun's first rays would wake up anyone inside.

The only other distinguishing feature of Sam's house was a tree that grew out front. It was a big pecan tree growing very close to the front porch, with branches hanging over the roof. Now no one else knew *this* bit of information about that tree: that tree was where the 'little people' lived. Even though they played there in the branches, no strange unusual noises came from the tree. On some days, early in the morning, you could hear a twittering in the tree. It sounded like the birds. Now you and I know that "they" were talking to each other in their little voices. On these days, "they" knew somehow when someone sick was going to visit. There would follow a scurrying of little feet across the roof of the house and a buzzing sound. When ol' Sam heard this kind of noise, he would come out the door and stand on the front porch. Then "they" would say in louder voices so he could hear, "Robin is coming today. Something is bothering his head". "They" would talk to each other to be sure of the next step. One little man would say to the next little man, "Tell him where to go in the woods to gather the herbs to cure those hurts". The second little man would speak to the docktor, "Go get this and that and little bit of this kind of herb and make him some *good* medicine." They would start chattering and giggling among themselves.

Later in the day, slow moving hoof-beats could be heard coming toward the house. It was Robin. He didn't look well either. The horse stopped, Robin slid down and left him to eat grass under the big tree. The docktor came out on the front porch. They exchanged greetings. This was done with few words and several gestures. He brought a little gift for the old man. This time it was a sack of Indian tobacco. Its a mixture of herbs that smokes harsh, but that's what the docktor enjoyed. They went inside the little house to have a cup of Indian coffee. They call it "ga-ve". Robin was a bigger man than Sam, so he had to stoop to enter the house. Stooping was followed by sitting on the floor. He was dizzy so it felt good to sit on a solid floor. The patient waited for the old man to make coffee at the fireplace. Ga-ve is made by boiling the coffee grounds in a blue porcelain pot. Adding a bit of cold water makes the grounds sink, then you drink it. Soon they were drinking ga-ve and the sick one was smiling!

After the coffee cups were emptied, the old man took out the little sack of tobacco and filled his pipe. Then he was ready to listen. As he lit his pipe and began to puff smoke into the air, Robin started to tell what was bothering him. It was something in his head. Ol' Sam didn't say a word. He put down the pipe and walked to the back of the house. Returning in a moment, he had the right medicine already made. Sam said a few words. It sounded like a brief chant in a very old language strange to the sick one. Robin drank it down. Little bit bitter but he knew some relief would follow.

Late into the evening the two men talked. It was good just to know the ol' docktor was always ready to take time out to talk with you. His head had hurt for days. For some reason, as they talked, that hurt had gone. His head was clear again. It *was* a little mystifying how the ol' docktor could have a medicine already prepared that worked so well.

Now it was time for Robin to leave for home. It was late, yet there seemed to be twittering of birds in the big tree. He knew the time was far beyond when the birds would be asleep for the night. Of course, you and I know that it's the 'little ones'. This is an important time for them. They watch very carefully to see if Sam will be paid cash for his work. Should Robin make excuses such as "I'll pay next time" would disappoint the 'little ones'. If excuses happened on several visits, there might not be any twittering in the trees before or after the sick one came to visit.

Were the patient to say, "I can pay in a few days" is not so bad. But you better keep your end of the bargain, or your illness will return. Most Indians don't have cash, so they pay with useful items such as coffee, flour or grease. Today, Robin pays with tobacco and a little cash. It's not much money but it's a lot for him. Those little people are so happy! They jump with great joy and slap each other on the back.

I will tell you a secret about those "little people". They don't care so much about money or payment. What is important to them is that Sam knows what "little people" like. Sam knows they like to eat sweets! So when you see an Indian man at the General Store in town, watch what he buys. There are the usual things that he will buy for himself such as cornmeal, flour and fresh chicken eggs. If he buys cookies or candy, too, you can bet that he has 'little people' to treat. The little people promote the old Indian ways, which includes paying back a gift with something special. The 'little ones' can see that to Robin money is special. It's a big sacrifice for him to give money as a gift.

After Robin went home that night, the 'little fellows' were so happy. One little man said to another, "Robin is going to remember this day. Maybe we can teach *him* how to docktor". They laughed and went to sleep dreaming about sweets! No more noise came from the tree until another day when some other visitor needed special medicine to cure his ills.

I Have Come to Help You
for the Rest of Your Life

Studying to be a Docktor

Most of the good Indian docktor's had died years ago. After docktor Sumogee died, many people doubted if any one could replace him. Every one knew the "little people" had picked him as a boy. Not to despair. One of the relatives had found the hiding place of the docktor's book of medical formulas. It might be valuable. He kept it for awhile deciding what to do. There was writing in what seemed to be an old Indian language. The tribes didn't write. When he sounded out the long words, he felt sure it was a name of plants. He couldn't tell which ones to use. The only thing left to do was to give the book to Sam Junior, Sumogee's son. It's not people who choose Indian docktors, so giving the book was like an invitation to chase after the 'little people'. Trouble began to brew from that moment.

Sam Jr. hadn't given a thought to being a docktor. Putting *that* book in his hands made him change direction. Carefully turning the yellowed pages, he found strange words. There was one mystic phrase "stee-lo-booch-go-gee". He wondered to himself, "What would happen if *I* spoke the same words that Dad used to make sick people well?" It was mumbled slowly at first, then repeated until it was firm. Once it was spoken, Sam realized this was a phrase that he knew. It meant "little people". Was this part of a spell or chant? What would happen? Speaking this phrase made chills ran up and down his spine. Nothing else happened, as far as he could tell. He knew that few talked openly about 'little people'. Who would teach him the meaning? His friend ChaBon had told him a little bit from his grandfather's stories. Yes! The old man might help.

There was no one near the house. Sam found the old man hoeing weeds from the young corn plants. As he walked across the field, the old man watched him. He kept hoeing. Sam was hoping to learn from the old man. Yet, his questions were about the hot weather or health. Couldn't seem to ask the questions that brought him here. Grandfather could feel his uneasiness. The corn needed care; he kept chopping. The silence bothered Sam. He left, the old man still hoeing.

After the aborted visit with grandfather, Sam was desperate to understand what the words in the book meant. What treasures were in this book? He had gone to school and made good grades; he would keep studying this book until the answers were clear. Sam began to read in earnest. There was something about songs to bring the deer from the woods. Hunters could use that. The words had been written with a soft pencil. Smudged. Other pages had a few words about healing wounds, frost-bites and bad dreams. He made out cryptic words on one page about catching big fish, growing tall corn, winning the stick-ball game. This was great knowledge!

He read daily. Something happened that was so subtle. Going to sleep was no longer easy. He lay awake far into the night. The bird's would wake him early in the morning. Lack of sleep began to muddle Sam's mind. It was hard to think yet not easy to go to sleep. That's what happens, if one goes chasing the 'little people'.

It was early in the morning a few days later. The birds had begun their twittering. Their daily task is to wake up the flowers.

Wild flowers have an important job. Man can't look at the bright sun's face without scowling. Flowers can look at the sun and smile all day. This morning the flowers seemed to be smiling at Sam, lying in the bed under the covers. He needed to be out of the bed, but kept dozing. Had trouble going to sleep last night after reading. Sleep hadn't come easy since he got *that* book. His bed was outdoors on the porch. Even with his head under the covers, he heard a buzzing sound. It seemed to be coming from beside the porch. At first the sound was like honey bees talking. His ears strained to make sense of the buzzing of the bees.

As he lay there half asleep, the thought crossed his mind, "That small buzzing voice is talking in my language." He opened one eye. Sitting there on the foot of the bed was a small man. He wore a hat. This was a very old man, his chin was covered with long white whiskers. He sat with his little legs crossed, patiently waiting for Sam to awaken. Sam sat up quickly in the bed. With both eyes open, he stared at the little man. He wiped the sleep granules from his eyes and looked again. No change. Same man sat there. The small buzzing voice in the Muscogea language had grown louder. It was his voice, only louder, "Sam, don't be afraid of me. I have come to help you for the rest of your life. Didn't you want me to come?"

Sam was excited at what his eyes saw. The thought flashed in his mind, " Isn't this one of the 'little people'? Isn't this what I needed to know about?" His eyes hungrily examined the little man. Sam nodded 'yes'. The 'little man' seemed to expect this answer and kept on talking, " I want to show you some things that you need to know—to be a docktor as good as your Dad. Listen hard, then do everything I say." Sam agreed but his thoughts were wandering to the book lying on the porch under the bed. He opened the book to brag a little, "This is my Dad's book. I've studied it well. I know many things already about docktoring. This is how to make sick people well. For a head hurt, you go to the woods and gather some of this and a little bit of that. Then you cook it all together. What else can you tell me?" Sam recalled the little man was looking him in the eye. Sniff. Sniff. The dogs came near the porch. Poof! The little man with the beard disappeared. The dogs were surprised too. They nosed all around the flowers by the porch, then walked away with tails up in the air.

Sam sat on the bed for a moment, then called out loud, "We weren't done talking". No answer. "Must have been a dream", he muttered. Soon, he was asleep again. When Sam awoke, he searched "the dream" but the 'little man' had given no instructions. He would just keep studying Dad's book for meaning.

Early in the morning a week or so later, Sam was sitting on the porch. He had been awake for an hour, wide awake. In the blink of an eye, there was a 'little man' standing there on the porch. Without mention of the last visit, he said, "Grey Beard was your Dad's helper." There was a long pause. This little man was bare-faced like most Indians. Sam was feeling his own bare face, remembering Grey Beard. He recalled,"*was* your Dad's helper." Dad had passed away but how would a stranger know? Answered by a nod, the little man told Sam, "When Grey Beard came to see you, I was with him, but you couldn't see me." Sam's eyes were spinning with questions to ask. So long! The 'little man 'disappeared.

That same morning, Grandfather was at the church grounds. Something always needed fixing. So he had arrived early before the Sunday meeting to do some tasks. There were sounds of huffing and puffing long before Sam came running from the woods. He acted as if something was chasing him. He stopped, exhaled and threw his hands in the air, "I've been looking for you! I must tell you about a 'little man' popping up before me!"

The old man laughed as he recalled what happened in the corn field. Knowing that a 'little man' was mixed up here explained the mystery. Grandfather asked, "How little would you say *he* was?" The old man was teasing to draw out what he knew. The young man replied, "Oh, about *this* tall." His hand cut the air below the knee. Grandfather asked, "What else was unusual?" Sam thought a moment, "Well, his toe nails were long and curved down, like a badger." He added, "It was odd the way he dressed". Grandfather heard the description. Yes, Sam had seen a 'little one'. (author's note: description is too sacred to repeat.)

Sam was speaking clearly, no more fuzzy thinking. He repeated what the little man told him, "they" talk in our language teaching what to say. Every word must be in line or the medicine won't help sick people. That's what 'good' medicine is." Grandfather nodded as Sam spoke, "I told Grey Beard that I had been studying Dad's medicine book." He was carrying *the* book. Sam asked the old man to help him read the hard passages. Grandfather scanned a few pages and returned the book, "It don't make sense, but what did Grey Beard say?"

Sam told what he said, 'I come to help you the rest of your life' and how the dogs scared him away. Grandfather asked, "Did he come back?" Sam answered, "Well, no, but a little bare-faced man told me that Grey Beard was my Dad's helper." Grandfather knew that a great thing had almost happened to Sam Jr. but something blocked the way. He had seen the words in the old book. Docktor Sumogee had written *part* of the secret recipe, enough to jog his memory. Sam Jr. was going by "the book" and "answers", not what the little people *said* to do. As Sam left, Grandfather observed, "Ol' Grey Beard really liked Docktor Sumogee a lot. He tried to find a way to use his boy, but his heart wasn't right."

That evening the children gathered around Grandfather to hear the newest 'little people' story. He told about the time when the Grand Daddy of all the 'little people' came to help the ol' docktor's son for the rest of his life. How the wisest one of all with knowledge way, way back cut short his offer when the boy wouldn't listen. The boy thought he knew too much from an old book that had half the answers left out. That old bearded one had much wisdom that would have been revealed to us. Now all the ol' time docktors are gone. The children were sad.

Grandfather smiled. His smile let the children know he had a story with a good ending. And this is what he told them. Long ago, our Tribe had lost the power of making sick people well. We needed to cross the big River We-of-gof-ke to get to Oklahoma. Our people were in such a bad way that they thought about singing the 'old songs' and walking into the raging river. The children's eyes got so big. The story continued. No one had seen 'little people' for a long time. When Great-Great Grandfather Jockogee as a boy had to cross the raging river, a 'little man' helped him. From that day, 'they' taught him about the plants and medicine for sick people. Even if we can't see them, the 'little people' are always watching us and protecting us. Maybe someday, the Grand Daddy of all of the 'little people', ol' Grey Beard himself, will come back and teach us what to do. Each child was excited. He might be chosen next. What they knew for sure is that people don't pick Indian docktors.

Legend of
Honeycomb Bluff

In Alabama, there was a Lower Creek town named "Eufaula". When they moved to Oklahoma Territory, the name came too, shortened to "Fallah". Fallah was noted for quite a few tall hills or short mountains. The hills are so close to each other that it's possible to go fifteen miles across the hill-tops. The ancient Indian trails were made in the days before the Creek's horses and wagons. The fastest way for a man to cross the country was to run the tops of the mountains. This unique feature was probably attractive to the ancient Indians who lived on the hills. On the north side of the mountain is a small bluff that overlooks the valley below. There are a lot of holes weathered in the rock. The holes may be a foot in diameter and several inches deep. From a distance, it looked like a giant honeycomb. This story is about a mountain laced with natural formations of tunnels and caves and how it came to be called "Honeycomb Bluff".

The M-K-T was the first railroad line in Oklahoma Territory, connecting St. Louis to Texas. They called it the "Katy" and it passed through Eufaula. The Katy was completed in 1872, followed by the Frisco line in 1882. By 1902, the Rock Island line connected Memphis to Amarillo via Indian Territory. Trains had become the main passage to the west. Many of the white settlers got off the train to live on Indian land. It wasn't theirs but they expected the US government to soon take the land. Stopping those trains at the Eufaula depot made them easy targets for the robbers lurking on that special mountain. After the Civil War ended and to the end of the 19th century, there was little law and order in Creek Country. Indian Territory was called "Hell's Fringe".[1] Many outlaws hid out in this area on one favorite mountain. With a reputation as an outlaw hangout, people seemed to notice the strangest things. For example, the mountain lined up with the rising or setting sun. This caused long shadows of trees to lay across the hill like prisoner stripes. Combined with the outlaw stories, those shadows made the mountain especially eerie in the light of a full moon.

As the 20th century began, there was great pressure on the tribal legislature to again give up their land. The Indians had set up a legislature similar to the United States with two houses of Congress. It would take a majority of votes by the Muscogea Legislature to sell tribal land. The Indians were divided in two factions. The "mixed bloods" wanting to sell the land were the "Progressives". They were betting Indian Territory would soon become a State of the Union. The opposing side, the full-blood traditional Indians, didn't want to sell tribal land—period. "That's all right," they said, "Make it a State of the Union and the Federal government will protect *all* of the citizens."

There was one full-blood man who took a hard stand to prevent the land sale. His name was Chitto Harjo. Chitto means "snake" and Harjo means "stumbling around" in our language. So Chitto Harjo means "crazy snake". Harjo wasn't as crazy as white people thought. He was a member[2] of the Tribal Legislature and the House of Kings. The people of each tribal district elected a "king" or principal chief. He was the King of the Fallah area. Everyone respected this old man. His kind of thinking went back to the "red sticks" of the early 1800's. Chitto was a full-blood and no full-blood could understand how anyone could take away or give land. The earth was like the sky, or the river, or birds or animals. No one could own something created by the Great Spirit. Indians only used what they needed and returned the rest to the Great Spirit. They were against selling Indian land. Years ago, General Andy Jackson had defeated the "red sticks" and took the Muscogea land in Alabama. The victory got Andy Jackson elected to be president of the United States. It also set the machine in motion that would force migration of the Muscogea people in 1836. In the 1836 agreement, they were given Oklahoma land in exchange for Alabama land. To the full-bloods, the way that white settlers wanted *their* land was no different than train robbers lusting after the gold on the trains that passed through Fallah.

The Federal government had a new "shell game" for the Indians. The Government set up the Dawes Commission to take back all the Indian Territory, then "give the title" of 160 acres to every "qualified" Indian. This was the "Dawes Roll". Underlying this "gift" was the fact they kept half of the land for the white settlers.

Chitto Harjo doubted the sincerity of either the white settlers or the government agents. Earlier he had testified before the US Congress in Washington DC:[3] He submitted a copy of the original removal treaty granting land to the tribe "for as long as the grass grows . . ." He argued that the whites were voiding their own treaties. They didn't like to hear the Indian's view. Then when Chitto got home from Washington DC, he learned the tribal legislature was voting to sell Indian land. Chitto's lone vote would swing the decision one way or the other. He wasn't going to change his mind. Neither was he going to let anyone cast his vote at the legislature. What could he do? Chitto chose to hide out in the heavy brush on that big mountain, the outlaw's hangout.

The US government is famous for ending complaints to their plans by hammering down the opposition and making examples for others to see the consequences. They went to great efforts to capture Harjo and drag him off that mountain to show people who was in control. We know the mountain was honey-combed with caves and escape routes. It seemed that every cave was filled with bears and rattlesnakes. Each time a troop of soldiers would ride up to a cave, there was a hissing rattlesnake. They would turn and ride away cursing under their breath, "Chitto Harjo".

Harjo escapes were legendary in Creek and Choctaw country, but undocumented in the White Man history books. How Chitto Harjo managed to escape capture for so long has remained concealed by silence. The soldiers thought that all the paths to Harjo were blocked. They weren't. Now we know that many relatives and friends knew the way to his hiding places. His visitors would bring him food and then stay to talk. Harjo loved to talk about what the agents tried yesterday. After the visitor left by the secret path, he retold the stories about Chitto. The Indians never needed television or telephone. This is because the fastest way to pass information was "tell-an-Indian". He tells the neighbors and they all laughed. As sure as you and I are sitting here, the "little people" had come to help Chitto Harjo hiding out on the mountain. The old Indians knew it. Can't you hear the 'little people' laughing and giggling at the sight of someone lost, circling the mountain over and over the same trail? Then finally, after weeks, helping them find their way out? The little fellows would have been telling Chitto Harjo when the men were coming and which cave to hide in. Who knows how those rattlesnakes got placed in the pathway of the soldiers? It's not important how Chitto escaped, it's simply that he avoided capture long enough to make it uncomfortable for the government men. They finally caught him, the leader of the Choctaw "snakes" as well as "snakes" from other tribes. The rebellion was crushed when 94 of the leaders went to prison for committing "violence against the government".[3]

All the full-blood Indians could see their loss in the land deal. They had suffered from every land deal with the White Man for 200 years. So when the government tried to haul Harjo off the mountain and failed, the Indians were laughing. As fast as the World was changing, all of a sudden everything screeched to a halt. No one could catch that sly old Indian man. That gave a bad image to the settlers waiting to get their free homestead land. They feared for their safety from "the hostiles" if the government couldn't control them now.

The Dawes Commissioners set up three or four white square tents along the well-traveled road connecting the Sand Creek road along the Canadian River. The Indians had four years to sign up for their "free" 160 acres. Many of the Progressive Party were the first to get their land. The old full-blood Indians delayed as long as possible. Some never signed the Dawes Roll even though they would have nothing nor anyplace to hunt and fish.

White man had taken their last hope for a life of freedom, independence and pride. It was a big loss of dignity to go before the officers who manned the Dawes Roll. They went with their heads bowed toward the ground, the Earth Mother, they all loved so much. They walked slowly, beaten in mortal battle without a shot being fired. After standing in line, the officers had another way to steal more dignity from these people. All Indian names were very long. Most of the full-blood Indians couldn't sign their names in English. Speaking through an interpreter, the officer would say, "I can't spell that long name. Can't you take a shorter name? Perhaps 'Jones' or 'Smith'? It don't matter."

Names are important, even to the Indian. Remember how the old Indians would give a new name when something important happened? Standing in line, the ol' Indian would look behind him to the other Indians. What name to use—to get the land? Why not use the name of their hero, the same name already stuck in their minds over getting land. Harjo! In tough situations, it's a time to respond with "Indian humor". That old man pleased his people by peacefully resisting the governments earnest efforts to take away their land. Harjo! Saying that name restored pride and dignity. So the name that many a full-blood put on the Dawes Roll was "Harjo" and an English name such as

"Billy". Some couldn't say "Harjo". They could say "Ha-jo" or "Had-jo". Nonetheless, many of the Muscogea people and the neighboring tribe, the Seminole, have last names "Harjo". Their descendants also named "Harjo" have multiplied several fold. All these Harjo names are a monument to Chitto Harjo.

In the 1830's when the Muscogea people first came to this new land, one group located five miles east of Fallah. "Oldtown" or "North Fork", as some called the place, was northeast of Fallah between two rivers, the South Canadian and the north fork of the Canadian. There was also a trading post licensed by the government. The Asbury Methodist built a Church in 1848. From this area an old Indian trail crosses Honeycomb Bluff and leads to the original home-place of ChaBon's ancestors. Although this route was a shortcut, it was still a long trip for groceries. So whoever went, took a wagon and hauled for all the neighbors. Still visible to this day, is a pair of wagon tracks going up Honeycomb Bluff. The iron-rimmed wheels have etched deep tracks in the rocks. Anyone starting the journey would suspect the ruts across the Bluff would remain well-marked all the way.

In the 1960's Uncle John was using the trail as a shortcut to the home-place after going to town for supplies. He got up on Honeycomb Bluff following the old wagon ruts. He seemed to go round and round that mountain. After three or four hours, he didn't know exactly where he was. When he got home, it was very late at night. All the people waiting on their food had gathered at his house. Someone asked, "Where you been?" It embarrassed him to appear so foolish, but he couldn't remember his pathway out. This story spread like wildfire when people remembered this was the place where the Feds tried to catch ol' Chitto Harjo.

More recently, someone else got lost. He was a college friend of a niece, home for the Thanksgiving turkey feast with the family. The friend wasn't Indian and hadn't been around this group before. It made him self conscious because the Indians, compared with White men, don't talk much with words. They do communicate non verbally. He soon tired of waiting for the big meal to be prepared. After excusing himself, he left to hunt on Honeycomb Bluff.

A lot of food was cooked for the feast. We waited and waited for the young man to return to eat with us. Everyone tired of waiting ate without him. The young man finally showed, but without any game in tow. He told about losing his way, going round and round the mountain for hours. Somehow he got out of the loop. It's a good thing there was plenty of leftovers. He was very hungry. No Indian spoke but all were communicating with their eyes, as they remembered the old stories of Chitto Harjo on Honeycomb Bluff. As you might suspect, that mountain was the favorite nesting place for the "little people". The little tricksters! Those same little people who helped Chitto Harjo stay hidden in the hills for years with the government agents lost for weeks at a time. Now they are playing tricks on unaware people.

Before Chitto Harjo, the mountain was known only as a robber's hangout. It was renamed "Honeycomb Bluff" to remind the people how Chitto Harjo dodged his enemies. The name "Harjo" was kind of a monument, a delaying tactic of a weak and oppressed people. It made the Indian people proud. As time passed and old Indians died, fewer people remembered how they or the mountain got named. Something must happen for the legend of Chitto Harjo and Honeycomb Bluff to survive!

Give Them All the Land!

The Crazy Snakes

Chitto Harjo was the man the Creeks and Choctaws called "Crazy Snake". He was trying to protect the "old Indian ways". This group of full-blood Indians wanted to keep the land undivided. Free for all to use. Back at the turn of the century, Harjo was hiding out from the soldiers who wanted the Indian's land for white settlers. His action was no crime in the eyes of the Indians. Harjo and GrandDad George had neighboring farms west of Fallah. As a good neighbor, GrandDad used to take good things to eat while Harjo was in hiding. Of course they would have taken the time to trade stories over a good meal. On his return, GrandDad would tell his family some of the ongoing battles of Chitto Harjo to protect Indian land—their land. Who would expect GrandDad to become involved.

GrandDad George had married Cindy, Jockogee's daughter. When the Katy railroad brought many white settlers to the community of Fallah, George didn't want to be around them. He had moved the family four miles west of Fallah to make a farm. This farm became one of the best in the area. Many Indians were not good ranchers or farmers. GrandDad George was good at both. He raised sheep. We sheared the sheep, then carried the wool to the "branch" to wash it. The wet wool is laid on blankets to dry in the sun. Then they would weave the woolen cloth to make clothing for everyone in the family. GrandDad also raised a big garden; filled with watermelons, squash, beans and corn. Corn was the big crop. The yellow ears would be put into the "corn crib" to dry naturally, so as not to mildew. Many of the neighbors depended on GrandDad's crop because he was such a good farmer.

The old Indians were smart and did a lot of things to avoid extra work. They made the corn crib out of the wood of the sassafras tree, built off the ground to keep out rodents. The sassafras had something in the wood that was real good about attracting the barn owls. They say the sassafras keeps the lice and bugs off the owls, so he stays around in the barn to eat any rodents brave enough to try to eat the corn.[1]

An Indian woman came one day to "choose" corn to take home. While she was "shopping" in the corn crib, three little boys came up behind her. There were saplings used in the fence for slats and the boys were looking through them. It was obvious to the ol' woman that they wanted something to eat. No one was talking. She would point at the yellow corn, lying in the crib. They would shake their heads "no". Lying beside the crib, were big juicy red watermelons. She pointed to them and again got a "no" signal. Likewise, other good things to eat were rejected, until she got to a bucket of milk. Oh, *this* was no good. It was clabbored and tasted sour! She didn't want to disappoint them with something bad. When she pointed at the bucket, that got them excited. They surely knew what was in the bucket. Their little heads started nodding up and down and they danced all around in glee. For certain, the old woman knew they liked the clabbored milk. She picked up the bucket and moved it around to the edge of the corn crib. All three of the little boys grabbed the handle and carried away the bucket of milk. She could hear the laughing as they carried away this "treasure". "Boy, they really liked that stuff", she said out loud. We don't know whether she knew these were the "little people", but they were.

The picket fence that the boys were peeking through was put up to keep the animals from strolling around the house and making a mess. There was a black lady, who lived just on the other side of the picket fence. She often came to work in and outside the house. It was so strange. Whenever we needed something done, this lady seemed to show up. After arriving, she didn't need to ask what to do. She just started working. It was a blessing to have her. Of course, she accepted the gifts of food to care for her family. So it was important to many neighbors that GrandDad could raise so much food. He cared for many who had no land to raise food.

In spite of being so important, GrandDad was a quiet man. He didn't tell what he was thinking nor change facial expressions to give away clues. If he liked someone, he would go stay the night and talk. The children would see him saddle and mount his favorite horse. They would go tell grandmother that he was gone. After his visit, there was no word given to say where he had been. He *was* a quiet man. Since he was the elder, no one in a traditional family questioned him. No one had to ask what happened. This is because in a few days the ol' Indian he visited would come by and continue the talk. They would build a fire in the fireplace and stay up all night—just talking. Your eyes adjust to the dim firelight and no lantern is needed. When hunger came they would bake a sweet potato or roast peanuts or parch corn over the hot coals. A little bit of food would get them ready for talking.

There was one subject that GrandDad had a passion to talk about. That was "playing stick-ball".[2] Stick ball was a team game played by all the Indian tribes in some fashion. Each player used two sticks, which had a little rawhide net on one end. A man couldn't touch the ball with his hands. The little net on the end of the stick was used to catch the ball in the air when thrown by a team-mate. It was harder yet to catch the ball because they ran at top speed up and down a long playing field. At either end were goal posts, like football or soccer today.

One stick could be used to throw the ball a long distance over a goal post. The second stick was a club used to fend off the defensive players. This game was not gentle and nobody wore "pads". Rather, the players would strip off their clothes to the waist—to stay cool. The game went on all day, which followed fasting and dancing the previous night. The pre-game activities lasted all night. It was a game of skill, strength and endurance. It was against the rules to hit anyone in anger, but there were always injuries and sometimes death on the playing field.

Another thing that made the game so exciting was the "whoop!". The Muscogea Creek learned long time ago to make a noise with his lungs and voice. His whoop can be heard a mile away. It's an art form that is highly developed. How would you feel with a band of painted warriors attacking in the middle of the night with the whoops that can be heard so far away. These same whoops were used in the stickball games as well as the stomp dances.

The worst part of the stickball game was that the people, spectators and team members, would gamble away family belongings. Some would lose everything! You can see how a good player could become excited about this game. It gets in your blood. When you get older, it's often wiser to just talk about the game. And that's what they did all night—talk.

Since GrandDad could see well in dim light, he didn't object to riding his horse at night. He knew all the trails like the back of his hand. One night after all the chores were done, he went to visit a special friend. This man lived two miles away. GrandDad was gone two days this time. They stayed up and talked the stickball game from its beginning to its end. Then it was time for GrandDad to go home.

As the horse carried him through the woods, they came to a barbed wire fence which the horse couldn't pass. The fence hadn't been there, two days before! GrandDad knew that the times were changing, when people were fencing in a country that had never known fences before. "Of course, it was some white man who did this!" he exclaimed. He turned his horse around and returned to the friend's house for cutters. Then back to the fence, he cut that barbed wire into tiny little pieces. He and the horse passed through and went home, but the white man was encroaching on *his* territory. To him, this affront was stealing his freedom. GrandDad was what they called "a loner". After that barbed wire incident, he joined a group of Indians. They called themselves "the followers of Crazy Snake".

In 1901, the U. S. Government formed the Dawes Commission to take back *all* the Oklahoma Indian Territory and return 160 acres to every Indian. This may have sounded like a lot of land. The government kept half of the land which was given to the white settlers. This was the same land given in total to the Tribe sixty years earlier. The Indian had to sign his name on what was called the "Dawes Roll". This had to be done by the year 1905. There near the old Fallah Church was where the soldiers set up three or four white square tents. They sat in their little tents and waited for the Indian to come sign the Dawes Roll. No reason for them to go out looking for Indians. The Indians must come to them, if they wanted the land.

GrandDad wasn't giving away any of the good farm land to a white man. He had worked too long. So he refused to sign up to receive less land with the "Indian Givers". GrandDad rode his horse to the soldier tents and dismounted. He was well known for being a quiet man. This time, his loud whoop shattered the quiet morning air. The sound reverberated off the trees in echoes. Everyone within earshot came running. He shouted out in anger for everyone to hear, "Give them all the land!" You could imagine him standing there bare to the waist, waving two ball sticks in the air. Ready to do battle with the sticks, war-clubs. Then he mounted his best horse and rode into the woods. The federal government had taken all the Indian land. He had refused to take *any* of the Dawes land. The only thing that he would not give up was his horse.

GrandDad George's wife and oldest daughter were sensible people. Each took a land allotment. GrandDad refused for both he and his youngest daughter, Susie. The white man who got the beautiful farm was told how GrandDad gave away his land. The new owner was told that he owed his prosperity to one of the "Crazy Snakes".

Oklahoma became a State in November 1907. In the Indian towns, this was a day of mourning. They were being absorbed into the white man's culture and would no longer be a tribe. One of the first laws passed was to outlaw the Indian stickball game. Those heathen savages were killing each other with clubs and gambling away their life savings! Just like them "Crazy Snakes"!

Aren't They Nice!

Big Pecan Tree

The children loved to hear the stories about Docktor Sum-o-gee and his son, young Sam. They wanted to hear more about the 'little people'. So Mother told about the time her niece took little Tamissa to gather pecans.

This story took place on the family's home-place north of Lake Fallah. On the south end of the land beyond GrandDad's house are a few pecan trees over one hundred feet tall. These big trees were planted from nuts long ago by the squirrels, blue jays and crows. They carry the nuts to the right place and bury close to other trees and thickets. When the trees grow the squirrels can jump from one tree to the next. Pretty smart animals. When the first frost comes in the Fall, it causes the green hulls to peel back, exposing the brown nut. The first winter wind rattles the branches and nuts fall to the ground below. It's a free-for-all time when the birds and animals come to collect *their* nuts. In some years the trees bear so many nuts that the birds and squirrels can't eat them all. They get fat and lazy and it's alright for people to have some of the nuts. This Fall was a very good year for the pecan nuts.

Mother's niece was going to gather nuts to sell to the General Store for extra money. She took along Tamissa, her two-year old daughter. You can't carry many nuts very far, so she drove the old truck. The pasture was bumpy from the cows walking around in the muddy field to eat the native grass. The old truck bumped down the rough road to the wire gate. Stopping the truck, she got out to unlatch the barbed wire gate and lay it down for the truck to pass through. It didn't take long, so the little girl waited in the truck. Her mother hurried back, fired up the engine, and drove through the gate. Again she shut off the truck's engine and left Tamissa inside the pickup. On the way to secure the wire gate to the fence post, she stopped to admire the field. The grass in the field was very short. The cows had done their job well, so finding nuts would be easy. Yes, it was good to have a truck to carry *all* the pecans they would find today!

The mother walked back to the truck. Her stomach had a strange feeling, as she opened the door. "Tamissa, ——" She couldn't see the little girl. "Oh, you are hiding from me. Now you come out!" mother said. Nothing moved. There was no noise.

Her eyes glanced out the truck windows to the field beyond. The grass was so short that if the little girl had somehow opened the door, then mother could see her scampering across the pasture. Not there! So she had to be inside the truck. This is a child's game, for sure. She first looked under the truck seat. No girl! Then she pulled down the back of the seat. No girl! How did little Tamissa open the door? How could she not hear the noise? She got down on her knees and looked under the truck, in the back, on top of the cab and everywhere. No girl! Even when both doors were opened to see all the way through the truck, there was no Tamissa to be found. Gone!

As fear settled in, the urge to scream was great. She would go for help. Turning to get in the truck, she saw the little girl was standing beside her. Tamissa was reaching out to hold on to mother's blue jeans. The mother peered in the little girl's eyes for clues. Was she alright? There was *no* fear in the little girl's eyes, as if nothing strange had happened. The girl turned and was pointing up to a big pecan tree. She giggled, then said, "aren't they nice?" The mother could see the work of pranksters. She knew about the 'little people' and how the smallest ones were full of mischief. There was no other way to explain what happened. How else could a little girl just disappear, then reappear as quickly?

Tamissa was alright. Firing up the old truck's engine, mother drove to the big pecan trees nearby. There were nuts laying all over the ground. Stopping the truck, they raced to the trees. Mother got down on her hands and knees to gather the fallen pecans. She put handfuls of nuts into the bucket. Then she emptied the nuts into big baskets in the back of the truck. Tamissa watched, giggling as she filled the little bucket with nuts. This was such fun!

Gathering nuts wasn't as easy as it appeared just because there were many nuts lying on the ground. Sometimes as mother was adding one last handful expecting to fill the bucket with pecans, there were none. They seemed to disappear. Finally discouraged, she called to Tamissa, "We are leaving now". The little girl was smiling and pointing at a spot behind mother. When mother turned around, there were nuts piled so high the bucket was covered. The big surprise was when she took the bucket to the truck to empty into the basket. The baskets were filled and running over with pecans. It seemed that someone was helping. They had gathered many nuts. Mother called out, loud, for all to hear, "I'm sure it was so easy to find nuts because the cows mowed the grass so low." No response. The only noise she heard was the leaves in the trees fluttering in the gentle wind. She remembered to search the branches for squirrels and squirrel nests hidden in the leaves. There were no squirrels in the trees. It was odd that with so many nuts, there were no squirrels.

Filled with baskets of nuts, the old pickup bumped across the pasture and out the barbed wire gate. She drove to the house to talk with GrandDad. First, he must see all the nuts in the back of the truck. "Oh, my goodness. There are so many nuts!" GrandDad exclaimed. Tamissa smiled because it pleased him. Then the mother gave GrandDad all the nuts that he cared to have. She helped him carry two big baskets of nuts to the house. They would be used for cooking to make many good things to eat.

Having shown respect to her elder with the gift of nuts, then she mentioned the strange things that happened today. The old man was often the only source of information on strange happenings. She needed his explanation. First, the mother told how Tamissa had disappeared into thin air and reappeared and how the pecan trees had squirrel holes, but no squirrels. Then, when the nuts disappeared, suddenly there were plenty. GrandDad scratched his head; this sure sounded like a strange thing. It was plain to see that she seemed to be in a hurry to go sell the nuts. All she wanted was an easy answer. Little Tamissa stopped before getting in the truck to leave with her mother. She smiled and waved her hand in the direction of the pecan trees. GrandDad took his hat and slapped it on his knee. He rolled his head back and laughed out. When the laughing slowed, he said, "Ho, Tamissa, now I see! Wait. I want to show you something!"

GrandDad turned and ran into the house. He came back with a big piece of paper, a sketch. "Tamissa" he said, "This picture was done by Johnnie". Johnnie was an older nephew who had drawn a special picture for his GrandDad. The sketch showed several of the 'little people' on a tree limb up in the big pecan tree in GrandDad's pasture. The little girl's eyes got *big*. She smiled and started nodding her head and pointing to the pecan tree.

Tamissa and her mother got into the truck. As they were driving away to sell the nuts in town, GrandDad remembered. Long ago, the ol' docktor Sum-o-gee used to live near those pecan trees. His house had long ago fallen down.

Cut Off the Braids

Sacrifice

There is always a battle between 'good' and' bad' medicine. You never know when something evil will happen. Often the 'witch docktor' can't find a way to cast a spell on good people. So he resorts to an attack on their children. Soon after gathering the pecans, little Tamissa came down with some terrible malady. "Someone" had seen them drive into town to sell all those pecans at the General Store. An envious person can't stand for someone to have more than him. He went to hunt the witch docktor. It took him a few days to figure out that his medicine wasn't working on the mother. Little Tamissa was the next victim. One morning her leg hurt so bad, she couldn't get out of bed. When an active child can't move, something is terribly wrong. Her mother was so worried and called all the relatives. They were worried too, fearing she could never walk. They took her to the ol' Indian docktor. He tried his best, but the leg kept hurting. When there is nothing that an Indian docktor can do, then you suspect right off that "black medicine" is involved. Nothing was working for Tamissa. She was getting worse.

As a last resort, her worried mother called the local physician and told him about Tamissa. Then she drove her child to the physician's office to inspect the leg. Oh, it looked bad to him. The next thing he did was to have Tamissa admitted to a large hospital in Tulsa. By the next day, the doctors at the hospital had run their medical tests. The results hurried them to take action. They told the mother, "It's bad. We will have to cut off the leg to save the child." Surgery was scheduled for the next Monday morning. Her mother and the family were afraid. All the relatives were contacted, including Grandfather. She needed much prayer!

All the relatives and others who were concerned gathered to pray at the Indian Baptist Church. The traditional Indians believe their hair should never be cut. Grandfather wore long braids, beautiful braids. God often recognizes sacrifices. What was needed here was a great sacrifice. He decided that the greatest sacrifice would be to cut off the braids. Grandfather called his wife. It seemed to be a voice in trouble. She came quickly to his side. His eyes showed a deep trouble inside. He told her "cut off the braids".

As she went to the kitchen for a knife, she thought, "This was something that he would never think about doing before". Why hadn't she thought about a sacrifice such as this for Tamissa? Grandfather sat on the chair and closed his eyes. She began cutting with her sharp butcher knife. One braid fell to the floor. Reverently, she stooped over to pick it up. Then as the second braid was cut, a big tear ran down his brown cheek. One tear. He loved this little granddaughter more than anything. She cared. God cares.

The Indian man and his wife got in the truck to drive to the Tulsa hospital. It was Sunday. Along the way, they knew of two other Indian Churches. No one knew they were coming but a stop was made. They asked the people to gather in prayer to ask God to save this little girl's leg. As they left the first church to drive on to the second, Grandmother remembered there were two braids cut. To her, this symbolized two churches that they were to ask for prayers. Soon they arrived at the second church. Again they asked the Indian people gathered here to pray for little Tamissa's leg. Oh, they were all touched. Then the truck's engine was started up. Not a word was said by either grandparent all the way to the hospital.

By the time the grandparents reached the hospital, the news was out. The little girl seemed to be better. The pain in her leg was gone. They had decided to reconsider on the decision to operate. Wait, blessed wait. Four days later, the little girl was up and running around. They let her go home without any operation— and walking on both legs. Six years later, she is eight years old and a normal happy little girl. No one knows how this little girl became so sick and then was healed and made well. All we know is that many prayed. In this operation, only two braids were cut off. It was worth the sacrifice!

Creek Dancer

Ancient Customs

This is a recent story of what happens to people who either don't believe or discount the spiritual world of the Indians. We don't think the "little people" have anything to do with this type of black medicine, but it's power is lasting. It is an example of the strength of Indian medicine, even if buried in the ground for ages.

When the Muscogea people were being relocated from the old country in Alabama, they were attracted to Fallah because of the water and country side. They could also see the signs of ancient burial grounds in the area. If this place was good enough for the ancient Indians, it was good enough for them. The ancient Indians buried the bones of their old people in hills of earth or mounds. The mounds were often built on higher grounds to protect from flood waters of their times. All the Indian children since the Muscogea people came to Oklahoma have enjoyed hunting artifacts whenever it rained. The rain washes the dirt from the flint tool and the morning sun makes the artifact glisten. It was such fun to find an arrowhead or two lying on the ground. Something that was buried long ago that waited until this moment to be found. Something precious to take home to show to mother and the other children. No one ever thought about digging into the dirt for anything else.

About thirty years ago, the US government decided to build a big lake. A big dam was made to create Lake Fallah. When the waters filled the lake, many of the ancient Indian burial grounds were flooded. Because the old mounds had been built on higher ground, the rising water left the tops of the mounds exposed usually at the shore line. The prevailing south wind washed waves across the north shore. After the waves have done their work cutting open the mounds and old burial grounds, flint arrowheads and fired clay pots are found lying on the shore.

There was a white man, who worked in the town's post office. He enjoyed digging along the shore line around Lake Fallah, searching for Indian artifacts. This man could not wait for the rains to come and the waves to do their work. Every weekend he would dig for artifacts.

Digging one weekend, he found a little clay pot. He had never seen one quite like it before. This pot was unusual because of the carving around the top. It had a little handle. It's opening was small, but what made the pot unusual was it's flattened shape. No one had found anything like this pot, so he was very curious. Probably worth a small fortune! He took it to an ol' Indian of the area, who knew about the old ways. He wanted an opinion, which came quickly. The Indian looked at the pot. Then he looked White Man in the eye and said, "This is a ceremonial pot. See the marking here and dried stuff inside?" White Man peered at the pot with his little 'squirrel eyes', which meant he didn't believe the Indian. The Indian said, "You shouldn't keep *this* pot. You have no use for it and it will bring you trouble." White Man still had those little squirrel eyes. He said, "I found it. It's mine to keep." The Indian shook his head at this man's bad decision against sound advice. They left each other's company.

Within the next few weeks, the Indian heard of many calamities in the other man's life. First, his car was wrecked when he ran into a telephone pole. Then he came down with some sickness after the wreck. Next he lost his job at the post office. Federal jobs are very hard to lose. Not long afterward, his wife left him. Then, one night his house caught on fire. No one arrived in time to help him put out the fire. He lost everything, including that little clay pot. Five bad things happened within a few short months. The little clay pot is now gone forever. It just makes you think twice about digging in the Earth that covered Indian burial grounds, then keeping strange Indian artifacts that don't belong to you.

Another story, about an Indian man, who was walking along the shore of Lake Fallah. He came upon the remains of an ancient fire. It was back away from the lake and hadn't been disturbed in a very long time. How do we know? Because these remains showed the signs of being on an old stomp ground.

The fire pit was rocked and blackened. Around the firepit, the earth had a slight dished shape of perhaps 75 feet in diameter. That's where the people would have danced, late at night, for three nights in a row. Their feet would have worn down the Earth. Don't you hear beating on the little water drum and the dancers moving and chanting? A-E-A, A-E-A, He-Hoe, He-Hoe!

Moving in three directions from the firepit, were piles of rotten sticks. That would have been the brush arbors. The east side of the firepit was open to let the dawn sun come in. In the olden days, the women would sweep and rake up everything off the grounds. They made a "clean ground". They would then make piles of brush and sticks at the edge of the clean grounds. The brush would be shaped like a giant serpent lying on the ground encircling the brush arbor and the fire pit. Its shape was curved like a giant snake's tracks in the sand.

What else is lacking? There should be some signs of a ball field nearby. Sure enough, it's *there*. By following the outline of the giant serpent's tracks away from the rotten sticks of the brush arbor, he found it. About a hundred feet from the firepit and the clean ground, there was a carved wooden fish. The fish was carved from black walnut. It was there on the ground. Lying beside it was a long wooden pole. It had rotted and was broken into three or four pieces. But the fish looked like it was carved yesterday! Then he could remember how his GrandDad had a passion for the game of Stick Ball. Two teams would be running up and down the field all day long. The men had two ball sticks. One stick was used to throw the ball at the wooden fish on top of the pole. The other stick was to fend away another man's ball-stick smashing his head. Sometimes women would be allowed to play the game too, but they didn't have to use the sticks. A women could dash into a crowd, pick up the ball and throw it over the fish. The game took great skill and courage to win.

One reason the stick ball game was so exciting was because with Indian medicine, either side could win. Each team had a medicine man. He had a whole bag of tricks to help his team win. The best players had great skill with the sticks, courage to be hit, and endurance—yet still be alert for anything strange and out of place. A curve ball or sudden rain storm. The great players had to sense something strange and avoid it!

The clue here was the carved fish. It had been laying on the ground for a long time, yet it looked freshly made. Danger! Don't touch it! Then the Indian's eyes followed the path of the broken pieces of pole used to hold the fish high in the air. The direction of the broken pieces lined up in a southwesterly direction, crossing right over the fish on the ground. Its strange how the stories told to us by the elders suddenly come back years later. In the old stories he remembered the old tribal grounds that lay in a south-westerly direction from this place. They called it Tuk-a-batchee Town. [1] It was located near the present village of Mellette, about ten miles southwest of Eufaula. He remembered being told that it was the only town built with the "round house, square ground, and four ceremonial buildings". In those days, the Chief of Tuk-a-batchee Town was the "principal medicine maker" of one of the old War Clans. His tracks that had been laid down many years ago were here today before our eyes.

The ol' Indian wisely decided not to touch the fish or the pieces of pole. He left it there on the lake shore for whatever fate it deserved. The Indian's house is still standing to this day. We wonder if anyone else has found the wooden fish and dared to take it home?

Going to Have Baby Soon

Little People's Baby

Introduction: *This is a story that takes place about 20 years ago in Chickasaw Country. Before Statehood the tribal lands of the Muscogea and Chickasaw were connected at the South Canadian River. Indian People have always crossed the river. At Statehood, both tribes lost most of their land. The Chickasaws were left with 640 acres, called "Kullihoma". This land is ten miles out in the country from Ada. Both tribes had docktors taught by "little people". None of the old docktors survived modern times. The Chickasaws are more progressive and know less about the old culture. Somehow the 'little people' survived and show up today in the strangest ways.*

This story is about wealth. Great wealth is an illusion. In Indian Country, no one has much money. Wealth comes in other forms as common as something good to eat, children, or even gifts of the 'little people'. It often takes the words of an admirer. When the 'rich one' finally sees his wealth in the eyes of an admirer, it sometimes causes him to act badly.

This story is about "Willie". He was one of those Chickasaws, from the tribe with round heads and little short noses. Willie lived east of town near Kullihoma, the only remaining tribal land. "Homa" means "home" but the meaning of the rest of the name is lost. The land is covered in 'scrub' oaks and too poor to farm. There was no work done out there, or nothing that paid money. Willie had been fortunate to find a job in Ada, washing dishes at the Barbecue Place. He had been doing this for years, not that dish-washers get paid big money. It was the food. The food that he liked to eat most of all was barbecued meat—pork was the best. Anytime he wanted some good barbecue, it was there to eat as ribs or brisket, sliced or in chunks. Most Indians like to eat barbecue. Willie was no different from other Indians, except that he had an endless supply. His only choice was to eat it 'mild' or add hot sauce to give it more taste. He liked it as hot as fire. You might say that Willie was *rich*—in barbecue. He was just the dishwasher but Willie knew that he had a good thing. Rich? He wouldn't have thought so.

Willie's first mistake was casually telling an Indian friend what he ate and how often. He had no idea what the effect would be from this comment. Word of mouth spread the news far and wide. No one talked about his ordinary job. They envied this 'rich Indian'. People will travel miles to eat good food. This makes a lot of dirty plates and forks. As Willie hauled dirty dishes to the kitchen, he overheard customers talking about him, the 'rich Indian'. The revelation electrified Willie. It made him feel important. At that moment, a change came over the simple dishwasher.

About that time, the US government was awarding money to Indian tribes to manage their own assets. The Chickasaws set up tribal headquarters in Ada. Government money was available to take care of tribal land; Kullihoma was all there was. No one went there anyhow. That made no difference to anyone in Washington DC. The problem was the tribe couldn't hire an Indian to care for the land who would drive twenty miles every day. Without a caretaker, the government money would have to be sacrificed. Someone at Tribal headquarters remembered that 'Willie' lived near Kullihoma. He was offered the new job of Grounds caretaker. Even though Indians get job preference, Willie didn't want to give up that barbecue to rake leaves and haul brush. It took a bit extra, but Willie, now the 'rich man', could be enticed. He could be the "boss" of the grounds. As "boss" that meant that he could hire a laborer.

It was a great task to clean brush from 640 acres of rough land. Willie hired a big strong man to do the work. Ben was a Muscogea Indian who lived in Wetumka, across the Canadian river. Because he was Muscogean, Ben preferred to live on his "home-place" and commute daily. He drove his pickup truck 35 miles one way to Kullihoma. It's a good thing he was hired, because Willie had much work to be done. One day, Ben couldn't finish all the chores. He would have to work late, then spend the night in his truck in the woods at Kullihoma.

Something unusual happened to him that night. Next morning Ben casually told Willie: "I got my work done. Then I went to my truck for the night. Just about to go off to sleep, I heard faint voices. I listened closely and heard little voices in the Creek language. Here I am in Chickasaw Country. Three 'little people' were talking to me in my language. The two little men I had seen before. This time there was a woman with a big belly. One of the little men said, 'She is big. Going to have baby soon'. They laughed and talked most of the night in my pickup."

Willie had heard brief stories about the 'little people'. He had always thought 'that stuff' was long gone. Now all that he remembered was how 'they' were helpers for life and brought good luck. He didn't know the 'little ones' take a long time to choose someone good before becoming visible. And since the little fellers that Ben saw spoke his language, we can figger they been around him a long time. As Ben told his story, Willie's eyes kept getting bigger and bigger. Good luck is about to fall! And if it does, a baby born on Chickasaw land oughta belong to a Chickasaw. It should be his! He wanted to make a deal with the Muscogea man. As the 'boss' he tried not to show excitement. Willie was sure this good fortune was following him since giving up the town job at the Barbecue Place.

Willie told Ben, "Say, when that baby comes along, give him to me. I will take good care of him. You still have the other three 'little people'. That would be fair!" Willie the 'rich man' was the 'boss'. He wanted that baby so bad! Ol' Greed was tugging at him now!

When you really want something bad, you get to wishing and dreaming about what's possible. He could hardly wait. When the little baby grew up, Willie could have anything in the World. He would be so rich with the things that this "little one" would do for him! He was going to the Barbecue Place in town and get twenty pounds of good barbecue ribs. No Indian man could resist barbecue. He'd have that baby! Ol' Greed got him now.

Willie bought a big brown bag filled with barbecue ribs. Rushing back to Kullihoma, he set the bag before Ben. He pulled out a big juicy rib and waved it. "Here! When the baby comes, he's mine!" Ben looked at Willie. At that moment, he decided to find another job closer to home. He thought, "Here's a guy who don't know nothing. I guess he didn't have a GrandDad to teach him. It's up to me to teach him something." Ben said,"You can't buy 'little people' like you buy a bag of spare-ribs. Ain't a way you can take advantage of them. If you even get a glance at one, something good will happen in your life. I quit!"

And many good things have happened to Ben, the young Muscogea man. He and Willie sat in his pickup and ate their way through *all* of the bag of barbecue. It was sure good eating. Willie felt better now and ol' Greed was gone. Ben got a better job in Wetumka. No one else has ever seen a 'little one' at Kullihoma. Maybe that baby is back in Muscogea Country.

Author's note: *This is the first ever report about "little people" having babies. If there are two sizes of 'little people' and some are older and some are younger, why wouldn't there be babies?*

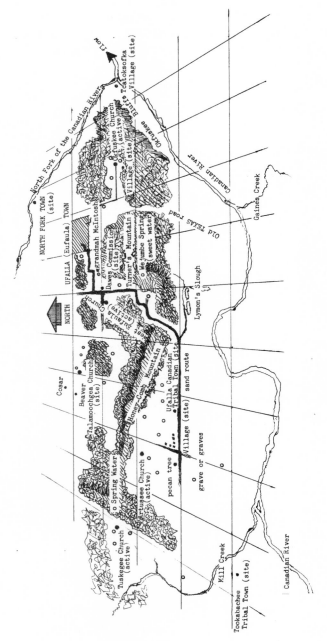

Eufaula, Oklahoma

Rattlesnake Tails

Today, a four-lane highway passes over Fallah in a north to south direction. It cuts through the middle of Aunt Loney's mountain. No one knows where to find "the place where the wild onion grows" down in the meadow. No one knows where to find the little spring of sweet "we-jumba" water seeping down the side of the mountain. Within one hundred yards of the cars roaring up and down the highway all hours of the day and night is the old McIntosh Cemetery. No one in those cars know this is the oldest cemetery in Oklahoma. This one has the grave markers. Visible in the distance from the highway is Lake Fallah. The water covers the ancient Indian graves in the mounds. We need to be quiet passing these old graveyards to keep from disturbing the old Indian spirits. This busy highway is passing over the home of the "little people".

You have probably heard before of elves, fairies and leprechauns. Maybe someone even told you about the Kobalds. All these tales came from Europe. Most likely you have never before heard of these brown-skinned versions living in America. The Indians have never believed in telling about sacred things. To this day, they are probably there in the heavy underbrush in the big, tall trees. Get off that highway and slow down the car. If you see a big nut tree, stop and park your car. Get out and look close and listen. There may be noises like squirrels fussing in the top branches or honey bees buzzing in the wild flowers. It's "them", waiting to talk to someone who wants to listen.

Sometimes "they" come out to play. We know this because unexplained things happen. Pranks. When the Federal agents were trying to catch ol' Chitto Harjo holed up in caves on Honeycomb Bluff, they were greeted by a big rattlesnake in front of every cave. They were hissing and shaking their big rattlesnake tails. Scared them away, too! Ol' Chitto Harjo and the "Redsticks" didn't want to give away this Indian land. Sure didn't want electrical power stations or highways on Indian land. There was a big electrical sub-station over in Bristow. That's north of Fallah, but still in Muscogea country.[1] A big rattlesnake crawled through the door of the sub-station. It shorted out the lights everywhere. Everyone wondered why the electricity went off. They worked all night to get the power restored. All that was found was the charred remains of what was identified as a big snake. It wasn't a snake!

Now you know that it's just the little ones playing their pranks. The only way to know for sure is to leave a little paper bag of candy under the tree. The hard and sweet ones, if you please. Don't look around as you leave the bag.

We can only speculate what might have happened if the Indians still had this land. Not only would we have the knowledge of the little people with the grey beards, we might all have good health care without hospitals and insurance. There would be lots of big tall trees and no pollution or crime. Sometimes we get to changing things too fast and mess up what God wanted for us.

When the Creeks came to this New Land in 1836, they delivered a formal message to the President of the United States. The War Clan told him the Tribe wanted to live in peace—if White

Man would let them. These old Indians knew a great deal about peace because that's the way they lived. White Man hasn't asked for any help from the Indians and created a big mess. The tribe has kept quiet so long, that the secret has almost become lost. We have had to use fiction to rebuild stories and put life back in because nothing is left.

Maybe we have lost the meaning that has been passed down from the ancients. As hard as we have tried to preserve just a tiny bit, maybe we have failed to find the most important parts. Nothing has been said about the Kobalds in hundreds of years and little is said today about leprechauns. By telling nothing about the "little people", we would make them fairy tales, too. Our revelations are not intended to release 'little people' from a prison of created secrecy. Words that bind and limit what's possible are yet another prison. The greatest prison is our minds by not reaching beyond the 'head-lights', and believing by faith.

In the stories, Grandfather tells us not to chase after the "little people". "Sam Jr." and "Willie" show us this is so. The little ones encourage discipline and following the rules to keep peace. Everything begins with this base. The suggestion is made that ol' Grey Beard has great wealth to bestow, if nothing more than wisdom and knowledge. Book learnin' isn't bad, unless it closes the mind to accepting new information and believing by faith. The suggestion that 'little people' procreate is a hope for the future. We have left a legacy for the children. If they know and they believe, then there is hope. When we have a terrible ordeal facing us—like swimming the Mississippi River, then a 'little man' may appear on the pony's head and steer us to safety. Otherwise, rattlesnake tails warn of danger.

Characteristics of the "Little People"

The Indian people didn't talk about anything sacred as to be limiting of a more powerful creature that man can not fully understood. What follows is for the reader and comes from the stories.

Physical Appearance

- Male and female.
- Same proportions as a man or woman but no taller than a normal man's knee.
- Two sizes. The smaller ones are pranksters. Larger ones are more serious, rarely play pranks.
- Always brown-skinned and usually bare-faced, like Indians.
- Always speaks the Native language of the person they favor, even in the country of another Indian tribe speaking a different language.
- Voices sound like birds or the buzzing of bees, yet they

can produce loud roaring noises. They are usually talk-ative, laugh, and easily show emotion.

- All are bare-foot. Some have long toe nails.
- Females have children.
- They seem to cross physical time and space in a twinkle of an eye. Pranks played on children and strangers hap-pen fast.
- Invisible to ordinary people, who probably don't believe in them anyhow.
- Probably a spirit, who have the power to help Indian people in weakened condition become healed. Espe-cially favor the "pure-blood" Indians. Infers little help to "Wannabe" Indians.
- Probably in the olden days, the "little people" had greater healing powers because people accepted them on faith.
- After helping a person for a lifetime, the little one grows a white beard.
- If not ageless, they live a very long time.
- Encourage taste standards for Indians different than White Man. Traditional foods are regarded over high-sugar foods which cause diabetes in many Indians. It's okay to eat a little bit of candy, in moderation.
- They eat and drink strange things to you and I, such as grasshoppers and clabbored milk. Taste is transformed by some illusion or it may be real, we don't know which.

Tribal or Social Acceptance

- Live in groups and favor big pecan trees or dark caves.
- "Little people" have sacred dance grounds to gather to-gether to overcome big problems.
- Since ancient times, the Muscogea tribe was known as peace-keepers and diplomats. It seems no accident the

"little people" chose to help the peace clans in times of need.

- "Little people" are guardians of children to keep them safe from harm. Even pester the rowdy ones to instill discipline toward traditional ways without guidance from parents.
- "Little people" have high standards and morals. They are great encouragers for good and perfect performance.
- "Little People" choose some of the brightest and curious children for secret training as herb docktors in a life-time service to Indian people. Likely the chosen one must also have the innate potential to connect sick people with the Creator or Great Spirit.
- Rowdy children are never selected by the "little people" to be a docktor. Children must accept 'their' discipline on faith alone.
- "Little people" don't like dogs. This is because dogs are more sensitive to spirits than people. Dogs were always part of the Indian community to detect spirits.
- "Little people" prefer to talk "eyeball-to-eyeball" to ensure that the student learns the first time. Their training requires a good memory for details. Their ways encourage the oral tradition, although some docktors learn enough to keep records in books.
- Just seeing "Little people" is considered to be good luck. To chase a 'little man' is certain to bring bad luck. Impossible for a anyone to seek or buy election.
- Great tribal honor to be a docktor. The strange ways of the "little people" are accepted by the tribe because they train docktors to heal sick people and guard against evil spirits.
- Parents must have faith that something good is happening whenever their child is gone for 1 to 4 days at a time, then returns healthy without explanation.

- Patients of the docktor must have the faith that healing can happen based on the use of indigenous herbs and native medicines.
- From the story "Jockogee", if the people accept the "old ways" which includes belief in healing with blind faith, healing can occur. This is the basis of the Christian belief in healing by faith alone.
- Even good docktor's didn't try to teach the art of healing to their children. Depended always on "little people" to select then train docktors. God heals, not man or "little people".
- Not all Indian docktors had "little people" for helpers. The best docktors had these helpers.
- Healing does not occur directly through the "little people" but always through a trained intermediary, highly respected in the community.
- Long ago, the "little people" taught songs to the hunters to entice deer from the woods for meat to feed the people. Part of the hunter's training was to kill no more than was needed.

Wacena Comes

Written history about the Muscogea migration of 1836 is difficult to understand, especially to the Indians[1,2]. What follows for them is a story. In a few pages we cover 200 years of their history through the 1836 migration. It tells where they came from and focuses on the last migrating party that brought horses to Oklahoma territory.

In the 1600's the first European traders came from Jamestown Colony to what is Georgia. They found Indian towns in strategic places surrounded by many villages. The people lived on Ochese Creek, the Okmulgee River today. Both sides likely asked, "Who are you?" The Indians called the traders "Wacena", meaning "the people that came from the Virginia country"[3]. When the Indians began naming their home villages, the names were long and confusing to Wacena. They also called themselves "Mus-co-gea". This was puzzling! In simple terms, they were called "Lower" and "Upper" Creeks to describe where the groups lived on Ochese Creek. That done, the Creek Chiefs were asked to tell where they came from. A picture legend was drawn on a buffalo skin, which was later sent to London in 1735 [4.] The legend told how four tribes or "sticks" came from the west, crossing a big muddy river. These "sticks" were the Ka-sih-ta and Co-we-ta, who lived on the Lower Creek; the Coo-sa and A-bih-ki tribes lived on the Upper Creek. Each Stick was responsible for either war or peace, symbolized on the hide drawing as red or white. Kasihta was red and the Coweta white. A fifth tribe, the Tuk-a-batchee, joined them later. In early days, the Muscogea were renown peace-keepers and diplomats in the region. Clever lads, the British. They chose to deal with the Chief of the Coweta, one of the peace tribes.

In 1770, the British counted 45 different Creek towns, each with several villages (see Figure 1). Little tribes, such as the Hit-chi-ti and Yu-chi, had joined the Muscogea Confederacy for protection. As more settlers came, the tribes were pushed further west. The Upper Creeks resettled on the Coosa and Tallapoosa branches of the Alabama River (Figure 2). Tukabatchee Town was the largest town of the Upper Creeks. The Lower Creeks settled along the Flint and Chattahoochee Rivers, near the present Alabama and Georgia border. The clamor to take their land was loud! President Jefferson knew how to satisfy settlers. In 1802, the US Congress passed a bill called "the Georgia Compact". This law was to remove the Indian tribes from Georgia, as soon as possible by peaceful means. Every one expected quick action.

The tribal elders were disturbed with the flight to learn the White Man's ways. Intermarriage led to the sale of tribal lands and the Red-Stick War of 1813–1814 [5.] This war pitted the "Red Sticks" against the "White Sticks". The Red Sticks opposed selling tribal land. Fearing the Red Sticks would win, the US government sent General Andy Jackson to "keep the peace". The US Army with Indians from enemy tribes killed 1,000 Creeks at the Battle of Horseshoe Bend. Then, fields were torched. "Peace" returned and the Creeks were forced to cede land in Southern Georgia (Figure 3).

The settlers were not satisfied with the ceded Indian land. They had been waiting since 1802 for *their* land. There was a half-breed Coweta Chief, William McIntosh. He fought at Horseshoe Bend under Jackson and made an enemy of Chief Menawa of the Upper Creeks. McIntosh had a powerful cousin, George McIntosh Troup, the Governor of Georgia. McIntosh ceded more "surplus" Creek land to Georgia in 1818 and 1821. The settlers were happy. McIntosh sold his land for $25,000, considered a fortune.[6] General Jackson gave him 640 acres, considered a bribe. The tribe quickly passed a law that revoked authority of any chief to sell tribal land. Selling land was subject to death, agreed by Chief McIntosh.

By 1825 the clamor for Indian land encouraged Governor Troup to ask for more. Chief McIntosh, his brother Roley and two other relatives agreed to cede Indian land in exchange for land out west. To them, the outcome was certain. Surely the rest of the tribe could see this. His house was set fire by a hundred Red Sticks. Running to escape, McIntosh was shot. Chief Menawa stabbed him. A son-in-law was assassinated and other executions followed.

The next year the treaty was rescinded. The Georgia land was still sold, but at a better price with a perpetual annuity. Individuals could exchange their land for Oklahom land, acre for acre. It's not said, the US Secretary of War and the Governor of Georgia were infuriated. After waiting years for the land, Indians were still there. Ceding Indian land had been voluntary, until the US Congress passed the Indian Removal Act of 1830. This would be a sword hanging over the Muscogea people, waiting to strike.

The McIntosh clan greatly feared the Red Sticks and white settlers. The land offer was accepted and the first group of 733 Creeks left for Oklahoma Territory. In Oklahoma, Roley McIntosh was made Chief. Life wasn't easy because the Osage Indians fought for the land they believed was theirs! The McIntosh clan couldn't return to Georgia. They fought. By 1830, other Creeks joined them increasing the population to 3,000.

Chief McIntosh was right, the outcome was inevitable. In 1832, the Creek Chiefs signed a treaty to give up 5.2 million acres in exchange for Oklahoma land. The US government agreed to pay removal costs and an annuity for one year subsistence. The Creeks could leave when ready. On arrival, the head of the family would receive a rifle, bullets and a blanket. With the treaty signed, everyone knew they had to leave. The land speculators believed it an honor to defraud land from the Indian: lease his land for $10, but move him off. Suck him into debt with high interest rates and sell or give liquor.`Four years of suffering preceded migration. "They could leave when ready" took on a new meaning. Everyone expected to be led by an old trusted Indian agent. Instead, an emigrating company was contracted with the speculators who were stealing their land! To top that insult, they were awarded twenty dollars a head to move the Indians. The Indians refused to go.

The first to give up was the Upper Creek Chief of Tukabatchee Town. With his people starving, the Chief set an early date and prepared to go. (See Figure 4). He conceded publically: "We will put out the old sacred fire—never to make it again, until we reach west of the Mississippi River—there never to quench it again."

Without a home or food, some 2,500 of the Lower Creeks went to live with the Cherokees in Tennessee and Northwest Georgia. The governor of Georgia was hostile against Indians; his volunteer militia fired on fifty of the Creeks. Trespassers! They killed and injured a few Indians. Others escaped across the Coosa River to Alabama, burning the toll bridge behind. The Georgia militia of 1,000 men crossed the river in pursuit. The Indians took revenge: they attacked Columbus, Georgia, a "rat's nest" of land speculators. A major Alabama newspaper correctly called the Creek War "a humbug" and blamed land speculators for the turmoil.

"Alarming reports" of the Indian attack on Columbus reached Washington DC. Three days later, the Secretary of War sent General Jesup and 11,000 troops into Alabama to stop the war and forcibly remove the Indians to the western lands. Jesup had been in Florida trying to subdue and move the Seminole Indians to Oklahoma. The white settlers in Alabama and Georgia were uneasy, because General Jesup had not subdued the Seminoles.

Since 1830, the sword of the Secretary of War was hanging over their heads awaiting the slightest excuse to fall. The sword first struck the peaceful Lower Creeks. Even fleeing, they were called "hostiles" and soldiers chased them like wolves. They caught 500 of the Lower Creeks from Eufaula and Chia-haw towns. Chief Emathla was brought in irons to Fort Mitchell. A few days later a thousand of his followers surrendered. The plan was to move the "hostiles" out west by steamboat. The nearest water was ninety miles away. Captain John Page believed that "chains are worse to Indians than death". The blacksmith began hammering handcuffs to shackle Indians in double file to a long chain. Chief Emathla was 84-years old. With chains rattling, the old man walked the ninety miles leading his people. The old chief never complained. To this day, the US government justifies military actions by branding their enemies as "hostiles".

The second time the "sword" struck was the Chief of the Upper Creeks. Ready to lead his people to the western land, the soldiers captured him. The charge was heavy debt against the tribe from rigged claims of the land speculators. The Indians had no money. They asked the government to advance payment on the lands sold. General Andy Jackson, now the President, intervened. Before loaning money to pay his "ransom", Jackson required the Chief provide 1,000 warriors to quell the upstart Seminoles in Florida. The Indians remember Jackson by the name "Sharp Nose".

The third time the "sword" struck was the rest of the Lower Creeks, who had "escaped" to live with the Cherokee. Many had married Cherokees and planted crops. The soldiers marched to Tennessee and demanded the return of the errant Creeks. The Cherokee refused! The soldiers pursued them to the hills. Many were found eating tree bark. There was no other food. About 500 prisoners were recovered and later joined Lt. Deas emigration party to the western lands. Even the soldiers wondered why these Creeks weren't allowed to emigrate with the Cherokee in 1837.

The soldiers rounded up all three "resisting" groups of the Creek tribe to be removed to Oklahoma. Chief Eneah Micco had signed the 1832 treaty. When the chief and 145 men were captured, General Jesup proclaimed, "The war is ended". It had taken less than a month to end the war. Nonetheless this action struck fear on all the Creeks and Indians of other tribes.

The hostiles were marched in chains to the riverboat landing at Montgomery. They were joined with Creeks captured from other towns, including 900 Yuchi and 500 Kasihta. Altogether 2,300 captives were loaded on two small steamboats with barges in tow. The boats descended the Alabama River to Mobile then up the Mississippi River. The contractors used old battered boats, heavily laden beyond their capacity of 600 passengers. Then the rains started, heavy blinding rains. The waves rocked the boats which frightened the Indians in the pitch-black hold. Worse yet, the cramped quarters spread the fever. At that time, there was no cure for yellow fever. Rampant deaths ended plans to move the rest of the tribe by steamboat to Memphis. The agent would be paid $20 for only live Indians.

By the end of July the hostiles were moved up the Mississippi River. West of Memphis, across the river, is an impassable swamp. The steamboats bypassed the swamp, ascend the White River to a landing at Rock Roe, Arkansas. Then, everyone waited eight days for the agent to buy wagons, ox and horses. Texas had declared independence from Mexico two months before. The Mexicans kept fighting. Soldiers in Oklahoma were rushed to protect the border to Texas, which depleted the supply of wagons and horses.

One good thing happened as they waited for the wagons and horses. In the boredom of the hot summer, the soldiers let the hostiles play their stick-ball game. Handcuffs and chains were unlocked and stored in empty barrels on the boat. The Indians were sent ashore to play the game, which lasted a long time. As everyone cheered the players, the Yuchi contingent sneaked aboard the ship. They rolled the barrels of chains into the river. The cheers were louder. When horses and wagons arrived, the people walked to Fort Gibson without chains or handcuffs. The Yuchi will be long remembered.

Hearing that hostiles were coming to Oklahoma, Chief Roley McIntosh was alarmed. The Red Sticks would kill him for revenge. When the hostiles arrived in early September, they were threatening. It looked bad until the soldiers warned the hostiles their annuity would be held unless they obeyed. Money talked. They accepted Chief McIntosh and the existing government as their leaders.

The initial plan was to move 12,500 non-hostile Indians by steam-boat to Memphis. The plan changed and everyone walked to Memphis (see Figure 5). The Creeks were divided into five big parties, each led by an agent and a military officer. From Memphis the parties would be hauled 100 miles down-river, up the White River to unload at Rock Roe, walking to Oklahoma.

Lt. J. T. Sprague of the US Marines led the last party, the Kasihta and Coweta Lower Creek towns (Figure 4). After Sprague arrived, it took one month to leave. His party with 500 horses reached Memphis on October 7, behind two other parties. They camped on the river bluffs waiting five days for the steam-boats. The first two parties were loaded and left for Rock Roe. As it turned out the boats were grounded in the shallow White River and blocked the way to Rock Roe. When it was time for Sprague's party to load, the men refused to leave. They chose to take horses across the swamp. The women, children and baggage would go by steam-boat up the Arkansas River, the next river west of the blocked White River. Even that plan was thwarted. The Arkansas River was too shallow. Half of the people and the baggage was unloaded to lighten the boat. After dropping its cargo in Little Rock, the boat returned for the balance of people. When the river level dropped suddenly, the boat was stuck in the sand the rest of the Winter.

From Chambers County, Alabama the trip was 800 miles by land and 425 miles by water in 96 days. Sprague's party was the last to leave but the second to reach Oklahoma. They left their home-land in a warm season thinly clad and endured many hardships with only 29 deaths. The soldiers handed out rations and blankets to the 2,000 who made the trip. On their arrival, Kasihta Town, the war clan, addressed Lt. Sprague. What's significant is that the Coweta Town, the peace clan, didn't speak. It was the Kasihta, who had decided to follow the white path of peace. Their message to the Lieutenant was meant to be delivered to the World:

"You have been with us many moons—you have heard the cries of our women and children—our road had been a long one—and on it we have laid the bones of our men, women and children. When we left our home the great General Jesup told us that we could get to our country as we wanted to. We wanted to gather our crops. We wanted to go in peace and friendship. Did we? No! We were drove off like wolves—lost our crops—and our people's feet were bleeding with long marches. Tell President Jackson if the White Man will let us, we will live in peace and friendship—but tell that these agents came not to treat us well, but make money. Tell our people behind not to be drove off like dogs. We are men. We have women and children, and why should we come like wild horse."

Later in December, 1836, General Arbuckle reported that the Chief of the Upper Creeks and 6000 of his people had arrived at Fort Gibson (Figure 6)without winter clothing. The contractor promised to bring clothing, but didn't. It was ironic. The Chief had put out the sacred fire in Alabama, not to be relit until reaching the new lands, then never allowing the light to go out. They were very cold now. More ironic was that long ago the tribe had migrated across the big muddy river "We-of-gof-ke" to a new land. After Wacena came, the Creeks tried to adapt to the ways of the White Man. In 200 years their paradise was lost. Even their migration legend enscribed on a buffalo hide had been stolen from the London Archives.

As the Creeks crossed the We-o-gof-ke, they were reminded that the Red Sticks said the White Man only wanted their land. After arriving in the new country, no Creek could claim to be a Christian without severe punishment. It wasn't until 1848 that the Creek Council realized their error. They had wrongly blamed God, when man was the problem. Then, they allowed Christian churches amongst their people again.

"To take a broad view of the thing, it really began with Andrew Jackson. If General Jackson hadn't run the Creeks up the creek, Simon Finch would never have paddled up the Alabama and where would we be if he hadn't?"

Harper Lee, To Kill a Mockingbird

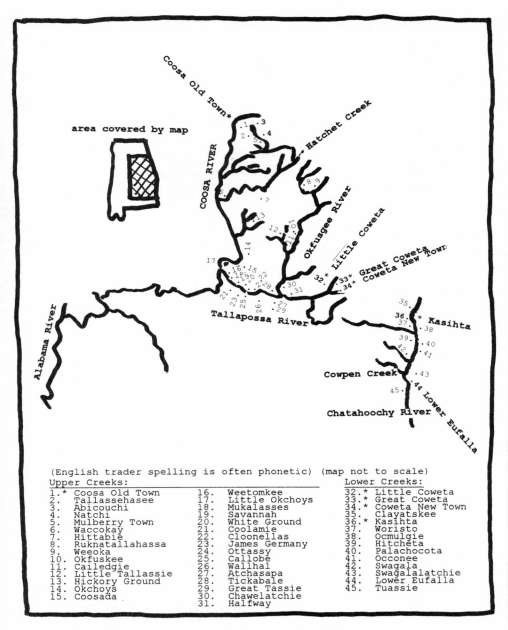

(English trader spelling is often phonetic) (map not to scale)

Upper Creeks:

1.* Coosa Old Town
2. Tallassehasee
3. Abicouchi
4. Natchi
5. Mulberry Town
6. Waccokay
7. Hittabie
8. Ruknatallahassa
9. Weeoka
10. Okfuskee
11. Cailedgie
12. Little Tallassie
13. Hickory Ground
14. Okchoys
15. Coosada

16. Weetomkee
17. Little Okchoys
18. Mukalasses
19. Savannah
20. White Ground
21. Coolamie
22. Cloonellas
23. James Germany
24. Ottassy
25. Callobe
26. Wallhal
27. Atchasapa
28. Tickabale
29. Great Tassie
30. Chawelatchie
31. Halfway

Lower Creeks:

32.* Little Coweta
33.* Great Coweta
34.* Coweta New Town
35. Clayatskee
36.* Kasihta
37. Woristo
38. Ocmulgie
39. Hitcheta
40. Palachocota
41. Occonee
42. Swagala
43. Swagalalatchie
44. Lower Eufalla
45. Tuassie

Fig. 1: The Creek Nation about 1770

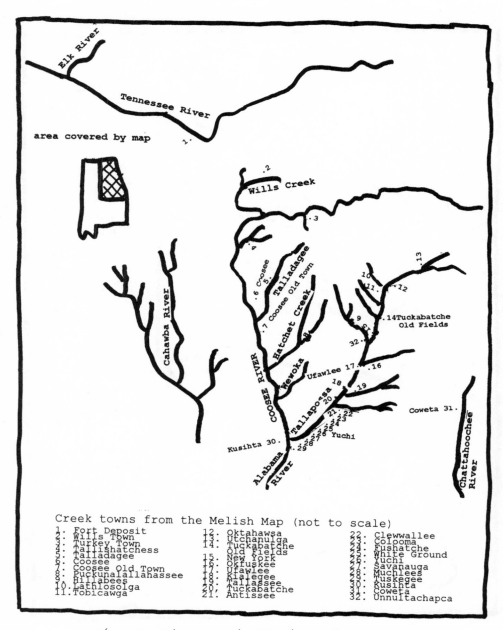

Creek towns from the Melish Map (not to scale)

1: Fort Deposit
2: Wills Town
3: Turkey Town
4: Tallishatchess
5: Talladagee
6: Coosee
7: Coosee Old Town
8: Puckunalallahassee
9: Hillabees
10: Lathlosolga
11: Tobicawga

12: Oktahawsa
13: Utchanulga
14: Tuckabatche
   Old Fields
15: New York
16: Okfuskee
17: Ufawlee
18: Kialegee
19: Tallassee
20: Tuckabatche
21: Antissee

22: Clewwallee
23: Coloома
24: Fushatche
25: White Ground
26: Yuchi
27: Savanauga
28: Muchlees
29: Tuskegee
30: Kusihta
31: Coweta
32: Unnultachapca

Fig. 2: The Creek Nation about 1814

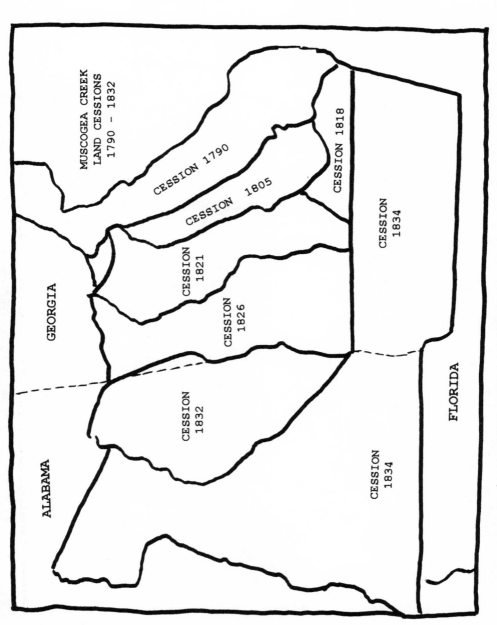

Fig. 3: The Creek Nation Land Cessions

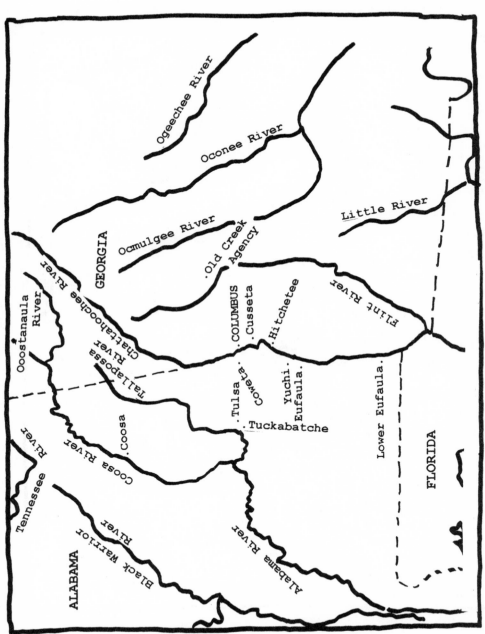

Fig. 4: The Creek Nation of 1832

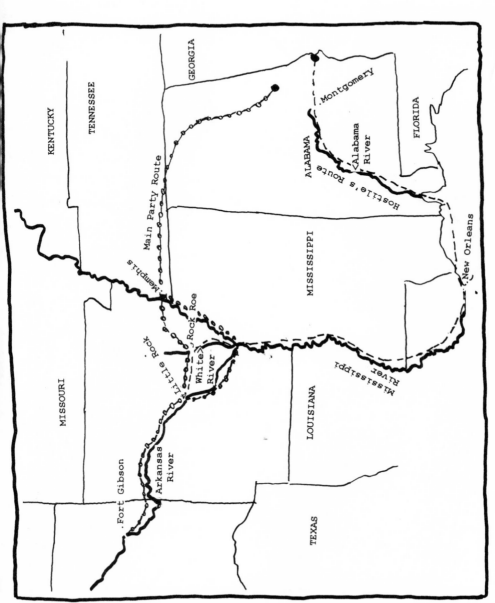

Fig. 5: Routes of Emigrating Indians

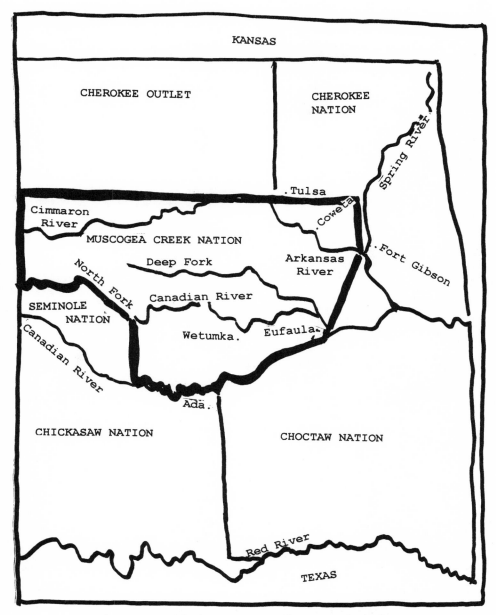

Fig. 6: Oklahoma Territory of 1880's

Glossary

Glossary: From the Muscogea language. These words are the long form likened to the "King's English", versus the common short form more popular in contemporary times.

People & Places:
Cha-bon . . . boy, a very curious boy.
Eu-faul-a or Fal-lah . . . they split up here and went to other places.
Jock-o-gee . . . Little Jack (name).
Gee . . . little
Har-jo . . . stumbling around, crazy.
Ma-to . . . thank you.
Steel-lo-booch-go-gee . . . little people.
Tul-la-much-kea . . . Indian church, meaning of name is lost.
Wa-cena . . . white men from early Virginia Colony.
We . . . waters, as in river.
We-o-gof-ke . . . muddy waters, referring to Mississippi River.
We-o-jum-ba . . . sweet water from certain natural spring.
We-tum-ka . . . leaping water

Foods:
Auh-push-kea . . . parched corn
Ga-ve . . . coffee
Tah-fum-be . . . onion
Tok-lake-dok-cea . . . sour bread

Birds:
Fus-wah . . . bird
Fus-wah doth-dah-ga . . . brown thrush
Fus-wah hoak-ho . . . wood thrush

Fus-wah ho-lot-toe-gee . . . little blue bird
Fus-wah ja-dea . . . red bird, cardinal
Fus-wah jo-lay-gotch-gee . . . little brown wren
Fus-wah loni . . . yellow bird, gold finch
Fus-wah sa-ha-ya . . . mocking bird
Chuck-bah-la-bah-la . . . night bird, whip-poor-will

Insects:
Gah-zuh-zah . . . the night time locust
Oke-we-yah . . . mosquito, having to do with water
Shu-we-sah-we . . . the daytime locust

Animals:
Chitto . . . snake
Chitto Harjo . . . Crazy Snake (name)
Chuffy . . . rabbit
Dah-lo-se . . . chicken
E-tho . . . squirrel
Thock-ko . . . horse
Thock-ko-bake-ka . . . mule

Bibliography

Introduction

1. Elizabeth Pennisi, Science News, Volume 144, December 18–25, 1993, Page 408–410, Temperate Treetops, Canopy Research Reaches New Latitudes.
2. Michael Lipske, National Wildlife, Dec/Jan 1994, Page 46–49, Animal Heal Thyself.
3. John A. Grim, Shaman, (Oklahoma U. Press, 1983).
4. G. Bernard Hughes, English, Scottish & Irish Table Glass, (Barnard House, 1956), Page 345–346. Courtesy of Charles S. Perry
5. Dr. Duane Niatum, January 1997, personal communication with author.
6. Elberton (Georgia) Star, 25 May 1889. A Little Race of Men and Women Who Once Inhabited Franklin County. Courtesy of Jerry King.
7. Joseph Bruchac, unpublished poetry shared with author.
8. J. J. Cornplanter, Legends of the Longhouse. Originally published by J. B. Lippincott (1938). See 1992 Reprint, page 67. Courtesy of Ross John, Sr.

Story 1—Little Jack

After the Muscogea people crossed the Mississippi River in 1836 to reach Oklahoma Territory, they tried to forget what happened. Two pieces of story remained: (a) After a small boy crossed the river on a horse, he was named "Jock-o-gee" and (b) from that day, the elders remembered seeing the "little people". The boy grew to adulthood and was a native docktor who healed the sick. The written history is filled with facts and dates but nothing as mundane as horses was clearly shown. It took a rewrite of the history as a story "Wacena Comes" to locate the proper party of Creeks that crossed the river by horse. This story confirms the elders story.

1. George E. Lankford, Native American Legends (August House), Page 96.

Story 2—Big Chicken

1. James C. Milligan, Oklahoma, A Regional History, Mesa Publishing Co. (1985), Pages 89–96.
2. James D. Morrison, The Social History of the Choctaw Nation: 1865–1907, Creative Informatics Press of Durant, OK (1988), Pages 45–49.
3. Robert J. Conley, The Witch of Goingsnake and Other Stories, U. of Oklahoma Press (1988), See "Wesley's Story, Pg 157.

Story 8—Intruder

1. Don Martini, Southeastern Indian Notebook, Ripley Printing (1986), Page 93–95. Page 61 gives the birthdate of 1850 for Robert Grayson, one of the Creek interpreters.

Story 9—Woman with Wagon

1. Jerry King, The Hart of Georgia, (1993), Page 11.

Story 11—Great Hunter

1. James Mooney, Myths of the Cherokee and Sacred Formula of the Cherokee, from 19th and 7th Annual Reports of the Bureau of American Ethnology, Elder-Booksellers Publishers of Nashville, TN (Reproduced 1982), Page 248.

Story 14—Studying to be a Docktor

1. James Mooney, Myths of the Cherokee and Sacred Formula of the Cherokee, from 19th and 7th Annual Reports of the Bu-

reau of American Ethnology, Elder-Booksellers Publishers of
Nashville, TN (Reproduced 1982), Pg 307–319. The Eastern
Band of Cherokee say that Mooney didn't get all the story
when he collected the medicine man's books.

Story 15—Legend of Honeycomb Bluff

1. James C. Milligan, Oklahoma, A Regional History, Mesa Publishing Co. (1985), Pages 140–144.
2. Muriel H. Wright, A Guide to the Indian Tribes of Oklahoma, University of Oklahoma Press (1951), Page 140.
3. Ibid, reference 1 above, Page 145–146.

Story 16—The Crazy Snakes

1. Jerry King, The Hart of Georgia, (1993), Page 10.
2. James Mooney (1890), "The Cherokee Ball Play", Journal of Cherokee Studies, Vol. VII,No. 1, Spring 1982, Pg 10–24.

Story 21—Rattlesnake Tails

1. March 13, 1993, The Tulsa (OK) World, Snake Causes Short in Bristow Substation.

Wacena Comes: History of Muscogea Nation

1. Muriel H. Wright, Guide to the Indian Tribes of Oklahoma, University of Oklahoma Press (1951), Pages 128–135.
2. Grant Foreman, Indian Removal, U. of Oklahoma Press (1932), Pg 107–177, The Emigration of the Five Civilized Tribes.
3. Jerry King, The Hart of Georgia, (1883), Page 11.
4. George E. Lankford, Native American Legends, August House, Pages 113–114.
5. Don Martini, Southeastern Indian Notebook, Ripley Printing Company (1986), Pages 93–98. Maps

6. James C. Milligan, Oklahoma, A Regional History, Mesa Publishing Co. of Durant, OK (1985), Page 75–77.
7. Harper Lee, To Kill a Mockingbird, Lipincott (1960), Page 1.

About the Author

Robert Perry is a son of Chickasaw Indian parents, raised in Chickasaw Country (Oklahoma). Bob is a member of Native Writers Circle of the Americas. He worked a career as a chemical engineer, specializing in long range business planning. To build management skills, his employer allowed him to be a volunteer tribal leader for 18 years. Early retirement opened the way to be an Indian. Bob learned from professional Native storytellers how to reach general audiences, including the National Association of Storytellers. Original material was provided by elder professional Indian artists of many tribes. A creation story of a lost band of Cherokee was accepted as a children's book. This manuscript was first written, followed by a biography of a famous artist, written as an epic of a modern day Indian hero.

My Dad was a full-blood Chickasaw Indian, a quiet man. He had gone through the eighth grade at Chilocco, a government school for Indians. The government's objective was to force Indians into the White culture. Students, who spoke their Native language, were punished. The punished ones, including Dad, spoke English but vowed to protect their language and culture. All Indians, especially 'full-bloods', feel the importance of imprinting cultural knowledge with their children. This is how the Tribe survived. Dad could also see that his children needed a good education to survive in the White Man's world. I was the oldest of four boys. He told me a crazy Indian story: Little brown-skinned men would secret away Indian children for days to teach them natural medicine. As adults, these native 'docktors' used the medicine to heal sick Indians. In any year, Dad would tell me a few words of this story. Never a warning to get out pencil and paper. I had to remember the words the way of the Indian people. I had to collect the new pieces and assemble. It took a dozen years to finish the story. I wondered why he bothered; all the old 'docktors' were dead. Too bad.

Dad observed us all during those early years. He knew that by age 12, I had decided to become a chemical engineer from books in the Public Library. No one in the small town knew enough to discourage me, except it would require a college degree. Ending high-school, there was no money for college. Dad said, "Join the Army. Let them pay you to learn instead of you paying for college." He knew his boys. No army; I worked my way through college. On graduation day his reward was a smile and a $10 bill. Two children and a secure engineering career followed.

Mom had told us about her Indian ancestors, but Dad's father had been adopted as a baby. When asked about his ancestors, he took me to the homes of the 'old ones' of our tribe. Dad spoke both the Chickasaw and Choctaw languages and they laughed about the old days. He was asking them about his father. When I asked in English, "What you know?" the old man laughed harder! His answer was in English; his laughs were because I couldn't speak my Indian language. The 'old ones' told stories in gales of laughter. From the bits of information, my research built a genealogy back to the earliest Perry. A British Tory who sought refuge in our Tribe to escape the American Revolution. My objective met, I remembered how peaceful were these old ones.

Through the years of a busy career, there was no time for Indian stories. After Dad died, I felt the pressure from the graves of the 'old ones'. Their death left me to pass on the stories to the next generation. The greatest realization was how my silent, un-educated father had touched me with a single Indian story. How it lay there inside me, even while laboring through college and a career. How wise he was.

Engineering ended with early retirement. It was a gift of time to think, write and search for the peace. This led me to a "pure-blood" Muskogea Creek man. He had painted and sold pictures, but quit this career 15 years ago. His favorite subject? Little brown men. I asked him to tell me more. Yellow caution lights seem to go off in his head. A test was devised to see if I was the right person to be entrusted with these stories and uphold the Muscogea honor. The test: find "Frankie". She was a patron who left town 15 years ago; no trail. We prayed together. In three weeks, Frankie was found. By marriage, she had twice changed her name and moved to different states. He didn't say this but if invisible spirits didn't approve, my way would be hidden. I passed the test. Or at least there seemed to be an innate ability inside that could be awakened.

Why me? A good example on a grander scale is in the Bible. Luke the physician was chosen. He was a learned man among the fishermen. His task was to write about what he saw for future generations. Through writing Luke learned about spiritual things, something new to him. He was chosen for an innate abil-ity that could be awakened.

About the Illustrator

Chester Scott is a pure-blood Muscogea Indian born of a traditional Indian family and raised in Eufaula, Oklahoma. Member of

Raccoon clan. These stories come from six generations of his family, since migration to Oklahoma. After high-school he attended Bacone College to hone art skills. Dating to 1891 Bacone is the highest citadel of Indian art. Bacone was the first college where professional Indian artists taught art to Indian art students.

After Bacone, Chester served with the US Marine Corps in Korea. He worked for the Bureau of Indian Affairs and spent some time in Macon, Georgia, the ancient Muscogea home. He has exhibited art in Santa Fe, Flagstaff, Phoenix Indian Fairs and New York City. Chester won the Creek Division Award and Creek Heritage Award in the 1979 Art Show at Five Civilized Tribes Museum. Then, he quit the art world. Many illustrations in this book were done more than 20 years ago. Many old clients and friends have asked for more of his work. Chester is a Native Writers Circle of the Americas (NWCA) member. He publishes a monthly letter to Indian People far beyond Oklahoma. One critic wrote recently that 'Chester is a raconteur like Garrison Keller'. Chester was ready to fight, before learning this was high praise. You can hear the "little people" cheering for him.

creative
photoshop
lighting
techniques

creative photoshop lighting techniques

Barry Huggins

LARK BOOKS

A Division of Sterling Publishing Co., Inc.
New York

Creative Photoshop Lighting Techniques

10 9 8 7 6 5 4 3 2 1

Published by Lark Books, a division of
Sterling Publishing Co., Inc.
387 Park Avenue South, New York, N.Y. 10016

© The Ilex Press Limited 2004

This book was conceived, designed,
and produced by:
ILEX
Cambridge,
England

Distributed in Canada by Sterling Publishing,
c/o Canadian Manda Group,
One Atlantic Ave., Suite 105
Toronto, Ontario, Canada M6K 3E7

If you have questions or comments about this book, please contact:
Lark Books
67 Broadway
Asheville, NC 28801
(828) 253-0467

Huggins, Barry.
  Creative Photoshop lighting techniques / Barry Huggins.
    p. cm.
  ISBN 1-57990-538-2 (pbk.)
  1. Photography--Lighting. 2. Photography--Digital techniques. 3.
Adobe Photoshop. I. Title.
TR590.H83 2004
006.6'86--dc22

                    2003024956

Printed in Hong Kong

For more information on Photoshop lighting techniques, see:
www.lifxus.web-linked.com

CONTENTS

INTRODUCTION

CREATING LOW-KEY IMAGES
Page 32

CREATING CANDLELIGHT
Page 44

Even the world's greatest photographers sometimes need a helping hand to capture the image that they see in their mind's eye. Nature has a habit of being at its most unaccommodating just at the moment you squeeze the shutter button. The speed at which the elements and lighting conditions change can leave all photographers, both professional and amateur, with a constant love-hate relationship with Mother Nature as she provides you with the image of a lifetime, only to snatch it away before you've had the chance to take the lens cap off.

The fact remains, that even with decades of experience, access to top of the range photographic equipment, location, timing, and a large slice of luck—the final image may be a poor reproduction of the original scene. This is where Photoshop can step in and put that "wow" factor back into your images.

CREATING NEON LIGHT
Page 48

CASTING LIGHT AND SHADOW THROUGH VENETIAN BLINDS
Page 86

With the know-how documented throughout this book, you will be capable not only of recapturing a lost moment, such as missing a sunset by a few seconds, or erasing bystanders reflected in your shots, but also of generating a believable scene that never actually existed.

The art of illusion is a skill in itself and the ability to create lightning, water, fog, moonlight, fire and a host of other natural and manmade atmospheric effects will be easily within your grasp as you work through the tutorials. The images displayed in this introduction are just a small selection of the effects that you will create as you work through the book.

CAST LIGHT THROUGH WINDOWS
Page 90

CREATING METAL REFLECTIONS
Page 102

CREATING REFLECTIONS IN WATER
Page 98

CREATING LIGHT THROUGH SMOKE & STEAM
Page 126

UNDERSTANDING LIGHT

WHAT IS LIGHT?

This is perhaps a question that few people consider in a lifetime. It's just another of those things we take for granted, like the air we breathe or water from a tap. Glibly we could say it is the thing that comes from the sun or a torch, but as someone involved in the field of digital imagery, you will find that a deeper knowledge will help your understanding not only of light and its quirks, but also of color, an essential requirement if you are to harness the full power of both in your images.

THIS PAGE

Above-right The color wheel displays all of the colors of the visible light spectrum in order of wavelength.

Below The full **electromagnetic spectrum** runs from short—as small as 0.003nm—gamma-rays at one end to long—sometimes several kilometers—radio waves at the other. The **visible light spectrum** occupies a short area of the electromagnetic spectrum, with wavelengths ranging from about 400 to 700nm.

FACING PAGE

Above-right The blue vase illustrates how we only see single colors, even though the light shining on an object contains a mix of colors.

Below-left CDs act as prisms, and can be used to show that the sun's light is made up of all of the colors of the visible spectrum.

Below-right These feathers reflect back only their own color wavelength, and absorb all others.

THE ELECTROMAGNETIC SPECTRUM

Light as we know it is just one small part of a greater entity known as the Electromagnetic Spectrum. The Electromagnetic Spectrum describes a range of energy in wave form, which we more commonly know as radiation. The range encompasses gamma-rays at one end of the spectrum where the wavelengths are short, to radio waves at the other end where wavelengths are long. The wavelength itself is defined as short, long, or somewhere in between by measuring from the crest of one wave to the crest of the adjacent wave.

Other wavelengths beyond gamma-rays and radio waves exist within the electromagnetic spectrum, and these are displayed in sequence in the diagram below.

The part that we are interested in is the section toward the center, called the visible light spectrum. Nestled between the Ultraviolet and Infrared wavelengths, which are not visible to the human eye, is the Visible Light Spectrum. The wavelengths here encompass all the colors visible to the human eye, ranging in wavelength from 400 nanometers (nm), which we perceive as the color violet to 700nm, which we perceive as red. One nanometer is equal to one thousand-millionth of a meter. All wavelengths outside this range are invisible to the naked eye.

So when we talk about color, we are actually discussing electromagnetic radiation wavelengths. Each color in the visible light spectrum conforms to a wavelength which can be seen in the diagram. Of course, no one sits in a romantic restaurant on a moonlit night and whispers to their date "Your eyes sparkle with a wavelength of 500 nanometers." They would say "Your eyes are so blue" and the evening might develop; the common words we use are better for widespread descriptive purposes.

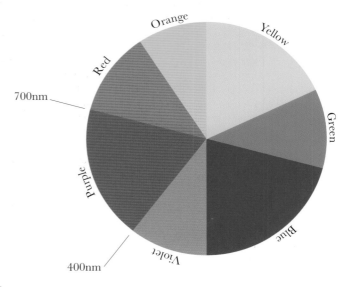

COLOR WHEEL

700nm

400nm

THE COLOR WHEEL

It was Sir Isaac Newton who created the first color wheel, which follows exactly the same configuration of color as the horizontally represented visible light spectrum. The color wheel remains a powerful aid to designers, photographers, and creative artists of all kinds. The wheel displays how analogous (adjacent) colors work well in combination, as do complimentary colors (those at opposite sides of the wheel). In the color wheel above, the color purple appears outside the visible wavelengths. This is because purple does not conform to a specific wavelength, but is instead created by mixing wavelengths of red and violet.

THE COLOR OF LIGHT

When all the colors of the visible spectrum are combined, the result is white light. If this sounds odd, you'll see the proof next time a rainbow appears in the sky. Water droplets in the air act as prisms and refract the white light generated by the sun, revealing the individual wavelengths, which we know as rainbows. The same effect can be witnessed by shining white light onto any object able to act as a prism, such as a CD.

You will notice that black is omitted from the visible light spectrum, as black is not a color wavelength in itself, but merely the absence of light.

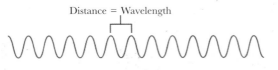

Radio Wave - Long Wavelength

Distance = Wavelength

Gamma-Ray - Short Wavelength

Distance = Wavelength

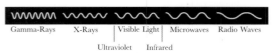

Electromagnetic Spectrum

Gamma-Rays   X-Rays   Visible Light   Microwaves   Radio Waves

Ultraviolet   Infrared

Visible Light Spectrum

(nm)
380   435   500   520   565   590   625   680   700

Violet   Blue   Cyan   Green   Yellow   Orange   Red

HOW OUR EYES SEE WAVELENGTHS AS COLOR

There may appear to be a missing link at this stage. We've discussed electromagnetic radiation wavelengths and how colors are assigned to specific wavelengths, but you may be wondering how our eyes and brains perceive red, yellow, green, or any color just by seeing a wavelength.

The answer lies in the eye itself. Photosensitive cells exist in the retina at the back of the eye that absorb light. These cells are categorized as either rods or cones. The rods are responsible for sensing light intensity and the cones for distinguishing color. Three sets of cones exist and are receptive to the different wavelengths of red, blue, and green. Although wavelengths of many frequencies are entering the eye, only the maximum wavelengths of red, green, and blue are responded to and therefore perceived as the color. In the case of yellow, you will notice from the electromagnetic spectrum that the yellow wavelength sits between the red and green wavelengths, so the red and green receptors in the retina receive equal stimulation with little impact being made on the blue receptor, resulting in the eye perceiving yellow.

THE COLOR OF OBJECTS

It is logical to say that we need light in order to see an object, but does it still sound logical if we say that in order to see the color of an object, the light falling on it must contain all of the necessary wavelengths? After all, isn't a red object always red? Well, not necessarily. If you cut your finger pruning roses in the garden in the afternoon, you will see red blood, whether it's sunny or cloudy. Cut your finger while scuba diving a few meters underwater, however, and your same blood will appear anything from green to near black, depending on how deep you are. While seeing green blood can be very disconcerting, physics can prevent you from going into panic. Upon encountering water, light wavelengths will be reflected right back, penetrate straight through it, or become absorbed. Which action takes place depends on the wavelength and the depth of the water. At relatively shallow depths, the longer red wavelengths are absorbed by the water. Objects too will also reflect, absorb, or enable light wavelengths to pass through them. So in order for the red blood to be perceived as red, it must reflect back the red wavelength and absorb all others, and therefore without the red wavelength underwater, the color we perceive is green-black.

It is important to recognize that the color of an object is not solely an intrinsic quality, but a combination of its color characteristics and the wavelength of the light that falls on it. When a white light falls on an object, the object will absorb all color wavelengths except for the color wavelength of its own appearance, which it will reflect back. If an object's surface reflects back all colors, it appears white; and if it absorbs all colors, it appears black.

The blue vase pictured is illuminated by the white light of the sun which, as we now know, is a combination of all the color wavelengths of the visible spectrum. Red, green, and blue in combination can create all of the other spectrum colors. The red and green wavelengths are absorbed by the blue vase, but the blue is reflected back, enabling the eye to perceive the object as blue. Similarly, the multicolored feathers are each reflecting back their own color wavelength only and absorbing all others.

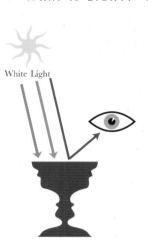

White Light

Kelvin Color Temperature Scale

Degrees Kelvin (K)

Above The Kelvin color temperature scale provides an accurate way of describing the color of light. The mean noon sunlight temperature of 5,400K is an arbitrary figure taken as the average direct midday temperature in Washington DC. Of course, daylight color temperatures can vary wildly, but 5,400K is a good base to work from.

Right These two images illustrate how much difference color temperature can make to our perceptions of a scene. The warm, welcoming yellows and oranges of the top picture evoke feelings of happiness and contentment, reflecting, from a purely temperature-based point of view, the warmth found in the reds and yellows of fire. The blues and violets of the lower image evoke a much cooler tone. They immediately conjure up visions of the cold light of daybreak and the freezing blues of ice. In both of these images it is easy to attribute the color of light to our perceptions of temperature and its associated feelings.

COLOR TEMPERATURE

The color of daylight can change throughout the day, having a major impact on an image. It would be useful to define these colors by a fixed unit of measurement, so accurate descriptions can be used when adjusting a light source to simulate a given lighting condition.

Such a measurement exists, and is called the **Kelvin** scale. The Kelvin scale uses a measurement of degrees Kelvin (K) to describe the apparent color of a light source relative to heating a black body source such as a piece of metal. Imagine applying a heat source to an ordinary metal key. As the key heats up, it first starts to glow red. As the heat source is maintained, the temperature increases and the key changes color accordingly to orange, then yellow, white, and finally a blue color. So the heat at any given point can be directly correlated to the color of the light emitted and denoted a numeric value.

The diagram displays typical Kelvin values for a range of common lighting conditions. Lower values are considered warm colors, higher values are cold colors. It should be noted that the color temperature is not influenced by the intensity of the light, but only the color.

With the Kelvin unit of measure as a base reference, it is now very easy to adjust different types of light sources so they match and produce a uniform light color. For instance if halogen bulbs are being used to supplement natural daylight, a color correction gel could be used to change the halogen bulb's 3000K temperature to something closer to the common daylight temperature of about 5000K.

COLOR TEMPERATURE, PERCEPTION, AND EMOTIONAL RESPONSE

If we remove the physics from the subject of light and color for a moment and look at the psychology, we will find that the descriptions of warm or cold colors have a great impact on our emotional response to an image. As a warm-blooded species, most humans are more comfortable in an environment that is warmer rather than colder. For many, the archetypal vision of relaxed, home comforts might be an image of a roaring log fire in a room diffused with a deep orange glow. It is natural, therefore, that images with warmer colors (lower temperatures as defined by the Kelvin scale) should have deep associations in the human psyche with comfort and an air of welcoming and desire.

Contrast this with images with an overall cold range of colors, and the human reaction is quite different. It's like pulling the welcome mat from under your feet. Take a look at the two pictures of the Taj Mahal. Although similar images in terms of content, the messages they convey are quite different. This has nothing to do with artistic merit or right and wrong. Both images are successful for their designated purpose. However the orange-colored version might inspire the viewer to kick off their shoes and walk lazily through the water, sipping cool drinks and dreaming of hot balmy nights. The tones of the blue version depict the first light of dawn, its colors reminiscent of the chill associated with the early morning. Though the ambient air temperature may, in fact, be similar to the ambient air temperature in the orange version of the image, our perception and therefore our emotional response will be quite different.

In these examples, we have looked at color temperature in the context of how it relates to ambient air temperature and this may seem a logical conclusion to form based on the knowledge

that fire is yellow-orange (warm colors) and generates heat, and ice is associated with a blue aura (cold color) and generates cold. If we now ignore the link with air temperature, psychology offers us further insights into how our emotions are affected by exposure to warm or cold colors.

Warm colors are considered to invoke such emotions as happiness, elation, and enthusiasm in the yellow to orange range and aggression and hostility in the red range. From within the cold color range, blue and green are associated with serenity and refuge, and black, brown, and gray with distress and despondency. Of course, these statements are an oversimplification and broad generalization because the perception of color temperature psychologically is, in fact, very subjective.

And yet we see examples of this psychology in practice everyday, principally in the field of advertising, where posters and television advertisements use orange and yellows to inject enthusiasm, joy, and vitality, blues and greens to inspire confidence and security, and, not unsurprisingly, there is a distinct lack of brown and gray. It would be imprudent, however, to implement these findings into an advertising campaign without first paying heed to such vital factors as fashion and cultural differences, which in extreme cases can turn much of the theory upside down.

Take the test yourself. Does the picture of the lake instill a sense of serenity in you inspired by the cold blue light?

Do you feel enthused and a sense of happiness when looking at the warm color of the yellow walls and orange doors?

Whatever your immediate feelings, the effect may be purely subliminal and if over the next hour you feel overwhelmingly elated or deeply peaceful, one or other of the images may have just kicked in.

Above and left The psychology of color is based upon many diverse factors and extensive testing, but different people still respond to color in entirely different ways. There are, though, some standard psychological responses to color that can be assumed to affect most people. For example, leaving aside the temperature response that people have to yellows and blues, look at the two images on this page and see if they stir any of the following emotions.

The yellows and oranges of the doors and walls evoke feelings of playfulness, creativity, and an easygoing attitude if bright, but duller yellows hint at caution and sickness. Yellow is also a difficult color on the eye, and its attention-grabbing properties can be overbearing at times.

The blues of the sky and water in the lower image are relaxing and harmonious. They indicate loyalty and trust, but also sadness and solitude. Perhaps the inherent tranquillity of this image is enhanced by the combination of the lonely blues and the contented oranges of the sunset?

DIFFERENT LIGHT TYPES

It would be easy to think of light as one generic entity that simply makes visibility possible, yet the different types of light are almost as diverse as night and day itself. Choosing the right kind of light for any given image is as critical and fundamental to the image as focusing the camera. Whether you are harnessing natural daylight or creating an artificial lighting setup, some thought needs to be given as to the final desired effect and the type of light that would be most appropriate to the project. In this section we will look at examples of the most commonly used types of light.

AMBIENT

Ambient is the most common form of light that we encounter in our daily lives. It is the overall light emanating from the sun or the artificial lights that illuminate a room. Often the direction of ambient light is vague, shadows are faint or limited, and the coverage of light is fairly widely distributed. Ambient light also consists of the light reflected from other objects in the environment. As a source for general photographic lighting, it merely provides illumination, but for more specific lighting scenarios props or additional lighting is required.

In the image of the pool ball, ambient light can be seen in the form of light from the sky as well as reflections from the concrete and the grass.

DIRECT LIGHT

Direct light can be from a natural source as in the sun, or from an artificial light source that projects light as a concentrated, directable beam, such as a spotlight or a torch. What both natural and artificial direct lights have in common is the fact that they are considered a small source light. Direct light results in what is termed as hard light falling on the subject, revealing hard-edged shadows and extremes of contrast. This makes it ideal for dramatic images and emphasis on specific areas of the photograph.

In the example, direct light is manifesting as rays of light because the direct sunlight is filtered though the foliage.

DIFFUSED LIGHT

As with direct light, diffused light can be from the sun or artificial lights. The common factor in this case is the fact that they are both categorized as large source lights. In the case of the sun, it hasn't physically changed size, but on an overcast day the cloud cover will disperse the light, converting the entire sky into the new source. Such conditions provide a flat, even light with little or soft-edged shadow. For artificial lights, even a spotlight can be converted to a diffused light by placing a semitransparent gel, tissue paper, or similar material over the light. This serves the same purpose as clouds where the sun is concerned. On days when there is no cloud cover and diffused light is desired, the same effect can be achieved by using a large white umbrella or similar prop to soften the light.

Mist rising from the water is adding to the overall diffusion in this river scene. The image also demonstrates the richness of the color of the grass. Greater saturation is a common feature of diffused lighting.

OMNI LIGHT

An omni light describes a light that radiates a circular, uniform spread of light, such as a household light bulb. This kind of light is fine for general lighting purposes but its nondirectional qualities mean that it can be difficult to control and produce creative effects.

HARD LIGHT

Hard light, as we have already seen, is generated from a small light source such as direct sun or a spotlight. The effect of hard light on the subject is to create hard-edged, well-defined shadows. Hard light can be considered severe and in some cases unflattering for portraits unless the desired effect is one of drama. This is where hard light excels, producing high-contrast, strong images with an interesting juxtaposition of light. Hard light is also successful at rendering texture when suitable light angles are employed and well suited to enhancing definition.

The picture of the roof terrace demonstrates the hard-edged, well-defined shadows of hard lighting.

The vividly colored buildings have caught the direct sun at such an angle that the corrugated surfaces are well defined revealing their true texture.

SOFT LIGHT

In the portrait of the girl, the silk scarf adds to the already diffused light where only her nose and lips show any discernable highlight. The softness of the shadow is highly complimentary to the girl's skin tone, suggesting an unblemished, porcelain-like surface.

As explained earlier soft light is generated from a large light source, such as an overcast sky. Soft light renders soft, subtle shadows that are flattering in portrait photography. Detail is minimized, with emphasis being on the overall form rather than the texture.

In the picture of the tree, the heavily diffused sun caused by a combination of cloud and mist has created an almost abstract image where most of the image information has been subdued except for the softened monotone branches, lending an eerie, timeless quality to the image.

HIGH KEY

High-key images are created by flooding the scene with a profusion of light. No one type of light source is solely responsible for the effect, although a diffused light will offer more pleasing results. A number of light sources can ideally be used for optimum effect with additional reflective surfaces making their own contribution to the image. Despite this abundance of light, shadow areas are an integral part of high-key images to prevent the image from being nothing more than an overexposed photograph.

All the ethereal qualities associated with high-key images are embodied in the photograph of the swans. The grace and poise of the airborne birds, although not essential to a high-key image, add to the heavenly dreaminess of the composition. The predominantly light tones are relieved only by the slightly deeper shade of sky at the top of the picture and the almost pure black beak, eyes and feet.

BACK LIGHT, RIM LIGHT & SILHOUETTES

This multiple category is, in fact, one type of light, namely, backlight. As the name suggests, the light source is positioned behind the subject and, depending on circumstances such as the intensity of the light and whether additional light sources or reflections are trained on the subject, the result could be a silhouette or a rim light resembling a halo effect.

In the picture of the girl, she is backlit, but the sun

LOW KEY

If high key is predominantly light, then low key is predominantly dark, but the same rules apply. A dark image risks being merely underexposed and uninteresting. As with the high-key image, it is the opposites that create the contrast and relief. In the case of a low-key image, strategically placed highlights create the mood and bring the image to life.

In the image of the door, the atmosphere is almost tangible. The small areas of light seem to be trying to burst forward, creating a tension and inviting anticipation in the viewer as to what may lie behind the door. The overriding sinister and mysterious aura is typical of successful low-key images.

is positioned at an angle to her. This enables its light to define her outline and also pass through the finer areas of her hair, forming a rim light effect.

The second photograph, taken from within a cave, is illuminated solely by light coming in from the background sky. This forces the framework of the cave and the lonely figure of the man into total silhouette.

LIGHT SOURCES

Of all the factors that determine the final quality of an image, the source of light is undoubtedly key. No other single part of a photographer's toolkit can so radically change the mood and context of a photograph.

The range of light sources itself is enormous, each source having its own characteristics and contributing its unique qualities to the finished work. The sun, the ultimate natural light source, has many characteristics. Its light is influenced by its position in the sky, cloud, and other atmospheric conditions. Choosing the right time of day and weather conditions for the type of desired image is a simple way of utilizing natural light to its best effect. Overcast days offer a flat diffused light with little shadow. On clear days, early morning and evenings provide a warm flattering light with long shadows and rich colors, while midday suffers from harsh direct light with little shadow to shape and mould subjects.

Although props can be used for a degree of control over natural daylight—such as white umbrellas or aluminium foil for diffusion and reflection, lens filters to correct or enhance color, and fill-in flash to minimize unwanted shadow—the true level of control is limited. This makes natural daylight sometimes unsuitable for certain situations, such as portraiture, still life and product advertising shots.

In these situations, the photographic studio provides a controlled environment where the full range of tones can be rendered with pinpoint precision through the use of blackouts, reflectors, photo lamps, and spotlights. Different factors now come into play, primarily the number of lights, their size, and their positions relative to the subject. A broad array of lighting configurations are possible but, perhaps surprisingly, a relatively small number are required to recreate most common lighting conditions.

This is demonstrated in the examples that follow, in which a statue is being used as the subject. The statue is a combination of both smooth and textured surfaces, with angular projections as well as soft contours, raised edges as well as deep recesses, and matt and shiny surfaces side by side. These extremes are not unlike many common subjects, such as a human face or a bowl of fruit, and the mood we create for that subject is all down to some basic decisions on how many lights to use, what size, and where to put them.

SINGLE SOURCE LIGHTING

For many photographers, the vast majority of their images will be taken under single source lighting conditions. Outdoor photography, for instance, is largely reliant upon the sun as the main, if not the only, source of light. Single source lighting needn't be considered inferior in itself. Some of the greatest images ever shot have used nothing more than natural daylight. It's not so much the number of lights used, but rather the quality of the light and what kind of atmosphere is intended.

Diffused Light
An example of a natural single diffused light source is a cloudy day, when the entire sky becomes the light source. The sun being shrouded by cloud is converted to a large source with the resultant light being even and generating either little shadow or shadows with soft edges.

In a studio, placing a semi-transparent material such as tissue paper or a translucent gel over a single spotlight or photo lamp will have the same effect. In the example, the minimal shadows and lack of definition combine to make the image uniform and simplified.

Direct Small Source Light
Direct sun is actually considered a small light source. Although it engulfs the earth with its size, the fact that it is over 93 million miles away reduces it to small source of light. This is mimicked in the studio with a single unobstructed light with a small concentrated focal point. Harsh shadows and removal of texture in the concentrated area are typical of this kind of light. The example shows a single light shining directly at the statue from the front, focusing on the face. The face area is almost completely washed out, with harsh shadows revealing detail in the peripheral areas around the lights concentration.

Top or Down lighting
Although this lighting condition is a very common one, particularly if you live in a country prone to overcast skies, it is generally unflattering from a portrait photography point of view. Small-source top lighting in particular will render harsh shadows down the face, darkening the area beneath the eyes, nose, and mouth and highlighting the brow and nose making a stark impression.

From a dramatic point of view, though, top lighting can convey a celestial air and a general aura of cascading light.

Bottom or Up lighting
As with top lighting, drama is the byword here. The unflattering nature of this form of lighting in respect of portraiture makes it less than ideal as a method for illuminating the human face, unless of course a sinister or stylized impression is desired.

Three Quarter lighting
This type of lighting achieves a good compromise between the depth of detail and shadow and highlight areas. The angle of the light is such that it illuminates the majority of the subject and still provides for a degree of shadow to mold and define the contours. This is equally true of peoples' faces or any subject with depth to its form.

Side Lighting
Single light source side lighting produces high-contrast images with strong detail where the shadow and light mix. Although detail is revealed, it should be noted that very little information is preserved in the extreme areas of highlight and shadow, making the image more of a curiosity piece rather than a detailed study of the subject.

Backlight
Backlighting would not generally be considered a prime source of lighting for classic composition, but for silhouettes, dramatic effect, and any situation where detail is less important than mood, it has great merit. Despite much of the subject being in shadow in the example, its contours are picking up light, providing highlighted areas of interest. These areas add to the mystique as small visual clues offer hints as to the image's form.

MULTIPLE LIGHT SOURCES

An extra light source adds another dimension to the subject. Rather than the decision being constrained to which side to have the shadow and which side to have the highlight, an additional light can be used to add additional highlights or, indeed, to cancel out shadows cast from the primary light.

This combination can realize a far better illuminated image with a generally more pleasing and flattering distribution of light and shadow. Compromise is no longer necessary as the full field of vision can be sculpted with the range of tones as desired.

Ambient & Direct Side light
This combination works well when good general lighting is required plus additional detail for information or dynamic interest. In the example, the ambient light is natural diffused daylight entering through the large studio windows. The second light is a small source direct light illuminating from the side. This immediately generates highlights, revealing a shiny surface and shadows that define the texture and contours of the statue.

**Diffused Front &
Three Quarter Light**
A perfect choice for flattering light, which offers good uniform illumination with strong detail. Whereas the single-source three-quarter light we saw earlier provided good detail for the subject, the degree of illumination was limited and fairly focussed. The addition of a large source diffused light located at the front of the subject, as in the example, expands the influence of light, making for an altogether more welcoming upbeat image.

Adding a Third Light Source
A third light source gives you the ability to create a perfectly balanced composition. Careful management of each light allows you to mold the subject through the interaction of highlight and shadow. Undesirable elements can be cloaked in shadow, while areas of interest can be bathed in light. For portraits, different lights can be used to place equal emphasis on the eyes, nose, and mouth. Another light can be used to define the jaw line with shadow. In the example, three large source diffused lights are used, two using three-quarter lighting on the left and right and the third shining down from the 11 o'clock position. This has produced highlights on both cheekbones, with a high quality of light illuminating the central facial area. The third light then serves to remove most of the heavy shadow area on the face generated from the other two lights.

Light and Photoshop Filter Presets

USING THE LIGHTING EFFECTS FILTER

Although far from being the only way to introduce light into images in Photoshop, the *Lighting Effects* filter does offer a fast and photorealistic way of creating an artificial light source. On first accessing the *Lighting Effects* filter, the array of settings and options can seem overwhelming, so in this section we are going to break down into bite-size chunks what each option does and how it affects the image.

To get you up and running quickly, the *Lighting Effects* filter comes with a number of preset lighting options that can be used in their original form or as a starting point for creating your own customized light. By way of demonstrating these presets, I am using a neutrally colored image with fairly flat, even light. The existing light conditions are such that each *Lighting Effects* preset will be able to demonstrate its effect without the complication of any extraneous light.

In all the examples that follow, the preset has been applied without any adjustment. It will be clear from some of the examples that further adjustments are necessary in order to make the light appear realistic.

The *Lighting Effects* filter can be accessed from the menus by going to *Filter > Render > **Lighting Effects***. It should be noted that the *Lighting Effects* filter works on image pixels only and will have no effect on transparent areas of a layer.

The presets are in the *Style* drop-down box at the top of the *Lighting Effects* dialog box. To apply a preset, select the one you want to use and click *OK*.

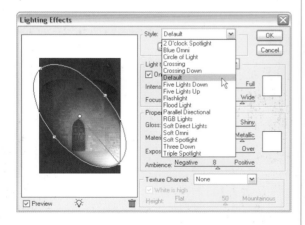

HERE'S HOW EACH OF THE PRESETS AFFECTS THE IMAGE OF THE ROOM.

Original without lighting

Default

2 O'clock Spotlight

Blue Omni

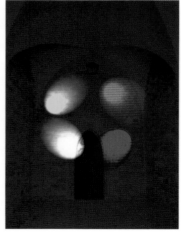

Circle of Light

Crossing

Crossing Down

Five Lights Down

Five Lights Up

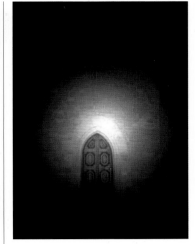

Flashlight

Flood Light

Parallel Directional

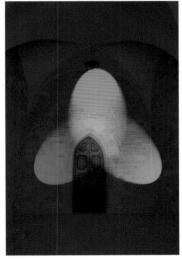

RGB Lights

Soft Direct Lights

Soft Omni

Soft Spotlight

Three Down

Triple Spotlight

CUSTOMIZING LIGHTS

The ability to control the lights offers you an endless variety of lighting situations that would not be possible by using the presets alone.

LIGHT TYPE

There are three types of lights to choose from. These can be accessed from the *Light type* drop-down box.

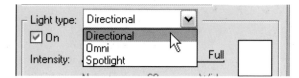

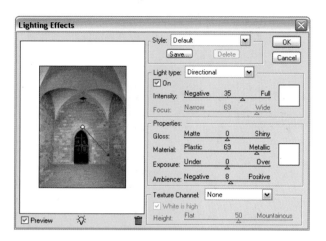

Directional Shines a light from a great distance, such as the way we receive light from the sun, so that the angle of the light doesn't change.

Omni Illuminates evenly from a central point in the same way as a light bulb would.

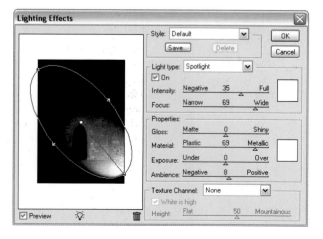

Spotlight Creates an elliptical beam of light that becomes weaker as it travels farther away from the source.

CHANGING THE LIGHT TYPE SETTINGS

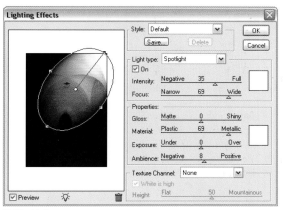

Field of Influence

Once a *Light type* has been chosen, it needs to be positioned and have its field of influence defined. This is the area that will be affected by the light. The example shows a spotlight with its field of influence defined by an elliptical shape. The white circle at the center of the ellipse defines the center point of the light and is used to reposition the light within the preview window. The light's source is defined by the point that connects to the center of the ellipse by the gray line. All four handles around the circumference of the ellipse can be used to change the ellipse's size and shape. In the example, the spotlight has been positioned so that its source is just out of the preview window, so the source will not appear in the image, only the light which it casts.

Intensity Regulates how much light emanates from the source. Drag the slider to the right to increase light, and to the left to decrease light.

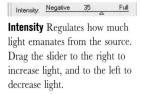

Focus Defines how much of the ellipse is filled with light. Drag the slider to the right to fill the ellipse, and to the left to restrict the spread of light.

Light Color Creates the effect of a colored filter being placed over a light. Click the white square in the *Light type* section to access the *Color Picker* where the desired color can be selected.

Properties

Gloss Defines how reflective the image should be in terms of the finish of a printed photograph. Drag toward *Matte* for low reflective and toward *Shiny* for high reflective properties.

Material Refers to the light's color reflection qualities. Drag toward *Plastic* if the light's color should be reflected, and toward *Metallic* if the object's color should be reflected.

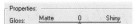

Exposure Has the effect of increasing or decreasing the overall light in the scene. Drag toward *Over* to increase light, and toward *Under* to decrease.

Texture Channel Can be used to create pseudo-3D effects through the use of grayscale alpha channels, which are used to map highlight, midtone, and shadow areas to different degrees of elevation. We will be using this technique to create some chrome 3D text later in the book.

Creating Additional Lights New lights can be created by clicking and dragging from the light bulb icon onto the preview area. A maximum of 16 lights can be created.

Deleting Lights To remove a light, drag it from its center point into the bin. There must be a minimum of one light left in the scene.

Duplicating Lights Press the Alt key and click and drag from an existing light to duplicate it with exactly the same settings.

Saving New Light Styles Having created a lighting setup, you may want to save it for future use with other images. Click the *Save* button and type a name in the *Save as* box that opens. The style can now be selected from the *Style* drop-down box in the same way as the presets.

Ambient Light Color In the same way as lights can be colored, so can the ambient light in the scene. To change the color, click the white square in the *Properties* section.

Ambience Takes into account other light sources in the scene, such as daylight or artificial lights, and diffuses the created light with those light sources. Drag toward *Positive* to increase light, and toward *Negative* to decrease light.

Deleting Light Styles Select a style and press the *Delete* button to remove it from Photoshop's folder.

Switching Lights On and Off For testing purposes, you may wish to switch one or more lights off to preview the effect. Select the desired light and uncheck the *On* box to switch it off. Click again to switch on.

Quality of Light

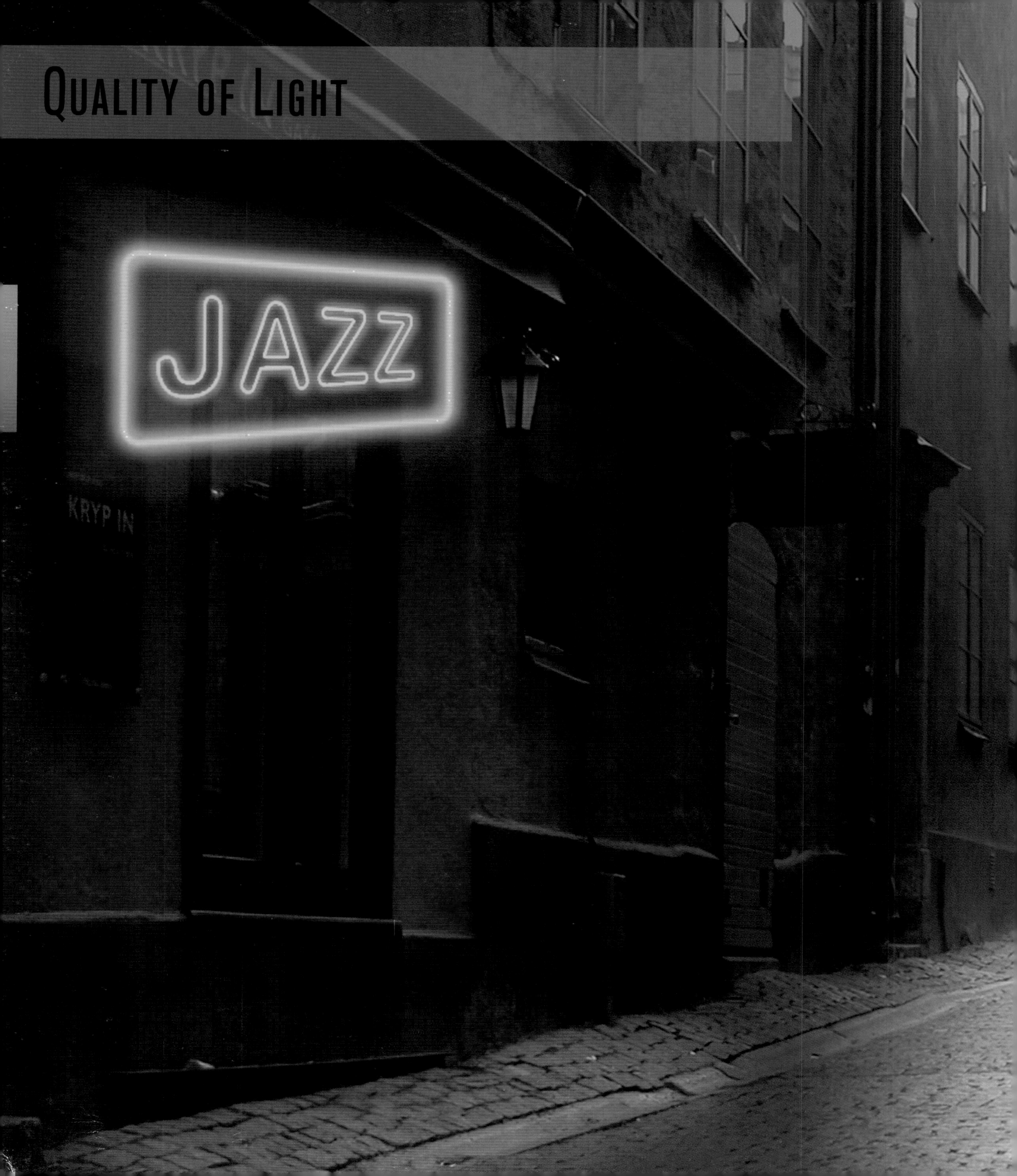

CREATING WARM LIGHT

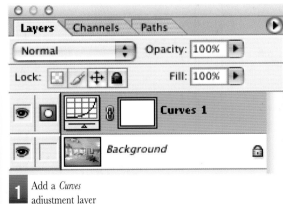

1 Add a *Curves* adjustment layer to the *Background* layer.

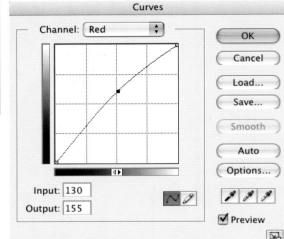

The link between the quality of light and human emotions cannot be understated. The world of sales and marketing observed and began to exploit this link many years ago. Whether selling a house, a hotel room, or the seat on a plane, warm light instantly conveys an impression of calmness, security, and all the creature comforts of home.

We'll now put this concept into practice by warming up the light in this interior setting.

2 Rather than applying the curve to the RGB composite, we are going to edit only the *Red* and *Blue* curves to warm up the overall light in the image. Apply the settings as shown to the relevant channels.

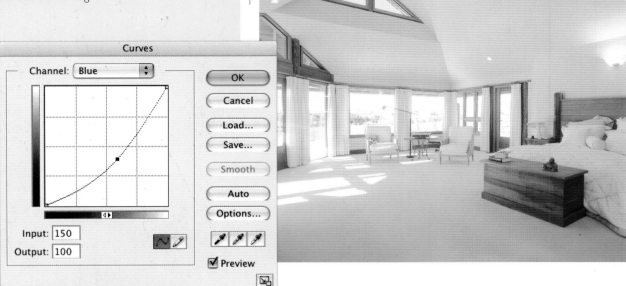

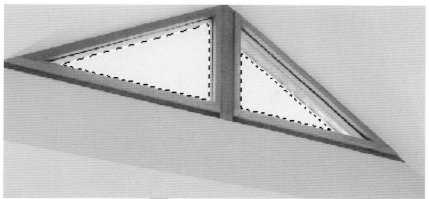

5 The final image displays a much more inviting feel purely as a result of warmer colors being introduced. You now have complete control over how warm the colors are by editing the *Curves* adjustment layer. Adjusting the curve to the whole RGB composite enables you to darken or lighten the image as desired.

3 The triangular shaped windows at the top of the room also need their color warming up to balance with the rest of the room. Use the *Magic Wand* tool to select both windows.

4 Go to *Image > Adjust >* **Color Balance**. Apply the displayed settings to the *Highlights* only.

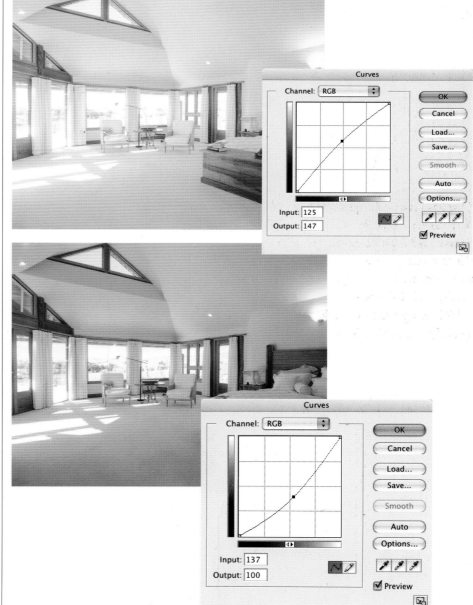

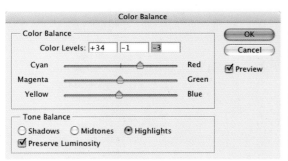

CREATING COLD LIGHT

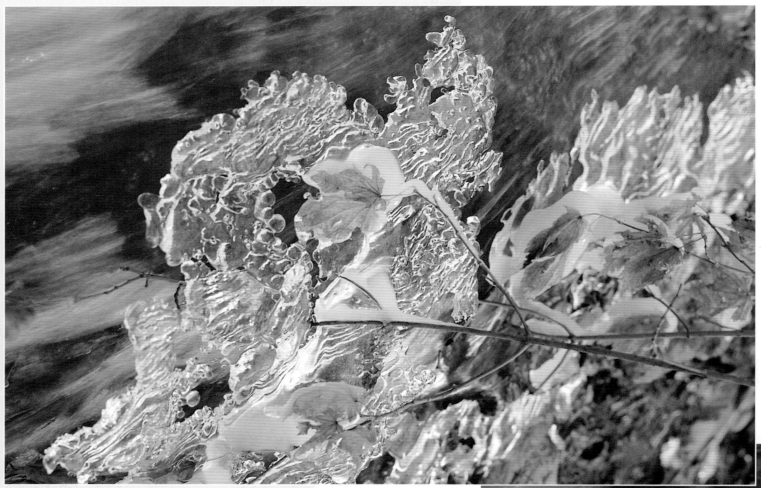

The first brief moment of dawn just before the sun emerges above the horizon is a prime time to photograph cold light. Although many conditions exist where cold light can be photographed successfully, few situations can match the primeval rawness of this time of day. However, if a warm bed is too inviting to leave at this hour, Photoshop has everything you need to reproduce it.

The fact that this image depicts ice suggests the scene is cold, yet the ambient light contradicts that fact: the colors are leaning toward the warm end of the spectrum. This in itself is not necessarily a bad thing, but if you are trying to instill in the viewer a sense of icy cold in the depths of winter, it doesn't really convey the message.

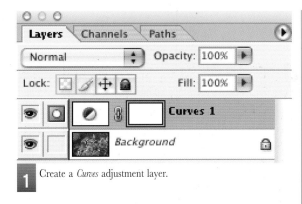

1 Create a *Curves* adjustment layer.

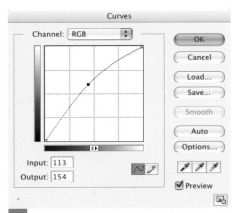

2 We'll make 3 adjustments to the curve. First, edit the curve for the RGB composite to lighten the overall scene.

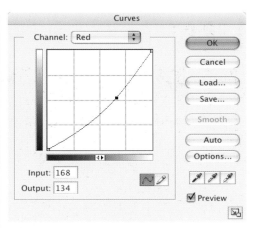

3 Now the *Red* curve can be edited to reduce the amount of red and suggest the introduction of blue light.

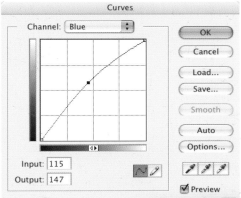

4 Finally, the *Blue* curve is raised slightly to strengthen the blue and add a little more light.

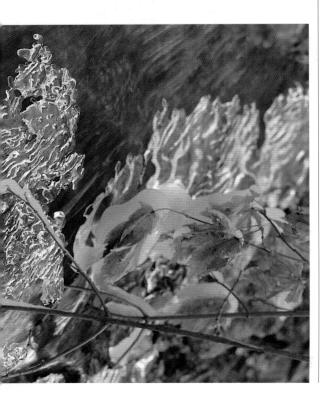

CREATING LOW-KEY IMAGES

The nature of a low-key image is one that consists primarily of dark tones with highlight areas to add dramatic contrast. The images are often moody and thought-provoking, and a world apart from the popular misconception that a low-key image is merely one that is underexposed. A truly classic low-key image, therefore, is one where the highlights shoulder as much importance as the shadows in determining the success of the finished image.

The original image.

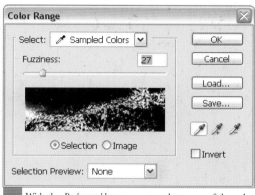

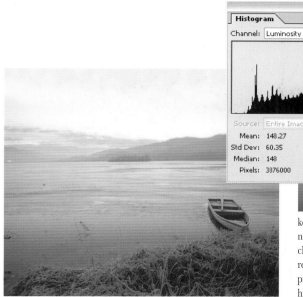

1 We can see that this image is clearly not low key. If confirmation were needed, checking the *Luminosity* channel in the *Histogram* palette reveals a broad distribution of pixels across the full range of highlights through to shadows.

5 With the *Background* layer active, go to *Select > Color Range* and use the eyedroppers to select some of the pale colored strands of foliage and click *OK* to confirm.

2 We first need to find the natural highlights in the image, which can be preserved and used later. Go to *Select > Color Range*. Choose *Highlights* from the *Select* drop-down box.

6 Press Ctrl (Cmd on a Mac) + J and rename the new layer *Foliage.*

7 The top edges of the boat and oar will also provide a stark contrast against a darkened background and provide added interest, so we'll isolate those onto their own layer too. Make a selection of the boat's top edge and oar.

3 Press Ctrl (Cmd on a Mac) + J to copy and paste the selection to a new layer. Once that's done, name the layer *Highlights*.

4 Make a rough, feathered selection of the foliage in the foreground. These too will be used to reveal some highlight areas shortly.

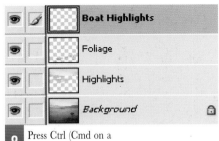

8 Press Ctrl (Cmd on a Mac) + J and rename the new layer *Boat highlights*.

9 All the highlight and midtone areas have now been isolated. Now the shadow areas need to be defined. Create a *Curves* adjustment layer above the *Background* layer.

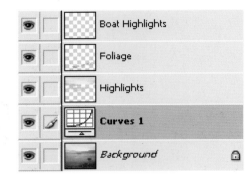

10 Create a curve similar to the one shown to darken the *Background* layer.

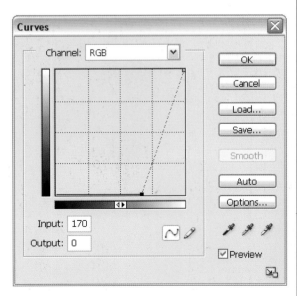

11 The result of super-imposing the highlight and midtone areas on top of the dark background has made the image too bright overall. We need to add some subtlety for a true low-key image.

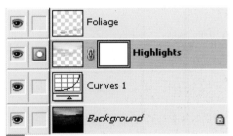

12 Add a layer mask to the *Highlights* layer.

13 Drag a *Black to White* linear gradient on the mask from top to about halfway down the image. This hides the top half of the *Highlights* layer, revealing the dark sky of the *Background* layer.

14 The foliage also is not subtle enough. In a similar way to the last step, add a layer mask to the *Foliage* layer and paint along the top edge with black to soften it.

15 Change the *Foliage* layer's blend mode to *Linear Dodge*.

16 Finally, the boat highlight looks a little false. Change the layer blend mode to *Pin Light* to unify it with the rest of the scene, and we're left with a classic low-key image.

CREATING HIGH-KEY IMAGES

1 Add a *Levels* adjustment layer to the *Background* layer.

C elestial light and dreaminess: two of the qualities that are the hallmarks of a high-key image. The soft flood of abundant light that permeates the shadows all but suffocates the image with its radiance, but as with low-key images, opposites are crucial to mastering the effect. The absence of any shadow detail would merely result in an overexposed image. So in this walkthrough we'll be concentrating on the creation of light, but also ensuring that some darker tones are preserved.

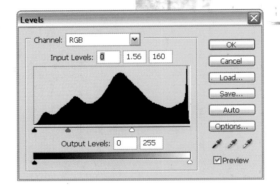

2 Drag the white and gray markers to the left to increase light in the highlight and midtone areas.

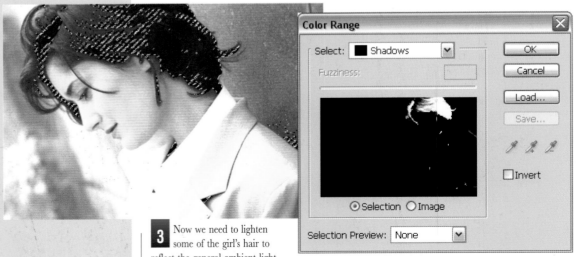

3 Now we need to lighten some of the girl's hair to reflect the general ambient light. Go to *Select* > **Color Range** and choose *Shadows* from the *Select* drop-down box.

4 To avoid any harsh lines, feather the selection by about 15 pixels for a high resolution file.

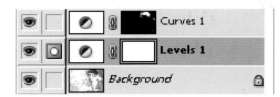

5 Create a *Curves* adjustment layer. The selection automatically becomes a mask for the *Curves* layer.

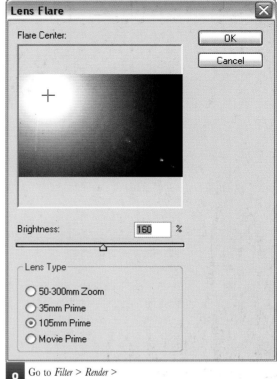

6 Drag the white point of the curve in a straight line to the left to lighten this area only.

8 Go to *Filter > Render > Lens Flare*. Apply the settings shown to the top-left corner of the preview window.

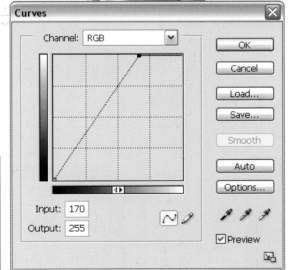

7 We already have a very effective high-key image, but to invoke that ethereal quality typical of so many high-key photographs, we need a soft wash of white light. Create a new black-filled layer called *White Light*.

9 Change the *White Light* layer blend mode to *Screen*. The amount of light flooding the scene can be controlled by using the layer opacity.

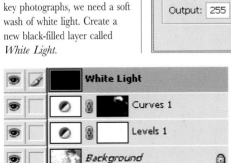

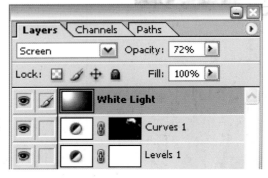

MIXING DIFFERENT TYPES OF LIGHT

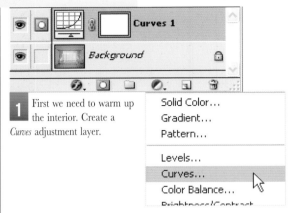

1 First we need to warm up the interior. Create a *Curves* adjustment layer.

Solid Color...
Gradient...
Pattern...

Levels...
Curves...
Color Balance...

2 I'm adjusting the *Red*, *Green*, and *Blue* channels independently, in each case leaving the highlight areas untouched and just changing the midtone to shadow areas. The result of the settings pictured is a warm tone, but with a natural looking distribution of the full range of tones from light to dark within the room. The windows, however, remain a fairly cold blue, which is what we want.

The difference between the blue color of natural daylight and the yellow color of incandescent light bulbs is virtually cancelled out by our eyes, as we adapt to lighting conditions very well. A white shirt will be perceived as white, although the shirt may well be tinged with blue or yellow depending on the light source. Cameras are not so adept at adjusting to these different conditions, although it must be said the latest crop come fitted with white balance adjustment to alleviate this problem. Nevertheless, for creative reasons you may wish to see both of these extremes of lighting conditions in one image. In the example we are going to work through, we'll convert an image to simulate the blue cast of daylight through the windows and the warm yellow of incandescent light within the interior of a room.

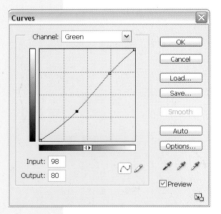

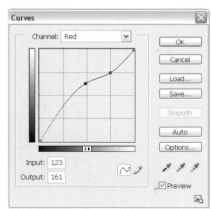

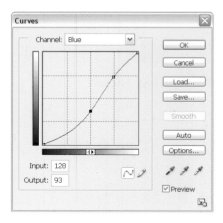

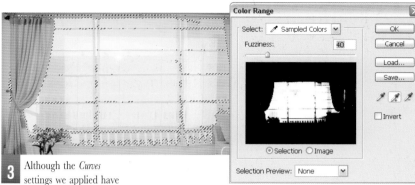

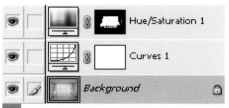

3 Although the *Curves* settings we applied have maintained a cool blue in the window area, the effect needs strengthening to make it more interesting. We don't want to change the interior, though, so we need to select the window area. Go to *Select > Color Range*. Use the eyedroppers to select most of the window area. It's fine to leave some of the wooden frames of the window unselected, as this will help avoid a strong uniform color change that can look unrealistic.

4 With the selection visible, add a *Hue/Saturation* adjustment layer. This automatically adds the selection to a layer mask that is linked to the adjustment layer. This means the color changes we make won't affect anything but the window area.

7 The main source of light in the room is supposed to be from artificial lighting with a few traces of sunlight, as seen on the floor and sofa. To emphasize this fact, we need to switch on the ceiling lights. In a new layer, create a circular selection filled with black.

8 Go to *Filter > Render > Lens Flare*, and use the settings shown.

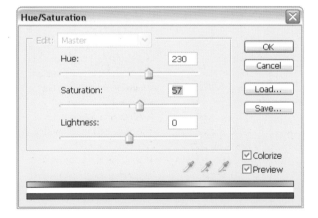

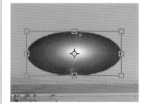

5 Apply the settings shown.

9 Press Ctrl (Cmd) + T to bring up the *Transform* bounding box and scale the circle nonproportionately to simulate looking at the light from an angle.

10 Change the layer blend mode to *Lighten* and position the flare over one of the ceiling lights.

6 The finished result has a good contrast between the warm and cold colors, and because we have used adjustment layers they can be edited until you get the color balance just right. The layer mask on the *Hue/Saturation* adjustment layer also enables you to edit the degree of blue on the window panels and walls behind the drapes.

11 Duplicate the layer twice to make the other two ceiling lights and drag into place.

CREATING MOONLIGHT

The ethereal qualities of moonlight make it a subject for photography in itself, as well as being an inspiring source of light. As with all forms of light, moonlight comes in a variety of tones, from soft, silvery light that molds long gentle shadows to strong directional rays that bathe the atmosphere in a calm blue haze. It is this powerful mental association with moonlight and strong silvery blues that renders so many attempts to capture moonlight on camera disappointing. Even the most sophisticated of cameras can struggle when it comes to immortalizing the essence of our perception of moonlight. This is not so much a criticism of camera technology, but rather a testament to the genius of the workings of the human eye. Photoshop can provide that link between what the camera captures and what we perceive as a glorious moonlit scene. In this section, we will look at two different ways of putting the romance back into moonlit images.

USING LIGHTING EFFECTS

1 Duplicate the *Background* layer, naming the duplicated layer *Moonlight*.

2 The expanse of white sky is ideally positioned to place the moon. The narrowness of the alley means that we'd expect to see quite a well-defined shaft of moonlight reflected on the cobblestones, with suitably shadowy areas on the buildings. The cobblestones are also quite moist, and this can be used to our advantage to emphasize reflected moonlight. Go to *Filter > Render > Lighting Effects*. Select the *Blue Omni* light from the *Style* drop-down. Set *Intensity* to 93 and the light color to R68 G98 B249. The real trick behind simulating moonlight with this filter is to perfectly balance the *Exposure* and *Ambience* properties. We need to reduce the exposure sufficiently to depict the soft, relatively small halo of light around the moon while maintaining the optimum ambient light to suggest low levels of generated moonlight without producing an overly dark image that lacks depth. Set the *Exposure* to –40 and *Ambience* to 14. All the settings are in the example pictured. Don't click *OK* yet, as we need a second light.

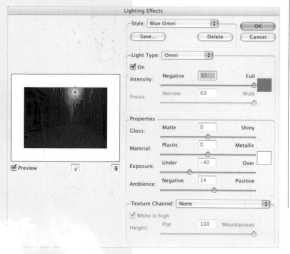

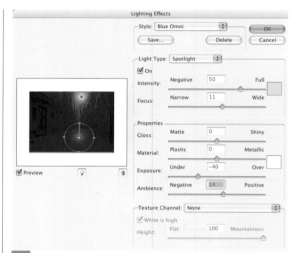

3 We now need to create a bold reflection from the moon on the cobblestones. Create a new light, choosing *Spotlight* from the *Light Type* menu. Apply the positioning and settings as in the example and click *OK*.

4 Here is the finished effect. If you're not completely satisfied with your result, simply undo the effect and return to the *Lighting Effects* filter, where you'll find the same settings that you just applied. It's very easy to adjust the depth of shadow if desired by increasing or decreasing the *Ambience* setting. I've left the shadow-filled area in the left of the image intentionally dark, as it will provide a perfect backdrop for some neon lights that we will produce in a later exercise.

USING GRADIENTS

Using the *Lighting Effects* filter is just one highly photorealistic way of simulating moonlight. A similar effect can also be achieved through the use of gradients. Ultimately it comes down to personal preference and the final desired effect. In the next example, we'll convert a bright daylight scene into a moonlit one with the help of gradients and some additional techniques to help the illusion.

It is important to remember when simulating lighting conditions that there should be no visible elements that conflict with the effect you are trying to achieve. A typical example would be a shadow that lies in the wrong direction for the light you have created. In this image, there is already a strong shadow being cast from the palm tree and umbrella, but if we place the false moonlight above and to the right of the tree and umbrella, the existing shadows will actually help the deception.

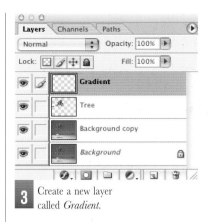

3 Create a new layer called *Gradient*.

4 Set up the *Gradient* tool with a radial gradient set to *Foreground to Background*. Use white for the foreground and a deep blue for the background. Drag the gradient from the top-right corner to create a gradient similar to the one shown.

5 Set the *Gradient* layer blending mode to *Multiply*.

1 Duplicate the *Background* layer in case any mistakes are made so it can be used again.

2 Make a selection of the palm tree and press Ctrl (Cmd) + J to copy and paste it onto a new layer named *Tree*. This layer will be used later to help with highlights.

6 Now we need an image of the moon. Nothing too perfect is required; in fact, a slightly out-of-focus image will be more realistic. Copy and paste the moon into the document and scale it accordingly.

7 The moon doesn't quite blend in well enough to its new background. Change the *Moon* layer blending mode to *Lighten* and reduce the *Opacity* to 60%.

8 To add further realism, we need to create some reflections from the moonlight. Drag the *Tree* layer to the top of the *Layers* palette, then go to *Image > Adjustments > Threshold*, applying the setting in the illustration.

9 Setting the *Threshold* level has defined the required highlights, but because it converts the artwork to 1-bit, either black or white, it has left it looking a little jagged. To counter this, use *Filter > Blur > Gaussian Blur* and apply the settings as pictured.

10 To bring the whole effect together, change the *Tree* layer blending mode to *Color Dodge* and reduce the layer's *Opacity* to 50%. It has left us with a subtle illusion of light being picked up from the moonlight.

11 To complete the scene, we need to add some surface reflection to the water. Use the *Pen* tool or *Lasso* tool to draw the outline of a likely surface reflection.

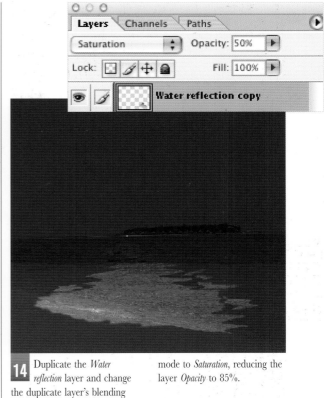

14 Duplicate the *Water reflection* layer and change the duplicate layer's blending mode to *Saturation*, reducing the layer *Opacity* to 85%.

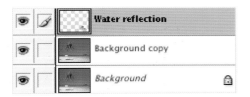

12 Activate the *Background copy* layer and press Ctrl (Cmd) + J to copy and paste the selection onto a new layer named *Water reflection.*

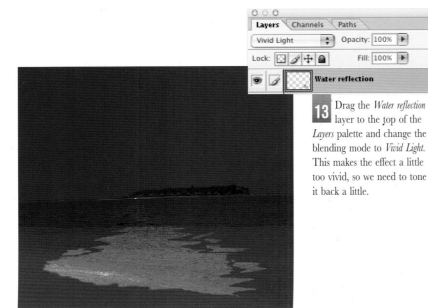

13 Drag the *Water reflection* layer to the top of the *Layers* palette and change the blending mode to *Vivid Light.* This makes the effect a little too vivid, so we need to tone it back a little.

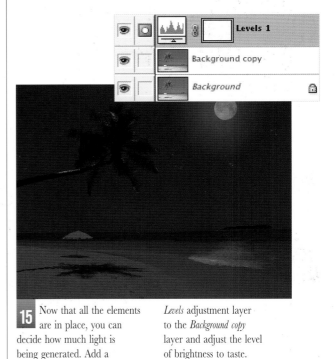

15 Now that all the elements are in place, you can decide how much light is being generated. Add a *Levels* adjustment layer to the *Background copy* layer and adjust the level of brightness to taste.

CREATING CANDLELIGHT

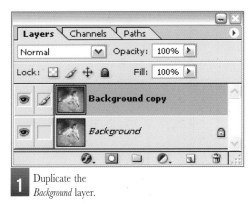

1 Duplicate the *Background* layer.

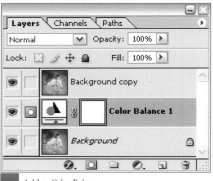

2 Add a *Color Balance* adjustment layer to the original *Background* layer.

Candlelight as a primary or supplementary source of light can offer a richness and depth of light matched only by a few other sources. It is not designed for capturing rapid movement, but still life scenes, or images where small amounts of blur are acceptable, are brought to life with the intensity of warmth generated by the glow of a candle.

Because of the limited range of candlelight, an image can be particularly striking when the candle is an additional light source in a room where other light sources are of a contrasting nature, such as cold evening light or moonlight. This is the effect we are going to produce where the secondary source of light in the form of cold blue light contrasts with the warm, inviting glow of the candlelight.

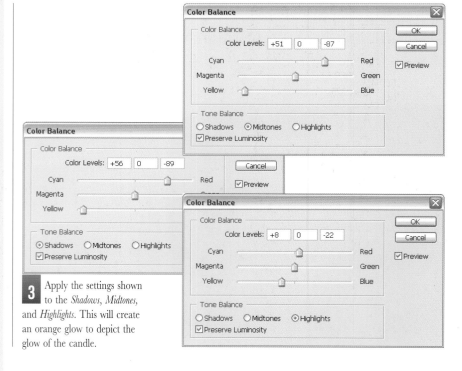

3 Apply the settings shown to the *Shadows*, *Midtones*, and *Highlights*. This will create an orange glow to depict the glow of the candle.

4 Hide the *Background copy* layer momentarily to see the effect of the *Color Balance* adjustment layer.

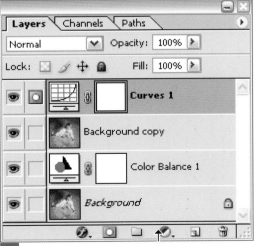

5 As the candlelight is supposed to be the main source of light, we need to darken the overall image. Add a *Curves* adjustment layer above the *Background copy* layer.

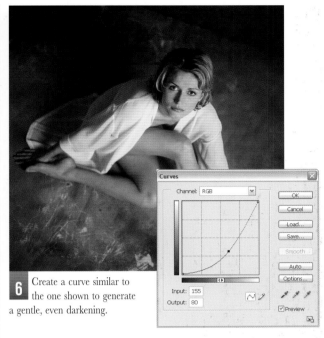

6 Create a curve similar to the one shown to generate a gentle, even darkening.

7 Make a selection of the candle image and drag it onto the image of the girl.

8 Scale the candle down to size and position it to the right of the girl.

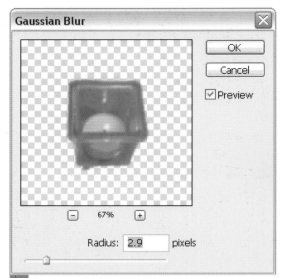

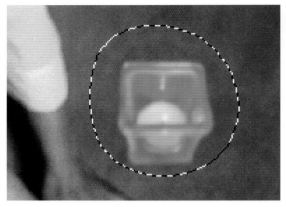

11 Although the candle will ultimately generate a relatively broad area of light, the immediate vicinity of the candle should display a soft, intense glow. Create a selection around the candle with a high feather setting. About 40 will work well for a high resolution file.

9 The photo of the girl was taken with a very limited depth of field, which explains why her face is in focus and her hands and feet are blurred. This causes problems for the candle, which sits on the same plane as the hands and feet and should therefore conform to the same degree of blur. We can easily fix this by adding some blur to the candle. Go to *Filter > Blur > **Gaussian Blur*** and apply the settings shown if you are using a high resolution file. For lower resolution files, reduce the setting accordingly.

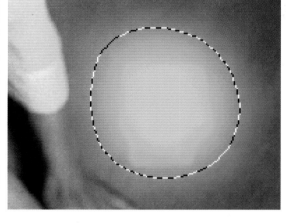

12 Fill the selection with orange. I'm using R245 G178 B52.

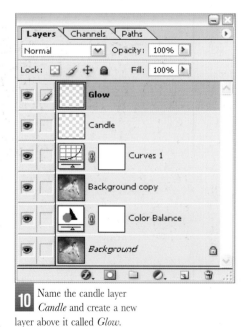

10 Name the candle layer *Candle* and create a new layer above it called *Glow.*

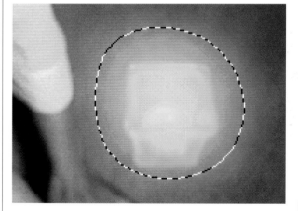

13 Change the layer blend mode to *Linear Light* to reveal the candle.

14 Now that we have the source of light in place, we can create the wider glow to illuminate the girl. Add a layer mask to the *Background copy* layer.

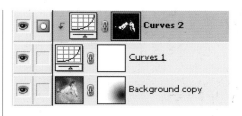

17 This has made a perfect selection of the high points of the girl and her clothing as well as of the candle itself. Activate the existing *Curves* adjustment layer and create another *Curves* adjustment layer, using the previous layer to create a clipping mask. This has the effect of making a mask from the selection that is automatically linked to the new *Curves* adjustment layer. This means that the adjustments we now make will affect only the areas that we highlighted.

15 Drag a *Black to White* radial gradient on the mask from point A to B. This lets the orange background layer show through.

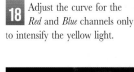

18 Adjust the curve for the *Red* and *Blue* channels only to intensify the yellow light.

16 That's created a nice soft wash of candlelight over the girl and the floor, but I really want to emphasize the concentrated glow of the candle and the stark cold of the room farther away from it. One way of doing this is to increase the intensity of the candlelight on the high points of the girl only, primarily her face and some of the clothing most exposed to the light. This would be a natural effect for anyone sitting so close to the candle. Go to *Select > Color Range*. Choose *Highlights* from the *Select* drop-down box.

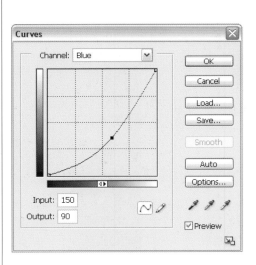

CREATING NEON LIGHT

In this exercise, we are going to create a neon text sign for a jazz club. Neon signs are synonymous with nightclubs, and their unique quality of light has a subtle and atmospheric effect on the surrounding night scene. Although not considered as a source of light to aid visibility, the light they emit will still illuminate the immediate environment, but with an almost ghostly air. It is this secondary light in addition to the fluorescent tubes themselves that will make our work convincing.

I'm using the finished image from one of the moonlight creation tutorials earlier in the book. The dark area in the bottom left of the image was left intentionally dark as a backdrop for the neon light.

1 Type the word *JAZZ* in black at 72 point with *Tracking* set to 75. Rounder fonts work best to depict the tubes of neon text. I'm using Arial Rounded MT Bold.

2 We need to change the perspective of the text to match the street, but first it is necessary to rasterize the text. To do this, go to *Layer > Rasterize > **Type***.

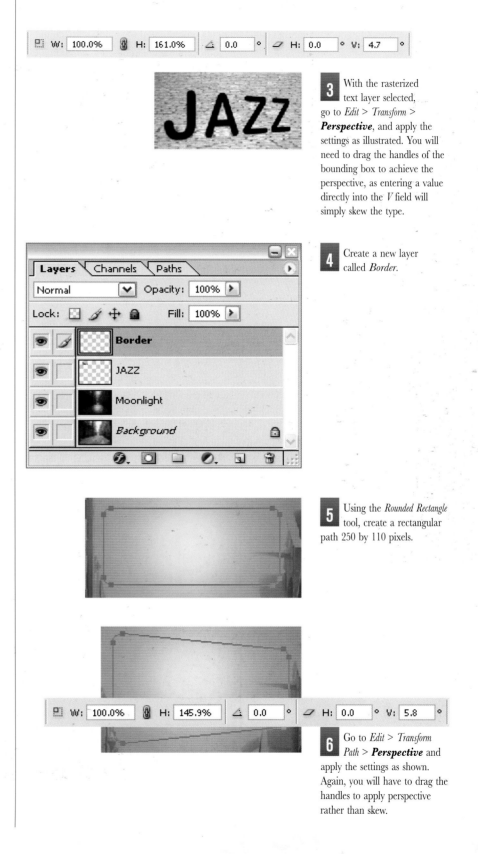

3 With the rasterized text layer selected, go to *Edit > Transform > **Perspective***, and apply the settings as illustrated. You will need to drag the handles of the bounding box to achieve the perspective, as entering a value directly into the *V* field will simply skew the type.

4 Create a new layer called *Border*.

5 Using the *Rounded Rectangle* tool, create a rectangular path 250 by 110 pixels.

6 Go to *Edit > Transform Path > **Perspective*** and apply the settings as shown. Again, you will have to drag the handles to apply perspective rather than skew.

7 Set up the brush tool with a soft-edged, 6 pixel, round brush and the foreground color set to R228 G230 B250.

8 Make sure the *Border* layer is still active, then stroke the path, using the icon at the bottom of the *Paths* palette.

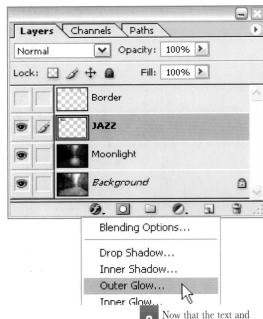

9 Now that the text and border of the sign are complete, we can start to apply the neon effect. Activate the *JAZZ* text layer and choose the *Outer Glow* option from the *Layer Style* icon at the bottom of the *Layers* palette.

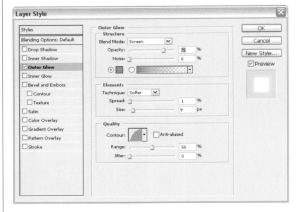

10 Apply the settings as shown in the *Layer Style* dialog box. I've used a bright color, as intense colors look most convincing. Don't click *OK* yet; we are going to add a couple more styles.

11 Click the *Inner Glow* option immediately below the *Outer Glow* and apply the illustrated settings.

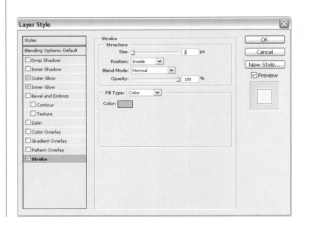

12 Finally click on the *Stroke* setting, which is the last style in the *Styles* list. The settings are pictured once again. The stroke color is a deep pink this time. Click *OK*.

13 Change the *Jazz* layer blend mode to *Screen*.

14 Repeat the process for the *Border* layer. The settings for each of the styles is displayed for you to copy. A midblue was used this time to contrast with the red text.

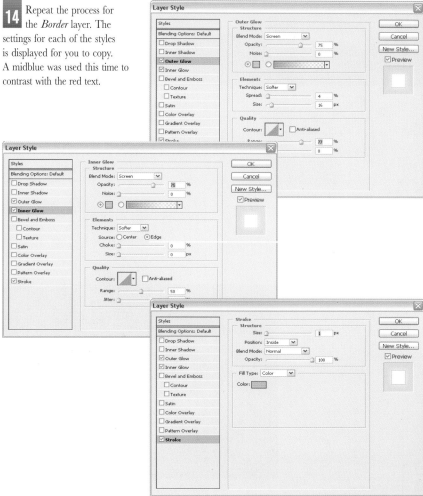

15 Position the text and border in the left of the image as if the sign is mounted on the wall.

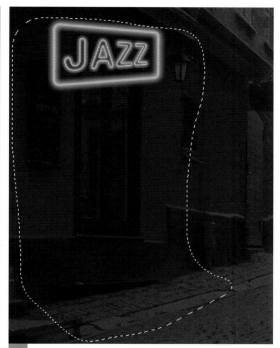

16 There would be a fair amount of ambient light generated from this kind of sign. The quality of the light would be quite subdued, though, as a consequence of the heavy coloring of the light. We will therefore use the original lighting of the image as the basis for the range of highlights and shadows. This should result in a very realistic projection of light. Make a 25 pixel, feathered selection with the *Lasso* tool as shown.

17 Activate the *Background* layer and then press Ctrl (Cmd) + J to copy and paste the selection to a new layer.

18 Name the layer *Ambient* and drag it above the *Moonlight* layer.

19 We now have the apparent light falloff in place, but we need to rectify the color. To do this, go to *Image > Adjustments > **Hue / Saturation***, and apply the settings as pictured.

20 To add the final touches, we need to create a soft blue glow to echo the blue border, and a slightly more intense red glow that radiates in the immediate vicinity of the text. Make a 30 pixel, feathered selection as shown.

21 As before, activate the *Background* layer and press Ctrl (Cmd) + J to copy and paste the selection to a new layer. Name the layer *Blue glow* and position it above the *Ambient* layer.

22 Use *Image > Adjustments > **Hue / Saturation***, and apply the settings as shown in the example.

23 Press Ctrl (Cmd) + click the *Blue glow* layer to load its selection and then contract it by 60 pixels by going to *Select > Modify > **Contract***.

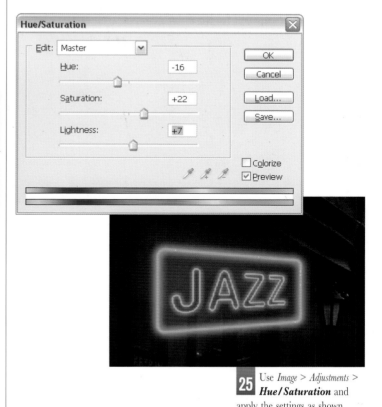

24 We now need to repeat the earlier process to copy the selection from the *Background* layer. Activate the *Background* layer and press Ctrl (Cmd) + J. Name the new layer *Red glow* and position it above the *Blue glow* layer.

25 Use *Image > Adjustments > **Hue/Saturation*** and apply the settings as shown.

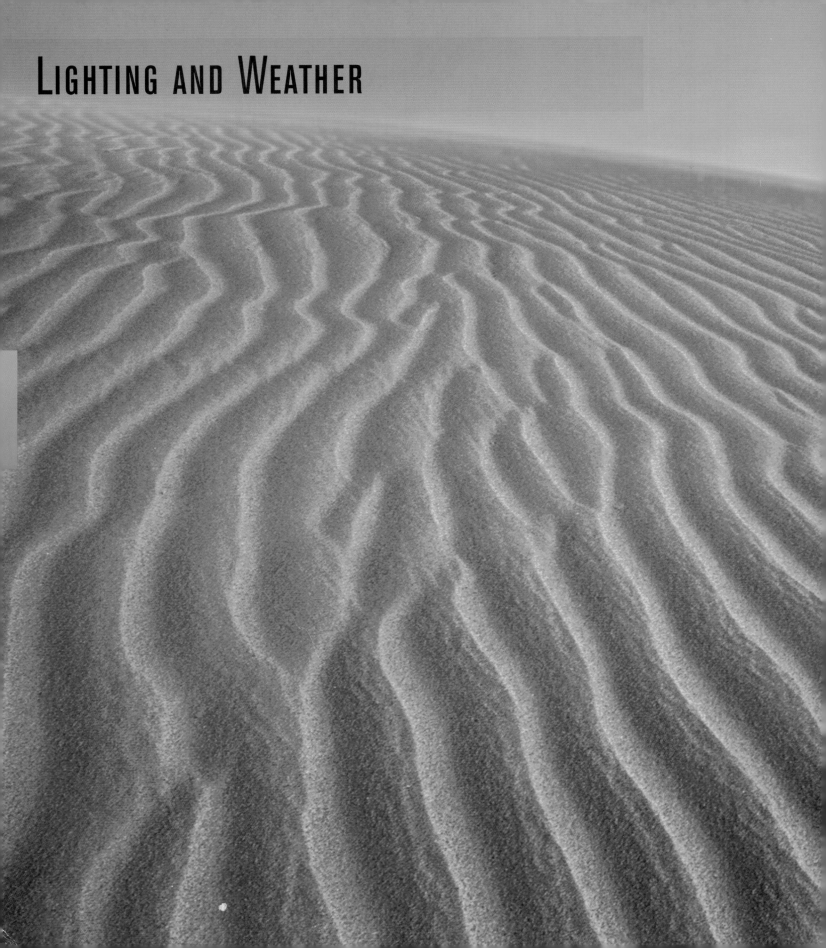

CREATING SUNSETS FROM DAYLIGHT SCENES

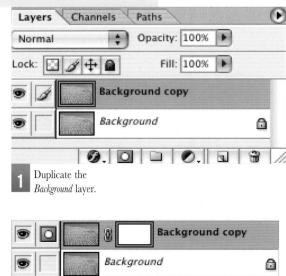

1 Duplicate the *Background* layer.

2 Add a layer mask to the *Background copy* layer.

It has been said that no two sunsets are the same. Whether or not you agree with that statement, one fact that is certainly beyond doubt is the sheer variety of sunsets that grace our skies. Sunsets appear as a result of the different colored light wavelengths traveling over a longer distance to reach your eyes as the sun sets lower in the sky. This increased distance means the light waves must travel through more atmosphere, whereupon the shorter blue wavelengths are scattered as they collide with particles of gas molecules and dust. This leaves only the longer wavelength colors such as yellow and red to reach your eyes. The most dramatic sunsets appear when there are increased particles in the air, such as during the aftermath of a storm. In this situation yellow light, which has a shorter wavelength than red, is also dispersed in the atmosphere, leaving only the longer red wavelengths as visible red light and thus producing rich red skies.

3 Drag a *Black to White* linear gradient on the mask from the top of the screen to about one fifth of the way down. This enables a small strip of the original blue from the background layer to be revealed at the top of the screen, and will prove very effective as the sunset is built up.

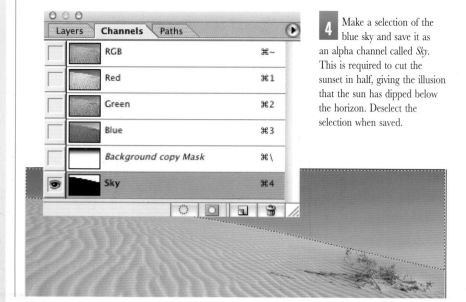

4 Make a selection of the blue sky and save it as an alpha channel called *Sky*. This is required to cut the sunset in half, giving the illusion that the sun has dipped below the horizon. Deselect the selection when saved.

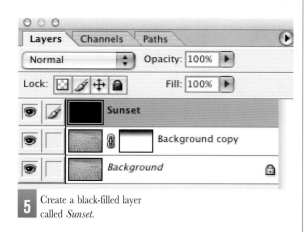

5 Create a black-filled layer called *Sunset*.

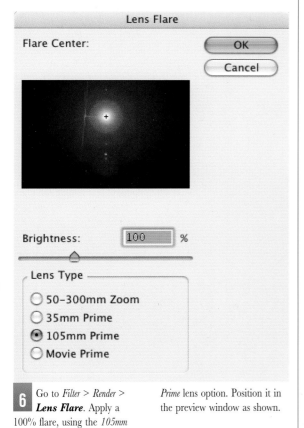

6 Go to *Filter > Render > Lens Flare*. Apply a 100% flare, using the *105mm Prime* lens option. Position it in the preview window as shown.

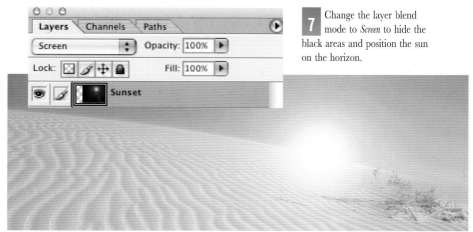

7 Change the layer blend mode to *Screen* to hide the black areas and position the sun on the horizon.

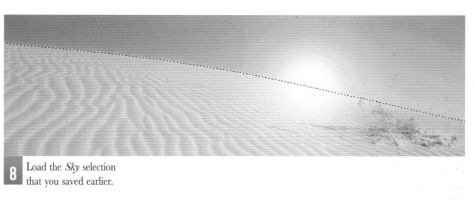

8 Load the *Sky* selection that you saved earlier.

9 Inverse the selection and press the Backspace key on the keyboard to delete the lens flare from the sand area of the image. Leave the selection loaded for the next step.

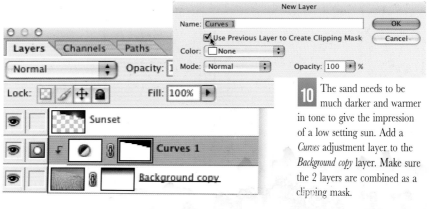

10 The sand needs to be much darker and warmer in tone to give the impression of a low setting sun. Add a *Curves* adjustment layer to the *Background copy* layer. Make sure the 2 layers are combined as a clipping mask.

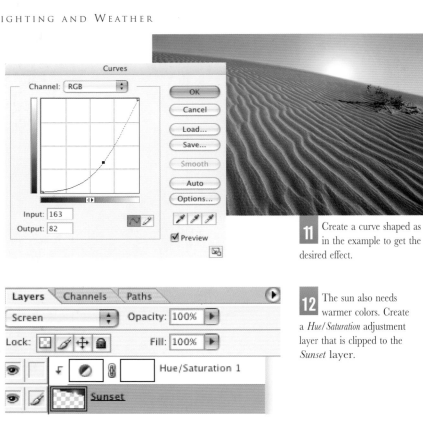

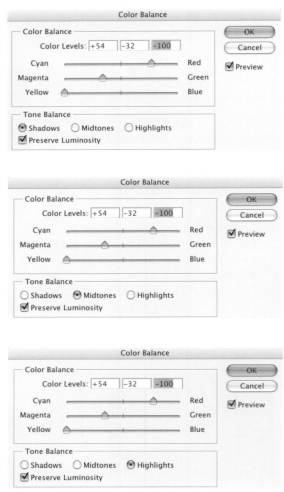

11 Create a curve shaped as in the example to get the desired effect.

12 The sun also needs warmer colors. Create a *Hue/Saturation* adjustment layer that is clipped to the *Sunset* layer.

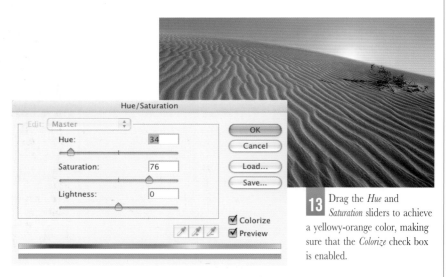

13 Drag the *Hue* and *Saturation* sliders to achieve a yellowy-orange color, making sure that the *Colorize* check box is enabled.

14 In order to add some real drama to our sunset, we are going to introduce a pink glow around the sun. Add a *Color Balance* adjustment layer that is clipped to the *Hue/Saturation* adjustment layer.

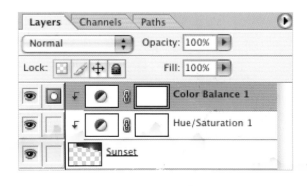

15 To create the dramatic changes of color, we need to change the *Shadows*, *Midtones*, and *Highlights* in the *Color Balance* dialog box.

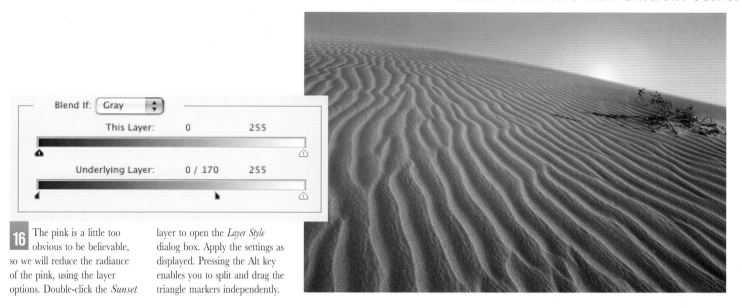

16 The pink is a little too obvious to be believable, so we will reduce the radiance of the pink, using the layer options. Double-click the *Sunset* layer to open the *Layer Style* dialog box. Apply the settings as displayed. Pressing the Alt key enables you to split and drag the triangle markers independently.

17 If we create a stronger degree of orange color to mingle with the pink, it will make for a much more complex and interesting wash of color, but also serve the purpose of generating a closer color match for the sand. These unifying techniques add considerably to the overall photographic realism. Load the selection that you saved previously.

18 Add a *Hue/Saturation* adjustment layer that is clipped to the *Curves* adjustment layer which we earlier attached to *Background copy*.

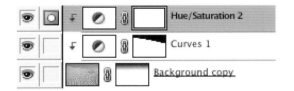

20 The great thing about the techniques used in this exercise is that you have complete control over the colors and brightness levels. By simply editing the adjustment layers, a huge array of sunset styles can be generated with just a few clicks. In the final image, the strong dark shadows from the bush have been removed with the *Patch* tool so as not to contradict the light direction, and the overall brightness of the sky has been toned down a little bit.

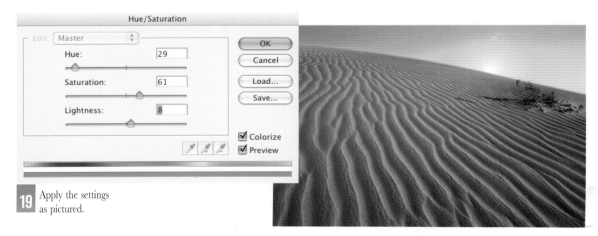

19 Apply the settings as pictured.

CONVERTING OVERCAST DAYS TO SUNNY DAYS

1 We'll start by generating some light and removing the strong blue cast that is overpowering the scene. Add a *Curves* adjustment layer.

How many photographs are now collecting dust in drawers and old boxes but would have been noteworthy images if only the sun had been shining when they were taken? Of the many things that can let a photographer down at the critical moment, the weather must be near the top of the list. Its sheer unpredictability makes it a force to be reckoned with. It's hardly surprising that over the millennia humanity has worshiped images of sun gods and rain gods in an attempt to appease the elements.

In the real world, the weather is its own master, in the digital world we can exercise a great deal of control, even to the extent of turning a drab, overcast day into one with bright sun and blue skies. This is exactly what we are going to do now.

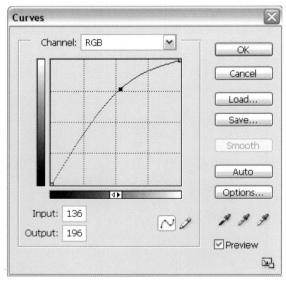

2 First adjust the *RGB* composite to lighten the image evenly.

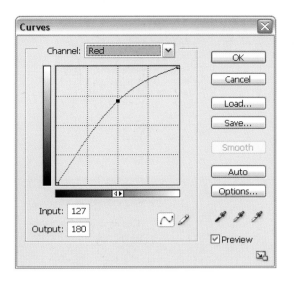

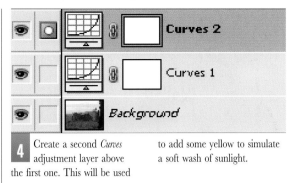

4 Create a second *Curves* adjustment layer above the first one. This will be used to add some yellow to simulate a soft wash of sunlight.

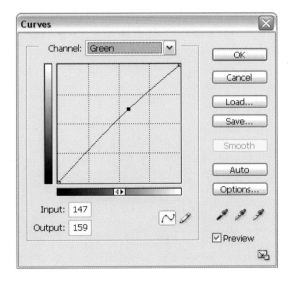

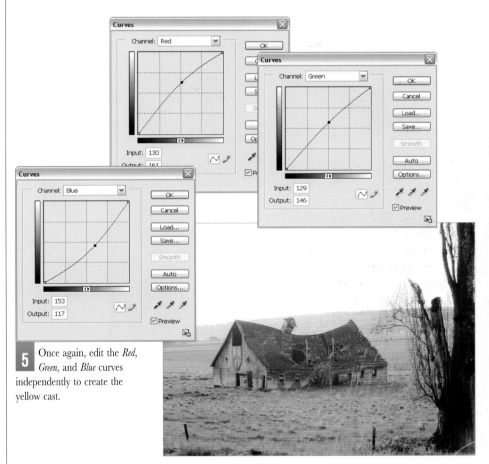

5 Once again, edit the *Red*, *Green*, and *Blue* curves independently to create the yellow cast.

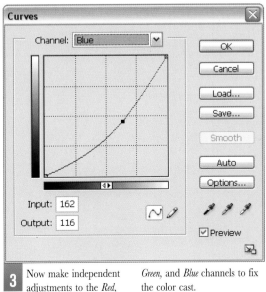

3 Now make independent adjustments to the *Red*, *Green*, and *Blue* channels to fix the color cast.

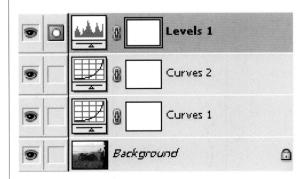

6 There's a slight haziness over the yellow cast, which is adversely affecting the illusion of bright sunlight. We'll fix this with levels. Add a *Levels* adjustment layer above *Curves 2*.

7 Drag the black and white input sliders toward each other to increase the contrast.

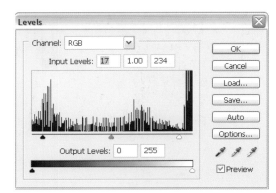

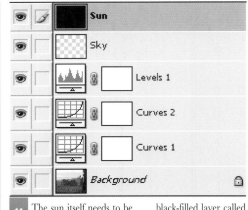

11 The sun itself needs to be introduced. Create a black-filled layer called *Sun* at the top of the *Layers* palette.

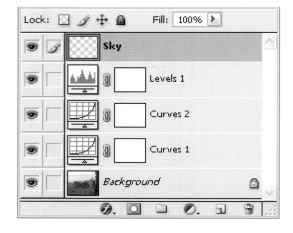

8 We now have a nice impression of strong sunlight and we've got rid of that dull, gray cloudy sky, which we can replace with a clear blue one. First make a selection of the white sky.

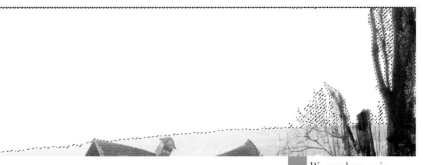

9 Create a new layer called *Sky*.

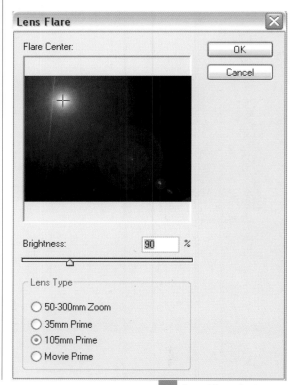

10 Drag a *Blue to Transparent* linear gradient through the selection, then deselect.

12 Go to *Filter > Render > **Lens Flare***. Apply the settings shown, clicking toward the top-left corner of the preview window.

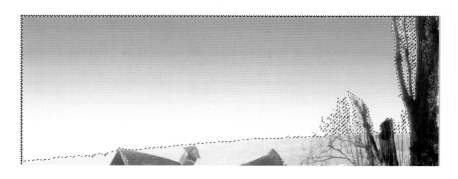

13 Change the layer blend mode to *Screen*.

14 To make the sun a bit more radiant, add a *Hue/Saturation* adjustment layer that is clipped to the *Sun* layer.

16 With the sun at this angle, the house would be casting a shadow. Create a feathered selection in front of the house.

15 Use the settings shown to create a larger sun with a hint of yellow.

Hue/Saturation

Edit: Master

Hue: 58

Saturation: 28

Lightness: 0

OK
Cancel
Load...
Save...

☑ Colorize
☑ Preview

17 On a new layer, fill the selection with a color sampled from a dark area of the grass. Setting the layer blend mode to *Multiply* at 75% will add to the realism.

Brush: 30   Range: Highlights   Exposure: 50%

18 Lastly, some of the edges of the branches in the top-right corner of the image stand out too much. Use the *Burn* tool set to *Highlights* to darken them.

CREATING DRAMATIC SKIES

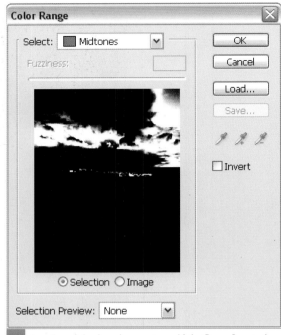

1 A section of cloud needs to be isolated so that we can create a layered file. Because of the wispy, undefined edges of these clouds, it is best to avoid the *Pen* or *Lasso* tools to make the selection. Instead, go to *Select* > **Color Range**, and choose *Midtones* from the *Select* drop-down box.

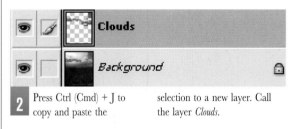

2 Press Ctrl (Cmd) + J to copy and paste the selection to a new layer. Call the layer *Clouds*.

Clouds and skyscapes have the distinction of being well suited to acting as the main subject in an image, or as a background to a more prominent focus of attention. As a subject in itself, the sky offers a rich, perpetually changing canvas of colors, shapes, and textures. Of all the possible variations, the most dramatic of skies must surely be the sunburst from behind darkened clouds. When this relatively rare phenomenon manifests itself, speed is of the essence if you intend to capture it, as it can all fade away just as suddenly as it appeared. But if time isn't on your side and you need a ready-made dramatic sky, we'll show you how to create one now.

3 A burst of light partially hidden behind the clouds will inject dramatic contrast into the scene. Create a black-filled layer beneath the *Clouds* layer, calling it *Light*.

4 Go to *Filter > Render > Lens Flare*, and use the settings as shown.

Lens Flare

Flare Center:

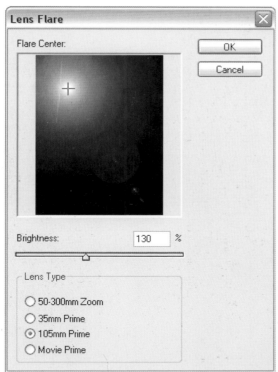

OK

Cancel

Brightness: 130 %

Lens Type

○ 50-300mm Zoom
○ 35mm Prime
● 105mm Prime
○ Movie Prime

Layers | Channels | Paths

Screen ▾ Opacity: 100% ▸

Lock: ☒ 🖉 ✛ 🔒   Fill: 100% ▸

👁 ☐ ☁ Clouds
👁 🖉 ◼ **Light**
👁 ☐ 🏞 *Background* 🔒

5 Change the layer blend mode to *Screen* to hide the black area, then reposition the central point of the flare, if necessary, so that it is tucked in behind the cloud.

👁 ◯ 🌟 🔗 ⬜ **Light**

6 Too much of the flare extends toward the bottom of the image. We could use the *Layer Options* sliders to reduce its radiance, but it's better to try and keep a smooth transition for this effect. Add a layer mask to the *Light* layer.

👁 ◯ 🌟 🔗 ◨ **Light**

7 Drag a *Black to White* linear gradient on the mask from the bottom to about halfway up the image so that the bottom half of the lens flare is hidden.

👁 ◯ ☁ 🔗 ⬜ **Clouds**

8 The flare has revealed some heavy outlining along the edges of the clouds, making it look false. Add a layer mask to the *Clouds* layer.

9 Using a soft-edged brush, paint with black on the mask along the edges of the clouds, hiding any obtrusive, heavy outlines.

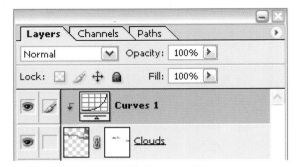

10 Now that we have a radiant background behind the clouds, we can darken the clouds to increase overall contrast and drama. Add a *Curves* adjustment layer that is clipped to the *Clouds* layer.

11 Make a small adjustment to the *RGB* curve to darken the clouds.

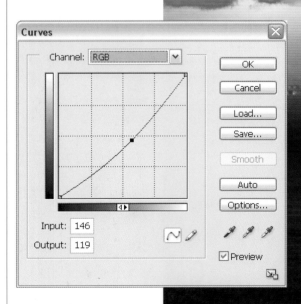

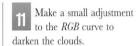

Input: 146

Output: 119

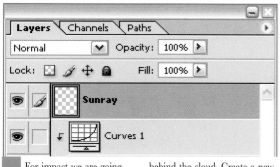

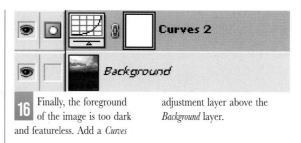

12 For impact we are going to create some rays of sharp sunlight emanating from behind the cloud. Create a new layer called *Sunray* above the *Curves* adjustment Layer.

16 Finally, the foreground of the image is too dark and featureless. Add a *Curves* adjustment layer above the *Background* layer.

17 Edit the curve to lighten the image.

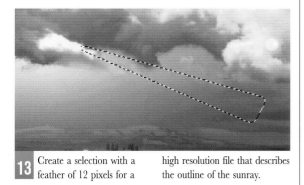

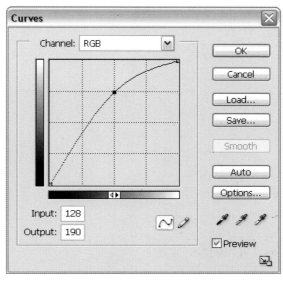

13 Create a selection with a feather of 12 pixels for a high resolution file that describes the outline of the sunray.

14 Drag a *White to Transparent* linear gradient about halfway through the selection, starting from the source of the light, then deselect the selection.

18 We want to lighten only the foreground, so drag a *Black to White* linear gradient on the *Curves* layer mask from the top of the image to about ⁴/₅ of the way down.

15 Repeat the same process for as many sunrays as you wish to create. If necessary, you can adjust the layer *Opacity* to make each sunray more subtle or less uniform.

CREATING LIGHTNING

Lightning must surely be one of the most dramatic phenomena of nature. From a photographic point of view, the sheer spectacle of a lightning storm makes it a highly desirable subject. Although capturing a lightning bolt on a modern camera is not a very difficult task, the finished image may not always match the drama of the original scene. Lightning is not the most cooperative of subjects. The average lightning bolt remains visible for less than a second and gives no warning of its appearance or position in the sky. Timed exposures are the usual method, but are easily prone to becoming overexposed if the ambient light is not favorable. From the point of view of image quality, the argument for creating your own lightning in Photoshop is a compelling one. It is also considerably safer.

Although we can simulate these conditions in Photoshop, a photograph with the right buildup of cloud will go a long way toward helping the illusion in the finished result. Choose an image that would be a likely setting for lightning. It doesn't have to be a stormy, dark image of course.

1 First we need to set up the initial layers. Duplicate the *Background* layer, naming the duplicate *Dark*, and create a new layer called *Lightning*.

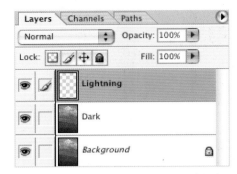

2 With the *Lightning* layer active, make a rectangular selection defining the region the lightning bolt should cover.

3 Fill the selection with a *Black to White* linear gradient at about a 45° angle. Gradients with more contrast, such as the one illustrated, result in lightning streaks that follow a straighter path.

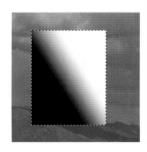

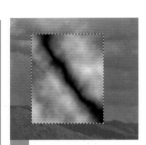

4 Go to *Filter > Render > **Difference Clouds**.*

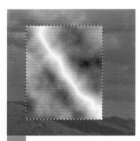

5 The lightning needs to be pale in color, so we actually need a negative version of the current image. Go to *Image > Adjustments > **Invert*** (Ctrl (Cmd) + I) and deselect the selection.

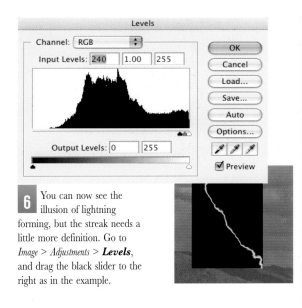

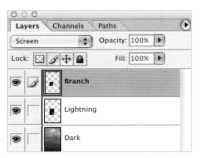

9 Lightning is often seen branching off into more than one streak. Now that the main streak has been created, it becomes very quick to create other sub-branches. Make a rectangular selection of part of the lightning.

6 You can now see the illusion of lightning forming, but the streak needs a little more definition. Go to *Image > Adjustments > **Levels***, and drag the black slider to the right as in the example.

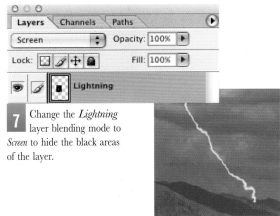

10 Go to *Layer > New > **Layer via Copy*** (Ctrl (Cmd) + J) to copy and paste the selection onto a new layer, and name the layer *Branch*.

7 Change the *Lightning* layer blending mode to *Screen* to hide the black areas of the layer.

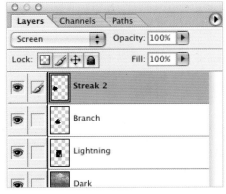

11 Press Ctrl (Cmd) + T to bring up the Transform bounding box and rotate and position the copied branch of lightning as shown.

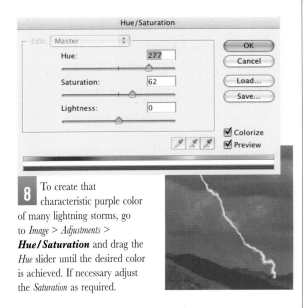

8 To create that characteristic purple color of many lightning storms, go to *Image > Adjustments > **Hue/Saturation*** and drag the *Hue* slider until the desired color is achieved. If necessary adjust the *Saturation* as required.

12 To create another independent lightning streak, duplicate the *Branch* layer and name the duplicate layer *Streak 2*.

13 Go to *Edit > Transform > **Flip Horizontal***. This helps to avoid the appearance of any uniformity between the different streaks. Position the flipped streak somewhere between the base of a cloud and the horizon.

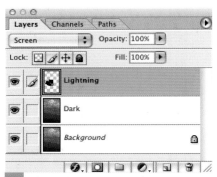

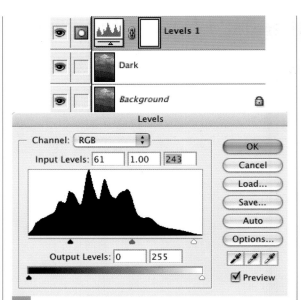

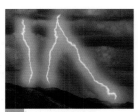

14 As long as you are happy with the final position of all the lightning streaks, you can merge the 3 lightning layers into one. Select the *Streak 2* layer and press Ctrl (Cmd) + E twice. This reduces the file size and gives us less layers to navigate around. You should now have just one *Lightning* layer.

15 Lightning usually appears to taper away, so we need some manual adjustment. Add a layer mask to the *Lightning* layer.

17 A little more overall contrast is required to make the lightning stand out and also to suggest dark, foreboding clouds. Add a *Levels* adjustment layer clipped to the layer called *Dark*, and apply the settings in the illustration.

19 Create a feathered selection with the *Lasso* tool around the perimeter of the lightning. The amount of feather depends on the resolution of your document. I am working on a 300ppi image and have used a 30 pixel feather. For lower resolution files, use a lower pixel feather.

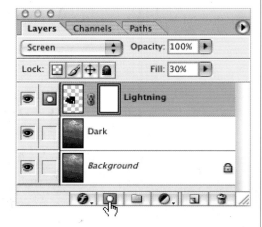

16 Using a small, hard-edged brush with low opacity, paint on the layer mask with black to simulate tapered edges at the ends of the lightning. You could, of course, simply use the *Eraser* tool to do this, but the benefit of the layer mask is that if you remove too much of the lightning by mistake, you can just use white paint to replace it, as the pixels have not been deleted.

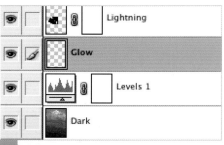

18 The sheer energy generated within a bolt of lightning creates a powerful glow around the core of the lightning streak. To simulate this, make a new layer called *Glow* and position it between the *Lightning* and the *Levels* adjustment layer.

20 Fill the selection with a pale purple color. I'm using R161 G134 B190. Deselect the selection.

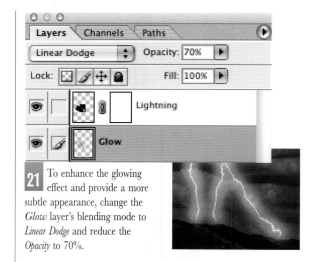

21 To enhance the glowing effect and provide a more subtle appearance, change the *Glow* layer's blending mode to *Linear Dodge* and reduce the *Opacity* to 70%.

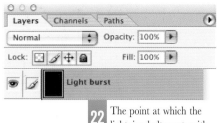

22 The point at which the lightning bolt meets with the base of the cloud sometimes appears as an explosive focal point. This can add greater impact to the final image. Create a black-filled layer at the top of the *Layers* palette called *Light burst*.

25 Position the lens flare at the top of the main lightning bolt.

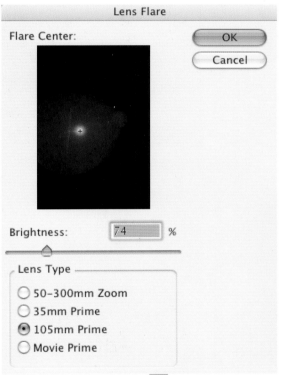

26 The darkened sky performs well as a backdrop to the lightning, but the overall darkness has made the foreground a little flat and featureless. This won't be a problem to fix, though, as we duplicated the *Background* layer right at the beginning. Add a layer mask to the *Dark* layer.

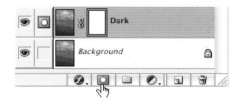

23 Go to *Filter > Render > Lens Flare*, and apply the settings as in the example.

27 Drag a *Black to White* linear gradient on the layer mask from the bottom of the image to about one quarter of the way up. This reveals the lower quarter of the original background image.

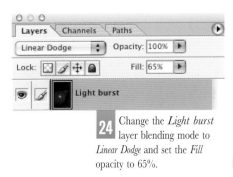

24 Change the *Light burst* layer blending mode to *Linear Dodge* and set the *Fill* opacity to 65%.

28 In the finished image, I have repeated the steps entailed in duplicating, scaling, rotating, and flipping the lightning bolts to achieve an apparently random flash of forked lightning without the need for any new artwork.

CREATING RAINBOWS

1 Create a new layer above the *Background* layer and name it *Rainbow*. We're going to create the rainbow on its own independent layer so we have more control over the final look.

A dding rainbows to your images is one of the easier Photoshop tasks thanks to the versatility of gradients. To make it easier still, Photoshop comes with a preset rainbow gradient ready for you to use straight out of the box. However, to make the rainbow really convincing and to avoid that "clip art" computer filter look, we need to use a little trickery to achieve photographic realism.

Most real rainbows are quite subtle in their appearance. Although the full visible spectrum is contained within the rainbow, the outlying colors are often much less visible than the colors at the center. Additionally, those perfect full semicircle rainbows are best left to fantasy movies.

The image we are going to use is a good candidate for a rainbow: a watery sky with lots of moisture in the air, and the sun is shining.

2 Select the *Gradient* tool in the toolbox, then click the *Gradient picker* drop-down box from the *Options* bar. Unless you have added or removed gradients previously, you will see the default Photoshop gradient set. We need to load another set.

3 Click the pop-up arrow in the top-right corner of the *Gradient picker* and select the *Special Effects* set.

4 Within this set, select the rainbow gradient named *Russell's Rainbow*, and choose the *Radial* option.

5 Make sure the *Rainbow* layer is selected. When the *Gradient* tool is used to apply the rainbow radial gradient, the point at which you first click becomes the center point of the gradient. Click and drag in approximately the same position as shown.

6 Depending on where you clicked and dragged, you should have a rainbow similar to the one shown. If you are not happy with the size or position, just click and drag again until you get the desired placement.

7 This rainbow has "computer generated" stamped all over it. To create some photographic realism, we are going to use a blending mode, which is one of the reasons we created the gradient on its own layer. From the *Layers* palette, make sure the *Rainbow* layer is active, then select *Screen* mode from the blend modes drop-down box.

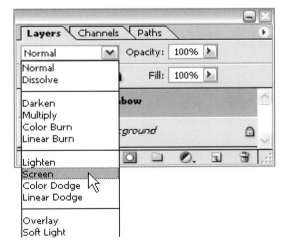

8 Now the effect is much more subtle and the outlying colors less visible, just like real rainbows. To complete the effect, we need to hide the part of the rainbow below the horizon, and at the same time achieve a realistic fading effect because few rainbows maintain full visibility all the way down to ground level. Add a layer mask to the *Rainbow* layer. The quickest way to do this is to click the icon at the bottom of the *Layers* palette.

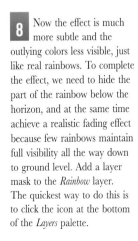

9 First we need to set up the gradient. Select the *Foreground to Background* gradient. You may have to reload the default gradient set if you replaced it with the special effects set. Make sure black is the foreground color and white the background color and use the *Linear* gradient option.

10 We are now going to create the gradient on the layer mask, so check that you have the mask thumbnail active in the *Layers* palette, and not the image thumbnail.

11 Position the cursor on the tree line and drag a short distance as shown.

12 If you are not happy with the degree of fading at the bottom of the rainbow, simply drag with the *Gradient* tool again. Each drag overrides the previous one, so you have complete control.

CREATING A HEAT HAZE

1 The source of heat for a heat haze is often fairly obvious, but there's no harm in emphasizing it to help the image along. The jet exhaust is clearly the source in this case, but we are going to boost it by a small amount.

Desert mirages, and watery, blurred images that dance in the wake of jet aircraft, or at the spout of a boiling kettle—all fall under the general term of "heat haze." This phenomenon is caused by light passing through air of different densities and therefore different refractivity. The heat of the sand in the desert or the exhaust of a jet engine heats up the air in the immediate vicinity, causing it to become less dense than the cooler air around it. Because this heated air is less dense, its refractive index is lowered, causing light to refract or bend as it passes from one density to another. The result is the classic wavy distortion, which we will now re-create near the exhaust outlet of a jet aircraft.

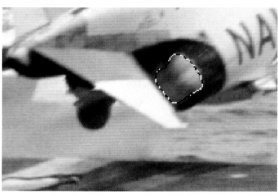

2 Make a feathered selection of the flames. Use a 3 pixel feather for a high resolution file.

3 Press Ctrl (Cmd) + J to copy and paste the selection to a new layer. Name the layer *Exhaust.*

4 Change the layer blend mode to *Linear Dodge*. This provides us with a more vibrant burst of heat and flames.

5 Make a feathered selection of the area to be affected by the haze. Let the selection run over the edge of the aircraft carrier deck, and into the sea. This will enable bits of the deck to appear to distort and dance above the deck itself, just as a real heat haze would do.

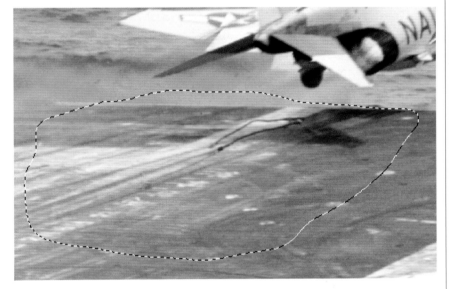

6 Activate the *Background* layer and press Ctrl (Cmd) + J. Once again, the selection is copied to another layer. Name this layer *Heat Haze*.

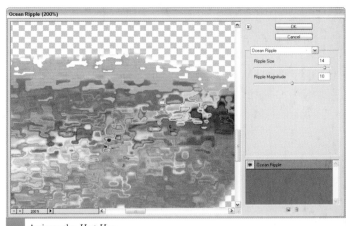

7 Activate the *Heat Haze* layer, then go to *Filter > Distort > **Ocean Ripple***. Apply the settings as pictured.

8 And that's all there is to it. Simple but effective and applicable to any situation where heat is involved.

CREATING FOG

1 Fog has the effect of drinking the color out of a scene, subduing even the most vibrant of colors. To simulate this effect, create a *Hue/Saturation* adjustment layer.

2 Drag the *Saturation* slider to the left to reduce the color intensity.

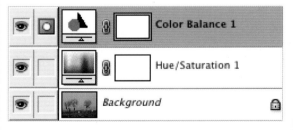

3 Fog is often associated with cooler weather conditions, and a little blue light will help to enforce this idea. Add a *Color Balance* adjustment layer to the *Background*.

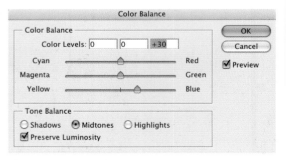

4 Add some blue to the *Midtones* only.

Weather and atmospheric conditions can change what would be a mundane image into a dramatic work of art. The more obvious examples, including lightning, tornadoes, and storms, speak for themselves, but less apocalyptic conditions, such as fog, have a lot of merit of their own. Logically, fog is associated with reduced visibility, and as such may be deemed a photographer's nightmare, but if you are trying to create an atmosphere to inspire a range of feelings from solitude to serenity, then fog is the perfect stage.

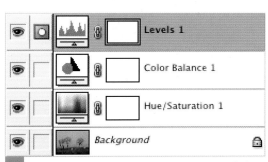

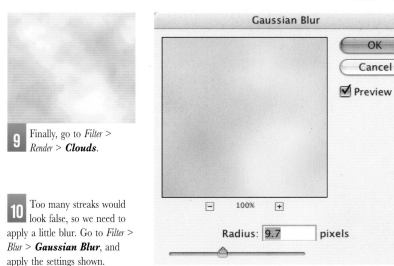

9 Finally, go to *Filter > Render > **Clouds***.

10 Too many streaks would look false, so we need to apply a little blur. Go to *Filter > Blur > **Gaussian Blur***, and apply the settings shown.

5 Definition also suffers from the effects of fog. This is one of those not so common situations when Photoshop can actually be used to decrease contrast rather than increase it. Add a *Levels* adjustment layer.

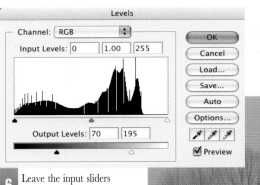

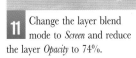

6 Leave the input sliders as they are, but bring the output sliders closer together to reduce contrast.

11 Change the layer blend mode to *Screen* and reduce the layer *Opacity* to 74%.

12 The *Clouds* filter is a little too patchy to be realistic, so we need to smooth it out without the scene becoming too uniform and flat. With the *Fog* layer active, go to *Filter > Artistic > **Neon Glow***. Apply the settings displayed, choosing a pale blue as the color.

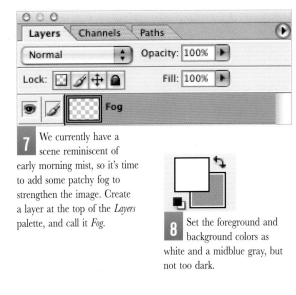

7 We currently have a scene reminiscent of early morning mist, so it's time to add some patchy fog to strengthen the image. Create a layer at the top of the *Layers* palette, and call it *Fog*.

8 Set the foreground and background colors as white and a midblue gray, but not too dark.

Shadows and Projections

CREATING DROP SHADOWS

The ubiquitous drop shadow has been around longer than many would imagine. Today it is associated with the computer graphics revolution and its seemingly obligatory use on titles in magazines and on webpages. However, watch the credits roll on old black-and-white movies from the 1930's and you'll often see the use of drop shadows on white text. This is what it was originally meant for, of course, to provide some contrast and aid legibility. Today it plays the same role, although its overuse has led it in some cases to be regarded as kitsch. Nevertheless, used correctly it provides a valuable asset to the photographer, artist, or designer as a means of emphasizing the subject.

1 The object that will cast the shadow needs to be isolated on its own layer. Make a selection of the key.

2 Press Ctrl (Cmd) + J to copy and paste the selection to a new layer.

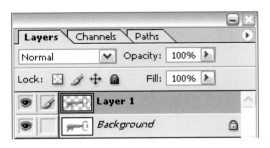

3 Click the *Layer Styles* icon at the bottom of the *Layers* palette and select *Drop Shadow*.

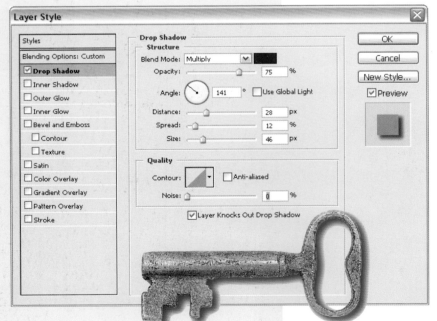

4 The settings in the dialog box that opens, enable you to edit the style of the shadow to your taste. *Blend Mode* and *Opacity* have the same effect as their counterparts in the *Layers* palette itself. *Angle* defines the direction of the light source. Tick the *Use Global Light* box to configure all styles to use the same direction for the light source. This will be applied to any styles applied where the check box is enabled. *Distance* is the offset for the shadow. This raises the apparent height of the object casting the shadow. *Spread* enlarges the mask that creates the shadow before it is blurred. This results in a larger, heavier shadow area. *Size* determines the final size of the shadow, which also softens the shadow as higher values are applied.

5 While the dialog box is open, it is possible to use the *Distance* setting to move the shadow away form the object, and also to click and drag the shadow in the image window itself.

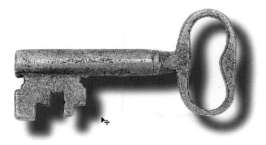

KNOCKING OUT DROP SHADOWS

The need to "knock out," or delete, a drop shadow is an important requirement where the object casting the shadow is transparent, such as in the case of colored glass, ice, and water drops. The Photoshop *Layer Style* dialog box provides a simple option to achieve this.

In this example, the colored glass is taken from another image and is on the top layer. It is not transparent and therefore doesn't reveal the girl on the bottom layer.

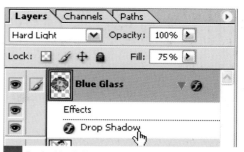

3 By double-clicking the *Drop Shadow* sublayer in the *Layers* palette, I can gain access to all the settings I previously applied.

4 At the bottom of the dialog box, tick the box labeled *Layer Knocks Out Drop Shadow*. This removes the shadow from any area of the layer containing pixels.

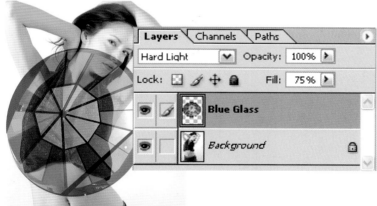

1 To make the glass transparent, I'm going to change the *Blue glass* layer's blending mode to *Hard Light* and reduce the *Fill* opacity to 75%. It's important to change the *Fill* opacity level and not the *Layer* opacity level because I want to reduce the opacity of the blue glass only, not the shadow.

2 I'll now add a drop shadow, using layer styles in the same way as with the key previously. The result gives a good impression of depth between the glass and the girl, but the shadow is now partially obscuring the girl and we've lost a lot of the transparency effect.

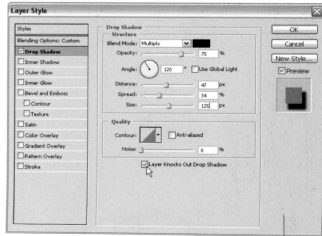

CREATING CAST SHADOWS

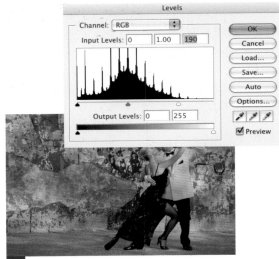

1 To emphasize the shadow, we are going to increase the level of sunlight, which will provide a better backdrop and more convincing final result. Add a *Levels* adjustment layer to the *Background* layer and apply the setting shown. It is better to use an adjustment layer in this instance, as we can change the degree of light later if necessary within the context of the finished shadow.

Although Photoshop makes the creation of drop shadows very easy, the automated process does have its limitations. In the example we are going to work through, a drop shadow in the traditional sense would be of little use. The dancers are some distance from the wall, so the shadow would appear on the ground first with just the tops of the dancers being cast onto the wall. Because of the distance involved, some distortion of the shadow would be apparent and the shadow would also bend where it meets the base of the wall and changes direction.

So we'll dispense with the automated method and work through a manual technique that will produce a perfectly photographic cast shadow.

2 Make a selection of the dancers, and feather the selection by 10 pixels if you are using a high resolution file. Lower resolutions will need a lower feather setting. Save the selection when finished.

3 Create a new layer, and call it *Shadow bottom*.

4 Fill the selection with a midgray. I am using R110 G109 B106.

5 Change the layer blending mode to *Multiply* and reduce the *Opacity* to 75%.

6 Deselect the current selection and go to *Edit > Transform > **Distort***. Drag the corner handles of the bounding box to achieve the shape pictured. The corner handles have been highlighted with red dots to aid in their visibility. Press Enter (Return) to confirm.

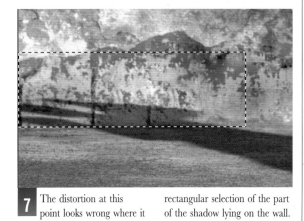

7 The distortion at this point looks wrong where it meets the wall. Make a rectangular selection of the part of the shadow lying on the wall.

8 Press Backspace to remove this part of the shadow.

9 Create a new layer called *Shadow top*.

10 Load the saved, feathered selection and fill it with the same gray as used previously.

11 Deselect and make a rectangular selection of the bottom half of the shadow.

12 Press Backspace to remove this half of the shadow.

13 Deselect, then drag the remaining shadow over to the wall so it sits on top of the distorted bottom half.

14 Change the layer blend mode to *Multiply* and reduce the *Opacity* to 75%.

CREATING SHADOWS FROM OBJECTS

Shadows can perform a role as the main subject or a supporting prop with equal success. In fact, some of the more moody, atmospheric images rely heavily on the interaction of shadows with the main theme. Shadows tend to be thought of as a background element, providing contrast and enabling the main subject to leap off the page or screen. In fact, considering a shadow as a foreground element can do much to raise the status of what might be an ordinary image. All you need is an image to cast the shadow and the simple techniques covered in the next few steps.

1 The intensity of a shadow is defined by the light source trained upon the object that casts it. This light source will also be evident in the area surrounding the shadow. It is therefore important that images

being used for the creation of false shadows should possess a degree of light that accurately matches the shadow. At times, it may be necessary to manufacture some additional light, but in the case of the

image we are going to use, the light is more than adequate. The object that will cast the shadow is the image of a palm. Make a selection of the palm.

2 Drag the selection onto the image of the girl.

3 Flip the palm vertically and rotate it so that it lies across the girl's face from left to right.

4 Press Ctrl (Cmd) and click the *Palm* layer to load its selection, then hide the visibility of the layer.

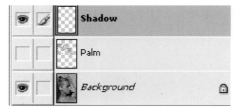

5 Create a new layer called *Shadow*.

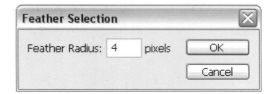

6 Feather the selection by 4 pixels for a high resolution image.

7 Fill the selection with 50% gray and deselect.

8 Change the layer blend mode to *Multiply* to see through the shadow.

9 The intensity of the shadow works well against the ambient light, but what gives the game away is the fact that we can still see the shadow on the blue water which is some distance away. A real shadow wouldn't be cast in this way onto the background, so we need to get rid of this element. Hide the *Shadow* layer.

10 Make a selection of the blue water. The *Magic Wand* tool with *Contiguous* switched off works well.

11 Activate the *Shadow* layer.

12 Press Backspace to remove the elements of the shadow lying on the water.

CASTING LIGHT AND SHADOW THROUGH VENETIAN BLINDS

1 First we need to make a grayscale file to be used as a displacement map. We are using a method that helps preserve the brightness of the image and so provides a better basis for the grayscale map. Duplicate the file and convert the duplicate to *Lab Color* mode.

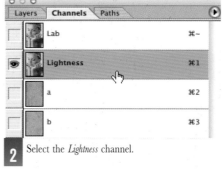

2 Select the *Lightness* channel.

The play of light and shadow on a subject can set the scene for some highly atmospheric imagery. From the point of view of realism, cast light and shadows bend and flow around the object they fall upon. As we are working in a 2-D environment in Photoshop, it may seem as if 3-D realism is beyond us, and yet we have a powerful tool at our disposal in the form of displacement maps. These highly versatile methods enable us to create photographic realism, even to the extent of wrapping light and shadows around the contours of an object.

A perfect subject to demonstrate this will be the light and shadow cast from window blinds onto a girl's face.

Duplicate Channel

Duplicate: Lightness
As: Alpha 1

Destination
Document: New
Name: Displace
☐ Invert

OK
Cancel

3 Duplicate the *Lightness* channel as a new grayscale document called *Displace*.

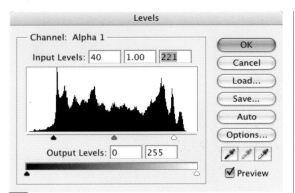

4 We now have 3 documents: the original RGB image, the duplicate Lab image, and a grayscale image. Close the Lab image, as we no longer need it. Its only purpose was to provide the *Lightness* channel as the basis for the grayscale document. Working in the grayscale document, go to *Image > Adjustments > **Levels*** to create a little more contrast. This will assist in bending the blinds around the contours of the girl's face and hands.

6 Because the girl is some distance from the wall behind her, any single shadows being cast, would appear to break up abruptly as the shadow falls away from her face onto the wall. This effect can be achieved by making the wall pure white in color, which contrasts strongly with the grays and blacks on the girl, thus resulting in more erratic distortion. This, incidentally, is just the effect we have taken great care to avoid on the soft contours of the girl's face. Make a selection of the wall and fill it with white.

5 Although a higher degree of light and dark areas is desirable, it is important that there are no sharp, distinctive lines between black and white. This can result in an unrealistic and fragmented warping of the image rather than the soft bending of light and shadow that we are trying to achieve. Go to *Filter > Blur > **Gaussian Blur***, and apply a *Radius* of 7.0.

8 Now add a *Color Balance* adjustment layer and increase the amount of yellow in the *Shadows*, *Midtones*, and *Highlights*. Do the same with the amount of red, but to a much lesser degree.

7 Save the *displace* document to update the changes and then close it. We now have just the original RGB document open. The RGB document's colors need warming up, and a little more contrast to suggest a flood of sunlight being cast onto the girl's face. Add a *Levels* adjustment layer to increase contrast.

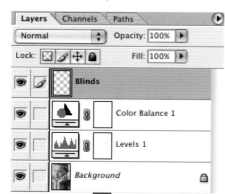

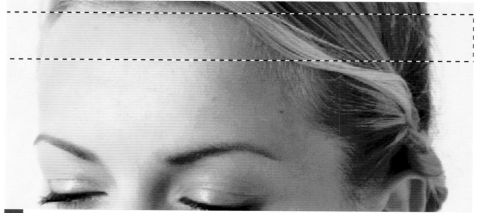

9 Now to create the shadow of the blinds: create a layer called *Blinds* at the top of the *Layers* palette.

10 Create a rectangular feathered selection outlining what will be one strip of the blind. For a high resolution file, use about 9 pixels for the feather.

11 Fill the selection with 50% gray and deselect.

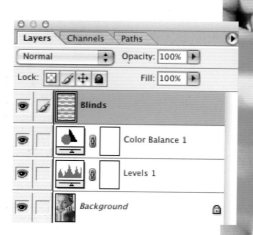

12 Duplicate the gray strip so that multiple strips fill the image window. All the gray strips should be on one layer.

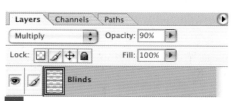

13 Now for the displacement map that will bend the shadow around the girl: with the *Blinds* layer selected go to *Filter > Distort > Displace*. Enter the settings as shown. We want to displace the image in the vertical plane only, hence the 0% setting for the *Horizontal Scale* option. Higher settings result in greater distortion.

14 After clicking *OK*, you will be presented with a dialog box prompting you to choose a displacement map. Choose the grayscale displacement map you saved earlier.

16 Finally, change the *Blinds* layer blend mode to *Multiply*, and reduce the *Opacity* to 90% to see the finished result. Notice how the shadow falling on the wall behind the girl is sufficiently offset to give a good impression of distance.

15 The displacement is clearly visible. Due to the blur we applied to soften the transition between white and black, the gray strips have gently molded themselves around the contours of the girl's face, hands, and arms. Although a certain amount of experimentation may be necessary according to the image, the basic principles remain the same and provide you with a great degree of control over the finished effect.

CAST LIGHT FROM WINDOWS

1 You can create your own design to act as a cast light object, but if you already have an image, then that too can be used with equal success. I am going to use the strong image of an arch window for a very bold effect. Make a rectangular selection of the area to be used. The method we are going to use for this effect will result in the arch window being tiled, so it does not matter if the window is much smaller than the image we are going to apply it to as we will have the ability to scale it later.

A light source can often have a more dramatic effect on a scene if it is constrained by some kind of aperture. In this way, it becomes similar to a stencil, providing a predefined shape which can then be projected onto the scene. Indeed, the shape of the projected light can itself be the focus of the image, becoming both the light source and the subject. But by combining such a light source with some existing subject matter, you can easily transform even the most mundane photograph into a work of artistic merit.

2 Light being projected onto another surface rarely has a sharp defined edge, so we need to soften the edges of the window to keep the effect realistic. Go to *Filter > Blur > **Gaussian Blur*** and apply a *Radius* of 2.0.

3 With the selection still active, go to *Edit > **Define Pattern***. Name the pattern *Arch* and click *OK*. This pattern will now be available for us to use with other images.

4 The image I am using on which to cast the light is a little darker than a well-balanced photograph would normally be. It also has quite well saturated colors. Both of these factors will compliment the finished result.

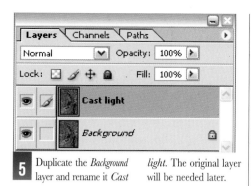

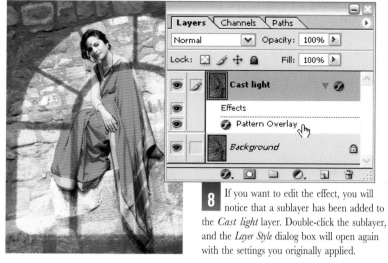

5 Duplicate the *Background* layer and rename it *Cast light*. The original layer will be needed later.

8 If you want to edit the effect, you will notice that a sublayer has been added to the *Cast light* layer. Double-click the sublayer, and the *Layer Style* dialog box will open again with the settings you originally applied.

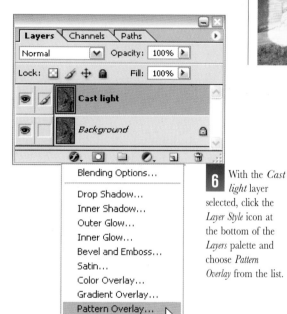

6 With the *Cast light* layer selected, click the *Layer Style* icon at the bottom of the *Layers* palette and choose *Pattern Overlay* from the list.

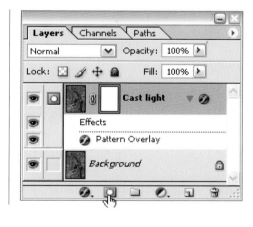

9 If you are happy with the result, there is nothing more to do, but if you are looking for a slightly less perfect window projection, then one more finishing touch will give it the right feel. Add a layer mask to the *Cast light* layer.

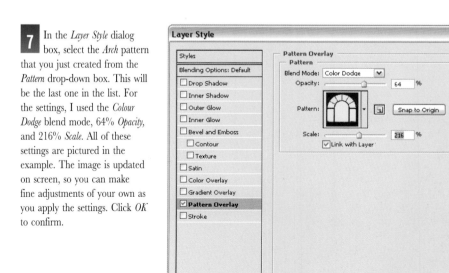

7 In the *Layer Style* dialog box, select the *Arch* pattern that you just created from the *Pattern* drop-down box. This will be the last one in the list. For the settings, I used the *Colour Dodge* blend mode, 64% *Opacity*, and 216% *Scale*. All of these settings are pictured in the example. The image is updated on screen, so you can make fine adjustments of your own as you apply the settings. Click *OK* to confirm.

10 Set up the *Gradient* tool with the *Black to White* linear gradient, and drag a short distance in the bottom-left corner of the image similar to the arrow in the example. Make sure you have the mask thumbnail selected before you drag the gradient. The final effect is a gradual fading away of the cast light, resulting in a less uniform, more realistic finish. This is achieved by way of the layer mask, which enables us to hide the corner of the *Cast light* layer, revealing the original *Background* layer underneath.

CREATING LIGHT CAST THROUGH STAINED GLASS WINDOWS

The beauty of a stained glass window is truly realized when it is flooded with strong directional light. Equally beautiful and yet not so obvious is the light that is cast from the window and the resulting projected image onto a nearby surface. In the right conditions, you have something akin to the world's largest slide projector. The right conditions, however, are not so easy to come by in terms of photographing such a scene. Such majestic windows are rarely positioned in locations with a perfect floor or wall space to act as a projecting screen. Equally rare is the chance of catching that fleeting moment when the sun's position is just right to create the beam of light without a group of tourists getting in the viewfinder.

So, we'll dispense with trying to capture the real thing on location and use Photoshop to make our own.

1 Make a selection of the stained glass window, using the *Polygon Lasso* tool and following the perspective of the window as in the example.

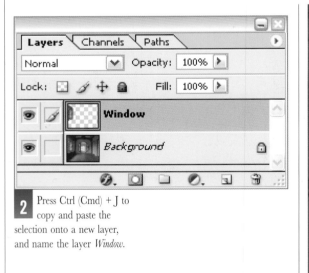

2 Press Ctrl (Cmd) + J to copy and paste the selection onto a new layer, and name the layer *Window*.

3 Go to *Edit > Transform > **Flip Vertical**.* This turns our duplicated window upside down.

4 Go to *Edit > Transform > Rotate 90° CCW*, and position the artwork on the floor as in the example.

5 Flipping the selection has created a perspective problem, but this is easily solved. Go to *Edit > Transform > Distort*. Drag the bottom-left handle horizontally to the left. Hold the Shift key down to help you do this as you drag. Keep dragging until you reach the line between the floor tiles. This gives you a perfect guide to mimic the actual perspective. Press the Enter (Return) key to confirm the distortion.

6 It currently looks a bit more like a rug than projected light, so to give it more of an airy feel, change the layer blending mode to *Screen*.

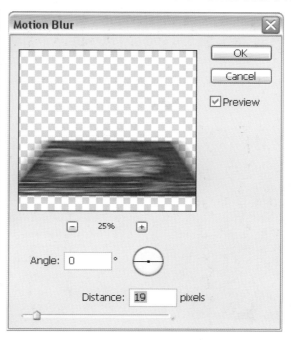

7 The window itself is not a perfect optical device as a projector lens would be, so we would expect to see a vague image rather than a crisp rendition of the window. Additionally because of the relationship between the angles of the light source, the window, and the floor onto which the light is projected, there should also be a stretched, distorted effect. To create this, click on *Filter > Blur > Motion Blur*, and set the *Angle* to 0 and the *Distance* to 19. I'm working on a high resolution document, but if you are working on lower resolution files, then you will need to reduce the *Distance* setting accordingly to achieve a similar look.

8 To create a really dynamic, ethereal feel, we are going to produce the beam of light being cast through the window onto the floor. First create a new layer called *Beam* and set the layer *Opacity* to 60%.

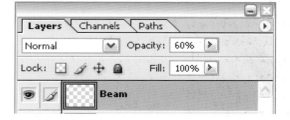

9 Using the *Polygon Lasso* tool, create the perimeter of the light beam from the window to the floor as in the example. Use a feather of 10, but lower if you are working with low resolution files.

10 Set up the *Gradient* tool to use the *Foreground to Transparent* linear option, making sure that white is the foreground color.

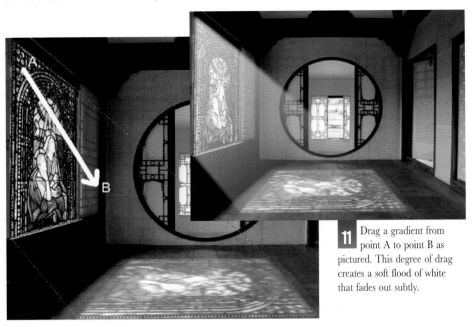

11 Drag a gradient from point A to point B as pictured. This degree of drag creates a soft flood of white that fades out subtly.

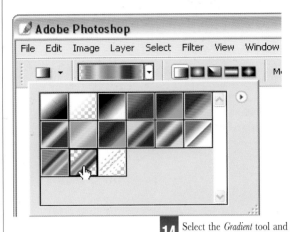

14 Select the *Gradient* tool and choose the *Transparent Rainbow* linear gradient option. This gradient is part of the default gradient set.

12 It should be remembered that the window has colored glass, and so light being transmitted through it would be expected to carry a hint of the colors. Create a new layer called *Color Beam* and set the *Opacity* to 25%, positioning the layer at the top of the *Layers* palette.

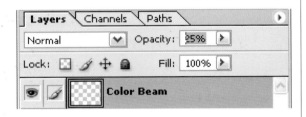

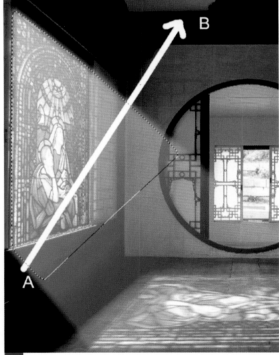

15 Drag the gradient from point A to point B as shown. The idea is to create the suggestion of colored light only.

13 Hold down the Ctrl (Cmd) key and click the *Beam* layer in the *Layers* palette. This loads the layer as a selection, which we will use reuse rather than creating a new one.

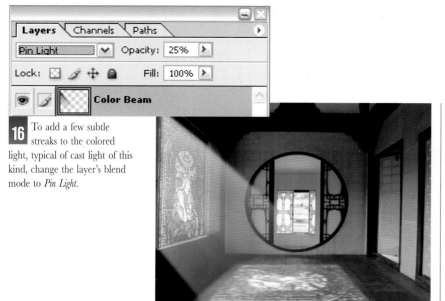

16 To add a few subtle streaks to the colored light, typical of cast light of this kind, change the layer's blend mode to *Pin Light*.

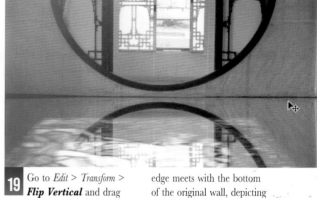

19 Go to *Edit > Transform > Flip Vertical* and drag the flipped artwork so its top edge meets with the bottom of the original wall, depicting a reflection in the floor.

17 Finally, a highly polished floor would really strengthen the illusion of the window being projected onto the floor. We will achieve this by creating a subtle reflection of the back wall. Make a rectangular selection of part of the rear wall on the background layer, as shown.

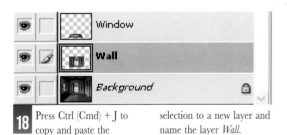

18 Press Ctrl (Cmd) + J to copy and paste the selection to a new layer and name the layer *Wall*.

20 Finally change the layer *Opacity* to 40% for the finished effect.

REFLECTIONS

CREATING REFLECTIONS IN WATER

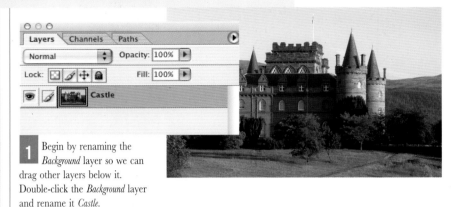

1 Begin by renaming the *Background* layer so we can drag other layers below it. Double-click the *Background* layer and rename it *Castle*.

Reflections in water have their own characteristics quite distinct from the perfect image reflected in a mirror. The calmer the body of water, the greater its ability to reflect an image, so a reflection in a smooth lake with no currents on a fine day would not be a very difficult task for Photoshop. At the other extreme, a stormy, turbulent sea would produce very little in the way of reflection. Complications set in when we start thinking about a body of water somewhere in between these two extremes. It's this in-between stage that accounts for most of the reflected water surfaces which we encounter in everyday life, whether it is a puddle in the street, the rippled surface of a lake, or water running into a bath. Add to this mixture the ambient light, the sky conditions, and what lies at the bottom of the water, and suddenly we have a bit more work on our hands than a simple flip vertical command.

If you have an image with a body of water already in place, things are much easier, but we are going to do something much more demanding and far more satisfying by creating the water as well.

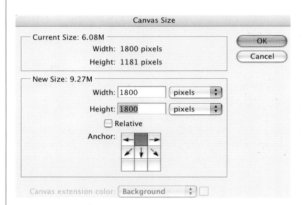

2 The canvas needs to be increased to accommodate the false reflection. To do this, go to *Image* > **Canvas Size**. The amount of canvas you add, will depend upon how much reflection you would like to see. I am adding about half of the original document height to make the new total image height 1800 pixels.

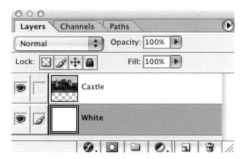

3 Create another white-filled layer that sits below the *Castle* layer.

4 Make a rectangular selection from the top of the document to just below the bottom of the castle. Try to line up with an element that should look natural as the starting point of the water, such as where the grass begins. My selection height is 970 pixels, which should convincingly simulate the division between the grassy bank and the water.

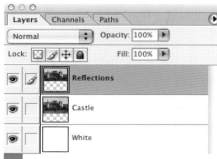

5 Now we need to copy and paste the selected area onto a new layer. Press Ctrl (Cmd) + J and name this new layer *Reflections*.

6 Ctrl (Cmd) click the *Reflections* layer in the *Layers* palette to load its selection and then inverse it (Ctrl (Cmd) + Shift + I).

7 Now activate the *Castle* layer and hit the Backspace key. This action trims away the lower portion of the *Castle* layer, which will not be needed, and enables the reflected layer to butt up to it perfectly. It also means we can reduce the opacity of the *Reflections* layer later without any unwanted elements showing through.

8 Activate the *Reflections* layer, then go to *Edit > Transform > **Flip Vertical***. Drag the reflected image to the bottom half of the document, keeping the Shift key pressed as you drag. This keeps the dragging movement perfectly vertical. Position the image so the edges meet in the center. It already looks quite convincing, but a little too perfect. One of the first casualties of water-reflected images is the depth of color. We need to desaturate the overall color of the reflection a little to add some authenticity.

9 Use *Image > Adjustments > **Hue/Saturation***. Drag the *Hue* slider to the left to reduce the saturation equally across the whole layer. I'm using a value of –40.

10 To reduce the strength of the reflection a little more, reduce the *Reflections* layer's *Opacity* to 80%

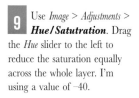

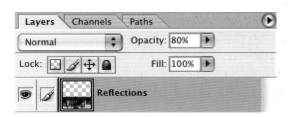

11 Now for some surface distortion to break up the uniformity: go to *Filter > Distort > **Ocean Ripple***. Some experimentation is required here. You can create everything from a gentle breeze over the water to a prelude to a hurricane. For this image, I have used fairly modest settings to create just a little surface disturbance.

12 Although the *Ocean Ripple* filter is good for appearing to break the surface tension of water, it doesn't really convey the impression of the rhythmic pattern of undulating ripples as the wind strokes the surface. For more convincing realism, we can use any grayscale image to simulate the current or ripple on the surface, but if you already have some rippled water in an existing image, why not use that and save yourself the tedium of creating a ripple pattern? This image of a canoe has a good ripple texture that will work well as a ready-made pattern for our reflection.

14 Make a feathered rectangular selection covering the lower ³/₄ of the *Reflections* layer. The amount of feather you use, will depend upon the resolution of your document. The higher the resolution, the higher the feather setting needs to be. I am working on a 300ppi image, so I have used a feather of 20 pixels.

15 Press Ctrl (Cmd) +J to copy and paste the selected area onto a new layer. Name the layer *Ripples* and reduce the layer *Opacity* to 82%.

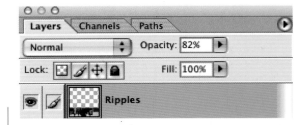

13 Make a rectangular selection of some of the ripples, then go to *Edit > Define Pattern*. Give the pattern a name and click *OK*. The pattern you have just made will be used as a pattern overlay in a moment, but before it is applied, some thought needs to be given to the characteristics of the reflection. In a body of water of this size, the reflection would typically be stronger closer to the bank where the water meets the land. Additionally, the ripples would appear to be less distinct as they travel farther away from the eye until the water appears almost flat. With this in mind, it will be more realistic if the pattern overlay is applied to only a selection of the water, leaving the water farthest from the eye unaffected.

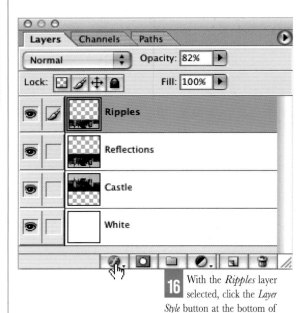

16 With the *Ripples* layer selected, click the *Layer Style* button at the bottom of the *Layers* palette, and select *Pattern Overlay*.

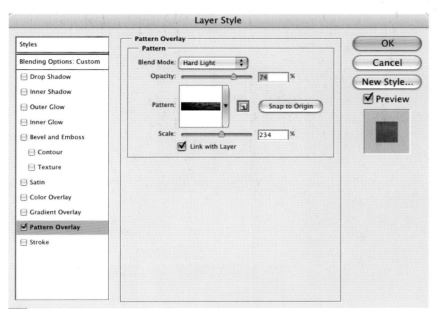

17 Select the last pattern from the *Pattern* drop-down box—this is the one you have just created. Use *Hard Light* as the blend mode, set to 74%

Opacity and 234% *Scale*. Finally, click the *Snap to Origin* button. This positions the pattern in the top-left corner of the image. All these settings are displayed in

the accompanying image. You may want to tweak these settings based on the images you are using and the depth of effect you are trying to achieve.

20 Use the *Magic Wand* tool to select the sky. It's quite uniform, so will be easy to select.

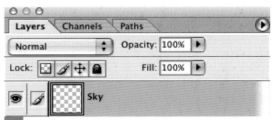

21 Make a new layer called *Sky* and position it at the top of the *Layers* palette.

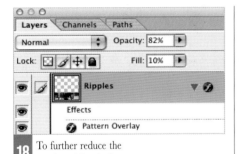

18 To further reduce the opacity of the pixels on the layer, strengthening the reflection effect but keeping the full opacity of the overlaid pattern, drag the *Fill* opacity slider to 10%. The only problem we are left with is the fact that the overriding color of the water should be dominated by the color of the sky. As we manufactured the water, there is a clear mismatch. Luckily, the sky is a little insipid anyway, so we are going to make a moodier sky color that would in real life inspire the darker color of the water.

19 Use the *Eyedropper* tool to sample a couple of blues from the water, one for foreground and one for background color. Use a deep blue and a pale blue. If you can't sample a blue that is pale enough, you can always manually adjust it to make it lighter.

22 Go to *Filter > Render > Clouds*. If the effect is too strong, press Shift + Ctrl (Cmd) + F to fade back the effect to the desired level.

CREATING METAL REFLECTIONS

Although the chrome element of the example image is highly reflective, the black bodywork isn't contributing greatly to the image. I really want to create a lustrous feel, with the black metal depicting an almost glasslike quality. We are going to create a false reflection that will simulate some distant hills with a sharp transition of light above the horizon.

1 Create a path with the *Pen* tool, as illustrated. You could alternatively use the *Lasso* selection tool, but the *Pen* will create smoother curves, and that is important for the effect we are trying to achieve.

2 Convert the path to a selection by pressing Ctrl (Cmd) + Enter (Return).

Far from being a standardized material, metal can possess a wide range of properties, each distinctive in the kind of reflection it displays. All of these properties can be simulated in Photoshop, from matte, dull surfaces to highly finished chrome. Car advertisements, in particular, are good examples of how a mundane metal shape can be made to look exotic and sophisticated by good use of light and reflection.

The environment in which metal is photographed is therefore critical, but conditions may not always be perfect for your particular project. This needn't necessarily be a problem, however, as some relatively simple techniques can completely transform your image.

3 Create a new layer called *Gradient.*

4 Drag a *White to Transparent* linear gradient as directed by the arrow, then deselect.

5 A *White to Transparent* gradient creates just the lustrous effect I was looking for, but pure black can add

an equally glossy finish. Create another path with the *Pen* tool, converting it to a selection as before.

6 Create a new layer called *Black* and fill the selection with pure black.

7 The black bodywork now has a smooth glassy finish, but to add some real impact we need some additional specular highlights reflecting imaginary points of light in the surrounding environment. Select the *Airbrush* tool and apply the settings as in the example. You will have to use a smaller brush size if you are working on a low resolution file.

10 From within this brush set, select the brush called *Crosshatch 4* and increase the size to 125 pixels for a high resolution file.

11 On new layer called *Sparkles*, click once with the *Brush* tool (not the *Airbrush*) over the center of one of the airbrushed highlights.

12 For a multisided sparkle, use the brush called *Starburst Large* from within the same brush set.

8 On a new layer called *Highlights*, apply bursts of white paint to some chrome areas, pressing the mouse button for half a second. We need only a subtle, soft circle of white. For the most dramatic effect, apply the airbrush to areas of the chrome that are dark or midtoned.

9 For that just polished feel, we are going to add a few sparkles that emanate from the center of some of the airbrushed highlights. From the *Brushes* palette, load the brush set called *Assorted Brushes*.

13 Here's the final image. You'll need to make a judgement on how many sparkles cross the boundary of good taste.

CREATING REFLECTIONS IN CURVED GLASS

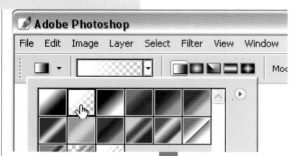

3 Select the *Gradient* tool and choose the *Foreground to Transparent* gradient using the linear gradient mode with white as the foreground color.

Some of the most attractive forms of glass reflections can be found in curved glass. Objects such as wine glasses, bottles, and bowls make perfect candidates for creating elegant reflected distortions of the surrounding environment. In the example of the rounded wine glass that we are going to work on, the glass itself is composed of a number of different surfaces, each acting as a separate entity, unlike a flat piece of glass such as a window. The bowl of the glass, the stem, and the base will all reflect the environment in their own unique way, molding the surrounding objects to conform to their own particular curves.

The cylindrical shape of the glass means that an area equal to approximately 180° is available for reflections from the viewer's standpoint. This offers the potential for multiple light sources to be reflected, often stemming from more than one window in different parts of the room.

Although the permutations are many and varied, Photoshop enables you to incorporate all these real world elements in photorealistic and controlled way.

1 We'll decide first of all that our room has three windows, two plain with glass and one colored glass. Begin by making a selection describing the first reflected shape. Although you can use the *Lasso* tool, the *Pen* tool will give you smoother curves and the smoothness is critical for the effect.

4 With the *Left reflect* layer active, drag a gradient through the selection from top to bottom. The white color should gradually fade out toward the bottom of the glass. If the effect isn't achieved first time, undo it and drag the gradient again. Deselect the selection (Ctrl (Cmd) + D).

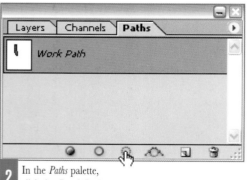

2 In the *Paths* palette, click the *Load Path as Selection* icon to convert the path to a selection. Make a new layer and name it *Left reflect*.

5 For the colored glass reflection, we are going to use an actual image of an ornate window. Make a selection of just the window portion of the image.

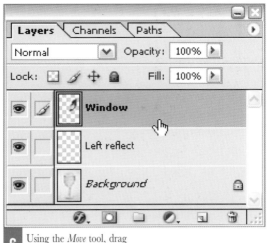

6 Using the *Move* tool, drag the selected artwork into the wine glass image, giving the automatically created layer the name *Window*.

7 Go to *Filter > Distort > **Polar Coordinates***, and choose the *Rectangular to Polar* option.

8 Position the distorted artwork over the bottom right of the glass and create a path defining the final reflected shape.

9 Load the path as a selection as you did in step 2. Activate the *Background* layer and press Ctrl (Cmd) + J. This copies and pastes part of the *Background* layer based on the selection onto a new layer.

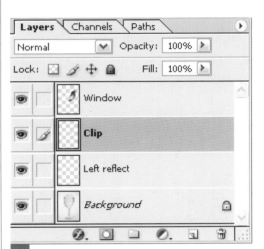

10 Name the newly created layer *Clip* and position it below the *Window* layer. This layer will be used as the basis for a clipping group combining it with the *Window* layer.

11 Activate the *Window* layer and go to *Layer > **Create Clipping Mask*** to make the clipping group.

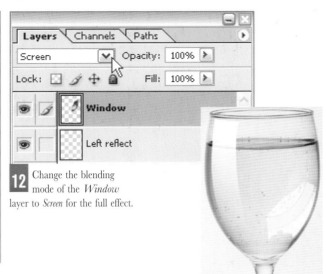

12 Change the blending mode of the *Window* layer to *Screen* for the full effect.

13 For the third and last window reflection, we need to repeat the process from step 1. Create a path toward the top of the glass.

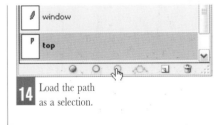

14 Load the path as a selection.

15 Create a new layer named *Top reflect* positioned at the top of the *Layers* palette. Using the *Gradient* tool and the same *White to Transparent* gradient, drag through the selected area at a 45° angle from top-left to bottom-right. This achieves a realistic fall-off of light as the glass curves away from the viewer.

CREATING REFLECTIONS IN SUNGLASSES

It's one of the all-time great movie and photographic clichés—the world as viewed through the eyes of another person, witnessed through a reflection in the darkened lenses of their sunglasses. The creative possibilities are endless, ranging from a startling juxtaposition to the recreation of a real scene.

Of course, to avoid the finished image looking like a couple of pictures stuck on top of the sunglasses, there are a number of factors to take into account, including curvature of the lens, reflection properties, light, shadow, and parallax, all of which will be considered as we work through the next steps.

1 Make a selection of the sunglass lens on the right of the image.

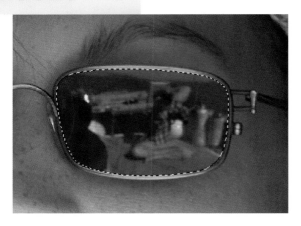

2 Create a new layer called *Right lens*.

3 Fill the selection with white and deselect.

4 Drag the palm tree image into the sunglasses image and name the layer *Palm tree*.

5 We are going to use the white shape on the *Right lens* layer as a mask for the image of the palm tree. This combination, known as a clipping mask or group, is ideal for the kind of illusion we are creating. One of its great benefits is the fact that it enables you to reposition one image within the other to get the right placement. With the *Palm tree* layer active, go to *Layer > Create Clipping Mask*.

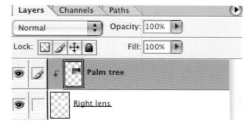

6 If necessary, you can reposition the image within the sunglasses shape so the palm tree is fully visible.

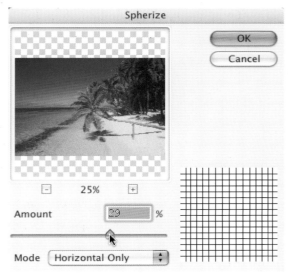

7 The lens is fairly flat, but is slightly convex in the horizontal plane. We need to distort the image accordingly to reflect this. With the *Palm tree* layer still selected, go to *Filter > Distort > Spherize*. Set the mode to *Horizontal only* and the *Amount* to 29%.

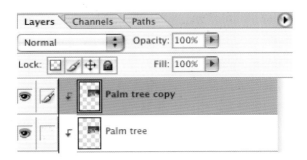

8 If you wanted a mirror type lens, we could leave it at that, but we'll make the lens a more conventional dark glass. Duplicate the *Palm tree* layer.

9 Change the duplicated layer blend mode to *Multiply*. You can now control the precise degree of lightness of the lens by editing the layer's opacity.

10 We need to emphasize the convex shape of the lens a little more and also strengthen the illusion of reflection. Press Ctrl (Cmd) and click the *Right lens* layer to load its selection.

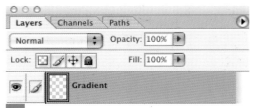

11 Create a new layer called *Gradient* positioned at the top of the *Layers* palette.

12 Drag a *White to Transparent* linear gradient diagonally from the top-left corner of the lens to about one quarter of the way through the selection.

13 Repeat the whole process for the other lens. Because the two lenses are viewing the scene from a slightly different angle, parallax should be visible in the lenses. Parallax is the apparent different position of objects when viewed from different angles, such as when viewing a scene through a compact camera. I have taken this into account and altered the position of the palm tree accordingly in the left lens. The left lens is also under the shade of the brim of the hat, which would prevent a bright highlight striking the top corner as with the right lens. Therefore I have compensated by

substituting the white gradient used on the first lens with a *Black to Transparent* gradient.

REMOVING UNWANTED REFLECTIONS

Removing reflections is as necessary a part of digital image manipulation as adding reflections can be. Before a scene has been photographed, the use of a polarizing filter is traditionally used to aid the removal of unwanted reflections, but you are presented with a different problem if the photograph has already been taken. So we are going to look at some techniques for eliminating reflections after the event.

1 This otherwise striking close-up image is ruined by the unwanted reflection of people nearby. We'll start by tackling the man's reflection on the wheel arch. Select the *Patch* tool, making sure the *Source* option is selected from the *Tool Options* bar.

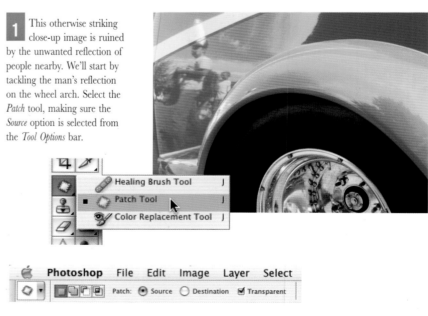

2 Drag around the area to be removed.

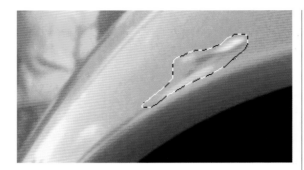

3 Drag the selection to a nearby area from where you want to copy pixels, then release the mouse.

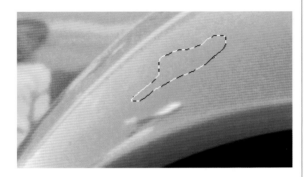

4 The result should be a smooth finish with no trace of the original reflection.

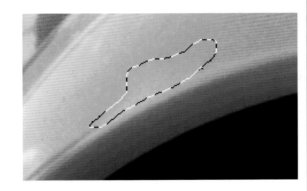

5 The *Patch* tool is a powerful addition to the Photoshop tool set, but of course every tool has its limitations. The bulk of the image is dominated by the main reflection of the man and boy. The *Patch* tool will be of little use here as we don't have enough suitable image area from which to copy pixels, so we'll use a different technique. Create a path around the area to be replaced. You could use a *Lasso* tool, but the finished result of a path created with the *Pen* tool will be much smoother. The path has been given a black stroke in the example just for greater visibility.

6 Convert the path to a selection by pressing Ctrl (Cmd) + Enter (Return).

7 Using the *Eyedropper* tool, sample a pale pink from the car for the foreground color and a deeper red for the background color. I am using R241 G111 B149 for the foreground and R187 G0 B17 for the background color.

8 Set up the *Gradient* tool to use the *Foreground to Background* radial gradient.

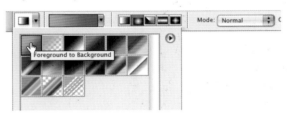

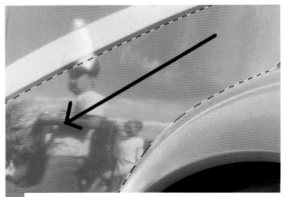

9 On a new layer called *Gradient*, drag the gradient as shown, then deselect the selection.

10 The completed gradient should leave you with a smooth, natural looking surface.

If the gradient doesn't have the right look, just drag again until you achieve a pleasing effect.

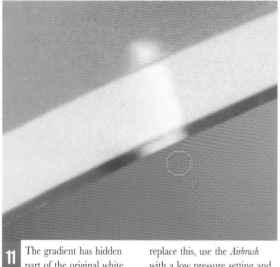

11 The gradient has hidden part of the original white specular highlight near the yellow and blue stripe. To replace this, use the *Airbrush* with a low pressure setting and an off-white paint color. Paint onto a new layer.

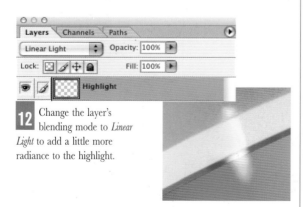

12 Change the layer's blending mode to *Linear Light* to add a little more radiance to the highlight.

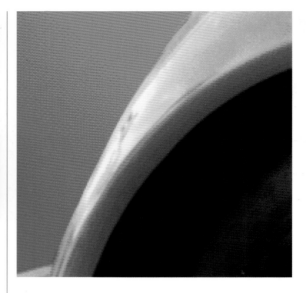

13 One more area remains with an unwanted reflection at the bottom of the wheel arch. This area is in a difficult position for the *Patch* tool as there are many colors in close proximity. The simplest and most effective tool to use here is the *Airbrush* tool.

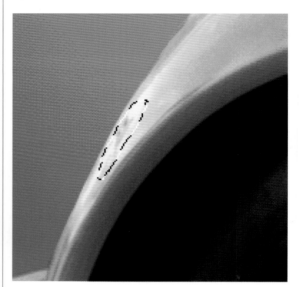

14 Make a feathered selection of the area to be hidden.

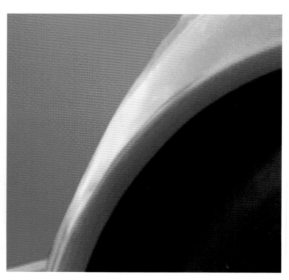

15 Sample an off-white color from within the selection, and use a low-pressure airbrush to brush several short strokes onto a new layer.

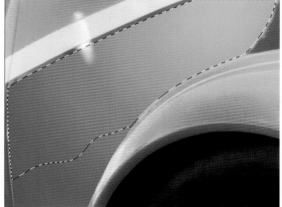

20 Set up the foreground and background colors with the same values as we used in step 7 for the gradient.

16 We could leave it at that, with a nice showroom finish to the car.

19 Draw a selection that subtracts an area from the bottom of the current loaded selection. This will result in a soft, wavy edge at the bottom of the edited selection, leaving the other edges crisp and well-defined.

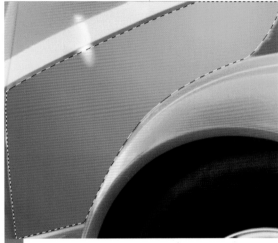

17 However, at this stage you may want to actually add a little reflection—nothing obvious, just a general reflection that adds to the sheen and realism. Press Ctrl (Cmd) + click the *Gradient* layer to load its selection.

18 Set up the *Lasso* tool with a high number pixel feather and in *Subtract* mode.

21 Create a new layer called *Clouds*, which sits between the *Highlight* and *Gradient* layers.

22 Go to *Filter > Render > **Clouds*** to give the reflection some texture.

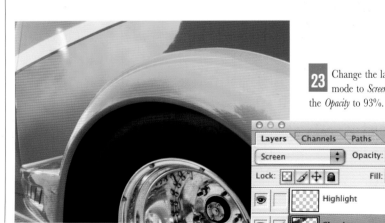

23 Change the layer blending mode to *Screen* and reduce the *Opacity* to 93%.

CREATING MULTIPLE COLORED LIGHTS

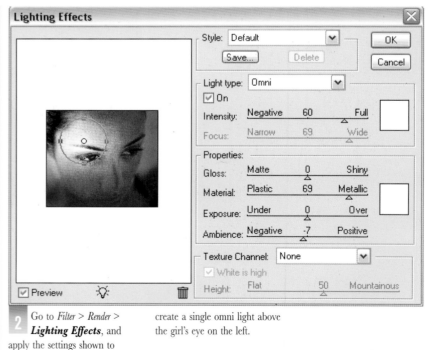

Duplicate the *Background* layer, and name the duplicate *Omni Light.*

D irecting more than one light source at the subject provides a degree of lighting options that could never be achieved with a single light. Add color filters to the lights, and an infinite variety of dynamic lighting possibilities opens up.

Photoshop, as we know, enables multiple and colored lights to be used within a single scene, but each additional light will impact on all the other lights that have been used. This can make it difficult to control the integrity of each light, sometimes resulting in over- or underexposing areas.

The technique we are going to use will overcome that problem, providing subtle transitions between each light and complete creative control.

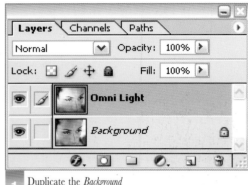

Go to *Filter > Render > Lighting Effects*, and apply the settings shown to create a single omni light above the girl's eye on the left.

3 Duplicate the *Background* layer again, and position it at the top of the *Layers* palette, calling it *Blue Light*.

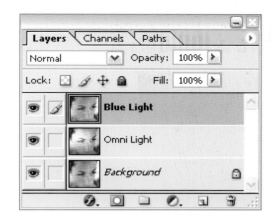

4 With the *Blue Light* layer active, go to *Filter > Render > **Lighting Effects*** again. Apply the settings pictured, using a deep blue as the light color.

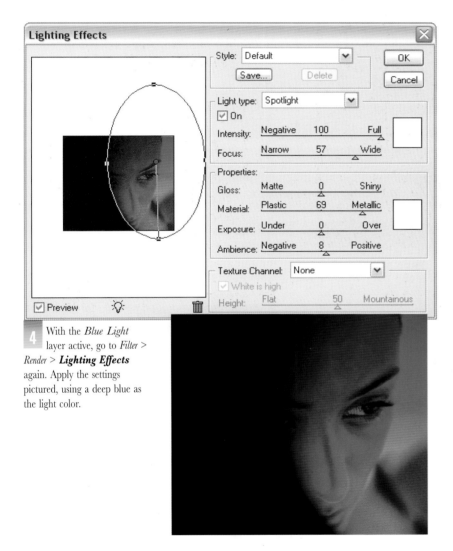

5 This layer now hides the layer beneath it containing the omni light effect.   Add a layer mask to the *Blue Light* layer.

6 Using a large, soft-edged brush, paint with black on the mask to hide the left side   of the layer, thereby revealing the left side of the *Omni Light* layer beneath.

7 Using different *Opacity* settings for the brush, you can now control exactly how   much of each layer is revealed to achieve the perfect blend of both lights.

CREATING RETRO STUDIO PORTRAIT LIGHTING

1 Make a selection of the white background area surrounding the girl.

The studio lighting setup for portrait photography is an entire and absorbing subject in itself. Some of the best examples of classic studio portraiture come from the film industry's heyday between the 1930's and 40's when the icons of Hollywood were immortalized on photographic paper as publicity material.

These black-and-white images were characterized by flattering lighting that drew sympathetic shadows, softening the skin tones and emphasizing the key features that transformed the artist into a star.

2 Rename the *Background* layer by double-clicking it, and call it *Base image*.

3 Press Backspace to remove the white selected area, revealing the transparency.

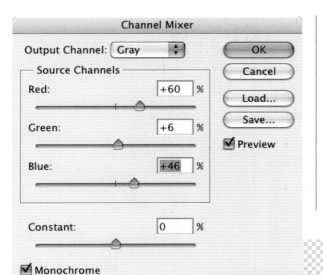

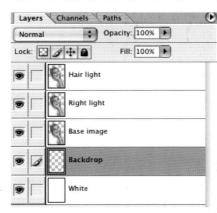

6 To achieve the retro look, our choice of background will be critical. Create 2 layers, one called *Backdrop* and the other, filled with white, called *White*. Position them below the existing layers with the *White* layer right at the bottom of the *Layers* palette.

4 We need to make the image grayscale. There are a number of ways of doing this. The method we are using is quick and offers great control over the distribution of grayscale values, from the shadows right through to highlights. Go to *Image > Adjustments > Channel Mixer*. Enable the *Monochrome* checkbox to create grayscale output. Apply the other settings as shown.

7 Activate the *Backdrop* layer and, making sure black and white are set as the foreground and background colors, go to *Filter > Render > Clouds*.

5 Duplicate the layer twice and name them from the top *Hair light* and *Right light*.

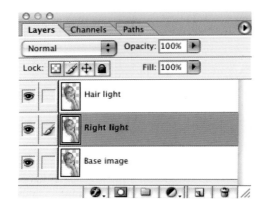

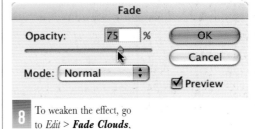

8 To weaken the effect, go to *Edit > Fade Clouds*, and reduce the *Opacity* to 75%.

Gaussian Blur

OK

Cancel

☑ Preview

⊟ 100% ⊞

Radius: 14 pixels

9 It still needs to be softer so as not to be distracting. Go to *Filter > Blur >* **Gaussian Blur**. Apply a *Radius* of 14.

10 The stage is now set to bring in the lights. Activate the *Right light* layer, and hide the *Hair light* layer.

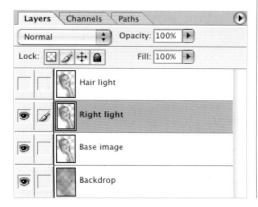

Layers Channels Paths

Normal   Opacity: 100%

Lock: ☒ ✓ ✛ 🔒   Fill: 100%

Hair light

Right light

Base image

Backdrop

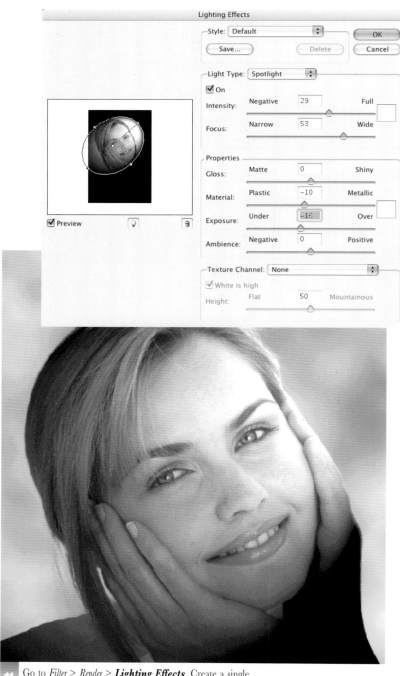

Lighting Effects

Style: Default   OK

Save...   Delete   Cancel

Light Type: Spotlight

☑ On

Intensity: Negative   29   Full

Focus: Narrow   53   Wide

Properties

Gloss: Matte   0   Shiny

Material: Plastic   −10   Metallic

Exposure: Under   −16   Over

Ambience: Negative   0   Positive

Texture Channel: None

☑ White is high

Height: Flat   50   Mountainous

☑ Preview

11 Go to *Filter > Render >* **Lighting Effects**. Create a single spotlight with its source originating from just to the right of the girl's forehead. All the settings used are displayed.

12 Activate the *Hair light* layer, then go to the *Lighting Effects* filter again. This time we need a spotlight coming from the top-left of the girl's head to light up the hair.

Lighting Effects

Style: Default

Save...   Delete   OK   Cancel

Light Type: Spotlight

☑ On

Intensity: Negative   52   Full

Focus: Narrow   53   Wide

Properties

Gloss: Matte   0   Shiny

Material: Plastic   −10   Metallic

Exposure: Under   −16   Over

Ambience: Negative   0   Positive

Texture Channel: None

☑ White is high

Height: Flat   50   Mountainous

☑ Preview

Layers   Channels   Paths

Normal   Opacity: 100%

Lock: Fill: 100%

Hair light

14 Using a soft-edged brush, paint with black on the mask of the *Hair light* layer to hide all but the spotlight area in the top-left corner.

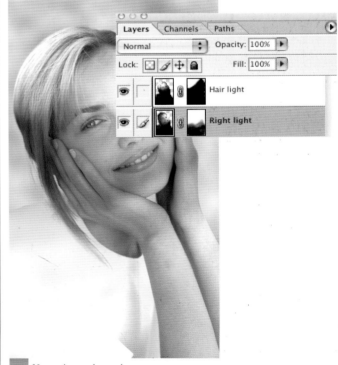

Layers   Channels   Paths

Normal   Opacity: 100%

Lock: Fill: 100%

Hair light

Right light

13 Both of the lights we are going to use are in place, and now we can selectively reveal parts of each layer as desired. Add layer masks to both of the light layers.

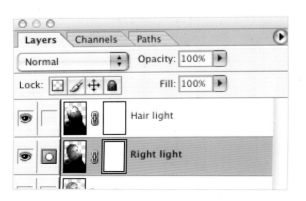

Layers   Channels   Paths

Normal   Opacity: 100%

Lock: Fill: 100%

Hair light

Right light

15 Now paint on the mask of the *Right light* layer, hiding the bottom half of it. This reveals some of the base layer, completing the image.

CREATING A FILM NOIR LIGHTING STYLE

T hat most evocative of movie genres, film noir, has left us with a legacy of imagery that inspires visions of dark secrets, espionage, and femmes fatales. Shadow is an integral part of this style, where the dark, ominous recesses invoke a sense of mystery and the soft, strategically placed light appears almost accidental. Of course, the success of this style is no accident. Careful planning and balancing the contradictions of light and dark are critical if the feel is to be faithfully reproduced.

1 We need a good strong grayscale image to give us a head start, and using the channel mixer offers a great degree of control. Go to *Image > Adjustments > **Channel Mixer**. Select the *Monochrome* checkbox to create gray output. Adjust the percentages of the *Red, Blue,* and *Green* sliders to achieve the required contrast. The settings shown will achieve a good range of tones for our working image.

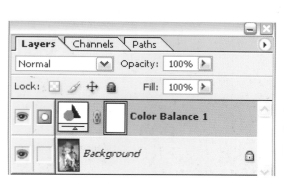

2 Film posters and publicity photographs of the period are sometimes seen with a blue tint. This elegant touch is still used today to add sophistication to grayscale images. Add a *Color Balance* adjustment layer.

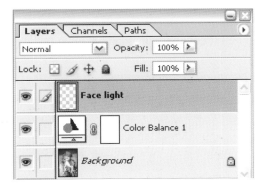

3 Apply the settings shown independently to the *Shadows*, *Midtones*, and *Highlights*.

4 The drama and enigmatic atmosphere is achieved through extremes of lighting. Strong directional light on the chosen focal points and heavy shadow elsewhere. The girl's face is going to be the main focal point. Create a new layer called *Face light*.

7 Finally we can enhance the focal point and deepen the shadows further to add a little more mystery by creating a directional light. This light can also be used to create a small ghostly blur of light in the background behind the girl's head. Create a new layer called *Direct light*.

8 Drag a *Black to White* reflected Gradient through the top-right corner of the image.

5 Drag a *White to Black* diamond gradient, starting from the center of the girl's face to the outside of her hat.

6 Change the layer blend mode to *Soft Light*.

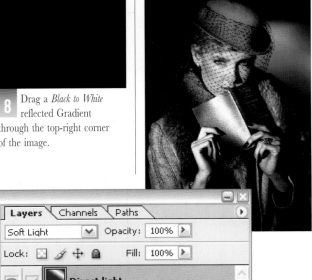

9 Change the layer blend mode to *Soft Light*. The gradient has the effect of throwing the nonfocal areas of the image into deeper shadow and simulating a soft directional light across the girl's face and hat. It also interacts with the diamond gradient below it, creating a nice play of light in the background.

CREATING SMOKE & STEAM

As with all intangible entities, smoke and steam create some unique problems when trying to simulate them in an image. Hard-edged objects can be relatively easy to create with great realism, but the nebulous qualities of smoke and steam can leave you hovering between something vague and watery and a solid, computer-generated object. With the techniques that follow, you'll be able to master the creation of both steam and smoke with a high degree of realism.

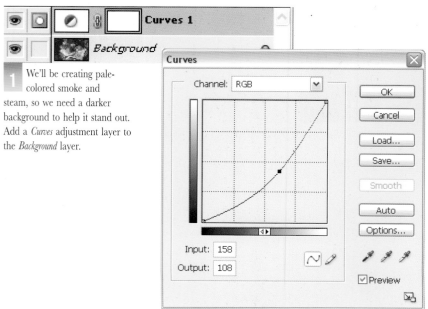

1 We'll be creating pale-colored smoke and steam, so we need a darker background to help it stand out. Add a *Curves* adjustment layer to the *Background* layer.

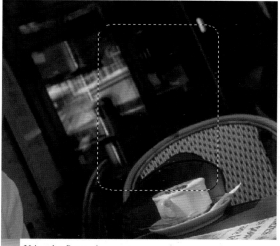

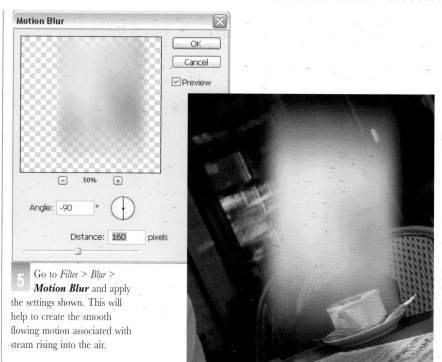

2 Using the *Rectangular Marquee* tool, create a feathered selection above the cup. I'm using a 15 pixel feather with a high resolution file.

3 Set up the foreground and background colors with midgray and white respectively.

5 Go to *Filter > Blur > Motion Blur* and apply the settings shown. This will help to create the smooth flowing motion associated with steam rising into the air.

4 On a new layer called *Clouds*, apply the *Clouds* filter. Go to *Filter > Render >* **Clouds**. This will become the basis for the steam and smoke.

6 The lightness of steam makes it very susceptible to even low levels of air currents, so a prevailing breeze at an outdoor café, the turning of a newspaper page, and a waiter walking by will all impact on the rising steam in their own way. This can result in a chaotic mass of steam fighting to flow in different directions. The *Wave* filter is an ideal method for simulating this condition. Go to *Filter > Distort > Wave*, and apply the settings displayed. The results can appear highly volatile, and small adjustments can make what appear to be disproportionate changes. Your result may be different to the one shown because the effect is influenced by many factors, including the degree of streakiness in the original clouds, the contrast between the colors, the feathering, and the resolution of the file.

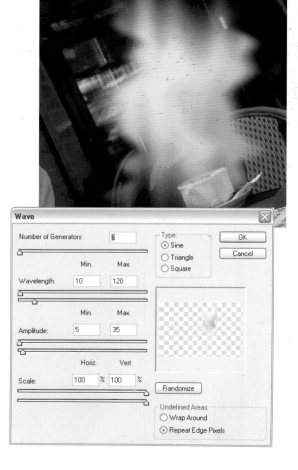

7 To breathe some photographic realism into the steam, change the layer blend mode to *Hard Light* and reduce the layer *Opacity* to 70%.

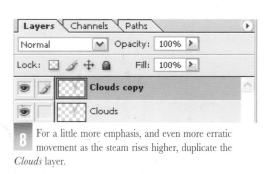

8 For a little more emphasis, and even more erratic movement as the steam rises higher, duplicate the *Clouds* layer.

9 It's important to avoid repeating patterns when using duplicate artwork, so to create a random appearance, go to *Edit > Transform > **Flip Horizontal*** and drag the flipped artwork to the top of the screen.

10 Reduce the *Clouds copy* layer's *Opacity* to 50% to keep the effect subtle.

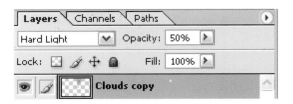

11 Now for the cigarette smoke: repeat steps 2 to 5 so you are left with some motion blurred clouds roughly approximating the area you wish the cigarette smoke to cover. This artwork should be on a new layer called *Smoke*.

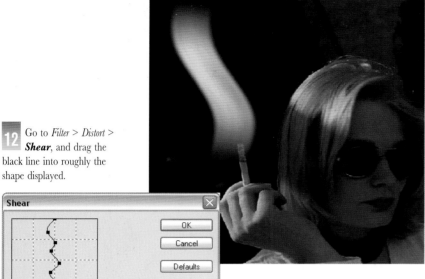

12 Go to *Filter > Distort >* **Shear**, and drag the black line into roughly the shape displayed.

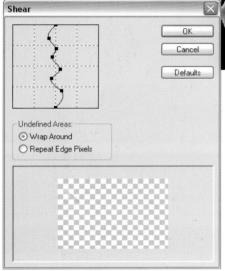

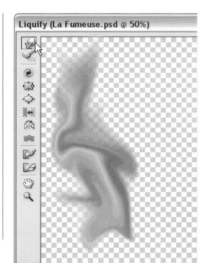

14 To give the smoke a more ethereal quality, change the layer blend mode to *Pin Light*.

13 The thin wispy strands of cigarette smoke are unmistakable and the *Liquify* filter will help us achieve this illusion. Go to *Filter > **Liquify***. Using the *Warp* tool from within the *Liquify* filter, click and drag the artwork in the preview window to distort it into a contorted shape resembling cigarette smoke. Don't try to achieve the exact effect as pictured; the result is based on many factors just as with the *Wave* filter earlier, not to mention your own, fine hand movements. Click *OK* when you have a suitable shape.

CREATING LIGHT THROUGH SMOKE & STEAM

Due to the inherent qualities of smoke—which range from full opacity to degrees of transparency and an ever-changing mass—creating a false light that appears to shine onto smoke can suffer greatly with credibility. The same may be said of any visible entity that is less than tangible. We are going to use a simple but effective technique to achieve this goal and then add some atmosphere to provide interest in the finished image.

2 Create a curve similar to the one shown, to provide a general darkening to the whole image.

1 To add greater impact to the final image, we're going to start by darkening the overall tone. Not only will this provide for a more dramatic scene but it will also offer a better platform for the light we create. Add a *Curves* adjustment layer to the *Background* layer. Using an adjustment layer enables you to change the level of brightness later in relation to the additional lighting effects.

3 Create a feathered selection defining a beam of light emanating from the landing light near the nose of the aircraft. This type of aircraft doesn't actually have a light in the position I have chosen, but a certain amount of creative license needs to be used for the benefit of the image.

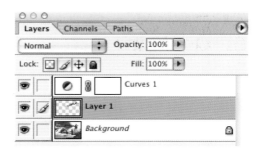

4 Activate the *Background* layer and press Ctrl (Cmd) + J to copy and paste the selection to a new layer.

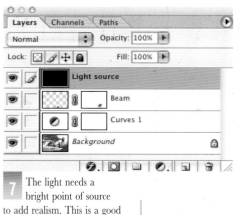

5 Drag the layer to the top of the *Layers* palette, then rename it *Beam* and change the layer blending mode to *Screen*.

7 The light needs a bright point of source to add realism. This is a good opportunity for the *Lens Flare* filter. Create a new black-filled layer called *Light source*, positioned at the top of the *Layers* palette.

8 Go to *Filter > Render > **Lens Flare***, and apply the settings as shown.

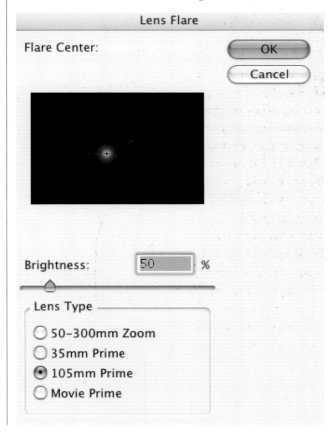

6 At the farthest point from the source of the light, the beam appears too white and washed out. We need to create the illusion of the light punching through some areas of the smoke. Add a layer mask to the *Beam* layer and use black to paint out some random areas on the mask.

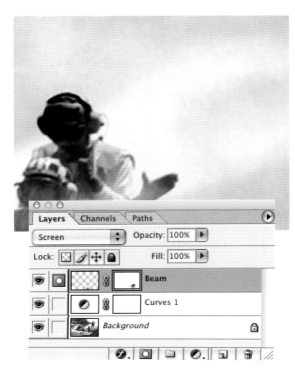

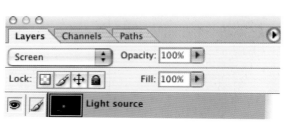

9 Change the layer blending mode to *Screen*. This lets only the flare be seen, and not the black area.

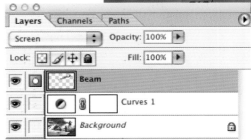

10 Now position the flare at the start of the light beam.

11 The light shining through the smoke effect is complete, but some further effects typically found in this sort of environment will really make the image stand out. We're going to switch on the starboard wing navigation light. Create a new black-filled layer called *Starboard* at the top of the *Layers* palette, and set the blend mode to *Screen* as you did in step 9.

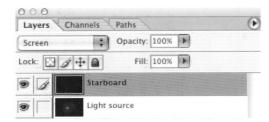

14 Any source of light will have an effect on the ambient light conditions in the area. We would expect to see a green glow on the ground immediately below the light and on some of the wing. Create a feathered selection on the ground below the light.

15 Activate the *Background* layer and press Ctrl (Cmd) + J to copy the selection to a new layer.

12 Go to *Filter > Render > **Lens Flare**, and apply the same settings as in step 8. To change the color, go to *Image > Adjustments > **Hue/Saturation** and apply the settings in the example to achieve a green color.

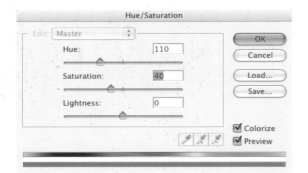

16 Rename the layer *Ground glow*.

13 Position the lens flare over the navigation light of the wing.

17 Use the *Hue/Saturation* command again to create a green similar to the navigation light.

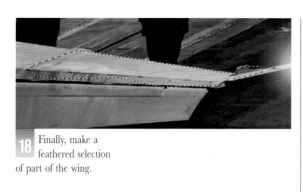

18 Finally, make a feathered selection of part of the wing.

19 Now it's a repeat procedure of the glow on the ground. Activate the background layer and press Ctrl (Cmd) + J. Name the new layer *Wing glow*.

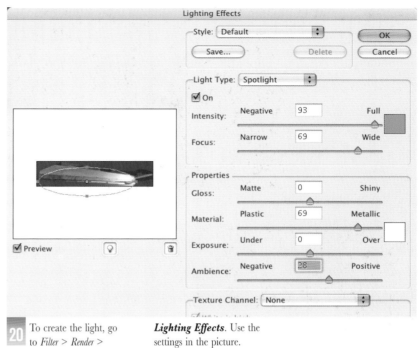

20 To create the light, go to *Filter > Render >* ***Lighting Effects***. Use the settings in the picture.

21 This has left a deep shadow area to the left of the light.

22 To remove this shadow, add a layer mask to the layer. Now use a soft brush with black paint at low opacity to paint over the mask and hide the dark area.

CREATING FILTERED LIGHT THROUGH DUST

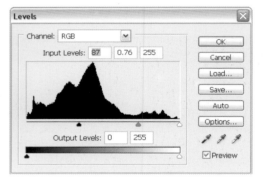

The image of the truck I am using for this effect provides plenty of scope for a dramatic picture. We can create the illusion of the truck throwing up clouds of billowing dust in its wake as strong evening sunlight is filtered randomly through the cloud. The composition of the original image is equally as important as the finished effect. In this example, the truck's placement within the image enables a broad area to the right to be used for the dust, making the dust cloud an integral part of the image rather than just some simple embellishment.

Dust, in a similar way to smoke, is composed of myriad tiny particles, each particle being light enough to be suspended in the air before slowly falling back to earth. Rarely does the density of a dust cloud form a solid uniform mass. Typically, random patches of dense dust are interspersed with more sparsely distributed particles. This phenomenon gives rise to some dramatic effects when strong directional light is applied to a dust cloud, resulting in the characteristic filtered effect as light falls on areas of different density. Where the dust is dense, light is completely or partially blocked, while in less packed areas light penetrates unhindered, revealing strong stripes or beams of light. Therefore to create this effect with any degree of photographic realism, we need to avoid uniformity at all costs.

1 We need to start by isolating the truck and placing it on its own layer. Use whichever tools you are most comfortable with to make a selection of the truck. There's not much color uniformity in this image, but the contrast between the truck and the background is reasonable, so the *Magnetic Lasso* will provide a good staring point. Alternatively, use the *Extract* command or *Pen* tool for most accuracy. With the selection completed, go to *Layer > New > **Layer via Copy*** or press Ctrl (Cmd) + J. This copies and pastes the selected artwork to a new layer. Name this layer *Truck*. To create more dramatic contrast between the truck and the dust and suggest

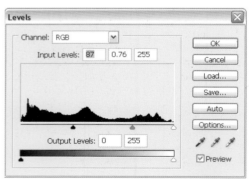

evening light, we need to darken both the *Background* and *Truck* layers by the same degree. Add a *Levels* adjustment layer to both the *Background* and *Truck* layers. Using adjustment layers enables you to fine-tune the level of brightness at a later stage within the context of the finished image. In the *Levels* dialog box, drag the black input slider to the right in both of the adjustment layers.

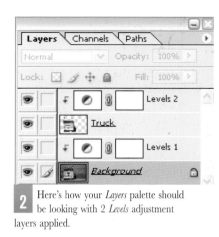

2 Here's how your *Layers* palette should be looking with 2 *Levels* adjustment layers applied.

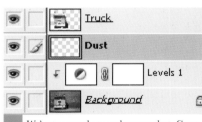

3 We're now ready to make some dust. Create a new layer named *Dust* and position it below the *Truck* layer.

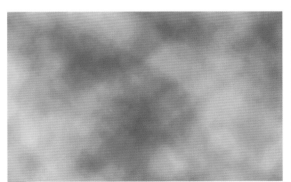

4 Set the foreground and background colors to two contrasting colors that reflect the sandy tones of a desert road. I am using R244, G224 B165 for the foreground, and R59, G55, B38 for the background color. Make sure the *Dust* layer is active and go to *Filter > Render > Clouds*.

Ideally we need a good random spread of light and dark areas. If you are not happy with the effect, just keep pressing Ctrl (Cmd) + F. This will keep reapplying the clouds in a different random configuration each time. When you are happy with the result, set the layer *Opacity* to 80%.

5 Duplicate the layer so we have 2 identical *Dust* layers, one on top of the other. The reason for this duplication will be apparent in a moment.

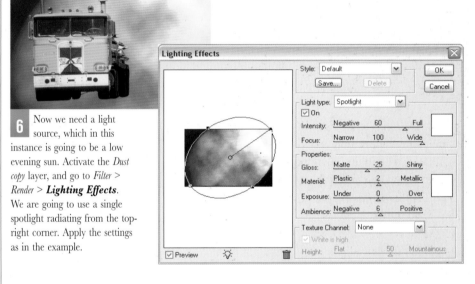

6 Now we need a light source, which in this instance is going to be a low evening sun. Activate the *Dust copy* layer, and go to *Filter > Render > Lighting Effects*. We are going to use a single spotlight radiating from the top-right corner. Apply the settings as in the example.

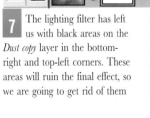

7 The lighting filter has left us with black areas on the *Dust copy* layer in the bottom-right and top-left corners. These areas will ruin the final effect, so we are going to get rid of them

first. This was the reason for duplicating the *Dust* layer. Apply a layer mask to the duplicated *Dust copy* layer, then paint on the mask in black until all the black areas have been hidden.

8 Once the corners have been painted out, merge the 2 dust layers together, using Ctrl (Cmd) + E. Duplicate the newly merged *Dust* layer and drag the duplicate layer to the top of the *Layers* palette. Make sure it is right at the top, above the *Levels* adjustment layer.

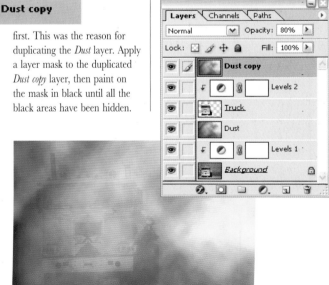

9 This *Dust copy* layer partially obscures the truck, so we need to reveal parts of it in such a way as to create the illusion of the dust cloud being generated from the rear and sides of the vehicle with just a little scattered around the front. Add a layer mask to the *Dust copy* layer, then paint on the mask with black, using a very low *Opacity* setting for the brush until the front of the truck starts to show through. You will need to use some creative license here, switching between black and white paint to reveal or hide the layer until the right degree of subtlety is achieved.

12 Make a rectangular feathered selection that goes from the top of the document to the horizon.

10 Add a layer mask to the original *Dust* layer too, and in the same way as before paint away some of the dust effect from the road area in front of the truck.

13 Make sure the *Sun* layer is active, then drag a linear gradient diagonally from top-left to bottom-right at about a 45° angle. If you are not happy with the spread of the gradient, keep dragging until you get the look that you want.

11 To create the streaks of filtered sunlight, make a new layer called *Sun* and position it below the *Truck* layer. Create a gradient similar to the one in the example using black and white. More instances of black and white results in more beams of light. Tightly packed black and white markers will create thinner beams with greater contrast.

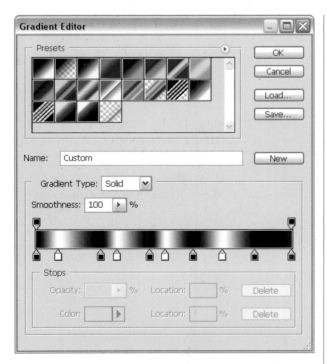

14 Set the *Sun* layer's blending mode to *Darken*.

15 To add a finishing touch, and reflect the fact that the sun is going down, we are going to turn on the headlights. Create a new layer called *Headlights* at the top of the layer stack and fill it with black. Go to *Filter > Render > **Lens Flare***, and use the settings as in the example.

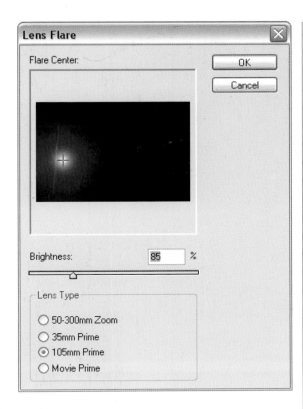

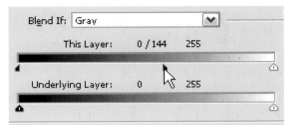

17 The lens flare has the effect of brightening the whole layer, though, which impacts negatively on the rest of the image. All we really want is the immediate burst of light from the headlight. Double-click the *Headlights* layer to reveal the *Layer Options* dialog box. At the bottom of the dialog box are the channel blending range mixers. We are going to use these to reduce the radiance of the lens flare. The *Blend If* field should be set to *Gray*. Working with the top row of range sliders and the left-hand pair, press and hold down the Alt key and then click and drag the right half of the pair to the right as in the example. The farther to the right you drag, the smaller the expanse of light from the lens flare becomes.

16 Set the layer blending mode of the *Headlights* layer to *Screen*. This removes the black areas of the layer, revealing only the headlights.

18 For the second headlight, duplicate the *Headlights* layer and drag the second light into position over the truck headlight.

19 If necessary, you may want to use the 2 *Levels* adjustments layers that are linked to the *Background* and *Truck* layers to fine-tune the brightness level now that you can see the finished image in its full context with the sunlight and headlights.

CREATING FIRE

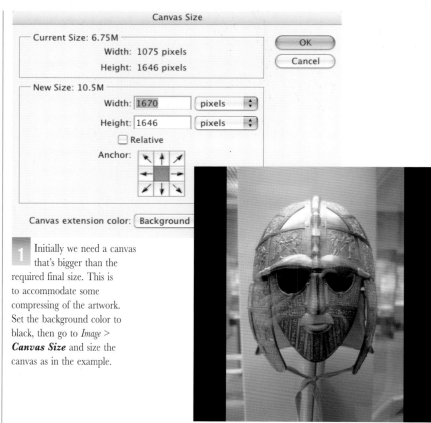

1 Initially we need a canvas that's bigger than the required final size. This is to accommodate some compressing of the artwork. Set the background color to black, then go to *Image > Canvas Size* and size the canvas as in the example.

Creating fire in Photoshop can be as satisfying as it probably was when man (or woman) created real fire for the very first time. The shapeless, random, and ever-changing form of fire makes it a challenging task for even the most accomplished of Photoshop users. Not only must we create the entity of fire itself, but also its inevitable generation of light as it paints the objects around it.

2 Make a selection of the mask and save it for later use.

3 Inverse the selection and fill the canvas with black before deselecting.

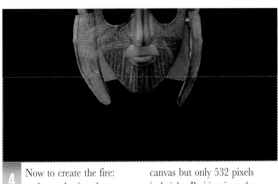

4 Now to create the fire: make a selection that covers the full width of the canvas but only 532 pixels in height. Position it at the bottom of the canvas.

5 Make a new layer called *Fire*.

6 Set up the foreground color with red R232 G44 B0 and the background color with yellow R255 G222 B3.

7 Go to *Filter > Render > **Clouds***.

8 The *Clouds* filter works quite well as fire, but we need it to be a bit more streaky. Go to *Filter > Render > **Difference Clouds***.

9 Press Ctrl (Cmd) + F. This will reapply the *Difference Clouds* filter, each time inverting the colors and applying a different random configuration. Keep doing this until you achieve a bold red/yellow pattern with fairly strong streaks. It may require around 10 repetitions or more.

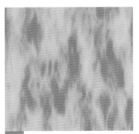

10 Deselect and press Ctrl (Cmd) + T to bring up the *Transform* bounding box. Drag the top-middle handle of the bounding box to the top of the canvas.

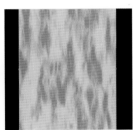

11 Now drag the bounding box's right handle to the left, and the left handle to the right, without revealing the mask picture beneath. The final width of the fire needs to be around 1275 pixels and roughly in the center of the canvas. Press the Enter (Return) key to confirm the transformation.

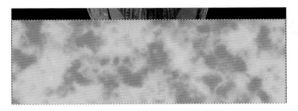

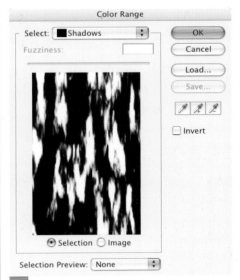

12 The red is too strong and flat and we need to create some breaks in the flames in order to see through them. Go to *Select > **Color Range***.

Select *Shadows* from the drop-down box. This selects all the shadow areas, which picks up all the red.

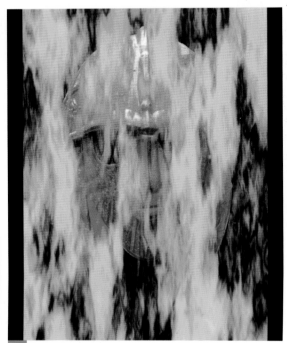

13 Press Backspace on the keyboard to delete the red areas.

14 I want the flames to appear to mingle and dance around the image of the metal mask, so we need to cut it out from the background. Load the mask that you saved earlier. I've hidden the *Fire* layer so as not to complicate the image.

15 With the *Background* layer active, press Ctrl (Cmd) + J to copy and paste the selection to a new layer. Name the new layer *Metal Mask*.

16 Drag the *Metal Mask* layer above the revealed *Fire* layer.

17 Duplicate the *Fire* layer and drag the duplicate above the *Metal Mask* layer.

18 To help avoid any repeated patterns from appearing, go to *Edit > Transform > **Flip Horizontal*** and drag the artwork down about 100 pixels.

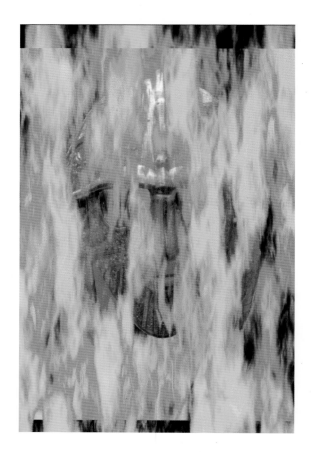

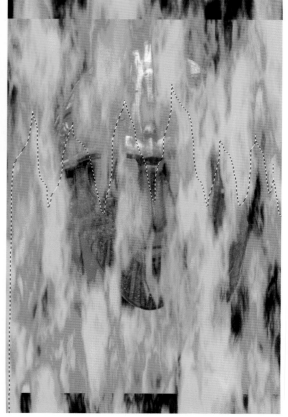

19 This has revealed a straight edge at the top of the canvas. With the *Lasso* tool, make a feathered selection describing some tapered flame shapes. Use a 15 pixel feather for high resolution files.

20 Make sure the *Fire copy* layer is active, then inverse the selection and press the Backspace key.

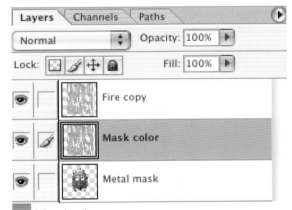

21 What gives the game away is the fact that the metal should be reflecting the color of the surrounding flames. We can use a quick and easy method to fix this. Duplicate one of the fire layers, naming the duplicate *Mask color*. Position this layer between the *Metal Mask* layer and the *Fire copy* layer.

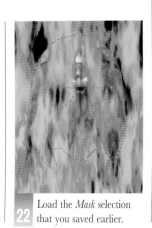

22 Load the *Mask* selection that you saved earlier.

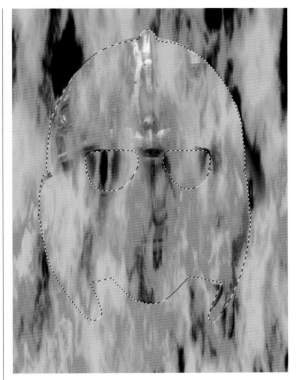

23 With the *Mask Color* layer active, inverse the selection and press Backspace. You won't see too much difference here, as we have only deleted the area around the outside of the metal mask. Change the layer blending mode to *Overlay* to create the effect of the metal reflecting the flames.

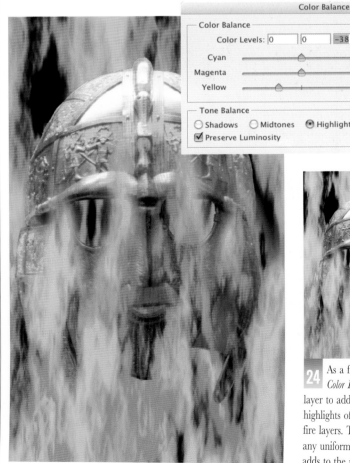

24 As a finishing touch, use a *Color Balance* adjustment layer to add some yellow to the highlights of one or all of the fire layers. This helps break up any uniformity of color and adds to the realism.

CREATING SILHOUETTES

1 Make a selection of the blue sky. We actually need a selection of the statue, but it's much easier to select the sky. Inverse the selection once made.

2 Press Ctrl (Cmd) + J to copy and paste the selection to a new layer. Name the layer *Statue*.

3 Change the layer blend mode to *Linear Burn* to darken the statue.

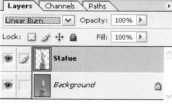

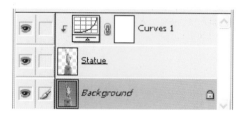

4 Although the statue is darker, it's not dark enough to qualify as a silhouette. Add a *Curves* adjustment layer that's clipped to the *Statue* layer.

It may be fair to say that many silhouette images are taken purely by accident, often when anything but a silhouette is desired. Strong backlighting and insufficient light on the subject, or setting the exposure for the wrong part of the image, can all result in an inadvertent silhouette.

However, if you do want to create a silhouette and it's based on an existing image, it could be very simple: just put a black cutout over the object and technically that's a silhouette. But it would also be very flat and boring, resembling a lifeless cardboard cutout with little artistic merit. Photographically, what makes a much more interesting silhouette is when a fraction of light is illuminating the subject, not really showing any detail, but enough to suggest we are looking at a 3-D form and not a flat 2-D cut-out.

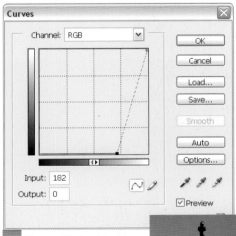

Curves dialog

Channel: RGB

Input: 182
Output: 0

5 Drag the black point horizontally to the right to radically darken the image while leaving a small amount of light in the lightest areas.

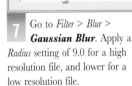

6 The extreme curves setting has resulted in some unflattering harshness and rough texture, but we can easily blur this away. Press Ctrl (Cmd) and click the *Statue* layer to load its selection, then inverse it so that the statue is the selected part of the layer.

7 Go to *Filter > Blur > Gaussian Blur*. Apply a *Radius* setting of 9.0 for a high resolution file, and lower for a low resolution file.

Gaussian Blur dialog

Radius: 9 pixels

8 Loading the selection before blurring meant the *Gaussian Blur* did not extend beyond the limits of the selection, so the statue is left with a well-defined edge with all the softening being applied to the inner of the statue where it is meant to be. The light areas now suggest a soft shaft of light falling on the statue.

Layers panel — Channels, Paths tabs. Screen, Opacity: 100%, Fill: 100%. Curves 1, Light, Statue, Background.

9 Our present blue background would not generate a silhouette of this kind as its intensity is not great enough. Create a new black filled layer below the *Statue* layer, and call it *Light*, then set its blend mode to *Screen*.

Lens Flare dialog — Flare Center, Brightness: 140 %, Lens Type: 50-300mm Zoom, 35mm Prime, 105mm Prime, Movie Prime.

10 Go to *Filter > Render > Lens Flare*. Apply the setting shown and click *OK*.

11 Repeat the process a second time to apply a second lens flare at 90% brightness and toward the top of the preview window to complete the effect.

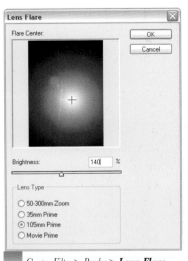

CASTING STAGE LIGHTING

It may be argued that the lighting for any concert or stage production is almost as important as the stage event itself. Just visit an afternoon rehearsal session to witness the difference that a full blown lighting setup makes to the impact of the overall performance. We are going to use just that scenario to turn a rehearsal session into the big night complete with laser show.

1 The ambient light pictured here is typical of a rehearsal session, so we need to darken the whole scene in such a way that it enables us to adjust the final lighting later, after the effects have been applied.

2 Add a *Curves* adjustment layer and create a curve as shown to darken the whole image.

3 Duplicate the *Background* layer and drag the copy above the *Curves* layer.

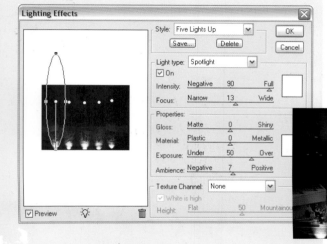

4 The duplicate layer will be used to place some footlights along the front of the stage. Go to *Filter > Render > Lighting Effects*. Select *Five Lights Up* from the *Style* drop-down box, and apply the other settings as shown. Position each light so that the source is just above the bottom edge of the window.

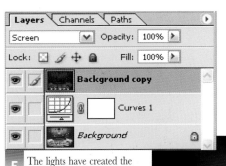

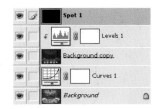

8 Now to create the spotlights: create a black-filled layer, naming the layer *Spot 1*.

5 The lights have created the right effect for footlights, but the rest of the image is now underexposed. Change the layer blend mode to *Screen* to reduce the visibility of the black.

9 Go to *Filter > Render > **Lens Flare***. Click in the bottom-left quarter of the preview window and use the other settings as shown.

Lens Flare

Flare Center:

OK
Cancel

Brightness: 100 %

Lens Type
○ 50-300mm Zoom
○ 35mm Prime
● 105mm Prime
○ Movie Prime

6 One of the problems with the *Lighting Effects* filter is the inability to adjust the lights once they have been applied, but we can easily overcome that problem by using adjustment layers. Add a *Levels* adjustment layer that is clipped to the *Background copy* layer.

10 Set the layer blend mode to *Screen* to hide the black area.

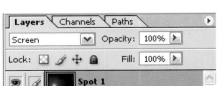

7 Apply a setting similar to the one shown to darken the image still further. The white and gray points can be adjusted to increase or decrease the strength of the footlights as desired.

Levels

Channel: RGB

Input Levels: 71 0.97 248

OK
Cancel
Load...
Save...
Auto
Options...

Output Levels: 0 255

☑ Preview

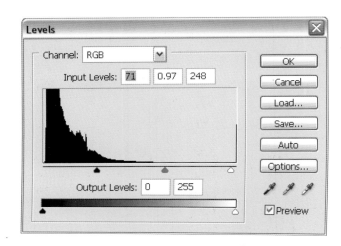

11 To save any repetition, we can make more lights by duplicating. Duplicate *Spot 1* and position it to the right of the original spot.

Hue/Saturation

Edit: Master

Hue: 270

Saturation: 27

Lightness: 0

OK
Cancel
Load...
Save...

☑ Colorize
☑ Preview

12 Stage lights are typically different colors, so we are going to tint the spotlights. Select the original *Spot 1* layer and go to *Image > Adjustments > Hue/Saturation*. Apply the settings, making sure that the *Colorize* checkbox is enabled.

15 Make a feathered selection describing the shape of the beam of light from the first spotlight.

13 Do the same with the duplicated spotlight layer, applying a different color this time.

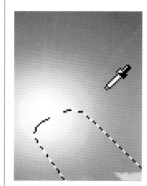

16 Using the *Eyedropper*, sample a color from the area of the spotlight.

17 Drag a linear gradient through the selection, using *Foreground to Transparent* colors, then deselect.

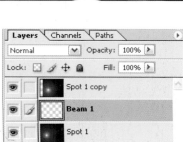

Layers Channels Paths

Normal   Opacity: 100%

Lock: ☐ ☑ ✦ ☐   Fill: 100%

👁 Spot 1 copy

👁 Beam 1

👁 Spot 1

14 For greater impact, we can make a beam of light that emanates from the spotlights. Create a layer called *Beam 1* above the *Spot 1* layer.

20 Repeat the same process until you have the desired amount of lights. The layers that contain the 2 spotlights shining on the conductor are set to the *Lighten* blend mode rather than *Screen*, as this mode generates less ambient light and prevents the scene becoming overly bright.

18 For the full effect, change the layer blend mode to *Linear Dodge*.

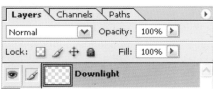

21 Smoke and atmospheric dust are particularly visible when caught in the light of a strong, vertical down-pointing beam. The result commonly manifests as a sharply defined outer edge to the light beam with a radically faded inner core. As well as being an interesting characteristic of light, this effect will add a subtle variation to our developing image. Create a new layer called *Downlight* at the top of the *Layers* palette.

22 Create a feathered selection outlining the beam of light as if emanating from one of the ceiling lights. I'm using a pixel feather of 10 in my high resolution file.

19 Repeat steps 14 to 18 to create a similar beam for the other spotlight.

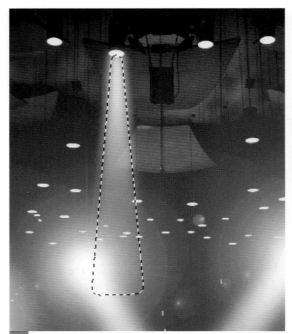

23 Drag a *White to Transparent* linear gradient through the selection.

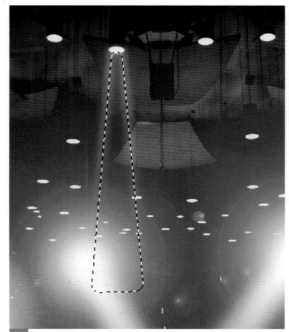

24 Delete the gradient you just applied, but leave the selection. Because of the high feather setting, a soft fringe of pixels has been left behind.

25 Using a different pale color, drag a *Foreground to Transparent* gradient through the selection, but drag only one quarter of the way through the selection.

26 Duplicate this layer and position the duplicate under one of the other ceiling lights.

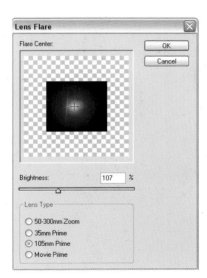

29 Apply the *Lens Flare* filter, using *105mm Prime* set to 107%.

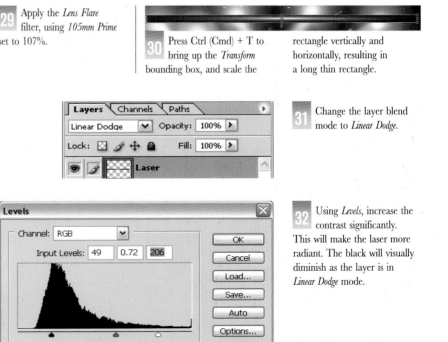

30 Press Ctrl (Cmd) + T to bring up the *Transform* bounding box, and scale the rectangle vertically and horizontally, resulting in a long thin rectangle.

31 Change the layer blend mode to *Linear Dodge*.

32 Using *Levels*, increase the contrast significantly. This will make the laser more radiant. The black will visually diminish as the layer is in *Linear Dodge* mode.

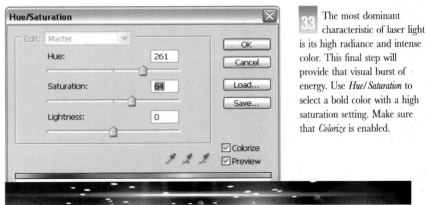

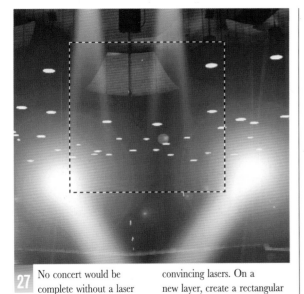

27 No concert would be complete without a laser light show, and Photoshop is very adept at creating highly convincing lasers. On a new layer, create a rectangular selection approximately 400 pixels square.

33 The most dominant characteristic of laser light is its high radiance and intense color. This final step will provide that visual burst of energy. Use *Hue/Saturation* to select a bold color with a high saturation setting. Make sure that *Colorize* is enabled.

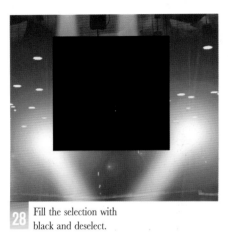

28 Fill the selection with black and deselect.

34 In the final step I have duplicated, rotated, scaled, and recolored the original laser. What really adds to the realism is the fact that real laser light will appear to merge and smudge when lights cross over each other, and this exact effect has been achieved through the use of the *Linear Dodge* layer blend mode.

CREATING GLASS AND REFRACTION

The way light refracts or bends through glass is an art form in itself. The wild, seemingly chaotic contortions of objects as their image is weaved through a glass shape seem to eclipse the imagination of even the most creative of abstract artists. Our task here is not only to distort the environment through a glass sphere, but actually to create the glass sphere itself.

1 Make a circular selection defining the outline of the glass sphere.

2 Press Ctrl (Cmd) + J to copy the selection a new layer. Name the layer *Distort*.

3 A popular method of distorting an image to simulate light refraction in glass is to use the *Spherize* filter. Although this gives acceptable results, it can result in blurring and too much degradation of the image. An alternative that we are going to use is the *Liquify* filter. While achieving similar results, the *Liquify* filter offers far greater control and a wider variety of distortions. Go to *Filter > Liquify*. Use the *Bloat* tool to create a similar distortion to the one shown.

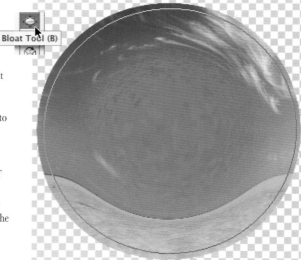

4 Now use the *Forward Warp* tool and distort just one element of the clouds to a rounded point. This will help with the illusion of the clouds bending to conform to the shape of the glass sphere.

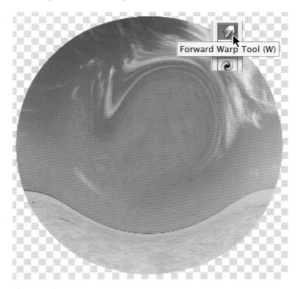

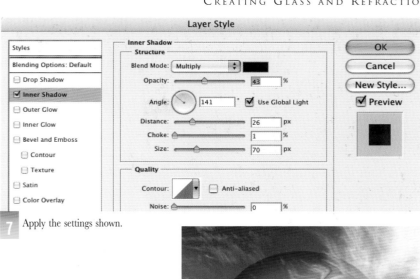

7 Apply the settings shown.

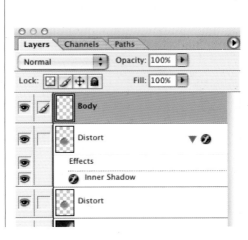

5 Finally, use the *Mirror* tool to increase the mass of the clouds and click *OK*.

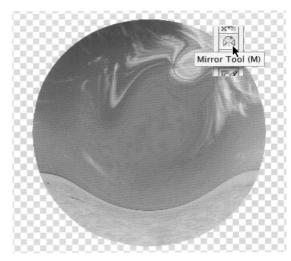

8 The shape already has a kind of bubble appearance, but a glass sphere would have a little more substance. Create a layer called *Body*.

6 The thing that defines a glass sphere to the viewer is a faint shadow around the perimeter. This needs to be subtle to avoid it looking like an outline. Click the *Layer Style* icon at the bottom of the *Layers* palette and select *Inner Shadow*.

9 Press Ctrl (Cmd) and click the *Distort* layer to load its selection.

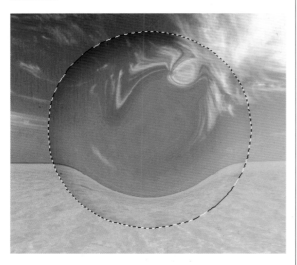

10 Drag a *White to Black* radial gradient through the selection, then deselect.

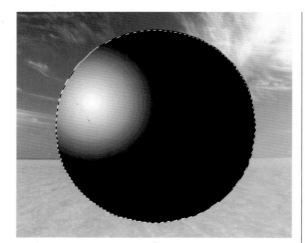
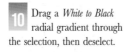

11 Change the layer blend mode to *Soft Light* and reduce the layer *Opacity* to 63%. This creates a more tangible object, and the visual strength can be controlled to taste.

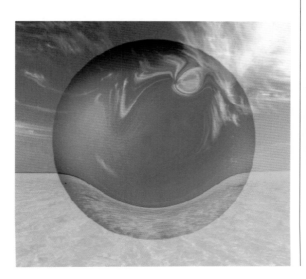

12 The shape is too dull to be highly polished glass, so we are going to add some highlights. On a new layer called *Left Highlight,* create a feathered selection that outlines a highlight area.

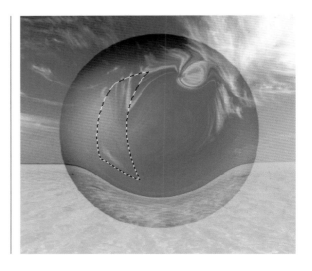

13 Drag a *White to Transparent* radial gradient halfway through the selection from top to middle.

14 On a new layer called *Airbrush*, add a burst of white with the *Airbrush* tool to create a specular highlight over the gradient.

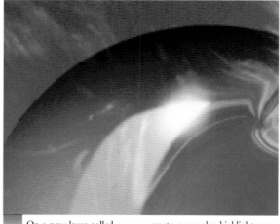

15 A similar highlight is needed for the bottom-right area. Make a feathered, crescent-shaped selection, leaving a gap of a few pixels between the selection and the outer edge of the glass.

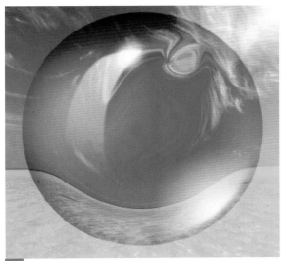

16 Drag a *White to Transparent* radial gradient a short distance to reveal a soft burst of white light.

17 Repeat the process to create another small eclipse of white in the top-left corner of the glass.

18 The image has quite a surreal feel, but we'll go one step farther and put a fish in the glass to finish. Add a fish image to the document, positioning the layer between the *Body* layer and the *Distort* layer.

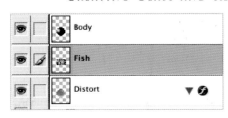

19 Add a layer mask to the *Fish* layer.

20 Using black paint, paint on the mask to subtly hide the rectangle edges so we see mainly the fish and some of the coral fading away.

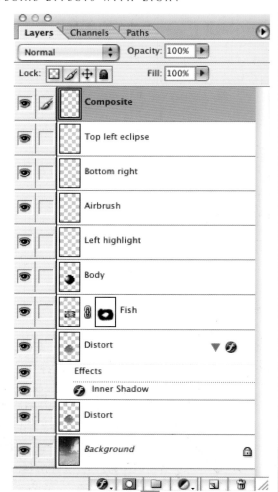

21 To help unify the whole image, we'll create a reflection and some ripples in the water just below the glass to suggest it is just bouncing along the surface. We need to make a composite layer from all the layers that make up the fish and glass. Hide the *Background* layer and create a new layer at the top of the palette, called *Composite*.

23 We now have a copy of the fish in a glass ball. Flip the copy vertically, using *Edit > Transform > **Flip Vertical**, and position it in the water.

22 Press Ctrl (Cmd) + Alt + Shift + E. This copies all visible layers and pastes them as one *Composite* layer into the layer at the top of the palette. It's now OK to reveal the *Background* layer.

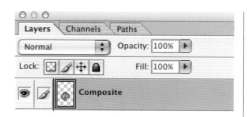

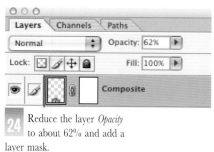

24 Reduce the layer *Opacity* to about 62% and add a layer mask.

25 Drag a *Black to White* gradient on the mask to hide the bottom portion of the fish reflection. This looks more realistic as water reflections fade away as the object moves farther away from the water surface.

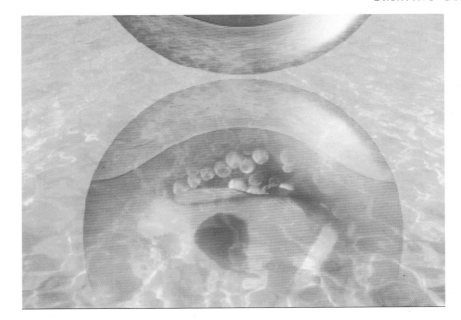

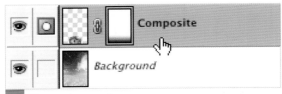

26 We are going to apply a ripple effect to both the water and the reflection at the same time. Reposition the *Composite* layer so it sits above the *Background* layer and press Ctrl (Cmd) + E to merge the two layers together.

27 Make a feathered selection outlining the perimeter of the water ripples.

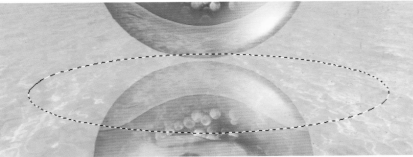

28 Go to *Filter > Distort > ZigZag* and apply the settings displayed.

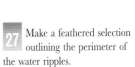

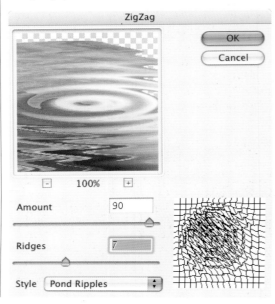

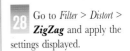

SIMULATING THE EFFECTS OF LIGHT UNDERWATER

2 Drag the selection into the underwater image and position as shown, naming the layer *Ship*.

3 You can probably see that a fair degree of work is required to make this ship look like an aging underwater wreck.

The first casualty will be most of the color and the sunlight. Go to *Image > Adjustments >* **Desaturate**.

The different wavelengths of light are absorbed differently depending on the depth of water. Red wavelengths are absorbed first, followed by green and lastly blue. This accounts for the predominant blue cast at greater depths underwater. Underwater photographers need to introduce artificial light at all but the shallowest depths if they are to capture the vivid colors that adorn marine flora and fauna.

In this section, we are going to create an image of an old ship wreck, simulating how its true color would be affected by the diminished light underwater. We'll also create some artificial light to reawaken some color in some coral.

1 Make a selection of the ship. You can ignore the rigging, as it's safe to assume this would not have survived many years on the ocean floor.

4 The crisp clarity of the ship is also a giveaway, so we need to apply a little judicial blurring. Go to *Filter > Blur >* **Gaussian Blur** and apply a *Radius* setting of 3.0 for a high resolution file.

5 To destroy clarity further, reduce the layer *Opacity* to 55%.

6 The ship is beginning to look a little more at home, but a very well-known characteristic of underwater visibility is how objects appear to fade out the farther they are from the eye. This ship has equal visibility from bow to stern, making it stand out too much. A layer mask will give us complete control over the visibility and apparent distance of the ship. Press Ctrl (Cmd) + click the *Ship* layer to load its selection.

7 Now go to *Layer > Add Layer Mask >* **Reveal Selection**.

8 Now it's time to get creative with the paintbrush. Use a large, soft-edged brush at very low opacity. Using black, paint on the mask to reduce the ship's visibility at different intensities. The rear of the ship should be less visible than the front. The relative clarity of the divers also helps to strengthen the illusion that the ship is farther away from the camera.

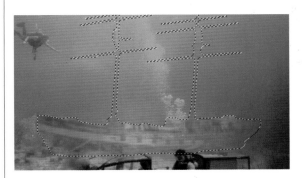

9 To unify the whole image, we are going to add a general color cast from the surrounding water. Load the ship's selection once again—Ctrl (Cmd) + clicking the ship thumbnail in the *Layers* palette.

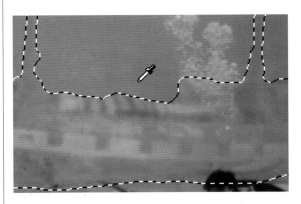

10 Use the *Eyedropper* to select a middle tone blue. I have used R0 G99 B159.

11 Create a new layer called *Color cast*.

12 Fill the selection with the sampled color and change the layer blend mode to *Pin Light*. The effect is subtle, but adds considerably to the realism.

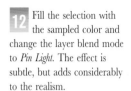

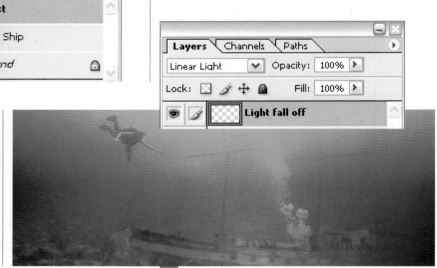

15 To make the gradient appear more radiant, change the layer blend mode to *Linear Light*.

13 The blue tone of underwater images can often appear monotonous, so we'll introduce some relief. The fall-off of light as the water depth increases is usually perceptible in wide-angle images such as this one. This effect can be visually appealing and provide a harmonious range of blues to lift the scene. Create a new layer called *Light fall off*.

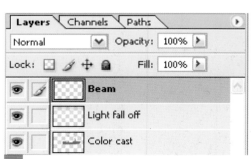

16 Rays from the sun, or any other large light source, can add dynamism to an image. The top-left corner of the image is a perfect background for some light rays. Create a new layer called *Beam*.

14 Choose a strong turquoise color for the foreground color; R7 G180 B196 works well. Set up the *Gradient* tool with the *Foreground to Transparent* linear option, and drag from the top of the screen to about one quarter of the way down.

17 Create a feathered selection describing a beam of light.

18 Using a pale blue/white color, drag a *Foreground to Transparent* linear gradient through the selection, then deselect.

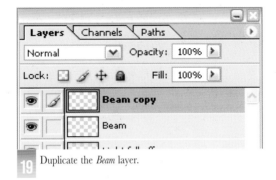

19 Duplicate the *Beam* layer.

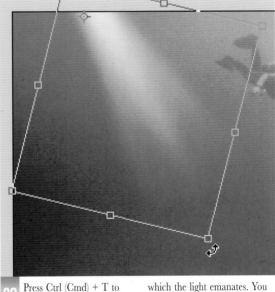

20 Press Ctrl (Cmd) + T to bring up the *Transform* bounding box, and change the point of origin to the point from which the light emanates. You can now rotate the selection clockwise to create a fanning out effect.

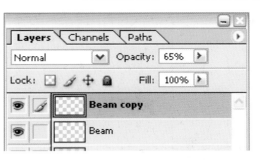

21 Change the layer *Opacity* to 65%.

22 Repeat this process, duplicating the last layer, rotating it from the new point of origin, and repositioning it if necessary to create a fan effect. Keep the layer *Opacity* at 100% until you have completed the sequence.

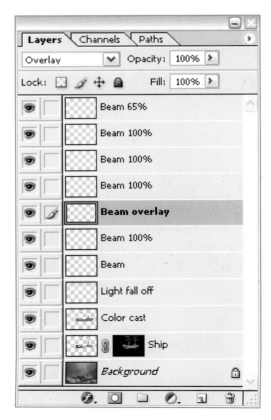

23 Now you can experiment with different opacity and layer blend modes for each of the beam layers. I changed the *Opacity* of just one layer to 65% and changed the blend mode of another to *Overlay*. This accounts for the nonuniform effect, which would be typical of light being filtered through water in this way.

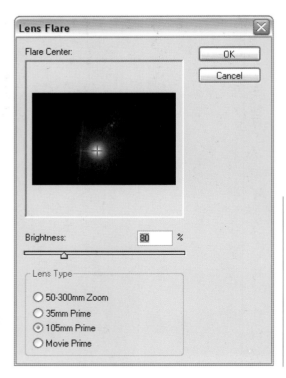

27 Go to *Filter > Render >* **Lens Flare** and apply the settings as shown.

Lens Flare

Flare Center:

OK

Cancel

Brightness: 80 %

Lens Type
○ 50-300mm Zoom
○ 35mm Prime
◉ 105mm Prime
○ Movie Prime

24 Artificial sources of light are critical for underwater photography, not only in terms of seeing but also to bring out the colors that don't appear at depth such as reds. We'll create a light source from the mini-sub to illuminate some coral. Create a new layer called *Sub light* and draw a feathered selection describing the shape of the cast light.

28 Press Ctrl (Cmd) + T to bring up the bounding box, and scale the layer non-proportionately so it is flattened in the vertical plane. This removes the roundness of the flare and gives the illusion that the light source is being viewed side on. The example picture's layer mode is *Normal*, so you can see the bounding box around the perimeter of the actual pixels.

25 Drag a *White to Transparent* linear gradient through the selection.

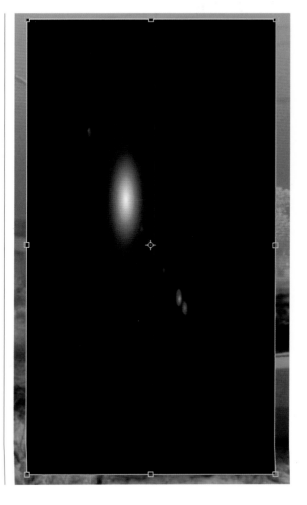

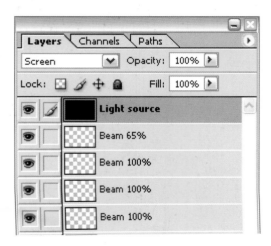

Layers Channels Paths

Screen Opacity: 100%

Lock: ☒ 🖉 ✛ 🔒 Fill: 100%

👁 🖉 ■ **Light source**
👁 ▢ Beam 65%
👁 ▢ Beam 100%
👁 ▢ Beam 100%
👁 ▢ Beam 100%

26 To make a more definite source of light for the beam, we'll add a distorted lens flare. Create a new black-filled layer called *Light source* set to *Screen* mode.

29 Position the lens flare as shown.

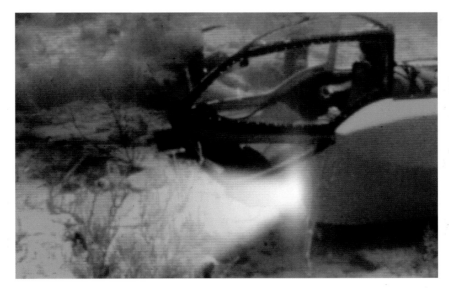

30 The underwater plant life or coral being illuminated by the light can now reveal its true colors. In this case, we'll make it red. Make a feathered selection of the plant area.

31 Activate the background layer and press Ctrl (Cmd) + J to copy and paste the selection to a new layer. Go to *Image > Adjustments > **Replace Color***. Use the *Eyedropper* tools to select just the branches of the plant, and apply the color settings as shown.

Replace Color

Selection

Color:

Fuzziness: 32

OK
Cancel
Load...
Save...

☑ Preview

● Selection ○ Image

Replacement

Hue: -180

Saturation: -14   Result

Lightness: 0

CREATING CAR LIGHT TRAILS

Levels

Channel: RGB

Input Levels: 57 1.00 255

OK
Cancel
Load...
Save...
Auto
Options...

Output Levels: 0 255

☑ Preview

1 Although the picture was taken as the sun was setting, it needs to be darker overall to add more impact to the light trails we are going to create. Add a *Levels* adjustment layer to the *Background* layer, and darken the image a little.

M oving lights captured with a slow exposure provide an infinite variety of seemingly hand drawn patterns. These "beams" of light seem almost independent from their source such as a car or aircraft. This phenomenon is due to the image of the light registering on film far quicker than the darker car, which requires either more light or a longer time exposure in order to register on film with equal intensity.

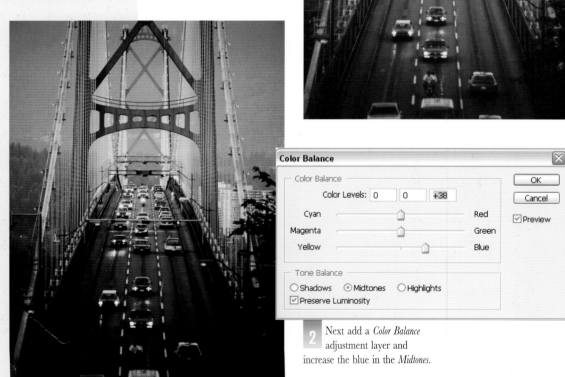

Color Balance

Color Balance

Color Levels: 0 0 +38

Cyan — Red
Magenta — Green
Yellow — Blue

Tone Balance
○ Shadows ● Midtones ○ Highlights
☑ Preserve Luminosity

OK
Cancel
☑ Preview

2 Next add a *Color Balance* adjustment layer and increase the blue in the *Midtones*.

3 There are a number of ways of creating light trails. One of the most realistic photographically is by using the *Pattern Stamp* tool. First make a rectangular selection of one of the car headlights.

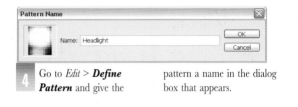

4 Go to *Edit* > **Define Pattern** and give the pattern a name in the dialog box that appears.

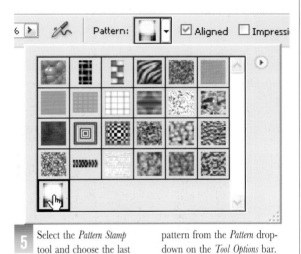

5 Select the *Pattern Stamp* tool and choose the last pattern from the *Pattern* drop-down on the *Tool Options* bar.

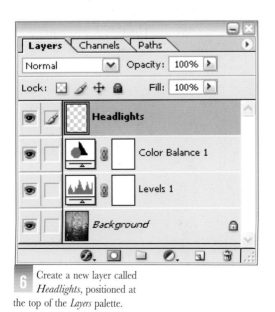

6 Create a new layer called *Headlights*, positioned at the top of the *Layers* palette.

7 Using a brush size about the same size as the original headlight, click with the *Pattern Stamp* tool exactly on top of one of the car headlights.

8 Holding down the Shift key, click again a short distance below the original click.

9 Repeat the process for the other headlight.

10 Go to *Filter > Blur > **Motion Blur*** and apply the settings as shown.

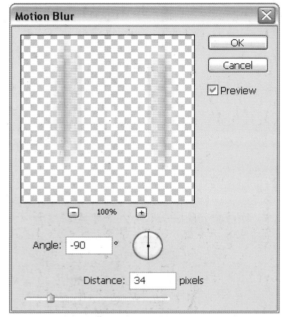

Motion Blur

OK

Cancel

☑ Preview

100%

Angle: -90 °

Distance: 34 pixels

Layers | Channels | Paths

Linear Dodge ▾ Opacity: 100% ▸

Lock: 🔲 ✏ ✛ 🔒 Fill: 100% ▸

👁 ✏ Headlights

11 Change the layer blending mode to *Linear Dodge*.

12 Repeat the process for the other headlights on a separate layer.

13 An alternative method of creating light streaks is to create a custom brush. This is particularly useful when creating a streak of light in one color. We'll use this method for the rear red lights. On a new layer, create a rectangular, 3 pixel, feathered selection and fill it with bright red. Use one of the rear red lights as a guide to how big to make the selection.

Name: Red light

OK

Cancel

26

14 Go to *Edit > **Define Brush*** and type a name for the brush.

15 Delete the layer on which the brush was created, as this is no longer needed. Select the *Brush* tool and open the *Brushes* palette. The last brush in the palette is the one you just created.

Brushes

Brush Presets

Brush Tip Shape

☐ Shape Dynamics
☐ Scattering
☐ Texture
☐ Dual Brush
☐ Color Dynamics
☐ Other Dynamics
☐ Noise
☐ Wet Edges
☐ Airbrush
☐ Smoothing
☐ Protect Texture

Watercolor Small Round Tip
11
Oil Heavy Flow Dry Edges
48
Oil Medium Wet Flow
32
Wet Sponge
55
Rough Round Bristle
100
Airbrush 75 Tilt Size and Ang
75
Airbrush Dual Brush Soft Rou
45
Red light

Master Diameter 20 px

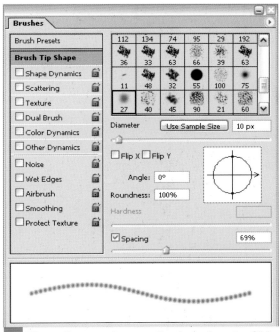

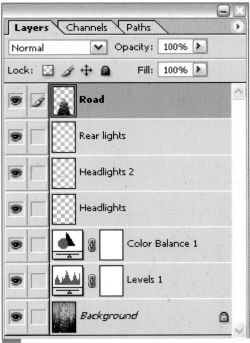

16 When traffic stops and starts during a time exposure, the light streak will have a characteristic staggered effect. To simulate this, we will adjust the brush spacing. Click the *Brush Tip Shape* option in the *Brushes* palette and set the *Spacing* to 69%.

17 On a new layer, apply one click with the *Brush* tool in red. Click on top of one of the existing rear lights.

18 As with the white headlight, hold down the Shift key and click a short distance below the first click to make a connecting brush stroke.

19 Repeat the process for the other light, and apply motion blur as with the white headlight. Do the same for a few of the other cars.

20 The type of slow exposure needed to generate light streaks of this kind would also result in a little more light being generated in the immediate vicinity of the main focus of car lights. If the camera was not on a tripod, there could also be a little camera shake. This is normally undesirable, but in this instance a little simulated camera shake will add to the dynamism of the image and emphasize the motion of the cars. Make a selection of the road area as pictured. I've hidden the adjustment layers in order to be able to see the road more clearly.

21 With the *Background* layer active, press Ctrl (Cmd) + J to copy and paste the selection onto a new layer. Name the new layer *Road* and drag it to the top of the *Layers* palette.

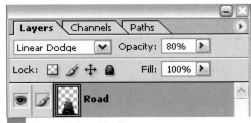

22 Change the layer blending mode to *Linear Dodge* and reduce the *Opacity* to 80%.

23 Using the keyboard arrow key, nudge the *Road* layer down by 12 pixels for the finished effect.

LIGHTING AND SWITCHING OFF TRAFFIC SIGNALS

The original picture.

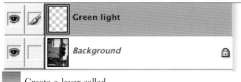

3 Create a layer called *Green Light*.

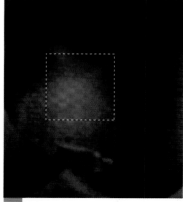

4 Using a 3-color radial gradient consisting of white, green, and dark green, drag from the center to the outside of the selection.

A lthough we are going to illuminate a traffic signal, this technique could apply equally to any kind of warning or hazard signal found on roads, airports, railroads, and other public areas. Lights of this kind are not designed to perform as a source of light to aid visibility, but rather to focus all their energy in one small point. No beam is created and, because of the intensity of the color, ambient light emission is limited.

In addition, we are going to extinguish a light that is currently switched on. This may appear as simple as slapping a black circle over it, but for the sake of realism we're going to do a more professional job.

1 Make a circular selection of the green light area.

2 Some of the brown metal hood intersects with the circular selection, so create another selection of this element to subtract from the circle selection.

5 Lights such as traffic lights have a textured or grid-like surface to the glass. This texture is usually visible and is a strong characteristic of lights of this type. Creating this texture will add greatly to the realism. Make a rectangular selection of the texture in the amber light.

6 Go to *Edit > **Define Pattern*** and name the pattern *Traffic light*.

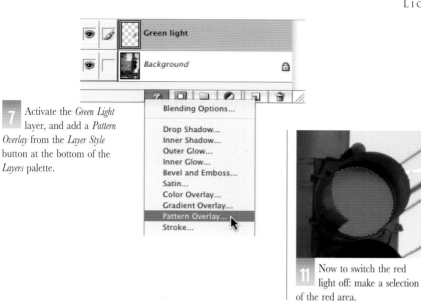

7 Activate the *Green Light* layer, and add a *Pattern Overlay* from the *Layer Style* button at the bottom of the *Layers* palette.

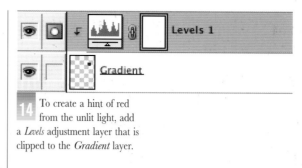

14 To create a hint of red from the unlit light, add a *Levels* adjustment layer that is clipped to the *Gradient* layer.

11 Now to switch the red light off: make a selection of the red area.

8 Select the last pattern from the *Pattern* drop-down box. This is the one you have just created. Apply the other settings shown.

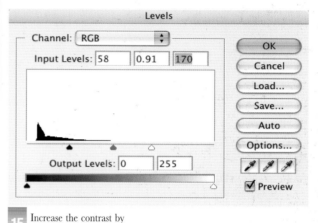

15 Increase the contrast by using the settings shown.

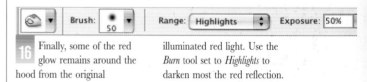

16 Finally, some of the red glow remains around the hood from the original illuminated red light. Use the *Burn* tool set to *Highlights* to darken most the red reflection.

9 As the hood is made of metal, there should be a faint green glow from the light on the inside of the hood. Make a feathered selection similar to the one shown.

10 Create a new layer called *Glow* and fill the selection with green to match the light.

12 Use the *Eyedropper* to sample 2 shades from the amber light. Choose a light and a dark shade.

13 On a new layer called *Gradient*, use these colors to drag a radial gradient through the selection from the center outward.

CREATING PROJECTED COMPUTER LIGHT

There are times when real life just doesn't live up to the expectations of film makers. Picture the scene for a moment: a computer hacker or a secret agent sits covertly at a computer terminal in a darkened room. The state secrets on the screen in front of her are tantalizingly projected onto her face. We can see the vivid text, but can't quite read it and the suspense mounts.

But it's all an illusion. No matter how dark the room or how bright the screen, the image just won't be projected onto the user's face. Does it really matter, though? It's visually a very striking effect, so let's see how it's done.

1 Duplicate the file, converting it to grayscale. The image needs to have fairly good contrast, so use *Levels* if necessary and apply a small amount of *Gaussian Blur* to soften edges. Save the file, naming it *Displacemap*, then close it.

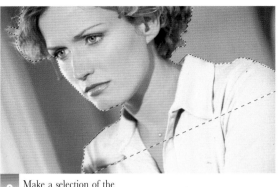

2 Make a selection of the girl's head and shoulders, and save it for later use.

3 Drag the computer screen image into the working document, and rotate and position it in place over the girl's face and shoulders.

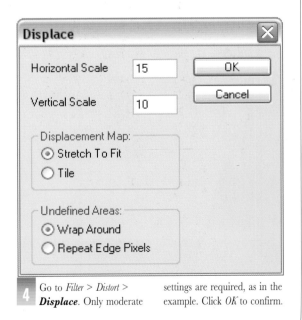

4 Go to *Filter > Distort > Displace*. Only moderate settings are required, as in the example. Click *OK* to confirm.

Displace dialog:
- Horizontal Scale: 15
- Vertical Scale: 10
- Displacement Map: ● Stretch To Fit ○ Tile
- Undefined Areas: ● Wrap Around ○ Repeat Edge Pixels

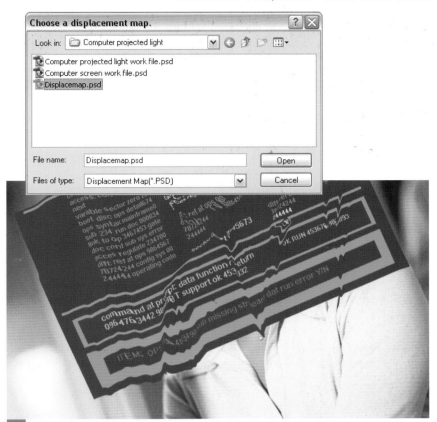

5 After clicking *OK*, the *Choose a displacement map* dialog box opens. Select the file called *displacemap* that you saved in step 1.

6 Change the layer blend mode to *Overlay*.

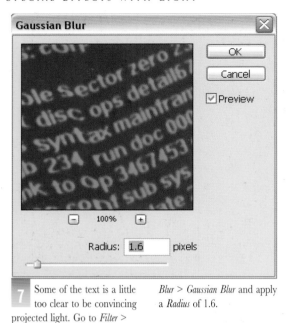

7 Some of the text is a little too clear to be convincing projected light. Go to *Filter >* *Blur > Gaussian Blur* and apply a *Radius* of 1.6.

8 The idea is that the screen's image is projected onto the girl only, not the background, and that's where the selection we saved earlier comes in. Load the selection.

9 Inverse the selection and press Backspace to remove the outer area of the computer screen image.

10 Even though we have distorted the screen image, some areas are a bit flat and straight, but we can easily fix that with the *Liquify* tool. Go to *Filter >* **Liquify**. Use the *Liquify* filter's *Warp* tool to distort some text and make the straight edge at the bottom wavy. Don't overdo it, though: we still need most of the text to be recognizable as text.

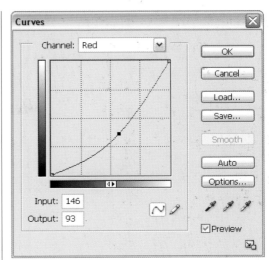

11 Any projected light would be much more obvious if the room's ambient light levels were low, so we are going to make the room darker and bluer, which will also enhance the impression of warm electronic light from the monitor. We want to affect only the room and the lower half of the girl, though. Load the selection and inverse it.

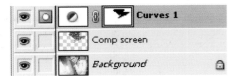

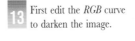

12 Create a *Curves* adjustment layer above the *Comp screen* layer. The selection is automatically made into a mask linked to the *Curves* layer. Now we can make changes to the selected area only.

13 First edit the *RGB* curve to darken the image.

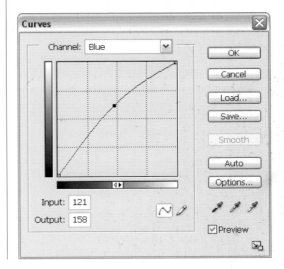

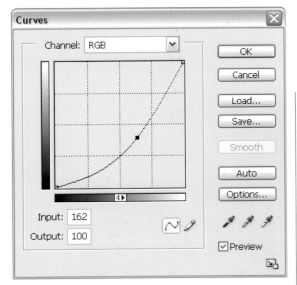

14 Now edit the *Red* and *Blue* curves independently to create the blue cast.

Creating a radioactive glow

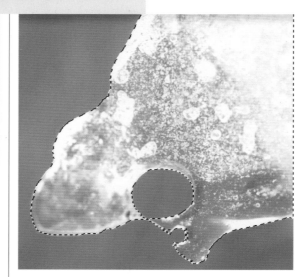

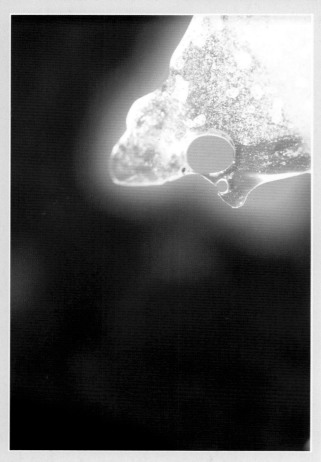

1 Make a selection of the ice.

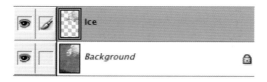

2 Press Ctrl (Cmd) + J to copy and paste the selection to a new layer. Name the layer *Ice*.

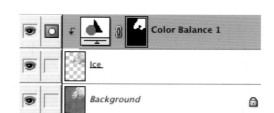

3 Press Ctrl (Cmd) and click the *Ice* layer to load the selection again. Add a *Color Balance* adjustment layer that is clipped to the *Ice* layer.

Although we are going to create what I loosely describe as a radioactive glow, the effect would be equally convincing with far less controversial (and safer) subject matter, such as deep sea marine life that emit vibrant light or any intense light trained on ice glass or other translucent materials.

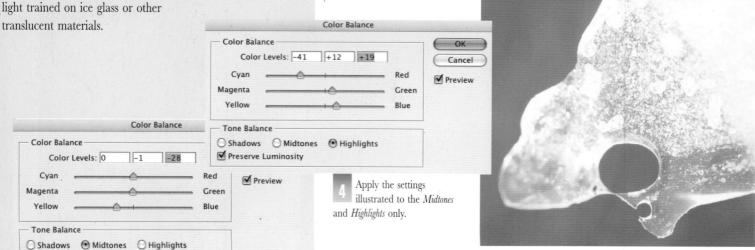

4 Apply the settings illustrated to the *Midtones* and *Highlights* only.

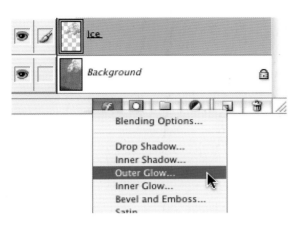

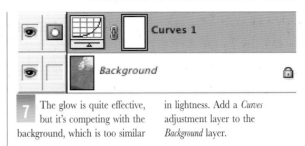

5 The intense light at the core of the object should give rise to a soft luminous glow around its perimeter, so apply an *Outer Glow* layer style to the *Ice* layer to achieve this.

7 The glow is quite effective, but it's competing with the background, which is too similar in lightness. Add a *Curves* adjustment layer to the *Background* layer.

6 Apply the settings displayed. Use a color sampled from the ice itself as the glow color.

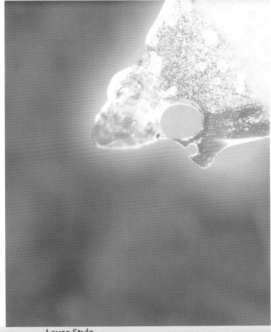

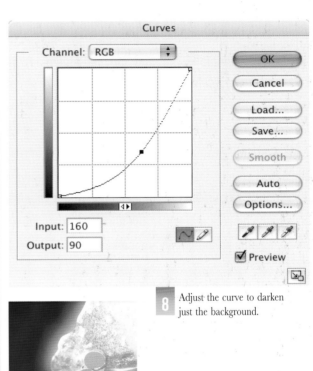

8 Adjust the curve to darken just the background.

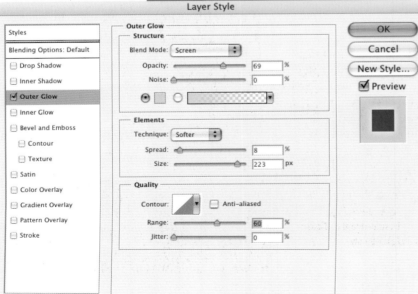

CREATING A STAR-FILLED NIGHT SKY

This desert city image is perfect for simulating a starry sky. There's a nice broad area of sky with relatively low levels of light emanating from the city. The low light level is achieved with the aid of the camera position, being far enough away for the ambient light to diminish sufficiently.

Photographing a star-studded night sky can be a daunting task at the best of times. Those stunning heavenly vistas can all too easily be transformed into a black void or a washed-out landscape when viewed on screen. The surreal, magical night sky scenes common to so many Hollywood movies are more often a product of clever software rather than a reflection of nature's own efforts. Apart from the technical pitfalls, location plays a major role in your ability to capture a good night sky. City-dwellers see only a fraction of what's really out there in deep space, due to the inherent ambient light of a city. If you're in the country or out at sea, or happen to find yourself in the middle of a desert, then with the right conditions you have the ultimate night sky at your disposal. For everyone else, there's Photoshop, and we will use it now to go one better than Mother Nature, by adding the Milky Way and a meteor on demand.

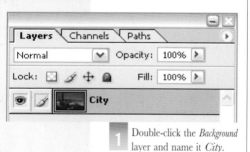

1 Double-click the *Background* layer and name it *City*.

2 Make a selection of the sky. The sky is fairly uniform, so 3 or 4 clicks with the *Magic Wand* tool should be sufficient.

3 Press the Backspace key to delete the selected sky, then deselect the selection.

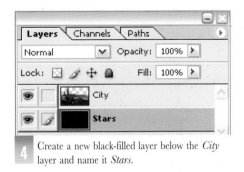

4 Create a new black-filled layer below the *City* layer and name it *Stars*.

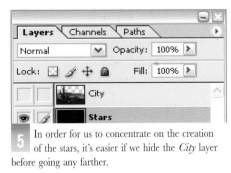

5 In order for us to concentrate on the creation of the stars, it's easier if we hide the *City* layer before going any farther.

Add Noise

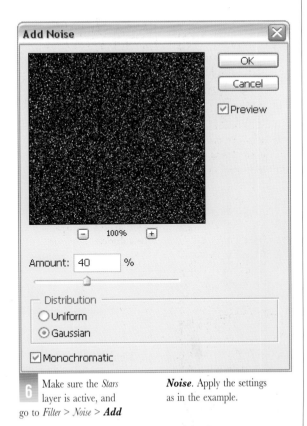

6 Make sure the *Stars* layer is active, and go to *Filter > Noise > Add* **Noise**. Apply the settings as in the example.

Gaussian Blur

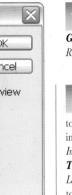

Radius: 0.3 pixels

Threshold Level: 162

Custom

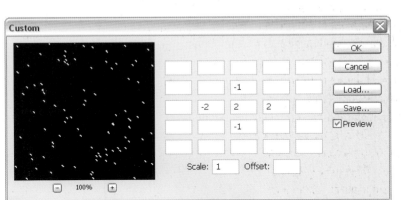

Scale: 1 Offset:

7 To soften the effect, go to *Filter > Blur >* **Gaussian Blur**, and apply a *Radius* setting of 0.3.

8 The result is a bit of a confused mass, so we need to pick out a random range of individual stars from it. Go to *Image > Adjustments >* **Threshold**, and use a *Threshold Level* of 162. Dragging the slider to the left increases the amount of stars, and dragging to the right decreases.

9 At this stage, you may decide you want either more or less, or bigger or smaller stars. This step lets you take control over the quantity and distribution of stars within the star field. Go to *Filter > Other >* **Custom**. In the dialog box, the center text box represents the pixel being evaluated. This pixel's brightness value can be multiplied by a range from –999 to +999. The other text boxes represent the adjacent pixels. Not all of the text boxes need to be used. By inputting different numeric values, we can create what appears to be a random distribution of stars at different sizes. Negative values reduce brightness and positive values increase brightness. Enter the values as in the example.

10 Make the *City* layer visible again to see how our image is developing.

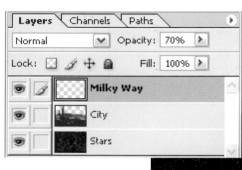

11 Now to create the Milky Way: the Milky Way is that band of heavily clustered stars which appear to form one gaseous mass. Make a new layer called *Milky way* and hide the *City* layer again. This is to prevent you creating the Milky Way over the top of the cactus.

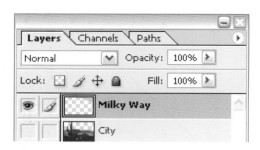

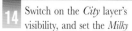

14 Switch on the *City* layer's visibility, and set the *Milky*   *Way* layer's *Opacity* to 70%.

12 Set up the *Gradient* tool with the following settings: *Foreground to Transparent, Reflected,* and a pale blue color as the foreground color. I am using R147 G163 B198.

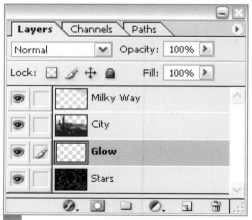

15 To introduce some real authenticity, we need to break up the large black background area a little. The perfect way to do this is to drop in the dying glow left by the sun as it sinks deeper below the horizon. Create a new layer called *Glow* and position it between the *Stars* and *City* layers.

13 Make sure the *Milky way* layer is active, and drag the gradient through the top-right corner of the image, as in the example, following the red arrow.

16 Set up the *Gradient* tool with the following settings: *Foreground to Transparent, Linear,* and a pale cyan/blue for the foreground color. I am using R173 G211 B211. Drag the gradient a short distance over the mountains as in the example.

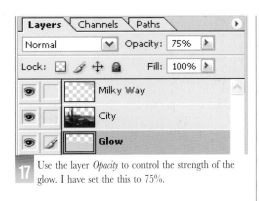

17 Use the layer *Opacity* to control the strength of the glow. I have set the this to 75%.

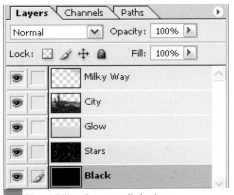

18 The visibility of stars usually begins to wane nearer to the horizon, especially over brightly lit cities. Our star field is a little too uniform in this respect, so we need to add a little fading. Create a new black-filled layer at the bottom of the *Layers* palette called *Black*.

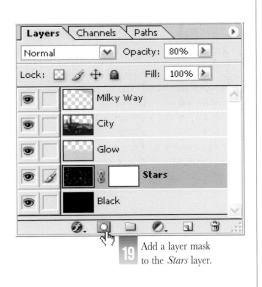

19 Add a layer mask to the *Stars* layer.

20 Set the *Gradient* tool to *Black to White* and drag a linear gradient in roughly the same direction and length as the *Glow* gradient that you dragged in step 16.

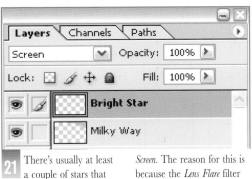

21 There's usually at least a couple of stars that outshine the others. We'll use a lens flare to depict one of these. At the top of the *Layers* palette, create a black-filled layer called *Bright star* and set the blend mode to *Screen*. The reason for this is because the *Lens Flare* filter can be applied only to an area filled with pixels. Applying *Screen* mode renders the black invisible, but allows the light-colored lens flare to show through.

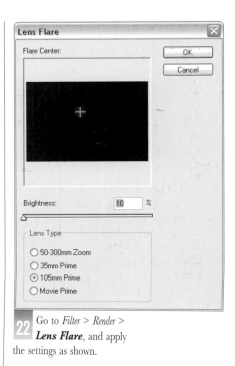

22 Go to *Filter > Render > Lens Flare*, and apply the settings as shown.

23 Use the *Move* tool to position the lens flare to your liking.

24 No star field is complete without a meteor, and the *Airbrush* is the perfect tool to create this particular illusion. Select the *Brush* tool and, using a soft-edged round brush, apply the settings from the *Tool Options* bar as pictured.

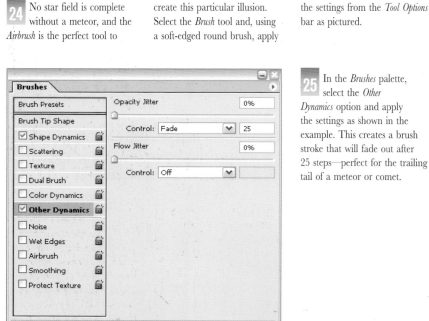

25 In the *Brushes* palette, select the *Other Dynamics* option and apply the settings as shown in the example. This creates a brush stroke that will fade out after 25 steps—perfect for the trailing tail of a meteor or comet.

26 Create a new layer called *Meteor* and drag a slightly curved brush stroke through the sky. The stroke automatically fades out into a subtle taper.

27 You may have noticed a faint pale outline around the cactus. This is a remnant from the original background. We can make light work of removing unwanted highlights such as these by using the *Burn* tool. Select this tool and apply the settings in the *Options* bar as pictured.

28 Start to drag over the highlight edge with the *Burn* tool, and the highlight will start to gradually disappear.

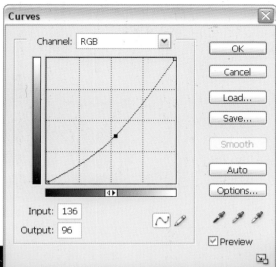

Curves

Channel: RGB

Input: 136
Output: 96

OK
Cancel
Load...
Save...
Smooth
Auto
Options...
☑ Preview

29 Finally, the mountains in the distance now look out of place with the new darker sky, so we need to gently darken the whole mountain range, concentrating chiefly on the midtones to give us a subtle effect. Make a selection of the mountains and go to *Image > Adjustments > **Curves***. Create a curve similar to the one pictured.

30 This is the finished result with an additional bright star applied using the *Lens Flare* filter again. Remember, the beauty of this process is that you have full control over the lightness and opacity of each element by simply changing the layer *Opacity*. This enables you to fine-tune each layer in relation to the other layers.

CREATING CHROME TEXT WITH THE LIGHTING EFFECTS FILTER

As well as using the *Lighting Effects* filter in its more traditional role as a method for casting light onto a scene, it can also be used for other less obvious applications. When used in combination with a grayscale channel, it turns Photoshop into a simple form of 3D program. Using the 3D concept of highlights and shadows to depict raised and depressed areas, the grayscale channel acts as a texture map. As light is applied via the *Lighting Effects* filter, the varying shades of gray are molded into a 3-D form.

We will use this technique now to create a 3-D text object, and then turn it into shiny chrome as part of a company logo image.

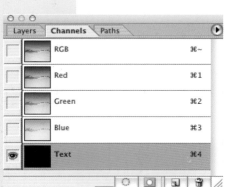

1 I am starting with a background image taken half in and half out of water. Create a new black-filled channel called *text*.

2 Type the words *club 100* in the channel in white. Large, rounded fonts work best for this effect. I'm using Arial rounded MT bold, point size 90 with anti-aliasing set to smooth.

3 To avoid any sharp edges appearing and to increase the height and roundness of the text, we need to blur the edges slightly. Go to *Filter > Blur > **Gaussian Blur***, and apply a *Radius* setting of 2.5.

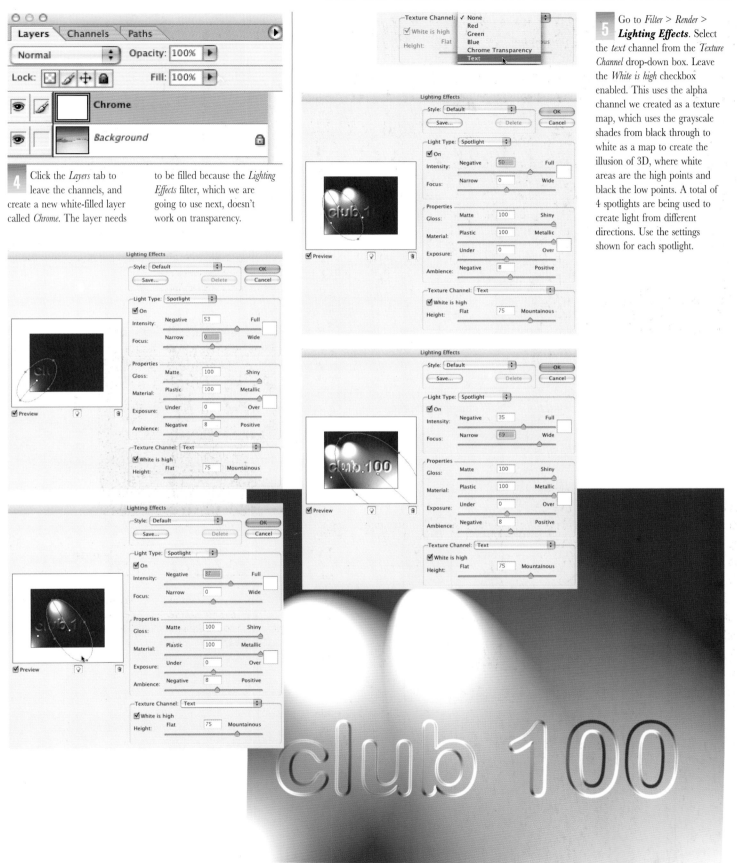

4 Click the *Layers* tab to leave the channels, and create a new white-filled layer called *Chrome*. The layer needs to be filled because the *Lighting Effects* filter, which we are going to use next, doesn't work on transparency.

5 Go to *Filter > Render > Lighting Effects*. Select the *text* channel from the *Texture Channel* drop-down box. Leave the *White is high* checkbox enabled. This uses the alpha channel we created as a texture map, which uses the grayscale shades from black through to white as a map to create the illusion of 3D, where white areas are the high points and black the low points. A total of 4 spotlights are being used to create light from different directions. Use the settings shown for each spotlight.

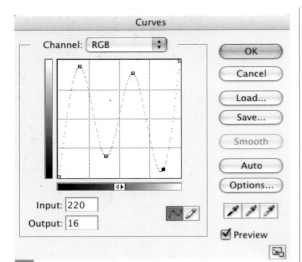

6 To create the shiny reflective surfaces of chrome, go to *Image > Adjustments > **Curves***. By creating the erratic shaped curve shown, we will be making extreme highlight and shadow areas in close proximity, which perfectly simulates the way light reacts when falling on chrome surfaces.

7 Now we need to cut the chrome text from its background. Load the selection from the original *text* channel. You can do this quickly by pressing Ctrl (Cmd) + Alt + 4, assuming that channel number 4 is your *text* channel.

8 As a consequence of the text becoming embossed, it is now bigger than its original selection. To increase the size of the selection, go to *Select > Modify > **Expand***. Expand by small increments to avoid softening the edge of the selection. For this text, I'm applying the command 4 times, expanding by 2 pixels 3 times, and by 1 pixel for the last time.

9 Press Ctrl (Cmd) + J to copy and paste the selection to a new layer.

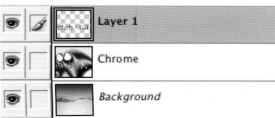

10 Drag the original *Chrome* layer into the bin, and name the newly created layer *Chrome text*.

11 Position the text above the water line.

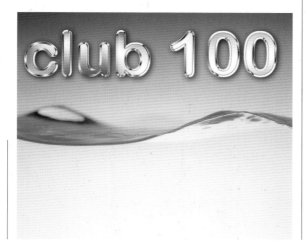

12 The chrome needs to pick up the blue from the surrounding area to help the illusion of reflection. Add a *Color Balance* adjustment layer that is clipped to the *Chrome text* layer.

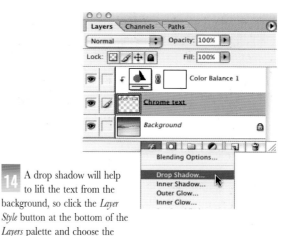

14 A drop shadow will help to lift the text from the background, so click the *Layer Style* button at the bottom of the *Layers* palette and choose the *Drop Shadow* style.

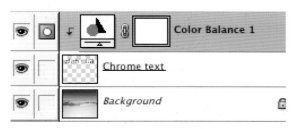

15 Use the settings shown to create a soft shadow.

13 Add small amounts of blue and cyan to the *Midtones* and *Highlights* only.

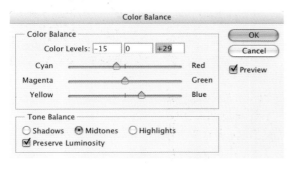

16 In the final image, a couple of star-shaped brush strokes have been applied for added sparkle.

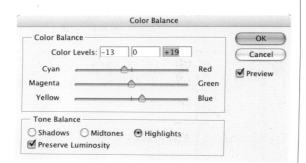

PHOTOSHOP KEYBOARD SHORTCUTS

Menu Command	Photoshop CS Macintosh	Photoshop CS Windows
Auto Color	Cmd+Shift+B	Ctrl+Shift+B
Auto Contrast	Cmd+Option+Shift+L	Ctrl+Alt+Shift+L
Auto Levels	Cmd+Shift+L	Ctrl+Shift+L
Bring Forward/Send Backward	Cmd+[or]	Ctrl+[or]
Bring to Front/Send to Back	Cmd+Shift+[or]	Ctrl+Shift+[or]
Browse	Cmd+Shift+O	Ctrl+Shift+O
Clear Selection	Backspace	Backspace
Close	Cmd+W	Ctrl+W
Close All	Cmd+Option+W	Ctrl+Alt+W
Color Balance	Cmd+B	Ctrl+B
Color Balance, use previous settings	Cmd+Option+B	Ctrl+Alt+B
Color Settings	Cmd+Shift+K	Ctrl+Shift+K
Copy	Cmd+C or F3	Ctrl+C or F3
Copy Merged	Cmd+Shift+C	Ctrl+Shift+C
Create Clipping Mask	Cmd+G	Ctrl+G
Curves	Cmd+M	Ctrl+M
Curves, use previous settings	Cmd+Option+M	Ctrl+Alt+M
Cut	Cmd+X or F2	Ctrl+X or F2
Desaturate	Cmd+Shift+U	Ctrl+Shift+U
Deselect	Cmd+D	Ctrl+D
Edit in ImageReady	Cmd+Shift+M	Ctrl+Shift+M
Exit	Cmd+Q	Ctrl+Q
Extract	Cmd+Option+X	Ctrl+Alt+X
Extras, show or hide	Cmd+H	Ctrl+H
Fade Filter	Cmd+Shift+F	Ctrl+Shift+F
Feather Selection	Cmd+Option+D or Shift+F6	Ctrl+Alt+D or Shift+F6
File Info	Cmd+Option+I	Ctrl+Alt+I
Fill	Shift+F5	Shift+F5
Fill from History	Cmd+Option+Delete	Ctrl+Alt+Backspace
Filter, repeat last	Cmd+F	Ctrl+F
Filter, repeat with new settings	Cmd+Option+F	Ctrl+Alt+F
Fit on Screen	Cmd+0 (zero)	Ctrl+0 (zero)
Free Transform	Cmd+T	Ctrl+T
Gamut Warning	Cmd+Shift+Y	Ctrl+Shift+Y
Grid, show or hide	Cmd+' (quote)	Ctrl+' (quote)

Menu Command	Photoshop CS Macintosh	Photoshop CS Windows
Guides, show or hide	Cmd+; (semicolon)	Ctrl+; (semicolon)
Help contents	Help	F1
Hue/Saturation	Cmd+U	Ctrl+U
Hue/Saturation, use previous settings	Cmd+Option+U	Ctrl+Alt+U
Inverse Selection	Cmd+Shift+I or Shift+F7	Ctrl+Shift+I or Shift+F7
Invert	Cmd+I	Ctrl+I
Keyboard Shortcuts	Cmd+Option+Shift+K	Ctrl+Alt+Shift+K
Layer Via Copy	Cmd+J	Ctrl+J
Layer Via Cut	Cmd+Shift+J	Ctrl+Shift+J
Levels	Cmd+L	Ctrl+L
Levels, use previous settings	Cmd+Option+L	Ctrl+Alt+L
Liquify	Cmd+Shift+X	Ctrl+Shift+X
Lock Guides	Cmd+Option+; (semicolon)	Ctrl+Alt+; (semicolon)
Merge Layers	Cmd+E	Ctrl+E
Merge Visible	Cmd+Shift+E	Ctrl+Shift+E
New	Cmd+N	Ctrl+N
New Layer	Cmd+Shift+N	Ctrl+Shift+N
New, with default settings	Cmd+Option+N	Ctrl+Alt+N
Open	Cmd+O	Ctrl+O
Open As		Ctrl+Alt+O
Page Setup	Cmd+Shift+P	Ctrl+Shift+P
Paste	Cmd+V or F4	Ctrl+V or F4
Paste Into	Cmd+Shift+V	Ctrl+Shift+V
Path, show or hide	Cmd+Shift+H	Ctrl+Shift+H
Pattern Maker	Cmd+Option+Shift+X	Ctrl+Alt+Shift+X
Preferences	Cmd+K	Ctrl+K
Preferences, last panel	Cmd+Option+K	Ctrl+Alt+K
Print	Cmd+P	Ctrl+P
Print One Copy	Cmd+Option+Shift+P	Ctrl+Alt+Shift+P
Print with Preview	Cmd+Option+P	Ctrl+Alt+P
Proof colors	Cmd+Y	Ctrl+Y
Release Clipping Mask	Cmd+Shift+G	Ctrl+Shift+G
Reselect	Cmd+Shift+D	Ctrl+Shift+D
Revert	F12	F12
Rulers, show or hide	Cmd+R	Ctrl+R

Painting	Photoshop CS Macintosh	Photoshop CS Windows
Save	Cmd+S	Ctrl+S
Save for web	Cmd+Shift+Option+S	Ctrl+Shift+Alt+S
Save As	Cmd+Shift+S	Ctrl+Shift+S
Select All	Cmd+A	Ctrl+A
Snap	Cmd+Shift+; (semicolon)	Ctrl+Shift+; (semicolon)
Step Backwards	Cmd+Option+Z	Ctrl+Alt+Z
Step Forwards	Cmd+Shift+Z	Ctrl+Shift+Z
Transform Again	Cmd+Shift+T	Ctrl+Shift+T
Undo/Redo, toggle	Cmd+Z or F1	Ctrl+Z
View Actual Pixels	Cmd+Option+0 (zero)	Ctrl+Alt+0 (zero)
Zoom In	Cmd++ (plus) or Cmd+= (equals)	Ctrl++ (plus) or Ctrl+= (equals)
Zoom Out	Cmd+- (minus)	Ctrl+- (minus)
Brush size, decrease/increase	[or]	[or]
Brush softness/hardness, decrease/increase	Shift+[or]	Shift+[or]
Cycle through Eraser functions	Option+click Eraser tool icon or Shift+E	Alt+click Eraser tool icon or Shift+E
Cycle through Focus tools	Option+click Focus tool icon or Shift+R	Alt+click Focus tool icon or Shift+R
Cycle through Rubber Stamp options	Option+click Rubber Stamp tool icon or Shift+S	Alt+click Rubber Stamp tool icon or Shift+S
Cycle through Toning tools	Option+click Toning tool icon or Shift+O	Alt+click Toning tool icon or Shift+O
Delete shape from Brushes palette	Option+click brush shape	Alt+click brush shape
Display crosshair cursor	Caps Lock	Caps Lock
Display Fill dialog box	Shift+Delete	Shift+Backspace
Paint or edit in a straight line	Click and then Shift+click	Click and then Shift+click
Reset to normal brush mode	Shift+Option+N	Shift+Alt+N
Rename brush	Double-click brush	Double-click brush
Cycle through Healing Brush tools	J to select, then Shift+J to cycle	J to select, then Shift+J to cycle
Cycle through Paintbrush tools	B to select, then Shift+B to cycle	B to select, then Shift+B to cycle
Select background color tool	Option+Eyedropper tool+click	Alt+Eyedropper tool+click
Set opacity, pressure or exposure	Any painting or editing tool+ number keys (e.g. 0=100%, 1=10%, 4 then 5 in quick succession=45%)	Any painting or editing tool+ number keys (e.g. 0=100%, 1=10%, 4 then 5 in quick succession=45%)

Applying Colors	Photoshop CS Macintosh	Photoshop CS Windows
Add new swatch to palette	Click in empty area of palette	Click in empty area of palette
Color palette, show/hide	F6	F6
Cycle through color choices	Shift+click color bar	Shift+click color bar
Delete swatch from palette	Option+click swatch	Alt+click swatch
Display Fill dialog box	Shift+Delete or Shift+F5	Shift+Backspace or Shift+F5
Fill layer with background color but preserve transparency	Shift+Cmd+Delete	Shift+Ctrl+Backspace
Fill layer with foreground color but preserve transparency	Shift+Option+Delete	Shift+Alt+Backspace
Fill selection on any layer with background color	Cmd+Delete	Ctrl+Backspace
Fill selection or layer with foreground color	Option+Delete	Alt+Backspace
Fill selection with source state in History palette	Cmd+Option+Delete	Ctrl+Alt+Backspace
Lift background color from color bar at bottom of Color palette	Option+click color bar	Alt+click color bar
Lift background color from Swatches palette	Cmd+click swatch	Ctrl+click swatch
Lift foreground color from color bar at bottom of Color palette	Click color bar	Click color bar
Lift foreground color from Swatches palette	Click swatch	Click swatch

PHOTOSHOP KEYBOARD SHORTCUTS

Type	Photoshop CS Macintosh	Photoshop CS Windows
Align left, centre or right	Horizontal type tool +Shift+Cmd+L, C or R	Horizontal type tool +Shift+Ctrl+L, C or R
Align top, centre or bottom	Vertical type tool +Shift+Cmd+L, C or R	Horizontal type tool +Shift+Ctrl+L, C or R
Edit text layer	Double-click on 'T' in Layers palette	Double-click on 'T' in Layers palette
Move type in image	Cmd+drag type when Type is selected	Cmd+drag type when Type is selected
Leading, increase/decrease by 2 pixels	Option+arrow key	Alt+arrow key
Leading, increase/decrease by 10 pixels	Cmd+Option+_ or _ (left or right arrow)	Ctrl+Alt+_ or _ (left or right arrow)
Select all text	Cmd+A	Ctrl+A
Select word, line, paragraph or story	Double-click, triple-click, quadruple-click or quintuple-click	Double-click, triple-click, quadruple-click or quintuple-click
Select word to left or right	Cmd+Shift+_ or _ (left or right arrow)	Ctrl+Shift+_ or _ (left or right arrow)
Toggle Underlining on/off	Cmd+Shift+U	Ctrl+Shift+U
Toggle Strikethrough on/off	Cmd+Shift+/	Ctrl+Shift+/
Toggle Uppercase on/off	Cmd+Shift+K	Ctrl+Shift+K
Toggle Superscript on/off	Cmd+Shift++ (plus)	Ctrl+Shift++ (plus)
Toggle Subscript on/off	Cmd+Option+Shift++ (plus)	Ctrl+Alt+Shift++ (plus)
Type size, increase/decrease by 2 pixels	Cmd+Shift+< or >	Ctrl+Shift+< or >
Type size, increase/decrease by 10 pixels	Cmd+Shift+Option+< or >	Ctrl+Shift+Alt+< or >

Making Selections	Photoshop CS Macintosh	Photoshop CS Windows
Add point to Magnetic selection	Click with Magnetic Lasso tool	Click with Magnetic Lasso tool
Add or subtract from selection	Any Selection tool+Shift or Option+drag	Any Selection tool+Shift or Alt+drag
Cancel Polygon or Magnetic selection	Escape	Escape
Change lasso tool to irregular Polygon tool	Option+click with Lasso tool	Alt+click with Lasso tool
Clone selection	Option+drag selection with Move tool or Cmd+Option+drag with other tool	Alt+drag selection with Move tool or Ctrl+Alt+drag with other tool
Clone selection in 1-pixel increments	Cmd+Option+arrow key	Ctrl+Alt++arrow key

Making Selections	Photoshop CS Macintosh	Photoshop CS Windows
Clone selection in 10-pixel increments	Cmd+Shift+Option+arrow key	Ctrl+Shift+Alt+arrow key
Close magnetic selection with straight segment	Option+double-click or Option+Return	Alt+double-click or Alt+Enter
Close polygon or magnetic selection	Double-click with respective Lasso tool or press Return	Double-click with respective Lasso tool or press Enter
Constrain marquee to square or circle	Press Shift while drawing shape	Press Shift while drawing shape
Constrain movement vertically, horizontally, or diagonally	Press Shift while dragging selection	Press Shift while dragging selection
Cycle through Lasso tools	Option+click Lasso tool icon or Shift+L	Alt+click Lasso tool icon or Shift+L
Cycle through Marquee tools	Option+click Marquee tool icon or Shift+M	Alt+click Marquee tool icon or Shift+M
Delete last point added with Magnetic Lasso tool	Delete	Backspace
Deselect all	Cmd+D	Ctrl+D
Draw out from centre with Marquee tool	Option+drag	Alt+drag
Feather selection	Cmd+Option+D or Shift+F6	Ctrl+Alt+D or Shift+F6
Increase or reduce magnetic lasso detection width	[or] (square brackets)	[or] (square brackets)
Move copy of selection	Drag with Move tool+Option	Drag with Move tool+Alt
Move selection in 1-pixel increments	Move tool+arrow key	Move tool+arrow key
Move selection in 10-pixel increments	Move tool+Shift+arrow key	Move tool+Shift+arrow key
Move selection area in 1-pixel increments	Any selection+arrow key	Any selection+arrow key
Move selection area in 10-pixel increments	Any selection+Shift+arrow key	Any selection+Shift+arrow key
Move selection outline independently of its contents	Drag with Selection tool	Drag with Selection tool
Reposition selection while creating	Spacebar+drag	Spacebar+drag
Reselect after deselecting	Cmd+Shift+D	Ctrl+Shift+D
Reverse selection	Cmd+Shift+I or Shift+F7	Ctrl+Shift+I or Shift+F7
Select all	Cmd+A	Ctrl+A
Select Move tool	V	V
Subtract from selection	Option+drag	Alt+drag

Layers and Channels	Photoshop CS Macintosh	Photoshop CS Windows
Add spot color channel	Cmd+click page icon at bottom of Channels palette	Ctrl+click page icon at bottom of Channels palette
Add to current layer selection	Shift+Cmd+click layer or thumbnail in Layers palette	Shift+Ctrl+click layer or thumbnail in Layers palette
Clone selection to new layer	Cmd+J	Ctrl+J
Convert floating selection to new layer	Cmd+Shift+J	Ctrl+Shift+J
Copy merged version of selection to Clipboard	Cmd+Shift+C	Ctrl+Shift+C
Create new layer, show layer options dialog box	Option+click page icon at bottom of Layers palette or Cmd+Shift+N	Alt+click page icon at bottom of Layers palette or Ctrl+Shift+N
Create new layer below target layer	Cmd+click page icon at bottom of Layers Palette	Ctrl+click page icon at bottom of Layers Palette
Create new layer below target layer, show layer options dialog box	Cmd+Option+click page icon at bottom of Layers palette	Ctrl+Alt+click page icon at bottom of Layers palette
Display or hide Layers palette	F7	F7
Disable specific layer effect/style	Option+choose command from Layer > Effects submenu	Alt+choose command from Layer > Effects submenu
Duplicate layer effect/style	Shift+drag effect/style to target layer	Shift+drag effect/style to target layer
Edit layer style	Double click layer	Double click layer
Edit layer effect/style	Double-click on layer effect/style	Double-click on layer effect/style
Go to background	Shift+Option+[	Shift+Alt+[
Go to top layer	Shift+Option+]	Shift+Alt+]
Group neighbouring layers	Option+click horizontal line in Layers palette or Cmd+G	Alt+click horizontal line in Layers palette or Ctrl+G
Intersect with current layer selection	Shift+Option+Cmd+click layer or thumbnail in Layers palette	Shift+Alt+Ctrl+click layer or thumbnail in Layers palette
Load layer as selection	Cmd+click layer or thumbnail in Layers palette	Ctrl+click layer or thumbnail in Layers palette
Merge all visible layers	Cmd+Shift+E	Ctrl+Shift+E

Layers and Channels	Photoshop CS Macintosh	Photoshop CS Windows
Merge layer with next layer down	Cmd+E	Ctrl+E
Merge linked layers	Cmd+E	Ctrl+E
Move contents of a layer	Drag with Move tool or Cmd +drag with other tool	Drag with Move tool or Ctrl +drag with other tool
Move contents of a layer in 1-pixel increments	Cmd+arrow key	Ctrl+arrow key
Move contents of a layer in 10-pixel increments	Cmd+Shift+arrow key	Ctrl+Shift+arrow key
Move shadow when Effect dialog box is open	Drag in image window	Drag in image window
Move to next layer above	Option+]	Alt+]
Move to next layer below	Option+[	Alt+[
Moves target layer down/up	Cmd+[or]	Ctrl+[or]
Moves target layer back/front	Cmd+Shift+[or]	Ctrl+Shift+[or]
Preserve transparency of active layer	/	/
Retain intersection of transparency mask and selection	Cmd+Shift+Option+click layer name	Ctrl+Shift+Alt+click layer name
Subtract transparency mask from selection	Cmd+Option+click layer name	Ctrl+Alt+click layer name
Subtract from current layer selection	Option+Cmd+click layer or thumbnail in Layers palette	Alt+Ctrl+click layer or thumbnail in Layers palette
Switch between independent color and mask channels	Cmd+1 through Cmd+9	Ctrl+1 through Ctrl+9
Switch between layer effects in Effects dialog box	Cmd+1 through Cmd+0 (zero)	Ctrl+1 through Ctrl+0 (zero)
Switch to composite color view	Cmd+~ (tilde)	Ctrl+~ (tilde)
Ungroup neighboring layers	Option+click dotted line in Layers palette or Cmd+Shift+G	Alt+click dotted line in Layers palette or Ctrl+Shift+G
View single layer by itself	Option+click eyeball icon in Layers palette	Alt+click eyeball icon in Layers palette

PHOTOSHOP KEYBOARD SHORTCUTS

Masks	Photoshop CS Macintosh	Photoshop CS Windows
Add channel mask to selection	Cmd+Shift+click channel name	Ctrl+Shift+click channel name
Add layer mask to selection	Cmd+Shift+click layer mask thumbnail	Ctrl+Shift+click layer mask thumbnail
Change Quick Mask color overlay	Double-click Quick Mask icon	Double-click Quick Mask icon
Convert channel mask to selection outline	Cmd+click channel name in Channels palette or Cmd+Option+number (1 through 0)	Ctrl+click channel name in Channels palette or Ctrl+Alt+number (1 through 0)
Convert layer mask to selection outline	Cmd+click layer mask thumbnail or Cmd+Option+\ (backslash)	Ctrl+click layer mask thumbnail or Ctrl+Alt+\ (backslash)
Create channel mask filled with black	Click page icon at bottom of Channels palette	Click page icon at bottom of Channels palette
Create channel mask filled with black and set options dialog	Option+click page icon at bottom of Channels palette	Alt+click page icon at bottom of Channels palette
Create channel mask from selection outline	Click mask icon at bottom of Channels palette	Click mask icon at bottom of Channels palette
Create channel mask from selection outline and set options dialog	Option+click mask icon at bottom of Channels palette	Alt+click mask icon at bottom of Channels palette
Create layer mask from selection outline	Click mask icon	Click mask icon
Create layer mask that hides selection	Option+click mask icon	Alt+click mask icon
Disable layer mask	Shift+click layer mask thumbnail	Shift+click layer mask thumbnail
Enter or exit Quick Mask mode	Q	Q
Intersect a channel mask and selection	Cmd+Shift+Option+click channel name	Ctrl+Shift+Alt+click channel name
Subtract channel mask from selection	Cmd+Option+click channel name	Ctrl+Alt+click channel name
Subtract layer mask from selection	Cmd+Option+click layer mask thumbnail	Ctrl+Alt+click layer mask thumbnail
Switch focus from image to layer mask	Cmd+\ (backslash)	Ctrl+\ (backslash)
Switch focus from layer mask to image	Cmd+~ (tilde)	Ctrl+~ (tilde)
Toggle link between layer and layer mask	Click between layer and mask thumbnails in Layers palette	Click between layer and mask thumbnails in Layers palette
View channel mask as Rubylith overlay	Click eyeball of channel mask in Channels palette	Click eyeball of channel mask in Channels palette
View layer mask as Rubylith overlay	Shift+Option+click layer mask thumbnail or press \ (backslash)	Shift+Alt+click layer mask thumbnail or press \ (backslash)
View layer mask independently of image	Option+click layer mask thumbnail in Layers palette or press \ (backslash) then ~ (tilde)	Alt+click layer mask thumbnail in Layers palette or press \ (backslash) then ~ (tilde)
View Quick Mask independently of image	Click top eyeball in Channels palette or press ~ (tilde)	Click top eyeball in Channels palette or press ~ (tilde)

Paths	Photoshop CS Macintosh	Photoshop CS Windows
Add cusp to path	Drag with Pen tool, then Option+drag same point	Drag with Pen tool, then Alt+drag same point
Add point to magnetic selection	Click with Magnetic Pen tool	Click with Magnetic Pen tool
Add smooth arc to path	Drag with Pen tool	Drag with Pen tool
Cancel magnetic or freeform selection	Escape	Escape
Close magnetic selection	Double-click with Magnetic Pen tool or click on first point in path	Double-click with Magnetic Pen tool or click on first point in path
Close magnetic selection with straight segment	Option+double-click	Alt+double-click
Deactivate path	Click in empty portion of Paths palette	Click in empty portion of Paths palette
Delete last point added with Pen tool or Magnetic Pen tool	Delete	Backspace
Draw freehand path segment	Drag with Freeform Pen tool or Option+drag with Magnetic Pen tool	Drag with Freeform Pen tool or Alt+drag with Magnetic Pen tool
Hide path toggle (it remains active)	Cmd+Shift+H	Ctrl+Shift+H
Move selected points	Drag point with Direct Selection tool or Cmd+drag with Pen tool	Drag point with Direct Selection tool or Ctrl+drag with Pen tool
Save path	Double-click Work Path item in Paths palette	Double-click Work Path item in Paths palette
Select arrow (direct selection) tool	A	A
Select entire path	Option+click path in Paths palette	Alt+click path in Paths palette
Select multiple points in path	Cmd+Shift+click with pen	Ctrl+Shift+click with pen
Select Pen tool	P	P
Make active path a selection	Cmd+Return	Ctrl+Enter

Crops and Transformations	Photoshop CS Macintosh	Photoshop CS Windows
Accept transformation	Double-click inside boundary or press Return	Double-click inside boundary or press Enter
Cancel crop	Escape	Escape
Cancel transformation	Escape	Escape
Constrained distort for perspective effect	Cmd+Shift+drag corner handle	Ctrl+Shift+drag corner handle
Constrained distort for symmetrical perspective effect	Cmd+Shift+Option+drag corner handle	Ctrl+Shift+Alt+drag corner handle
Freely transform with duplicate data	Cmd+Option+T	Ctrl+Alt+T
Replay last transformation with duplicate data	Cmd+Shift+Option+T	Ctrl+Shift+Alt+T
Freely transform selection or layer	Cmd+T	Ctrl+T
Replay last transformation	Cmd+Shift+T	Ctrl+Shift+T
Rotate image (always with respect to origin)	Drag outside boundary	Drag outside boundary

Crops and Transformations	Photoshop CS Macintosh	Photoshop CS Windows
Select Crop tool	C	C
Skew image	Cmd+drag side handle	Ctrl+drag side handle
Skew image along constrained axis	Cmd+Shift+drag side handle	Ctrl+Shift+drag side handle
Skew image with respect to origin	Cmd+Option+drag side handle	Ctrl+Alt+drag side handle
Skew image along constrained axis with respect to origin	Cmd+Shift+Option+drag side handle	Ctrl+Shift+Alt+drag side handle
Distort corner	Cmd+drag corner handle	Ctrl+drag corner handle
Symmetrically distort opposite corners	Cmd+Option+drag corner handle	Ctrl+Alt+drag corner handle

Rulers, measurements and Guides	Photoshop CS Macintosh	Photoshop CS Windows
Create guide	Drag from ruler	Drag from ruler
Display or hide grid	Cmd+" (quote)	Ctrl+" (quote)
Display or hide guides	Cmd+; (semicolon)	Ctrl+; (semicolon)
Display or hide Info palette	F8	F8
Display or hide rulers	Cmd+R	Ctrl+R
Lock or unlock guides	Cmd+Option+; (semicolon)	Ctrl+Alt+; (semicolon)
Snap guide to ruler tick marks	Press Shift while dragging guide	Press Shift while dragging guide
Toggle grid magnetism	Cmd+Shift+" (quote)	Ctrl+Shift+" (quote)
Toggle horizontal guide to vertical or vice versa	Press Option while dragging guide	Press Alt while dragging guide

Slicing and Optimizing	Photoshop CS Macintosh	Photoshop CS Windows
Draw square slice	Shift+drag	Shift+drag
Draw from centre outward	Option+drag	Alt+drag
Draw square slice from centre outward	Option+Shift+drag	Alt+Shift+drag
Open slice's contextual menu	Control+click on slice	Right mouse button on slice
Reposition slice while creating slice	Spacebar+drag	Spacebar+drag
Toggle snap to slices on/off	Control while drawing slice	Ctrl while drawing slice
Toggle between Slice tool and Slice selection tool	Cmd	Ctrl

Filters	Photoshop CS Macintosh	Photoshop CS Windows
Adjust angle of light without affecting size of footprint	Cmd+drag handle	Ctrl+drag handle
Clone light in Lighting Effects dialog box	Option+drag light	Alt+drag light
Delete Lighting Effects light	Delete	Delete
Repeat filter with different settings	Cmd+Option+F	Ctrl+Alt+F
Repeat filter with previous settings	Cmd+F	Ctrl+F
Reset options inside Corrective Filter dialog boxes	Option+click Cancel button	Alt+click Cancel button

Hide and Undo	Photoshop CS Macintosh	Photoshop CS Windows
Display or hide Actions palette	Option+F9	F9 or Alt+F9
Display or hide all palettes, toolbox, status bar	Tab	Tab
Display or hide palettes except toolbox	Shift+Tab	Shift+Tab
Hide toolbox and status bar	Tab, Shift+Tab	Tab, Shift+Tab
Move a panel out of a palette	Drag panel tab	Drag panel tab
Revert to saved image	F12	F12
Undo or redo last operation	Cmd+Z	Ctrl+Z

Viewing	Photoshop CS Macintosh	Photoshop CS Windows
100% magnification	Double-click Zoom tool or Cmd+Option+0 (zero)	Double-click Zoom tool or Ctrl+Alt+0 (zero)
Applies zoom percentage and keeps zoom percentage box active	Shift+Return in Navigator palette	Shift+Enter in Navigator palette
Fits image in window	Double-click Hand tool or Cmd+0 (zero)	Double-click Hand tool or Ctrl+0 (zero)
Moves view to upper left corner or lower right corner	Home or End	Home or End
Scrolls image with hand tool	Spacebar+drag or drag view area box in Navigator palette	Spacebar+drag or drag view area box in Navigator palette
Scrolls up or down 1 screen	Page Up or Page Down	Page Up or Page Down
Scrolls up or down 10 units	Shift+Page Up or Page Down	Shift+Page Up or Page Down
Zooms in or out	Cmd++ (plus) or - (minus)	Ctrl++ (plus) or - (minus)
Zooms in on specified area of an image	Cmd+drag over preview in Navigator palette	Ctrl+drag over preview in Navigator palette

Function keys	Photoshop CS Macintosh	Photoshop CS Windows
Undo/redo, toggle	F1	F1
Cut	F2	F2
Copy	F3	F3
Paste	F4	F4
Display or hide Brushes palette	F5	F5
Display or hide Color palette	F6	F6
Display or hide Layers palette	F7	F7
Display or hide Info palette	F8	F8
Display or hide Actions palette	F9	F9
Revert to saved image	F12	F12

GLOSSARY

Adjustment layer A specialized layer that can be handled as a conventional layer but designed to enact effects upon all those layers below it in the image "stack." Effects that can be applied via an adjustment layer include changes in levels, brightness/contrast, color balance, and even posterization. These changes do not actually affect the underlying pixels. If the adjustment layer is removed the image will revert to its previous appearance. Conversely, an adjustment layer's adjustments can be permanently embedded in the image (or in the underlying layers) by selecting the appropriate layer merge command (such as Merge Down).

Alpha channel A specific channel in which information on the transparency of a pixel is kept. In image files, alpha channels can be stored as a separate channel additional to the standard three RGB or four CMYK channels. Image masks are stored in alpha channels.

Ambient light An alternate name for available light. This is the light (natural, artificial or both) that lights the photographic subject. It is specifically that illumination not provided by the photographer.

Artificial light Strictly, any light source not naturally occurring in the environment, but usually a term to describe incandescent, tungsten or fluorescent lighting.

Backlighting The principal light sources shine from behind the subject and are directed (broadly) towards the camera lens. This tends to produce results that have a lot of contrast, with silhouettes. A specific form of backlighting is called contre jour. Many cameras feature backlight controls that increase aperture (or exposure time) to compensate for backlighting and to prevent the silhouetting of foreground objects.

Base lighting Sometimes known as "ground lighting," this is the technique of lighting a subject from below with an upward-pointing light source. Often used for still-life photography of glassware and metallic objects to provide full lighting but without the flash highlights that would occur with front or side lighting. Causes a reversal of normal shadow profiles. Synonymous with ground light, although the latter term is sometimes reserved for ground-mounted lighting designed to up-light a background, rather than the subject.

Bézier curve A curved line between two Bézier control points. Each point is a tiny database, or "vector," which stores information about the line, such as its thickness, color, length, and direction. Complex shapes can be applied to the curve by manipulating "handles," which are dragged out from the control points. In image-editing applications, Bézier curves are used to define very precise shapes on a path.

Blending mode In Photoshop, individual layers can be blended with those underneath using blending modes. Some examples of these mode are: Normal, Behind, Clear, Dissolve, Multiply, Screen, Soft Light, Hard Light, Color Dodge, Color Burn, Darken, Lighten, Difference, Exclusion, Overlay, Saturation, Color, and Luminosity. Blending modes enact changes upon the original pixels in an image (sometimes called the base layer) by means of an applied blend color (or "paint" layer). This produces a resultant color based on the original color and on the nature of the blend. Many users find that blending mode results can be unpredictable and use trial and error to get the desired effects.

Blur filter The conventional blur effect filter, designed to detect noise around color transitions and remove it. It does this by detecting pixels close to boundaries and averaging their values, effectively eliminating noise and random color variations. Blur More is identical but applies the effect more strongly. Somewhat crude, the Blur filter is now joined in many image-editing filter sets with more controllable filters such as the Gaussian Blur and Smart Blur filters.

Brightness The relative lightness or darkness of the color, usually measured as a percentage from 0% (black) all the way up to 100% (white).

Capture The action of "getting" an image, by taking a photograph, scanning an image into a computer, or "grabbing" an image using a frame grabber.

Channels A conventional RGB color image is usually composed of three separate single-color images, one each for red, green, and blue, called channels. Each color channel contains a monochrome representation of the parts of the image that include that color. In the case of the RGB image channels containing the red, green, and blue colors, images are combined to produce a full-color image, but each of these individual channels can be manipulated in much the same way as a complete image. Channels can be merged or split using the Merge Channels or Split Channels commands. Additional channels exist to perform specific tasks: grayscale channels that save selections for masking are known as alpha channels; spot color channels are used to provide separate channels for specific ink colors known as spot colors (premixed inks used either in addition to or in place of CMYK inks).

CIE L*a*b* color space Three-dimensional color model based on a system devised by the CIE organization for measuring color. The L*a*b* color model is designed to be device independent when it comes to maintaining consistent color. Results should be consistent regardless of the device used, whether scanner, monitor or printer.

L*a*b* color consists of a luminance or lightness component (L) and two chromatic components: a (green to red) and b (blue to yellow).

Clipping Limiting an image or piece of art to within the bounds of a particular area.

Clipping group A stack of image layers that produce a resultant image or effect that is a net composite of the constituents. For example, where the base layer is a selection shape (say, an ellipse), the next layer a transparent texture (such as craquelure) and the top layer a pattern, the clipping group would produce a textured pattern in the shape of an ellipse.

Clipping path A Bézier outline that can be drawn around a subject or image element to determine which areas of an image should be considered transparent or "clipped." Using a clipping path, an object can be isolated from the remainder of the image, which is then rendered transparent, enabling background elements in an image composite to show through. A particular application is when cut-out images are to be placed on top of a tint background in a page layout. When a clipping path is created it can be embedded into the image file, normally when saved to the EPS format.

Clouds filter Creates a cloudscape using random values between those of the foreground and background colors. Care is therefore needed in selecting sensible colors in order to create a realistic effect. When aiming to create a realistic sky, background and foreground colors are completely interchangeable. This filter does not depend on the currently active image, unlike the Difference Clouds filter, which subsequently blends the clouds with the underlying image.

Color The visual interpretation of the various wavelengths of reflected or refracted light.

Color cast A bias in a color image which can be either intentionally introduced or the undesirable consequence of a lighting problem. Intentional color casts tend to be introduced to enhance an effect (such as accentuating the reds and oranges of a sunset, or applying a sepia tone to imply an aged photo) and can be done via an appropriate command in an image-editing application. Alternatively it can be done at the proof stage to enhance the color in an image. Undesirable casts arise from a number of causes but are typically due to an imbalance between the lighting source and the response of the film (or that of the CCD in the case of a digital camera). Using daylight film under tungsten lighting causes an amber color cast while setting the color balance of a digital camera for indoor scenes can give a flat blue cast outdoors.

Color temperature A measure of the composition of light. This is defined as the temperature—measured in degrees Kelvin—to which a black object would need to be heated to produce a particular color of light. The color temperature is based on a scale that sets zero as absolute darkness and increases with an object's—for example a light bulb filament's—brightness. A tungsten lamp, for example, has a color temperature of 2,900K, while the temperature of direct sunlight is around 5,000K and is considered the ideal viewing standard in the graphic arts.

Color wheel The complete spectrum of visible colors represented as a circular diagram and used as the basis of some color pickers. The HSB (hue, saturation, brightness) color model determines hue as the angular position on the color wheel and saturation as the corresponding radial position.

Complementary colors Any pair of colors directly opposite each other on a color wheel, that, when combined, form white (or black depending on the color model, subtractive or additive).

Contrast The degree of difference between adjacent tones in an image (or computer monitor) from the lightest to the darkest. "High contrast" describes an image with light highlights and dark shadows, but with few shades in between, while a "low contrast" image is one with even tones and few dark areas or highlights.

Crop To trim or mask an image so that it fits a given area, or to discard unwanted portions of an image.

Definition The overall quality—or clarity—of an image, determined by the combined subjective effect of graininess (resolution in a digital image) and sharpness.

Density The darkness of tone or color in any image. In a transparency this refers to the amount of light which can pass through it, thus determining the darkness of shadows and the saturation of color. A printed highlight cannot be any lighter in color than the color of the paper it is printed on, while the shadows cannot be any darker than the quality and volume of ink that the printing process will allow.

Density range The maximum range of tones in an image, measured as the difference between the maximum and minimum densities (the darkest and lightest tones).

Difference Clouds filter A Render filter like the "Clouds" filter, Difference Clouds creates cloudscapes using random color values between those of the foreground and background colors. It then blends these "clouds" with the underlying image using the same technique as the Difference blending mode.

Diffuse lighting Light that has low contrast and no obvious highlights or "hotspots." Bounce lighting can be diffuse if well spread. Overcast skies also represent a natural diffuse light source.

Dots Per Inch (dpi) A unit of measurement used to represent the resolution of devices such as printers and imagesetters. The closer the dots or pixels (the more there are to each inch) the better the quality. A typical resolution for a laser printer is 600dpi .

Drop shadow Effect (available as a filter, plug-in or layer feature) that produces a shadow beneath a selection conforming to the selection outline. This shadow (depending on the filter) can be moved relative to the selection, given variable opacity or even tilted. In the last case a drop shadow can be applied to a selection (say, a person) and that shadow will mimic a sunlight shadow.

Existing light Alternative name for available light, the term describes all natural and environmental light sources (those not specifically for the purpose of photography).

Eyedropper tool Conventionally used to select the foreground or background color from those colors in the image or in a selectable color swatch set. Eyedroppers can normally be accurate to one pixel or a larger area (such as a 3 x 3 pixel matrix) which is then averaged to give the selected color.

Feather Command or option that blurs or softens the edges of selections. This helps blend these selections when they are pasted into different backgrounds, giving less of a "cut-out" effect.

Flat lighting Lighting that is usually low in contrast and low in shadows.

Gaussian Blur filter Blur filter that applies a weighted average (based on the bell-shaped curve of the Gaussian distribution) when identifying and softening boundaries. It also introduces low-frequency detail and a mild "mistiness" to the image which is ideal for covering (blending out) discrete image information, such as noise and artefacts. A useful tool for applying variable degrees of blur and a more controllable tool than conventional blur filters. It can be accessed through the Filter > Blur > Gaussian Blur menu.

Gradient tool Tool permitting the creation of a gradual blend between two or more colors within a selection. There are several different types of gradient fills offered, those of Photoshop are typical: Linear, Radial, Angular, Diamond, and Reflected. A selection of gradient presets are usually provided, but user-defined options can be used to create custom gradients.

Graduation/Gradation The smooth transition from one color or tone to another.

Hard Light A blending mode that creates an effect similar to directing a bright light at the subject. Depending on the base color, the paint color will be multiplied or screened. Base color is lightened if the paint color is light, and darkened if the paint color is dark. Contrast tends to be emphasized and highlights exaggerated. Somewhat similar to Overlay but with a more pronounced effect.

Hex(adecimal) The use of the number 16 as the basis of a counting system, as distinct from our conventional decimal (base ten) system or the binary (base two) system used by basic computer processes. The figures are represented by the numbers 1 to 9, followed by the letters A to F. Thus decimal 9 is still hex 9, while decimal 10 becomes hex A, decimal 16 becomes hex 10, decimal 255 becomes hex FF, and so on.

High key An image comprising predominantly light tones and often imparting an ethereal or romantic appearance.

Histogram A graphic representation of the distribution of brightness values in an image, normally ranging from black at the left-hand vertex to white at the right. Analysis of the shape of the histogram (either by the user or an automatic algorithm) can be used to evaluate criteria, such as tonal range, and establishes whether there is sufficient detail to make corrections.

Image size A description of the dimensions of an image. Depending on the type of image being measured, this can be in terms of linear dimensions, resolution, or digtal file size.

Kelvin temperature scale (K) A unit of measurement that describes the color of a light source, based on absolute darkness rising to incandescence.

Lab color Lab color (as opposed to the CIE L*a*b* color model) is the internal color model used by Photoshop when converting from one color mode to another. "Lab mode" is useful for working with PhotoCD images.

Lasso The freehand selection tool indicated by a lasso icon in the Toolbar. there are many other variations on the basic lasso, such as the Magnetic Lasso (that can identify the edges nearest to the selection path, aiding accurate selection of discrete objects) and the Polygon Lasso (that allows straight-edged selections to be made). In the case of the latter, to draw a straight line, place the cursor point at the end of the first line and click. Place the cursor at the end of the next line and click again to select the second segment.

Layer Method of producing composite images by "suspending" image elements on separate "overlays." It mimics the method used by a cartoon animator wherein an opaque background is overlaid with the transparent "cells" (layers) upon which pixels can be painted or copied. Once layers have been created they can then be re-ordered, blended and have their transparency (opacity) altered. The power of using layers is that effects or manipulations can be applied to individual layers (or to groups of layers) independent of the others. When changes need to be made to the image only the relevant layer need be worked upon. Adjustment layers are specialized layers that perform modifications to the underlying layers without being visible themselves.

Layer effects/layer styles Series of effects, such as Drop Shadow, Inner Glow, Emboss, and Bevel, enacted on the contents of a layer.

Layer mask A mask that can be applied to the elements of an image in a particular layer. The layer mask can be modified to create different effects but such changes do not alter the pixels of that layer. As with adjustment layers (of which this is a close relation), a layer mask can be applied to the "host" layer (to make the changes permanent) or removed, along with any changes.

Layer menu Menu dedicated to layer manipulations. Options allow you to create, delete or duplicate layers, link, group, and arrange layers, and flatten an image.

Lens Flare filter A Render filter that introduces (controllable) lens flare into images that previously had none. Lens flare can often be simulated for a variety of lenses (for example, using multiple artefacts for multi-element zoom lenses).

Lighting Effects filter Powerful set of rendering filter effects that can be used to alter or introduce new lighting effects into an image. Most of these include an extensive range of tools to achieve credible effects. For example, the Photoshop implementation uses four sets of light properties, three light types and 17 styles to produce endless variations of lighting effects. "Bump Maps" (texture grayscale files) can be linked to the image to create contour-line three-dimensional effects.

Linear Gradient Option of most Gradient tools. Shades uniformly along a line drawn across the selection. The start point is colored in the first color (or foreground color, in a foreground to background gradient) and the end point in the last color (or background). A gentle gradient is achieved by drawing a long line over the selection (which can extend beyond the selection at either extreme); a harsher gradient will result from drawing a short line within the selection.

Liquify Photoshop 6 and above. An image distortion "filter" or filter set that allows a series of tools to be used to alter the characteristics and linearity of an image. Distorting tools include Twist, Bloat, and Pucker, the last giving a pinched, pincushion effect. Reconstruction modes are provided to undo or alter the effect of the distorting tools. The three modes of reconstruction are known as Amplitwist, Affine, and Displace. A Warp Mesh is drawn over the surface of the image to enable distortions to be easily seen and monitored. Image areas can also be masked at any point (prior to distorting, prior to reconstruction or otherwise) to prevent the tools taking effect in those areas. In Liquify this masking, and the consequent unmasking, is known as freezing and thawing.

Low key A photographic image comprising predominantly dark tones either as a result of lighting, processing or image editing.

Mask In the printing industry a mask was a material used to protect all or part of an image or page in photomechanical reproduction, photography, illustration or layout. Image-editor applications feature a digital equivalent that enables users to apply a mask to all or selected parts of an image. Such masks are often stored in an "alpha channel."

Mean noon sunlight An arbitrary color temperature to which most daylight color films are balanced, based on the average color temperature of direct sunlight at midday in Washington DC (5,400K).

Midtones/middletones The range of tonal values in an image anywhere between the darkest "shadow" tones and lightest "highlights." Usually refers to the central band of a histogram.

Mixed lighting Lighting comprising several different sources—such as tungsten and fluorescent artificial sources mixed with daylight. Such mixes are difficult to compensate for, but can be used to creative effect.

Motion Blur filter One of the blur filters, Motion Blur creates a linear blur (implying movement) at any angle. The degree of blur can be altered between arbitrary levels that introduce mild through to excessive blurs. Works most effectively when applied to an inverted selection: a selection is made of an object (say, a car, a runner or a train), the selection is inverted (to select the surroundings) and the filter applied to the inverse selection.

Multiply Useful tool for creating or enhancing shadow effects. Uses the paint pixel values to multiply those of the base. The resultant color is always darker than the original except when white is the paint color. Using a light paint imparts a gentler, but similar, effect to using darker colors.

Ocean Ripple filter Distort filter that places random ripple effects across the image, simulating the appearance of an object through the media of a changing refractive index, as distinct from "ripple" filters. The latter create the effect of ripples on the surface of water, such as when a pebble is dropped in an (idealized) stream. Also useful for creating image edge effects.

Opacity The degree of transparency that each layer of an image has in relation to the layer beneath. Layer opacities can be adjusted using an opacity control in the Layers palette.

Overlay Retains black and white in their original forms but darkens dark areas and lightens light areas. The base color is mixed with the blend color but retains the luminosity values of the original image

Path A line, curve, or shape drawn using the Pen tool Paths typically comprise anchor points linked by curved (or straight) line segments. The anchor points can be repositioned to alter a path if required. Each anchor features a direction line (Bézier line) and (normally) a pair of direction points. These can be pulled and moved to smoothly reshape the curve. Closed paths can easily be converted into selections and vice versa.

Pen tool Tool used to create paths. The basic Pen tool is used to draw around an intended selection, adding anchor points that are connected to make the path. You can add as many or as few anchor points as required to draw the path; simple, basic shapes will require few anchor points, while more complex selections will need more. Closed paths are completed by clicking on the original starting point. Open paths (for example, a straight line) are completed by clicking in the Pen tool icon in the Toolbar. The Magnetic Pen uses the same technique as the Magnetic Lasso: it identifies the "edge" closest to the track being described by the user and snaps the path to it. Anchor points are automatically added as the path progresses and can be added, removed, or moved later. The Freeform pen provides a means of drawing a freeform path. Use this to draw paths when the selection outline is not critical or you are confident of your drawing abilities. Again, anchor points are added along the path automatically. Additional options for these tools (that appear in dialog boxes or on pull-out menus) include the Add/Delete Point tools, Direct Selection tool (selects points on a path) and Convert Point tool (converts corner points into curve points and vice versa).

Perspective Command used principally to aid the correction of perspective effects in images, but also for the introduction of such effects for creative effect. The most common use is to remove converging verticals in buildings when the original image was taken with a conventional lens (relatively) close up.

Polar Coordinates filter Distort filter that converts an image's coordinates from conventional rectangular x–y axis to polar, and vice versa. The rectangular-to-polar conversion produces cylindrical anamorphoses—images that make no obvious logical sense until a mirrored cylinder is placed over the centre, when the image is displayed in conventional form again.

Quick mask Provides a quick method of creating a mask around a selection. The mask can be drawn and precisely defined by using any of the painting tools or the eraser respectively.

Radial gradient Option of most Gradient tools. Shades along a radius line in a circular manner. The start point of the line is the "origin" and is colored in the first, or start, color, while the end point defines the circumference and is colored with the end color.

Raster image An image defined as rows of pixels or dots.

Raster(ization) Deriving from the Latin word "rastrum," meaning "rake," the method of displaying (and creating) images employed by video screens, and thus computer monitors, in which the screen image is made up of a pattern of several hundred parallel lines created by an electron beam "raking" the screen from top to bottom at a speed of about one–sixtieth of a second. An image is created by varying the intensity of the beam at successive points along the raster. The speed at which a complete screen image, or frame, is created is called the "frame" or "refresh" rate.

Reflected gradient Option of most Gradient tools. Produces a symmetrical pattern of linear gradients to either side of the start point. The effect is one of a "ridge" or "furrow."

Resolution The degree of quality, definition, or clarity with which an image is reproduced or displayed, for example in a photograph, or via a scanner, monitor screen, printer, or other output device. The more pixels in an image, the sharper that image will be and the greater the detail. The likelihood of jaggies is also reduced the higher the image resolution.

Rim lighting A variation on backlighting where a strong light source is placed behind (and completely concealed by) the subject. In portraiture situations, this light is diffused through the hair to create a rim of bright light—the rim light. Careful metering is often called for to balance the rim light with that directed at the subject from the front.

Ripple filter Distort Simulates random pond-like ripples. The Wave filter provides similar results but provides more control.

Rubber Stamp tool Sometimes called the cloning tool (on account of its action), the Rubber Stamp tool is often considered by newcomers to be the fundamental tool, in as much as it provides the image-editing principle of "removing unwanted image elements." Later Photoshop versions (and some other editors) feature two Rubber Stamp tools, the basic tool, and the Pattern Stamp. The basic tool is normally used as a brush (and shares the common Brushes palette for brush type selection) but "paints" with image elements drawn from another part of the image, or a separate image. Choose the point you wish to use as the origination point for painting, and Alt-click or Option-click on it. Now move to the image element you wish to cover or remove and click the mouse to paint on the pixels from the origination point. When you click and drag the selection point can be set to move also, thus providing an exact copy of the original area. Careful use of the opacity setting in the Rubber Stamp Options palette can provide more subtle results and further options.

Screen Calculates the inverse of the blend and multiplies this with the base pixel values. The resultant color is always lighter than the original with the darkest parts of the base removed to give a bleached effect. There is no bleaching only if the blend color is black. This mode has been likened to printing a positive image from two negatives sandwiched together.

Sidelighting Lighting that hits the subject from the side, causing sharp, and often very profound, shadows.

Soft Light A more gentle, but similar, effect to Overlay. A light paint or layer color lightens the base color, a dark one darkens the base color. Luminosity values in the base are preserved. If the blend paint or layer is lighter than 50% gray, the image is lightened in the same manner as would result from photographic dodging. Blends darker than 50% produce a burned effect.

Specular highlight An intense highlight usually resulting from reflection of a light source from a convex section reflector. Specular highlights are plentiful on photographs of cars, for example, where curved brightwork produces such highlights. Also used for the lightest highlighted area in a reproduced photograph, usually reproduced as unprinted white paper.

Stroke path The Stroke Path command in Photoshop enables a previously constructed path to be painted using one of the painting tools.

Unsharp Mask filter One of the most potent Sharpening filters, Unsharp Mask can sharpen edges whose definition has been softened by scanning, resampling or resizing. Differing adjacent pixels are identified and the contrast between them increased. The Unsharp Mask uses three control parameters: Amount, Radius, and Threshold. Amount determines the amount of contrast added to boundary (edge) pixels. Radius describes the number of pixels adjacent to that boundary that are affected by the sharpening and Threshold sets a minimum value for pixel contrast below which the filter will have no effect. Once mastered it is a powerful filter and can achieve more subtle, but more effective, results than any other normal sharpening filter.

Wave filter Version of the Ripple Distortion filter that features customizable controls. Using "wave generators," ripples are created. The number of wave generators can be specified, as can wavelength and wave height. Though waves are conventionally sinusoidal, i.e., following the shape of a sine curve, they can also be triangular or square.

White balance "White" light is rarely pure white and tends to have unequal levels of red, green, or blue, resulting in a color cast. This color cast may not be visible to the human eye but can become very pronounced when a scene is recorded digitally. Almost all video cameras and many digital cameras feature a "white balance" setting that enables these to be neutralized, either by reference to a neutral white surface or against presets (precalibrated settings for tungsten lighting, overcast sky, fluorescent lighting, etc.). An auto white balance (AWB) setting ensures that the white balance is neutral by continuous or periodic monitoring (for example, prior to exposure) of environmental lighting conditions.

White light The color of light that results from red, blue, and green being combined in equal proportions at full saturation. If the saturations are anything less than full (and the proportions remain equal), then the color gray results.

White point Point on a histogram denoting where those pixels that define white are. Though nominally at the extreme end of the histogram, the white point should normally be moved to the position of the first "white" pixels in the histogram.

INDEX

ACKNOWLEDGMENTS

Thanks to the National Oceanic and Atmospheric Administration/Department of Commerce for the underwater source image on page 152.

ONLINE RESOURCES

Note that website addresses can change, and sites can appear and disappear almost daily. Use a search engine to help you find new arrivals or check old addresses that have moved.

Absolute Cross Tutorials (including plug-ins)
www.absolutecross.com/tutorials/photoshop.htm

The Complete Guide to Digital Photography
www.completeguidetodigitalphotography.com

creativepro.com: news and resources for creative professionals
www.creativepro.com

The Digital Camera Resource Page: consumer-oriented resource site
www.dcresource.com

Digital Photography: news, reviews, etc.
www.digital-photography.org

Digital Photography Review: products, reviews
www.dpreview.com

ePHOTOzine
www.ephotozine.com

The Imaging Resource: news, reviews, etc.
www.imaging-resource.com

Laurie McCanna's Photoshop Tips
www.mccannas.com/pshop/photosh0.htm

panoguide.com: panoramic photography
www.panoguide.com

photo.net: photography resource site - community, advice, gallery, tutorials, etc.
www.photo.net

Photolink International: education in photography and other related fields
www.photoeducation.net

Photoshop Today
www.photoshoptoday.com

Planet Photoshop (portal for all things Photoshop)
www.planetphotoshop.com

Royal Photographic Society (information, links)
www.rps.org